SHE WAS FOOLISH?

SHE WAS FOOLISH?

Ifedinma Dimbo

Library of Congress Control Number: 2012908528
ISBN: Hardcover   978-1-4771-1180-2
              Softcover   978-1-4771-1179-6
              Ebook   978-1-4771-1181-9

This is a work of fiction. Names, characters, places and incidents either are the product of the author's imagination or are used fictitiously, and any resemblance to any actual persons, living or dead, events, or locales is entirely coincidental.

This book was printed in the United States of America.

Cover Designer: Maeve Clancy *www.maeveclancy.com*
Author photograph: Leonard Photography *www.leonard-photo.com*

To order additional copies of this book, contact:
Xlibris Corporation
1-888-795-4274
www.Xlibris.com
Orders@Xlibris.com
116191

Contents

PART FOUR

PART FIVE

PART SIX

Dedication

This effort is dedicated to the Holy Spirit of God and our mother, the Virgin Mary, for ceaselessly interceding regardless.

Acknowledgement

This book would not have been written without the substantial help from the following people: Ms. Ifeyinwa Onyechi who implanted the idea of being an author in me; Ms. Chidi Ngoka for her generous suggestions.; Lady Celia Otubu for making me 'see' how it is done in the courts; Ms. Joan Arbery for the initial copy-editing when the book was a tortuous read. To the members of Irish Writers' Exchange who prevailed upon me when it looked like I couldn't keep it together anymore; To my Literary Agent, Roslyn Fuller, for her astute, concise and infectious drives, you are a find. To Ifunanya Ibegbu for that Laptop that got things started. To my family who believed even though they are not exactly sure of what I was talking about. To all of you, I say may you live long!

To my father for always being proud of me, but is no longer here to see this feather on my cap.

And finally to my boys; the people of the 'United States of Amiri' whose ever increasing impatience kept me striving, Ethelbert-Anthony my husband, and George-Jordan our son—it is done.

References

Sometimes you read, watch or listen to things that inform or shape your perceptions. In respect of this book, these include: The Book of Psalms in the Holy Bible, Oprah Winfrey's show on 'Who Am I,' Joyce Meyers' 'Radical Obedience' in Enjoying Everyday Life and Alive! a Catholic Monthly Newspaper.

Preface

A few years back, I got a dream assignment from *The New York Times*—to travel the world and document the changes being wrought by human migration. Ireland offered an especially vivid example. Once a racially homogenous capital of red-haired Marys and blue-eyed Seans, Dublin had been transformed into a showcase of multicultural splendor—a city thrumming with Polish plumbers, Lithuanian nannies, Filipino nurses, Chinese traders, and sub-Saharan asylum seekers. My travels took me to a dingy government hostel and a bright—in both senses of the word—Nigerian woman with a compelling story to tell. Stories, I should say. They poured forth like agitated champagne, sparkling, plentiful, and funny.

Ifedinma Dimbo and her husband, Tony, faced the threat of deportation under a convoluted case that had made its way to the Irish Supreme Court. She had come to Cork a decade before as a graduate student, given birth to a son, gone home to Lagos and returned to Dublin, thinking that her child's status as an Irish citizen gave her and her husband residency rights. The Irish government argued otherwise and left them languishing in a dormitory for three years. Barred from working, they shared a single room, lined up for meals, and watched their life savings disappear—a story she told in wry tones, absent self-pity.

Impossibly polite, their son, George-Jordan, was top to toe an Irish lad, who studied Gaelic and papered the wall with parochial school awards. "Dear Justice Minister," he wrote when he was nine, "I heard my Mommy and Daddy whispering about deportation. Please do not deport us. Remember, I am also an Irish child." Ife was unmistakable in her visits to the parochial school—the only parent in a Yoruba headdress—and beamed as the teachers marveled at George-Jordan's manners. The Synge Street School was pulling for them. The Dimbos won their case.

During our visit, Ife told me she had overheard an intriguing snippet of conversation. A Nigerian man at the hostel said that he had come to Ireland to find a woman who had abandoned him. Ife's restless imagination went to work. Why would a woman leave such a man? What would spill forth in her side of the story? Stuck in legal limbo, Ife started writing, and from a small, dull room a long, lively story flowed. Among the territories it covers are sex, love, greed, borders, betrayal and redemption. With the characters traveling from Lagos, London, Italy, and Ireland, I tend to think of it as a novel that is partly about migration. Ife sees it through a feminist lens.

At its heart is a woman as striking as a Yoruba headdress in a Dublin parochial school. Her name is Gift.

—Jason DeParle
The New York Times
Washington, D.C.

Prologue

The cry of death does not need invitation; when you hear it you go and say *ndo*, for you do not know when it'll be your turn. Under this umbrella the people of my town turned out to bury my father. But some of the mourners' umbrellas, in addition, covered the hope of filling up their stomach, now that *garri* was no longer poor people's food. Even *garri biko nu? Tufiakwa,* Nigeria *emebisi go nnoo.* My father was a good man who would not eat while a brother's stomach was empty; a pillar of Saint Alphonsus Catholic Church and the community. "If you want to hear it as it is, go to Abraham, he does not stand with the crooked." He was not rich from the strength of his hand, but his son had defied the Ofoedu poverty legacy, so in the end he was rich by begetting ThankGod. My father refused to take up the subtle nudgings from our parish priest, Father Augustine Obidi, to go for knighthood. And we, the inner caucus of the Ofoedu family, knew why he resisted the nudge. ThankGod my brother had made it; yet my father and mother went about with a colorless air enveloping them, the air of failure; failure at their duty as parents. This kind of air does not allow you to breathe with your head held up. It's strange how what one has done tends to impact the lives of close relatives, it should be a course of study in the university, to really examine the implications of action and effect, maybe then one would be armed before taking any step towards action.

Thump! Thump! Thump!

Shivers ran round my body causing me to swallow hard hurting my throat. The putting into the ground part of burial must have commenced, but that did not get me to open my eyes. What was there to see?

Then a feathery touch, which became firm, announced itself on my shoulder. I twitched, but still did not open my eyes. I was not ready to see my mother's eyes: reproachful. But the touch persisted. That'd be ThankGod then.

'Gi, it's your turn.' I nodded but made no move. Gently he nudged and then propelled. So I moved, one leg placed in front of the other, alongside him till we got to the mouth of the grave. I shivered but had to do what I had to do while I still had the iron-rod that had inserted itself into my spine since I got the news. It was a good thing that I had the iron-rod, anything less would have made me create more fodder for gossip: maybe this time that I was the one that killed my father. Maybe it was even being said already, right here in the graveyard. Swiftly I opened my eyes and stole a look around and then at my mother; but she was already being led away, so my eyes encountered only her black-clad droopy shoulders.

I took the proffered shovel and plucked a little soil from the heap beside the freshly dug grave and threw it in. The sharp thump turned out to be a galvanizer; because a deep-seated emotion buried somewhere in my core became dislodged and broke through to the surface. It tore at my throat ferociously, I staggered, dazed. Quickly I gathered myself but that effort was too late, it had spread across my shoulders, down to my arms, my stomach, my spine, my whole being and, very hard to comprehend, to the iron-rod, melting it along with my resolve and, unlike anything I had ever done in my entire twenty-eight years of existence, I howled. That howl braced me as I geared to launch my body into the grave. But my brother probably anticipated this reaction for he pulled me back sharply and held me against his chest preventing my throwing myself in. I twisted, took a good look at him and shouted 'that is my father down there, alone!'

'I know,' he murmured, 'I know,' while rubbing the nape of my neck with the fingers of his left hand as he pulled me well away from the gaping mouth of the grave while he gripped me tighter with his right hand. I couldn't breathe, I couldn't move. That was ThankGod for you; always full of gusto.

The pain in my heart was inexpressible: My father was gone.

And I had failed to wipe out the ridges of pain I had caused to appear on his forehead. Initially I had believed that money could do it, but it didn't. He died with the pain of my iniquity in his heart. How would I ever know that he truly forgave me? What could I do to atone for my actions? Who would tell me? At this point guilt, a very heavy emptiness, firmly draped itself around me, squeezing before finally making itself comfortable in my soul. This made the flow of my tears increase, running down freely, collecting mucous from my snout on its way. After a long while, the deep keening lessened and my silent tears stopped flowing and blinking rapidly, my vision cleared. It was only then I realized that we were the only two people left in the burial ground.

I stepped out of my brother's hold and turned to look into his eyes. I always believed that when you pinned people down, eye to eye, they'd be careful about lying because you'd know. Not that ThankGod would lie to me, but there's always a first time.

'Tha, did he ever say anything about me?'

My brother looked at me with surprise before his brows rose, doubtfully, like I was speaking a foreign language. Finally he shook his head dispersing the various emotions, looking at me steadily he sighed, heavily, and then he said,

'Gi, you are his mother, remember?'

'Did he forgive me ThankGod?' I was not going to make do with a roundabout answer; an answer that was based on assumptions.

'You must be asking about something else,' ThankGod added.

'But he never looked me in the eyes again afterwards.'

I decided to continue on the path that was safe. A path that was easy to deal with while ignoring what he was really saying. However, ThankGod, the recalcitrant mule of our childhood days, ignored me: If I wanted to play games he had the tenacity of an elephant. I had never won.

'But . . .' I trailed off.

'Gi, you know what is troubling you.' He paused and then nodded as if we had just agreed on that, before he continued, 'Face it.'

'Tha, what am I going to do?'

'Nobody will tell you that.'

'Tha . . . I am truly lost.'

And that was when my brother held my gaze in return, a gaze that said: you got lost because you allowed yourself to, but you could also retrace your steps if you wanted to. Then he asked me, as if to confirm the look, 'Are you?'

He must have intended the question to spur me into action, into making me desire to retrace those steps I took to ruination . . .

'Keep walking, Gi.' His right hand now draped over my shoulder was used to exert a subtle pressure that propelled me forward yet again.

PART ONE

"The Woman Issue"

We cannot reflect about the nature of anything without considering carefully how it can act on other things and they in turn on it. To pursue the enquiry without doing so would be like the progress of a blind man.

Plato

He Found Me

CASTLEKNOCK, DUBLIN

2005

A cold finger of something roused me. Slowly I opened one eye to see if I could see through the cobweb of sleep, to size the situation. Then I remembered and sighed deeply. Of course, it's Lucky. I yawned, following it immediately with an extended stretch that woke up all the bones in my body and the itches. With great relish I scratched abandonedly, farting to round up the bliss.

Fully awake now, I sat up to await my turn after master Lucky. As I sat there I tried to wake up my brain, which for some reason was still slumbering, by trying to organize the morning's activities. Suddenly it clicked. It was Saturday. 'Oh my goodness! Isn't life just sweet?' But surprisingly, I didn't feel the full sweetness of a work-free Saturday because that earlier finger of something did not disappear but sat solemnly somewhere in my lungs breathing with me. Occasionally it'd release these things that would wash over me in waves. Premonition? Fear? But why?

The bang of the toilet seat heralded Lucky's arrival as it reverberated, nipping my thoughts, as he launched himself on me, but I was already sitting up, prepared. I had learnt from the past.

'Mummy I love you.' He murmured in a crotchety voice that could only be Lucky's as he landed.

'I love you too, baby. Did you sleep well?' He nodded yes and snuggled behind my back, enfolding my waist. I turned to gaze at my son, smiled and kissed his forehead. I extricated myself and went into the bathroom to get ready for our Saturday morning tradition: when the girls would join Lucky in my bed and we'd all have a lazy hour.

I love our time together; it gives us the opportunity to get to know and understand each other: bonding. I had to smile at that: *bonding!* White people eh! They have name and time for everything. But . . . it works for them though, as it should, affirming the saying that the type of firewood found in a given place cooked their food.

Engrossed with my children, I emptied my mind of all thoughts. One did not need sophisticated thoughts to be with children: just be there, answer *complicated* questions as best as you could and mediate wars that erupted incessantly. Now I am a master at being at a balance with my children and their ways. Initially it wasn't easy. Now . . . Well . . . Now life couldn't be better.

As we played, a sharp chiming of the doorbell pierced the air. I raised my brows, surprised; not because our doorbell rang but because I knew of nobody that would be calling on us this early and on a Saturday at that! I was still trying to savor the taste of not having to engage in the chaotic rushing about that was characteristic of our weekday mornings: getting everybody ready to leave before 8.30am. Now that would be scuttled by whomever.

I thought of sending Frances, my seven-year-old daughter, to find out who had encroached into the sacredness of our Saturday morning uninvited, but decided to go myself. I'd still be required to attend to the *visitor* anyway.

I sighed as I got up and tried to make myself presentable. Looking in the mirror I beheld this ragamuffin looking back at me and shook my head, plucked a brush from the dressing table and attacked my hair with all the might I could muster at that hour to untangle the beehive. The hair extensions remained kitten soft and were touted to be 100% human hair until sewn into your hair, then they change form. I kept promising myself to go easy on these extensions. The problem however was that the hair salons operated by our people here in Dublin were only interested in weaving, plaiting, twisting, sewing, and so on, because that's where the money came from, wash and set or anything that had to do with just your natural hair? Forget it; they'd kill your hair to deter you from doing just that so as to push you into the extension vice.

Heading out of the room, poised to descend the stairs the doorbell rang again and I stopped. How dare whomever? Did this caller think we had lain awake all night awaiting the visit? For some reason, I returned to the room and instructed my children to stay in there and watch television. Then I closed the door firmly, before starting to descend the stairs, mumbling to myself while struggling to put my housecoat on.

At the verge of unlocking the front door, I swallowed my anger and rearranged my demeanor. It wouldn't be good manners to face a visitor, however unwanted, with a frowning face. Besides, it was too early for one's hackles to be up. I opened the door, poked my head out and froze. *It was a good thing I came down myself* darted through my mind as soon as my eyes fell on the caller. Rooted on the spot I stared at him in shock: struck dumb, as it's said. My eyes must be playing tricks on me, so I shook my head, and then blinked in rapid succession to clear the woozy feelings. Now with crystal vision I peered again at the man on my doorstep. Yes it was him alright. Just as I confirmed this to myself, survival instinct, born out of years of looking over my shoulders, kicked in and quickly I withdrew my head and slammed the door shut along with my eyes. I was surprised at how fast I rallied round because I was sure that I had turned into a statue. I leaned on the door for support, my breathing, a short gasping noise, harshly escaping my contracted nostrils, accompanied my slide down to the floor that ended with a sharp heavy thump, as my legs gave way.

'It couldn't possibly be, could it?' I murmured, bewildered. Of course, it couldn't be. I was still asleep. It had to be. But hadn't I woken up earlier? I thought I had. So how come then I was seeing things while awake? For the possibility of him being here was far too remote. Very cautiously I opened my eyes, stood up and moved the window curtains, ever so slightly. Then with narrowed eyes, for a clearer vision, I took a peek, through the clear-glassed part of the window.

Good God in heaven! It was him alright. Osahon was standing on my front porch, as tall and as majestic as ever! Quickly, I closed the curtain and slid down on the floor again, closing my eyes, hoping to ward off what I saw and all it could mean.

This was unbelievable. What on earth was Osahon doing here? What could possibly bring him across forests, mountains and oceans to my doorstep? It did not make any sense. If I remembered correctly, he had delivered a harsh ultimatum to not come within breathing distance of him or die. Now he was here himself, breaching his own instructions. Aaaah, Osahon!

Hadn't I steered clear since then? Or had I inadvertently disobeyed him? But how and when? Then I started to really panic as a thought flickered past: Oh my God, did he come here to kill me? *Don't be silly Gift, this is abroad.* But I was not reassured. My body had started to tremble badly, even as these thoughts assailed me. My mind was whirling perilously like a washing machine in a spin mode and my heart was keeping pace, thundering, threatening to crush my ribs. A vicious woodpecker was tugging persistently at a vein on my forehead, which caused a squeezing and releasing sensation that brought on an instant headache of dizzying proportions from the jaw up. That finger of something that had sat sedately in my lungs since morning had exploded into a nightmare in broad daylight!

But as all these disorders were settling themselves on the various parts of my body, it also dawned on me that I had to face him someday, sometime. Acknowledging then that all these physical ailments would not help me in any way, I decided to do something much more than trembling and cowering behind my door!

I stood up again and very cautiously opened the door, took the key out of the lock, went outside and closed the door behind me while pocketing the key. It would not do to lock myself out at the point of retreating grandly. Besides that, I would not want the children to get a whiff of what was going on.

I composed myself, smoothened my askew housecoat, then standing erect to my God-given height of 5ft 9" pretending to be calm, I took a very long wither-inducing-kind of look at my ex-husband's chin. I had aimed for his eyes forgetting that Osahon was one of those men who happened to tower over me. But no matter, I did not need my height to be able to emit animosity. For everything that had happened to me since I met Osahon flashed through my mind at a high speed, one by one, and they were more than enough to ignite an inferno that could sear him to cinders.

But it seemed really surreal that the source of these emotions was standing before me and I couldn't do more than stare at him in stupefied terror. I also realized that I did not hate him, not anymore. Maybe I never had, but I could not love him either, not anymore. Nonetheless, very strangely, I felt the vestiges of his hold on me tug, ever so slightly, but I squashed them.

I squared my shoulders and stood erect again, then with a voice full of venom, designed to shred to pieces, I inquired of him, 'Osahon what are you doing here?'

Osahon, who had up to then been staring at me intently, abandoned that task and raised his face up to the clouds, as if to seek divine wisdom, then slowly creased his face into a frown. Finally, concluding the rituals with a great sigh, he brought his face down, but instead of answering he just stared at me. I lifted my brows questioningly but said nothing. So we stood there and stared at each other, like two adversarial cockerels over a hen. Eventually in a voice filled with pain, probably designed to elicit appeasement and more he answered me. Sort of.

'You look ever so beautiful, Princess.' He tilted his head to one side, probably to lend credence to his appeal, before he continued, 'Can you ever find it in your heart to forgive me?'

Still numb from shock, but gradually gathering my scattered wits, I shook my head before I managed to ask him again.

'What do you want from me, Osahon?'

Without wasting time he said, 'To ask for your forgiveness. To see if I could ever make it up to you.'

This is beyond belief, I thought, before venturing in a whisper, 'Do you think that that is a possibility?'

I could not believe what I was hearing. This Osahon must be crazy. He had to be. I shook my head, puzzled. Or he must think that I was a fool. But of course, how could I ever forget? That I made myself the greatest of fools all because of love and see where it landed me. It just went to show that you could never predict what would be.

Though I was staring at Osahon, I was neither seeing him nor listening to him. I was on the familiar outskirts of the footpath to the memory forest; gearing to embark on a remembering-discovery trip. But then I brought myself back, quickly. I needed to dismiss him now that he had supposedly told me what he came for. As I refocused, I caught the tail-end of his further misguided suppositions.

' . . . If we both work at it, it is possible. You see, that was my singular purpose of undertaking this journey: to wipe clean the hurt that I had put in your soul.' He took a deep breath and then requested, 'May I come in then?' He paused again, probably to gauge my demeanor before he zoomed in, 'your neighbors are beginning to twitch their curtains. We can discuss this properly seated you know? Please.'

I nodded as if in agreement before I released the sum of my feelings on him,

'Let me make myself very clear, Osahon Osanobua Iguedia, if that is your name, I do not know you, and in my book of life you do not exist, not anymore. So you are dead. And as far as I know, my children were not fathered by you. If my knowledge is anything to go by, I do not have anything that might possibly interest you. Therefore, you are wasting your time with me. Remember? I am an *ashawo*.' I paused, wondering if it might do any good to add a threat or two, decided that it might give my words a punch, so I threatened, 'I do not want you to come back here to pester us again, but if you do, that will be at your own peril.' I was satisfied to see Osahon cringe from the whiplash before I banged and locked the door behind me.

I leaned on the door, then slowly slid to the floor again, but without the jarring thump of earlier, my tail-bone was still smarting from that mistake. I pulled my legs up and tucked my knees firmly under my chin, circling my legs with my arms, my eyes clenched tightly shut. I saw my mother, her mouth always tightly clenched in objection, especially when she did not want any words to escape. Then my thought shifted to the anus of a tortoise, reputed to be so tight that if you had your finger stuck in it, you either had the tortoise killed or cut your finger to free yourself. *Good Heavens! Gift, have you gone mad? How can you be thinking of the anus of a tortoise and your mother's mouth at this calamitous time?* I smiled. Nothing unusual there. I had long since realized that the mind enjoyed playing games: When you need to be at your sharpest, with all your wits around you, to tackle *untackleable* problems, your mind wanders off and your thought processes latch onto silly, mundane and illogical pastures. I suppose it is a self-protective mechanism, devised by the body to keep pressures at bay, otherwise the mind—or is it the brain?—would explode. So it had to wander, perambulate to softer grounds, graze lazily at lush pastures, gathering strength and strategies.

I had always wondered and worried about what my reactions would be if I ever saw him again, all these years. Now I know. Nothing! Well . . . Almost nothing.

How many times in one's life could a problem wrestle one literally to the ground? Wasn't it said somewhere that problems would come, that was a given, but it was your ability to rise above them that made you the person you were? Good talk. And I did it. I rose above my problems. Didn't I? And emerged victorious. I had squashed my challenges to the ground, reduced them to rubble, to dust, to nothing. So I had assumed.

Suddenly, unbidden, the image of the triumphant Virgin Mary appeared in the landscape of my mind: Pulping the head of the traitorous snake. I smiled, thoughtful. *Wouldn't it be nice to possess a pinch of divine alliance, a wee bit, just enough . . . To enable me to mince this obstinate problem into oblivion, permanently?*

Because I obviously didn't get it right the first time.

I heaved myself up and like a drunk stumbled into the living room, plonked myself on the sofa and rubbed my eyes with the heel of my palm and then pinched my cheeks, for no discernible reason, before continuing my mental meanderings. I knew that I had stepped on the proverbial tail of a lion because there was no way Osahon would let go. If he could locate me, several thousands of miles away from home, sniff me out and came calling, then mere words would not send him away. But I had to find out what exactly was going on before embarking on any plan of action whatsoever.

As I sat stiffly on the sofa pondering in despair, sadness gradually took on a larger proportion.

'Why is Osahon here?' I asked out loud. The last I remembered he was riding the waves of success at my expense. He had got himself a new wife, whom he loved according to him, and they were expecting their first issue. He had told me so himself. First issue indeed! Well, my children and I had ceased to exist for him, so it was alright for him to be expecting his first issue with his *wife whom he loves*. He was on top of the world then. So what was it all about now?

The heavy brocade curtains guarding the windows gave the living room a dark hue which not only suited the occasion but also nurtured my bruised soul. As I sat there I felt my heart constrict by this overwhelming sadness, the squeezing pain finally erupted and became a torrent of tears that gushed from my eyes.

All the emotions, which I thought I had killed and buried, came crashing down as hot-bitter tears streamed down my face. Shamelessly, I gave full vent to the sorrow, my body shaking in full support. I could not stop crying, not even when my son, Lucky, clambered up the sofa and started whimpering, then his face crumpled and his whimpering graduated to full-blown crying. This summoned his sisters to the living room, and they promptly joined the melee.

Why now?

I continued to cry, ignoring the presence of my children, while searching for the elusive answers. Now that my life was beginning to assume a semblance of normality: I had my children with me; I had trained and found a job in the financial sector as a fund administrator; I was living anonymously as much as I could; and the thread of life was being woven somehow in my favor, once again. Now this? Why should Osahon consistently choose to wipe laughter from my soul? I wailed while gathering my children to myself. We continued to cry until Lucky imperiously demanded to have the TV switched on so that he could watch Barney and Friends. This request caught us unawares, breaking the spell of gloom. Releasing my children from my tight clutch, I switched on the television as I went into the kitchen.

In the kitchen I found myself frantically cleaning everything with Domestos bleach mixed with warm water, from the worktops to gas cooker to cupboards, shelves, microwave, washing machine, then on all fours scrubbing the kitchen floor. At this point it occurred to me that something was not right; why should I be on my knees washing my kitchen floor? So I got up and severely admonished; *Gift what you do not need right now is altered mental state alright? Get hold of yourself now!* I nodded and washed my hands before wiping my eyes that still had tears streaming down from them. With a sense of purpose I went about gathering what I'd need for our Saturday breakfast-special; *akara* and *akamu*, which had been relegated by the furore.

Then I heard the gentle fall of tiny footsteps on the passageway to the kitchen and smiled. Frances. I had wondered what took her so long. She may be only seven, but she was a very discerning seven year old, wise beyond her years. Maybe, being the oldest she had witnessed me suffer then in far away Donegal. I shook my head again. Only God knew what she thought was amiss then in our lives. But one thing was for sure; Frances had made it her duty since then to look out for me; fierce frown creasing her little face, whenever she saw my face clouded. Thereafter she'd stick to me like a leech, a protective leech that is; until she felt that the storm had passed.

I busied myself with assembling the makings of *akara* and *akamu*, pretending not to have noticed her presence, until I felt a gentle tug and looked down.

'Yes Fran.'

'Mum.' . . . She hesitated and at my nod, she spoke gently. 'Mum, why are we crying?'

'Fran dear, you will not understand. Not now anyway,' I said as I drew her close to my bosom rubbing her head distractingly, soothingly, and then stretching my fingers to straighten the fat braids on her head. I made to shoo her away, but changed my mind, it'd be better to allay her fears. 'Maybe when you are a little older I will tell you everything. But you must promise me that you will not let whatever I tell you then colour your life, okay?'

Frances nodded, but a little frown appeared on her forehead. You could almost see her grapple with the problem.

'Was that why we are crying mum? Our life was coloured? But is colouring not good? Is life a picture book that you colour? But how do you colour life, mum?'

'When bad things happen to you, sometimes, it may change the way you look at things.'

'Oh . . . I hope nothing bad happens to us, mum. I do not want our life to be coloured if it is from a bad thing. I love you mum. Will the colour be black or red?'

'Fran, that is why you have to be older to understand. Go to the living room and supervise your brother. You know he is very stubborn especially if he thinks Eudora is *playing* big sister.'

'Okay, mum, but tell me first.'

'Alright. Life can be coloured, red or black; it all depends on how serious the bad thing is.'

'Can life be coloured yellow? You know, yellow is bright and it has a funny smiley face.'

'Yes Fran.'

'Then it won't be bad again, will it?'

I bent down and drew up her face with my palms and looking straight into her eyes, really seeing her, I smiled before saying, 'No it won't, and you are very correct. You can have a yellow-coloured life with a smiling face. We can say then that bright colours are for good things, while moody and dark colours are for bad things. But do not be afraid, our life will be coloured yellow from now onwards and we will all be happy, I promise ok.'

She nodded.

Bless the child, I mused, she had actually provided me with an easy way to explain it to her. There was no need to plant unnecessary apprehension in my children's life, thereby *colouring* it!

'Now go, they are screeching in there.' Frances nodded again before trotting off while I settled down to cook our breakfast.

I fed, bathed, clothed and settled my children, then went into my room with very reluctant feet. I didn't want to be alone with my thoughts. I needed to be busy. But what could I do? Reaching my room I sat down heavily on the bed and gazed into space. My thoughts immediately sprang into action: releasing themselves. Unwilling as it was, I had hardly set foot to the memory forest before I was besieged by various images of my past, baying and snapping at my heels like a pack of evil and vicious mutant rats of my nightmares of yesteryears. Which one would start first? Which aspect of my life would push forward? Hadn't I regained my space in the cosmic arrangement that was life? Am I going to continue to pay for a single misstep? Surely not! I had paid, and paid in full. There was nothing more to extract from me so there must be a mistake somewhere, a mix up. Osahon was not here to see me. He was only passing by.

If only . . . I closed my eyes and sighed as I stared at the panoramic greys, reds, blacks, yellows and the greenery pictures of my life flying past . . .

The Stranger

OYI TOWN, ANAMBRA STATE, NIGERIA
1982

I was born to bring light to the Ofoedu clan. This gleaned from the numerous talks that usually swirled around my head growing up. It was the miracle of my being in this realm in the first place that gave rise to this deduction. It was told that my brother ThankGod, with that coconut head of his, had torn our mother's womb into shreds while exiting, thus putting paid to any further child-bearing for Celina. This was vintage Egenti, the local midwife, whose penchant to see beyond the realms of this world irritated my father no end.

Whenever I did anything supposedly beyond my years I was lauded, with my father going *Ifechukwu anyi g'eji wee f'uzo!* The light from God; that will brighten our way, while every other member of my family would nod sagely in agreement as if they were privy to the handing down ceremony of this enlightenment. So I grew up knowing that I was special and that my efforts would advance my family.

My Town, Oyi, etched at the tail-end of a valley-like plain was a one-horse town that boasted of four villages. During the rainy season, Oyi Town would be drenched. But the rains cleansed the village from her coat of red-paint. Then the enterprising fingers of farmers would set to work, preparing their farmlands: cutting and burning of grasses, trees and anything that would constitute a hindrance. The tilling of the soil and the final preparation of ridges and mounds for planting of the main staples, yam and cassava, would follow thereafter. Minor crops like, tomatoe, okra, *akidi, anyala,* cocoyam, corn, planted amongst the kings and queens of crops would be the first to mature. Ears of corn and pears were roasted on smouldering charcoal and hot ashes, respectively, and were eaten with such relish.

Aku—the ant-like flying insects, flushed out by the rains from their home—constituted another rainy season delicacy. All we needed to do was keep a wide basin outside that would soon fill up with rain water and you'd get as many of the insects as you'd ever need: for when they flew out of their home, the rain would beat them down into our basin trap and then their water-soaked wings would fall off trapped in our basin destined to our greedy mouths. Dry-fried and slightly salted, they'd become fodder for our teeth as we crunched away, like popcorn.

All sorts of green vegetables would be in bloom. I wouldn't say that I quite appreciated their abundancy because my mother, in addition to using them as base for every food, would cook them on their own with a sliver of onion and a strip of liver and we were made to eat it just like that: for nutrition and vitamins, she said. Yuck! My mother was not a book woman so how did she come about this knowledge? But you swallow your entire portion without as much as a frown. Half of the known fruits would ripen; *udala,* cashew, guava and we'd gorge ourselves like there was no tomorrow.

But my father was a palmwine tapper and not a farmer so I was only trying to say what I believed happens from having my eyes on the ground—one of my mother's constant admonitions—and my mother's pepper shrub could not be equated to a farm. It was beside her kitchen and there she produced all her vegetables and the rookie crops.

Then the harmattan season would set in from around November through to February when the sun would turn us into seasoned walnuts, dry and lifeless. All of us in the village, including the grasshoppers, the lizards, the trees and the streams would be the walking dead. The sun was that merciless. The vibrancy from the rainy season would turn into fine-red fires during the dry season. For my village was blessed with this fine-red soil. If you climbed up a tree and surveyed the village during this time, you'd see a dried-up red desert with no oasis in sight. But then, it was my village and I loved it, before I came to ache for much more, all because a stranger passed by.

Abraham nodded in the general direction of his daughter Gift, in acknowledgement of her chattering, as he worked away. They had just returned from their palmwine collecting rounds, and as soon as he had let go of her hand she skipped off but as usual maintained an uninterrupted stream of one-sided conversations with him. He settled down and got busy mixing and pouring palmwine into gourds of various sizes and shapes to be collected by his customers later in the morning. Gift's jabbering, in-tune with the droning of the bees and the buzzing of the flies, kept him company. With the underlying knowledge that he had trained his ears to always cover her, he went about his business unworried. He lost track of time as he hummed to himself, oblivious of the racket from the bees and the flies jostling for position to sip the nectar that was his palmwine. He never whisked off the flies; there was no need to, they were part and parcel of palmwine.

Suddenly he was wrenched back to the present by an ear-throbbing scream. What has happened to his Gift? He stood up and gazed towards her, she had fallen and grazed her knee. He nodded as if that was inevitable. Rubbing his palms on his bush khaki-shorts, he walked over, scooped her into the crook of his arms and gently murmured words of endearment as he strode towards his shed. But she was wailing and flailing so much that he had to sit down to dandle her on his knees before delving into the intricacies of first-aid.

At last he got up, with Gift, now tucked under his armpit, reasonably calmed, to rummage for the bitterleaf leaves he had kept on the raffia roof that morning: to be used in addition to the palm fruits as stoppers to prevent the fiery and foaming palmwine from overflowing their gourds. Some of it would now be employed for other uses. He did not relish the result of this other uses of the bitterleaf, good as it may be, if he knew his Gift well. He sat back down having taken the quantity he felt he needed and crushed it in his palm to soften it, stopping to spit generously into it. Finally it formed a soggy mush, then he squeezed the liquid onto Gift's grazed knee. She howled lustily from the sting. Abraham nodded, he did not expect any less from her, but he must seal the wound and prevent infection. Abraham shook his head in amused mystification as his daughter continued to shriek. One would think, at the rate she was carrying on, that she was being killed.

Abraham refocused at the sound of a throat being cleared and beheld a stranger who had obviously requested to be served, if the scowl on his face was anything to judge by. He put Gift down whom, having sufficiently calmed down, scampered off once more as soon as her legs touched the ground.

*   *   *

I had left, but quickly doubled back, and hid behind one of the big and already filled palmwine gourds to observe the stranger, the warning, to not listen in to adult conversations, was buried. It was a rare thing to see a stranger. Ours was a town that led to nowhere, so nobody got lost on their way to anywhere. The sudden appearance in our village of a strange man therefore, was a wonder, a newness that must be absorbed. So I watched, eyes as wide as the setting sun, as my father served the stranger.

*   *   *

Abraham also cleared phlegm from his own throat, as if in retaliation, while studying the man that seemed to have appeared from nowhere from beneath his hooded eyes, as he served him. The stranger snatched the proffered palmwine and downed it in one gulp, without a break, and stretched the cup for another helping. It was after the third drink that he slowed down.

What could have brought this man to this part of the world and how could he have worked up this much thirst so early in the morning? Determined to find out, he cleared his throat, yet again, but this time as a prelude to opening up a conversation.

'You are not from these parts then?' he asked, knowing fully well that the thirsty man from nowhere was not.

'No. I am only visiting. I came to inform my brother of our mother's passing.'

'*Ewuu*,' Abraham exclaimed as was expected before continuing, '*Aru ona anwuia?*' Was she sick?

'*Mbao, onaba nno nwuru.*' No, she went to bed and died.

'*Eyi yaa. Ndo nnu.*' A pity. My condolences.

'I hope she did not suffer?' Abraham added as he rearranged his face sorrowfully, to suit the news.

'No, you'd think she was asleep. God rest her soul. She was a good woman.'

'*Onya nu, onwu ndi aka fa kwuoto, okosi adi.*' That is it, that is how the deaths of good people are, Abraham informed the stranger, then kept quiet, mulling over his comment and after what he considered a respectful time, to have honoured the dead, had elapsed, he continued, 'You must be Josiah Igbene's brother then?'

Of course he was. Everybody knew everybody in the village and Josiah was the only settler, though he had stayed long enough to be counted a native. Abraham had often wondered why Josiah or anybody at that must leave his place of birth to settle in another village as a watch repairer! A village where you could count on one hand the number of people that owned wrist watches worth repairing inclusive of him Abraham. That went to show how people upstage themselves, set themselves up to be permanently poor. Not that he Abraham fared any better, but he was at least in his own father's homestead surrounded by his kith and kin. If you must leave your homeland for greener pastures, at least aim for pastures that have the wherewithal to support your chosen trade.

'Yes,' the stranger answered to Abraham's long forgotten question.

'Oh. I suspected as much. Greet him for me. Tell him that I will pass by later to greet him myself.'

'Thank you,' murmured the stranger and drained his fourth drink, smacked his lips in appreciation of the quality and then commented, 'I say, it is only in the village that you can get palmwine worthy of that name. If it is in the Township, those sons of goats would have watered it down, that you'd wonder why they still bother to call it palmwine,' he ended bitterly while rooting in his back pocket for money to pay for the drinks.

So he lives in the Township then, Abraham thought wryly. It was comments like this that made him count his blessings for not venturing out.

He chuckled expansively, as was expected, at such comments, then looked at the stranger again before deciding to take the edge off the stranger's anger with a mild comment, an appropriate response as it happened, because a flicker of smile lifted the stranger's lips.

'That is Township for you, where anything goes,' was the magic wand.

'I will bring some palmwine with me when I come around later,' Abraham added, rubbing his palms together. That, brought yet another flicker, but this time a softer smile that spreads up to the stranger's eyes.

'Thank you very much, my brother, you are very kind indeed,' the stranger intoned thinly before striking out decisively towards Josiah's homestead. Abraham nodded with a smile, while turning to scout for Gift.

*   *   *

As the conversation had wound down, I had crept away from my hiding place, to delight in all that I had overheard. Township, where sons of goats water palmwine? What kind of place was that? My heart had ricocheted up and down while my imagination went wild, presenting me with all sorts of imagery.

That encounter had planted a seed of adventure in my little mind then, remembering how I sat swinging my legs in pace with my thoughts afterwards, thereupon I had caught sight of one of my friends, the lizard, scuttling by, and I jumped down and scuttled after it in search of information, it might know. It looked well traveled.

Oyi Town 1988

POOR VILLAGE URCHIN

Then my brother ThankGod started school. Even though I had watched the preparation that preceded the actual event—getting his uniform, his metal school box, chalk and slate—it did not dawn on me what it was all about until that day and I was told that I would not be going with him!

'But why?' I had wailed fiercely before rounding on the culprit, 'Tha, where are you going without me?' He shrugged, deepening the mystery. But off he went, to school. I had flung myself on the mud floor with a loud thump and shrieked, rebuffing my father's attempt to console me. Finally he gave me a job; to go on palmwine-rounds with him: To first collect and mix then taste to ascertain the potency of his palmwine.

So every morning, I held my father's last two fingers like my life depended on my holding them, as we struggled along the footpath, dodging early morning dews that perched precariously on the long green grasses, looking for who to drench, to get to my father's palm trees. My father explained to me that palmwine came from making a hole on the upper trunk of the palm tree towards the branches, and then gourds were positioned to catch the juices that would flow out of the hole. If the juices so collected were too sweet you mixed them with water, if they were not sweet you mixed them with saccharine, if they were too strong you add water or you sold them like that at a premium if you had good paying customers which was rare anyway so you mixed them to have plenty. So each day when we returned from our collection rounds my father would start on his next job, mixing, and I on mine, playing.

One day dawned as usual but different. I was excited, so excited that I couldn't keep my breakfast down. My turn had come to start school.

*　　*　　*

I had believed that playing was the soul of life, then I started school, made more friends and played harder. But then my desire to acquire knowledge overturned playing. I loved school. To read, learn, explore, to add to what I knew was given full throttle and to crown it all I was a model student. ThankGod was not interested in the nitty gritty of school even though his brain was hot according to his friends and classmates. He was also a fearless soul and as such I was a fearless soul. I tagged along to everywhere and that was how he landed us somewhere which ingrained another insight into my soul. It was during the Christmas season when the whole village was agog with activities, and everybody was out in full force. ThankGod had left the usual gathering of singing and dancing outed by one group or the other and sidled out and so I sidled after him. The events that caused the gatherings were usually the fulcrum of the Christmas season and may be organized by different associations of our town, an age-grade: men or women born within a given age range which served as a social support group for members; one could get a loan from the purse of the age-grade if you were a full and active member, or members could help you cultivate or weed your farm at a reduced price than employed labour. Or the events could be organized by the yet to be married daughters of the villages, grouped through the cleaning and sweeping of the village stream, which one joined from around the age of nine, to showcase new dance steps. Or yet still the groupings could be the CWO, Catholic Womens Organization, an umbrella shading all women in the Catholic Church, outing one thing or the other. The Anglican Church people must have their own thing, but I had never witnessed any, besides we always saw them as left-handed people, so I wouldn't be surprised if they didn't. Old Masquerades with new apparels could be on show organized by men, again through any of the age-grades. Also lots of people living abroad (by abroad I meant outside the bounds of our Town) came home for Christmas celebration, so there were lots of activities going on and as a result a lot of places to visit.

Usually, on the day of no activities or activities to be showcased much later in the evenings, we would go round for treats by way of visiting returnees. One did not need any invitation; you'd be fed anyway, showered with presents from abroad like Our Lady's bread, cabin biscuits—Oxford brand, chin-chin, powdered sachet soft drinks which you had to mix the contents of with water to get the drink and so many other things.

But we had seen it all before and so we had left and inadvertently strayed beyond our estimate and landed in front of a big black wrought-iron gate guarding a big palace, it must be. We stood rooted in front of the gate and could only stare in shock. ThankGod finally made a move dispelling the shock and indecision. We pushed the small side-gate that was already half-open and went in. We had strolled far into the compound before really taking in the size of the house and that smacked into us, knocking the air out of our lungs. Then I felt ThankGod's courage seep out and on its way it collected mine and they then were scattered in the compound by the gentle breeze. What had we got ourselves into? Whose house was this? It was big and raised half-way up to the sky, in two levels, that was all I could say. The outside walls of the building looked like they were made out of real rocks! We could not glimpse the inside of the house proper, because it was heavily guarded by glass doors and windows with heavy curtains.

I felt ThankGod twitch and followed the ripples of the twitch to the pointed front-end of a shoe. I nudged my eyes upwards and beheld the richest of fabrics, up still, past the swell of breasts to a face. I expected a woman's face, but not that of a black Angel. It took the remainder of my breath away. I didn't know how to describe beauty, but she was it. I looked up to the sky to take in her head-gear—definitely conjured from the land of the spirits. Yet again I couldn't describe what I saw. The black Angel was drenched in jewelries: necklace, bangles, earrings and one was twinkling atop her nose! As if these were not enough, the gold jewelries were accompanied by heavy-duty beadings, which must have come straight from the intricate artifacts associated with the then famed ancient Benin kingdom of mid-western Nigeria.

I found my face wreathed in a beatific smile at these beautiful things encountered, because they were the kind of things that would sit well with me. Then the smile was interrupted by a voice followed by the presence of a bulldog of a man: Tall and heavy, like a solid Iroko tree, but with triple jowls instead of branches. His protruding belly not quite concealed by the well-tailored caftan. The material was like liquid silver. He was a big-man or a representative of what a big-man should be. By big-man I mean a rich man.

'My dear, you see my car keys?' he asked the black Angel. Then he was stopped by our presence. 'Who are these, these . . . ?' The big-man bellowed, the bellow tapering into a stutter and a dismissive hand wave.

'On top of the fridge dear. I believe they are Abraham's.'

'What?!'

'Your car key is on top of the fridge. The children belong to Abraham, the tapper.'

'Oh. You confused me for a moment there. What a . . .' A pause, then, 'I mean their family being poor, you know.'

'Be kind dear, poverty could be overcome as you know,' the black Angel replied scowling at the Iroko tree.

'I haven't said anything bad. I only . . .'

'Be kind all the same.' Clapping, she called out, 'Come on children we are late,' and then swinging round she asked, 'do you want to eat rice?'

Suddenly my tongue swung into action and firmly responded. 'No ma, we are fine thank you.'

'You,' pointing at ThankGod, the Iroko tree bellowed, 'tell your father to come and see me.' *Your father* thrown at us with such carelessness that it made my father insignificant. My pa! I could feel my hurt flowing out of me like blood. I was wounded.

'Why?' the black Angel asked.

'To order palmwine for the family meeting, he may be poor but he knows his way around palmwine.'

I nudged ThankGod and stepped closer to rub my courage into him and heard him murmur, 'Yes sir.'

The big-man looked at me with a deep frown, then a smile flickered past his rough features, before he shook his head as if to disperse any spell I might be trying to cast on him.

We stood there and watched as two children, a boy and a girl close to our age came out and went into a giant car while staring at us curiously. The boy finally smiled and waved at me. I ignored this gesture. The big man and the black Angel went into the car too and they drove out of the compound.

I grabbed ThankGod and clumsily we ran, barely scrambling through the main gate that had opened on its own to let the family drive out, and was now laboriously closing itself again. Panting from the narrow escape we walked home. Any residual joy of Christmashood was snuffed out, like cold harmattan water had been poured on our feverish enthusiasm of earlier. I never discussed it with my brother, but I was quite sure that it stood out in his memory like it did on mine.

However, I started daydreaming more and more; sometimes I'd be the daughter of the big-man, dressed up in fine clothes and good shoes. Or I'd be a different persona but always, always richly dressed and being driven about in a big car with nobody ever asking for my father, just so he'd be sent on an errand like he was nothing!

As if my mother suspected our unguarded and daring wanderings, she banished me from them, festivities or not, for according to her, I had now reached the age to be reckoned with as a woman. I had just crested ten then, a gangly ten at that. I was not sure of why anybody, least of all my mother, should think that I was now a woman. But I had learnt not to argue—my mother's ear-twisting technique was matchless. When administered it'd first of all constrict my throat so that no sound could escape, my nose would start running, then my eyes would cloud up, hot with tears, and spilt without decorum. All these before she had completed the first twisting-circle! I had wished, times without number, that our punishments would be reversed, because ThankGod's own consisted of a sharp knock exactly above the groove on the nape that tapered up to his coconut head. But he had warned me to not even breathe that out. "If ma gives you the knock, your head will shatter." I believed him but it didn't stop me from wishing: He carried it off with such aplomb that I suspected it couldn't be that painful.

*   *   *

An itch twinged my ankle and that brought me back to the problem at hand, Osahon!

I stood and stretched as the twinging heel seemed to be going numb. I sat down again and shook my head. Where did it all go wrong then, eh? For surely it must be rooted in my past. Nowadays, every bad behaviour or failure was eventually traced to the person's growing up years; irrespective of anything. Either they were locked up in dark cupboards, or were smacked or were told off sometimes by their nanny or their parents or somebody or something. I should be able to locate that something and when it occured, for it was said that if you did not know when rain started to beat you, you'd not know when it ceased to beat you either. There must be a beginning and an end, otherwise, I would not find answers, thus solutions and finally closure to what happened to me.

My Brother ThankGod

1990

Our house, a four bedroom bungalow, was built with mud and had a thatched roof. Our pit toilet located at the back of the bungalow was hidden in the dense foliage after my mother's pepper shrub. It was fenced with raffia palm but did not have any door so it faced the forest to ward off prying eyes and for the wind to carry away the smell. I slept with my mother on a mud bed and ThankGod with my father. My brother Obumneme and his wife occupied one room but one had to go round to the backyard to enter this room and this gave them their privacy. My mother said Obumneme's wife was lazy so I forgot about them most of the time, but they were there and later they had children, five of them and my mother and father provided for us all.

My life, at any point in time, growing up, would have paled into nothing if it was not for my brother ThankGod. I loved him and I loved being with him, which was nearly always. He took me hunting. He taught me everything that needed to be taught. I knew how to trap grasshoppers through to birds, lizards, rats, even grasscutters. I smiled which turned into chuckling, shaking my head at the scene playing out in the window of my eyes, imagining being a hunter of monkeys in Dublin! The animal rights people would haunt me out of Europe, that'd be guaranteed.

I had never liked that I was not allowed to go for moonlight playing in the village square. My mother vehemently refused and my father concurred. I knew I missed out on a whole lot that took place out there and I also knew that ThankGod sneaked out to go, but I would not tell, so as to leave a window of opportunity to be regaled afterwards about the happenings out there. It was my pa that offered some sort of explanation for their refusal; '*Nnem*, children learn bad things out *there*, especially young girls.'

'Mmm . . .' I had snorted then, masking my tears, more determined not to betray ThankGod.

I untangled the phone's extension chord absently, half a smile etched on my face: I had to smile for I had since come to know that moonlight playing did not amount to anything different from our regular playing just that it was under the silvery, made-shadowy-by-the-trees light of the moon. It offered some sort of unnamable tantalizing delights to be outside at that time where the stars of heaven jostle to outshine each other, the atmosphere so created bestowing and infusing calmness and joy on the soul. Oooh! Moonlit nights were the best, but really as an adult, it wouldn't necessarily have invoked such level of heartache I had suffered then at not being let out. During the moon phase, some villages used that time to learn new dance steps, women or men or the youths. But then all sorts of other hanky panky also went on, too, some girls that got pregnant were living testimonies to my pa's inference then for their refusal to let me go.

I loved it best when ThankGod and I went to fetch firewood: because then we'd play without interruption in *our* haven—the *Ogbaligodo* forest. Nobody expected us to come home early and this was usually once a week, every Thursday. Celina, our mother, knew to have at least a day's supply to cook with when she sent us. I looked forward to every Thursday with the same intensity of anticipation. ThankGod and I would be uncharacteristically home early from school: our usual tortoise-speed would transform to hare-speed. One would expect children to be reluctant about going on errands, especially such strenuous errands like going to the forest to fetch firewood, but not ThankGod and I. We loved going to fetch firewood! It's like going away to a magical land and on the day, as soon as we were home, our school boxes made from rusted corrugated iron sheets thrown to a corner, we would swoop down on our lunch.

When we had sufficiently recovered from throwing it down our throats, we would then collect our head-pads, ThankGod's own already made from banana fronds while mine to be made later with our mother's old wrapper. The wrapper head-pad was softer, but ThankGod couldn't be bothered one way or the other about what he used to carry the firewood. We would collect the machete for cutting the firewood into manageable sizes, then waving to our pa, who'd be at the height of his snoozing in his shed at that time, skip off through the winding footpath, trailing the back of our compound, past all the homesteads, the forked road that would take us away from the village, and continued deeper into the forest until we reached *Nmili Ezu* which flowed serenely in the bowel of the *Ogbaligodo*, with a look of invitation to take a dip about it. But we would not, not then. Giant trees blessed with abundant leafy branches, lined both sides of the stream. It looked purposely shaded, a particular giant tree became our friend, as its branches were comfortably curved, designed for sleeping, an embodiment of a relaxation spot. But firstly, we'd cast ballot about what exactly we would do after collecting the firewood; forage for fruits? which, depending on the season could be *udala, icheku, ala-nkita, ugili,* and mango, or hunt for grasshoppers, lizards, birds, etc, or just trade stories, before swimming and finally settling down for our siesta, a much deserved rest, our spines curved on the branches of our tree friend. But first the firewood.

With the machete we would cut and trim branches, which we had cut on our previous trip into manageable sizes; if they were too long they'd snag the tangled forest here and there and make our journey home tiresome, that was, if the force of the snagging did not snap our neck in the process. After we had trimmed enough woods, we would arrange them on top of two ropes made from the fingers of raffia palm fronds, one on each end. Having piled enough heap, we would then tie the two ends of the rope across the firewood on both ends, as tight as we could, before inserting and then twisting a hard small stick in-between the end-knots to firm the bundle further before pushing the sticks onto the side of the ropes: it'd not do to have your firewood falling around your ears on the way home.

Our official reason for being in the forest now over, we'd move on to the next item on the agenda in the agreed order—look for fruits, hunt, swim, sleep and eat, but before we left, we'd ensure to cut branches for our next trip, otherwise we would be forced to bring home firewood that was not dry, which would smoke and not burst into flame at use and then only God would know what our mother would do to us.

At a younger age we used the back road to church then later to school, but as we got bolder ThankGod took us to school or to catechism classes through the village main thoroughfare, and this opened my eyes about many things. That electricity was not only in the Church but everywhere! And that we did not have it in our house because the electric poles and cables allocated to our village were insufficient. Families out of range could contribute and buy, some did, but our family living so far out could not, it was too dear for our pa to buy three poles and the cables to draw the electricity into our compound and that was that.

This main major thoroughfare traversed the length and breadth of our town leading to Onitsha, with rickety mini-buses, held in places with ropes, plying it at intervals. Houses, well built with high walls and wrought iron gates, dotted the village. The village itself had a kind of a rainbow-flavoured vibrancy of activities; a daily *mammy* market for all sorts of food items stood opposite a bank, this part could be considered a mini city center of my village. One end of a long one-story building with many lock-up shops stood beside the mammy market while the other end of it jutted onto the main road so much so that it constituted a sharp bend with its head, and had been the cause of several accidents, one or two fatal. The lock-up shops included; a barber shop; a hair dressing saloon; a butchers; a seamstress; a kind of off-license that also stocked school uniforms, bicycle tubes, puff-puff—a local doughnut—fried chicken, bread, minerals—coke, fanta, sprite—curtains, door locks, all sorts of things.

My father's palmwine trade, I began to realize, was not lucrative because people had celebrations with other drinks besides palmwine. I saw drinking shops or beer parlours where music blared out of their music box and stacks upon stacks of cartons and crates of beer and minerals outside but then only about 2 or 3 gallon palmwine kegs. People sat inside and outside eating goat-meat, fish or bush-meat pepper soup and drinking beer or palmwine. So palmwine was like an afterthought that was drunk once in a while.

But we had never gone without food and my mother was rabid about neatness. So you'd never catch us with a single strand of hair out of place; our bodies scrubbed and maintained with Premiere soap and Stella pomade and we always had our head held high literally, my mother's instructions. We always read our books, because that was the only sure route of escape from poverty in this our country, my mother again, and believe it or not we were a respectful and respected family. Yes, but what of when some of my classmates traded stories of what they had seen on television like *Sesame Street, Tales by the Moonlight, Ichoku, Robin Hood, Village Headmaster, Mirror in the Sun, Cock Crow at Dawn, Mind your Grammar, Speak Out,* drama of *Things fall Apart, The New Masquerade, Night Rider, The Cosby Show,* and so on, what would 'head held up' do here? Initially I didn't believe them, I was sure they were lying, then I visited Eziamaka at the appointed time and truly there she was, on the floor, her legs stretched out in front of her, engrossed with *Mind your Grammar,* watched from a small televion, and they were not even as neat as us! But they had light and so she watched television and I was suffocated with envy. Afterwards I began to sneak out, whenever I could, to visit any of my friends at the time they would be watching something. I liked watching everything and anything; news, advertisement, it didn't matter. And when they showed all those foreign programmes, I'd be lost in dreams of being there physically one day. I was now convinced that you could only get to abroad through book otherwise how could one cope, my mother must be right. When I couldn't sneak out, I would borrow my fathers' radio to listen to all manners of reporting.

However, my brother ThankGod did not have any fire in him; he was content and met my incessant complaint about our situation with a stoic wall of silence. If he was not out in the field playing his blasted football, being a team *member* of ManU, he'd be visiting his friends to watch their TV without any thought at all about his future. So on one of our firewood fetching days I decided to speak with him to ignite the firewood in his belly into a blaze that'd set him right. For me I already knew what I would want to be. I itched all the way to the stream but refused to indulge in our usual ritual until I got it out of the way. ThankGod was mystified.

'Gi, is anything the matter?'

'No, what are you going to be when you grow up?'

He looked at me clearly confused.

'I don't know.'

'You don't know? What do you mean you don't know? You have to know.'

He nodded assent and then embarked on this extended thinking that was getting us nowhere.

'Tha, hurry up.'

'I'm thinking.' Finally he came up with, 'Ok. Maybe a carpenter then?'

'It took this long to think about being a carpenter, Tha?' He shrugged and looked away. ThankGod did not engage in idle chitchat like wanting to line up your future.

'Anyway, me I will be a leader, a leader of women like ma.' At this declaration he turned and eyed me, like he was weary from having to point out the obvious absurdity of the statement, but he did at the end of the eying.

'But you don't want to live in the village when you grow up?'

'I know that.'

'Also ma is already the leader of the Saturday-Eke church cleaning women, St Agnes group,'

I nodded my confirmation. Baffled, he continued, 'How are you going to lead the women then?'

'No. What I mean is that I will go to University so that I can speak for the women to our Government, then they will get all they needed. Remember ma complained they needed the machine that grind cassava for making Garri, but nobody listened to them. But if I go to University I will just go to Government and tell them, you know, the way they said you can on that programme *Speak Out*?' I concluded watching him as he nodded, his eyelashes, that competed with mine in length if not longer, lowered to shield his eyeballs, like I had made perfect sense, even though I knew he did not watch *Speak Out*. Then he nodded again and said, 'That will be good, our ma *dem* will really be happy. I will help to build the machine.'

'As a carpenter?' I frowned at him, sometimes ThankGod can be really testing.

'Well . . . maybe I will be a mechanic then or both.'

'OK.'

He had nodded Ok too but with this aura of unconvinced floating around, like my little drama was of no benefit. But ThankGod liked to think about things later. Today that brother of mine is wealthy as an interior designer and furniture merchant. His furniture designs and accessories are unrivalled and are ordered from all over Nigeria and he did not do any unsavoury stunts to get there. It was sheer hard work, assured talent and contentedness. But I will not digress.

Our lives did not change much after the receipt of the first Holy Communion, not that I could discern anyway. But I made it my duty to obey all the requirements of God's commandments as I understood them. And also not to forget my mother's constant admonition to not forget that I was a girl and stop trying to do everything ThankGod did. The final rounds of catechism classes culminated in our receipt of the Sacrament of Confirmation—the receipt of the Holy Spirit, with its attendant gifts. Now we had finally made it into the inner circle of God's chosen children; integral and bona fide members of Saint Alphonsus Catholic Church, Oyi Parish. My joy was complete.

Some people would say, 'My mother is my best friend, I confide everything to her.', but Celina, my mother, did not occupy that position in my life. She was a tall, beautiful woman, full-breasted and slender like a gazelle, the gazelle aspect was according to my father. She had married the strapping and enterprising Abraham Ofoedu as a young girl of eighteen to the envy of her mates. At twenty-two years then,

Abraham, was already a skilled tapper with the rumour that he could coerce the sweetest of palmwine from the most onerous of palm trees. This was when palmwine was the be all and end all in the drinking choice and the foreign beers and minerals were in ones and twos and mostly exclusive to the well-to-dos. Now every lizard and rat can buy beer. In marrying my father, Celina had expected so much in life, but didn't get it so she had occupied her position gracefully waiting to be elevated through me, while selling *akara* and *akamu* at the edge of my father's compound. Looking back, her lips must have been clenched out of bitterness then and out of sorrow now.

When ThankGod finished primary school he went to *boys* as our towns' Boys' High School was called but after one year declared that he was not going back to school as he was more inclined towards 'doing things with his hands'. He was such a brilliant student, lamented his class teacher when he came to find out why he did not return after the long vacation. Our pa ignored ThankGod and so he just roamed about in the village and possibly beyond until our pa finally gave up and found him a place to learn a trade. He was sent to Onitsha Urban to learn carpentry. By the time ThankGod came home the second time, the subtle hint of dissatisfaction which I had glimpsed during his last visit had surfaced and taken residence on his mannerisms. He was dissatisfied with life as an apprentice carpenter cum houseboy.

It was the application of the code of apprenticeship that was ThankGod's undoing. It was agreed, as was the usual practice, that he would live in his master's house while in training so he was also a houseboy of sorts running errands in his master's house when they returned from the workshop in the evenings. But this time, the errands were according to the needs and dictates of the master's wife. ThankGod complained that the woman seemed to find work at every nook and cranny of the house and just as he had settled down to sleep, it was already morning and he was being shaken awake to go and fetch water before resuming at the workshop.

He had returned to his master and endured a full year of the five years he was to train, but then declared that he would rather be an electrician and returned home. He was not particularly keen on being rich or anything like that, but he was also not interested in being anybody's servant. Enough was enough. Vintage ThankGod!

My pa raised the roof, but my ma intervened and after three months of *loafing* about in the village, my pa went to see his friend, Ozo Akunne Ezenwata Odiari, because after much contemplation he had come to the conclusion that he was not so versed in this intricate business of master/apprentice knot. Akunne would steer him in the right direction. Because if you were unfortunate to get a wicked master he could cheat you out of your due, if you were not careful, by sacking you just as you were about to *free*, claiming one bad behaviour or the other, or that you were stealing from him.

When Akunne sighted his friend, walking down the lane to his compound one mid-morning, he was happy and hoped against hope that Abraham would not be rushing back to that village of his right away, as had always been the case. "A family man should not sleep outside his homestead, doing so is delinquent. But if he must, it should be for a matter of life and death." So Abraham had claimed so long ago. Akunne was happy to see his friend whichever way, he needed the *talk* of an old friend; they rubbed each other the right way. He was therefore, very surprised when Abraham came prepared to stay overnight.

'I need your help to thrash out an issue that has been troubling me for sometime now,' Abraham announced as soon as he had finished shaking his friend's hand.

'Wonders shall never cease to happen,' Akunne observed, 'this must be a matter of life and death I take it?' he queried on the same breath, with a twinkle in his eyes, for he had not discerned any aura of sadness around his friend. Abraham chuckled at the fact that his friend had not forgotten.

But he was newly married and had barely tasted her before he was drafted to go to the Nigerian/Biafran civil war so nobody should blame him, besides no responsible Igboman slept outside his homestead. Abraham shook his head as he chuckled in remembrance. Finally he turned his attention back to his friend and answered his earlier question.

'It may well be. ThankGod my son is really trying me.'

'ThankGod? Well . . . *nnoa* first, welcome. Are other members of your family in good health then?'

'Oh yes. We thank God. And yours?'

'We are well, thank you. Though Awele's diabetes acted up last week, it has been brought under control again. She finds it difficult to adjust to her new diet; she loves her food you see. But I have warned her that I will not cherish being alive without her. If she must die then she has to devise a way to take me with her.'

'Nobody is talking about death for now Akunne, so put it far from your mind. Have we eaten from our grandchildren's hands?'

'*Manchadu!*' Akunne vehemently concurred to his friend's question, sighing heavily as he sat down.

'Then what is this you are saying?'

'Aah, that I will tell you my friend. My father, now with his maker, has always said that you talk about life and death on the same breath. And a wise person will choose to live well for you do not know when death will strike.' And so they continued to banter until they were called to the table by Iyom Awele.

After attacking a well appointed *Nni-oka* with *Ogbono* soup, they settled down in Akunne's *Iba*—a building like a *properly* built gazebo, usually preceding the main house but on the corner of the compound, for the exclusive use of the head of the household where he entertained his esteemed, elderly guests or any male guest for that matter. Women were not welcome in an *Iba* except to clean it or to bring kolanut.

Akunne's wife certainly knew how to please the stomach of a man thought Abraham as he lowered himself on a rocker in the *Iba*. They drank, in companionable silence, each to his thoughts, reminiscing about the good old days when the world was a better place. This vein of thinking brought him round to the day he met Ozo Akunne. It was during the Nigerian/Biafran civil war at the Abaganaa sector where their battalion was sectored. On this particular day shelling and bombing was too much, blood was flowing like stream from corpses strewn everywhere. At this point the fight for liberation and freedom had left him. He had seen enough, the price of this freedom was becoming too much, so he decided to take refuge from the onslaught and had clawed along on his belly towards a clump of trees ahead, where he hoped to burrow beneath the roots and never come out untill after the war.

When he heard a voice laden with agony asking for help, he ignored it. When the man cried out again Abraham looked back and was shocked at the intensity of pain and terror from another's eyes as it bored into him.

Their friendship endured after the war but Abraham had to cut through the veneer of Akunne's arrogance to reveal the pearl of a man lurking there. In later years when they had had to discuss the meeting, they agreed that they were both glad that Abraham took that reluctant backward-crawl in that dim and shadowy past.

Ozo Akunne Odiari heard his friend out and, as it was said that two heads were better than one, they tackled the problem as old friends and came up with a solution. Akunne was not really familiar with the finer details of building materials business as a lawyer and a politician, but his friend Chief Ezenwa Omifukwu, *Agu Eji Eje Mba* 1 of Okide had firmly dominated the sector, he just hoped that he'd be able to help. Later that evening based on their mutual judgment and Abraham's decision, Akunne took Abraham to see Chief Osungwa.

*   *   *

Before they left for Chief Osungwa's place Ozo Akunne felt that it was only fair to tell Abraham about a rumour that was peddled about Chief Osungwa's wealth in case he decided to place ThankGod with him.

'You know, my friend Chief Osungwa was accused of sacrificing his maternal uncle to make money.'

'*Alu!*' Abraham exclaimed before asking, '*ona bu eziokwu?*' Is that true then? As he waited for the story to unfold, he hoped that it was not true, but then if Ozo had continued to maintain friendship with him, it probably wasn't.

'No, but at that time his money had started to pour in and you know how our people think, they concluded that the money could not have been from any other source than *mago mago*, especially when said riches started flowing in shortly after his uncle Dick Nwude, his mother's eldest brother, died. You see, Emma had lived with him after his own father died.' Akunne coughed to clear phlegm from his throat and called out to the housemaid for a glass of cold water. A maid appeared with a tray of water and placed it beside Akunne. He drank the cold water but rolled his tongue round it as if seeking for its taste. Not finding whatever he sought from the water, he swallowed it and continued with his tale.

When he finished Abraham shrugged as he commented, 'weren't every rich man in Nigeria accused of either using juju or spilling blood to make his money by the way?' Akunne nodded reiterating Abraham's comment with, '*I n'ege fa nti.*'

Do you listen to them?

Later in the evening after listening to NTA's six o'Clock news Ozo Akunne hurried them off to Emma Osungwa's new residence in *Omoba* Layout area of Onitsha, not too far from Ozo Akunne's family villa in *Enu*-Onitsha. Chief Osungwa had since built his mansion and moved from Omegana. Akunne expertly negotiated a sharp corner and brought his car to a stop in front of a high-gated imposing compound and honked his horn. Abraham winced before asking.

'Is this house all his own?'

Akunne smiled.

'It will put you off the first time, but you have to remember that most of these traders feel inadequate because of their lack of education and to make up for what they perceived as a shortcoming in their lives, they build such showy gigantic houses. It is supposed to bestow a sense of adequacy or *something* on their personality.'

Abraham nodded but did not comment. He simply wondered why his own sense of inadequacy or *something* never galvanized him into action, for he was neither educated nor wealthy. But he suppressed the thought while thinking that it was a good thing they had had their earlier discussion while still at home, because however much Chief Osungwa had overcome the malicious labeling in the past, Abraham was not too sure that he'd appreciate such a conversation in his house, on his dinner table. Akunne finished parking the car and said,

'I think we had better go in and see Emma, that we can do without much hypothesizing,' as he fumbled to get out of the car. Abraham chuckled, opened the door on his side and joined his friend.

They were ushered into a massive parlour by a maid and on to the corner that had leather couches arranged in a semi-circle in front of a huge television. As they were being swallowed by the couch, Chief Osungwa came in and they had to struggle out and up for greetings. Chief Osungwa embraced Ozo Akunne and shook hands with Abraham, he then turned and called out, 'Oliaku', the generic name for most married Igbo women that means, she who came to eat wealth, '*biakwa na anyi nwelu ndi obia*'—come, we have guests. At that Abraham decided not to sit back in until he had greeted Oliaku, so he looked around instead and then settled on looking at Chief Osungwa surreptitiously, who was attired only in a singlet that stretched tightly across his massive stomach, and a wrapper around his waist. He had obviously dressed down for the evening.

Chief Osungwa's wife came in and greeted them on bended knees with bowed head, saying '*ndi nannyi nnonu*'—our fathers, welcome. She was then patted on the shoulder first by Ozo Akunne, with his *akupe*—a hand fan made from cow hide carried by titled Igbo men with their title name written on it—then Abraham patted her shoulder with his open palm, he never carried his own *akupe*. As Oliaku got up and left, Abraham gingerly tried to sit down, but all that carefulness was in vain as in he slid into the bowel of the couch once again. But thanks to his height he could at least make out Ozo Akunne's head next to him, who, inspite of being in the bowel of the couch himself, still managed to sit regally, while their host, Chief Osungwa sat on a high-backed dining chair, giving him a towering advantage over them.

Oliaku returned with the housemaid who was carrying *Oji* including the kola nuts, *Nkpulu-anyala*—garden eggs—and *ose-oji*—groundnut paste with pepper—for eating the kola nuts.

'*Oliaku igbayalibaa iche oji na anyasi a?*' Oliaku did you have to run around to entertain us this night? Chief Osungwa answered instead with, '*Ozo Akunne, Abraham, Oji abiakwa nu.*' Kola has come.

'*Dalu.*' Ozo Akunne and Abraham expressed their thanks in unison.

'Ozo Akunne, *ngwanu walu anyi Oji a.*' Chief Osungwa said, asking Ozo Akunne to break the kolanut for them.

Ozo Akunne touched the plate and then pushed it back to Chief Osungwa saying, 'Omifukwu *Oji Eze di Eze n'aka, m'enya k'esiemie.*' The king's kola is in his hands, so do the norm. Chief Osungwa took one kolanut and stretched his hands out and upwards to heaven, head raised and eyes in a supplication mode, closed, then he prayed, '*O wetalu oji wetalu ndu,*' he who brought kola brings life.

'*Isee,*' chorused Ozo Akunne and Abraham in agreement.

'*Nna nna anyi fa nekwa nu oji,*' our forefathers look at kola.

'*Isee.*'

'*Egbe belu Ugo belu nkesi ibie ebena nku kwalia,*' Let the Kite and Eagle perch, whoever does not accept that, let its wings break (live and let live).

'*Isee.*'

'*Onye lie onye nwa nnie.*' When you eat, you should also give your brother to eat.

'*Isee.*'

'*Chineke nye anyi ndu nye anyi aru isi ike.*' Lord, give us life and health.

'*Ami.*' Amen.

'*Nekwa umu anyi mekwaa kafa malife,*' See our children let them have wisdom.'

'*Ami.*'

'*Ka Chineke gozie Oji'a anyi tanya k'ozua anyi aru na mkpulobi nafa Jesus.*' May God bless this Kolanut so that when we eat it, it will nourish our body and soul in Jesus name.

'Amen.'

'*Omifukwu igoka kwa oji'a.*' That was a powerful prayer, Ozo Akunne commended.

'*O nyanu.*' Indeed. Accepted Chief Osungwa.

'*Omifikwu,*' Abraham limited his own commendation to just hailing him.

'*Nnoa nu.*' Chief Osungwa in turn welcomed them again. These were the ceremonies that went with the breaking of kolanut and the prayers over the kolanut, it was said, must always be in Igbo language as kolanut did not understand any other language.

After the kolanut had been offered and eaten, having declined to eat proper meal or peppersoup and fried meat that was offered, Akunne cleared his throat and hailed his friend by all his titled names, before he then went to the heart of the matter for he was not one to mince his words.

'I came with my friend Abraham Ofoedu from Oyi . . .'

'*Nnoa nu,*', you are welcome, responded Chief Osungwa, then he bellowed, '*bia, kedu umuaka?*'—Come, where are these children?—meaning his servants, 'Bring drinks here!' As soon as Chief Osungwa had quietened down, Ozo Akunne continued immediately.

'What I have to say on his behalf could have been on my behalf maybe, but God did not bless me with a male child as you know, so whatever you could have done for me do it for Abraham.' Akunne declared massaging his wounded thigh while he stared at Chief Osungwa to signify that it was his turn to give appropriate responses before he continued.

'Akunne, since you will not bring bad thing to me, if it is what I can do, consider it done. Our friend Abraham welcome to my house.'

'Thank you,' responded Akunne and Abraham together before Akunne continued,'Omifukwu, his second son, ThankGod, has finished primary school and had trained for a year as a carpenter here in Onitsha, but suddenly three months ago he returned and said that he does not want to be a carpenter anymore. When Abraham told me all these, I knew that you will be able to take him in and set him on the right course. You know children of nowadays do not always know what is good for them, they need direction.'

Abraham nodded while Akunne stopped speaking to pour Guinness Stout into his tumbler, from a trayful of drinks that had been set before them. He took a sip and put his tumbler down before he continued, 'You know, I have not been able to determine the exact condiments used in making this Guinness Stout but, whatever it is, it quietens my stomach whenever it is unsettled.'

'Aaaah,' exclaimed Chief Osungwa, 'I say, it is a combination of various roots. Guinness Stout is a very medicinal drink. Throughout my mother's life time, she swore to the efficacy of stout in quenching all stomach problems and was inclined to taking a bottle or two herself everyday even when I could not discern any signs of stomach upset.' He smiled rubbing his extensive stomach and probably thinking of his deceased mother.

Abraham did not want to contribute to this very discussion, but if they asked him, he would have told them that Palmwine was more efficient when it came to calming upset stomachs but he kept his counsel. Comparing the efficacy of drinks in their ability to quench upset stomach was not why he had come all the way from Oyi to Onitsha.

Chief Osungwa must have read his mind, or his face, as the case may be, for he steered the conversation back. '*Ozo* Akunne, that is why I like you, you tell it as it is,' referring to their reason for the visit. He then turned to Abraham, '*Oyi anyi* Abraham does your son do strong-head?'—is he stubborn.

'Yes,' Abraham intoned simply but firmly, believing that there was no need to beat about the bush. 'But he is a good boy,' he added.

'I ask this now so that I will know exactly what I am getting into.'

'You are in order there Omifukwu,' Abraham solemnly concurred, before adding, 'I will do the same if I were you. But I want to assure you that ThankGod has a lot of goodness in him, all he needs is a good but firm hand to point him in the right direction.'

'In that case there is no problem, but to be sure that it is clear to you, as I know that you are not in my line of business, I must explain certain things to you. Apprenticeship for somebody his age will be for up to five years. He will live with me as most of my boys do. Usually it will be required of him to take a blood-oath in any shrine of our choice, but I am a Christian and so do not dabble into such *dark* activities. When he gains his freedom I will give him his due. But ask me why blood-oath? And I will answer you immediately.'

Chief Osungwa asked and answered the questions because he did not expect the answer to come from Abraham.

'Children of nowadays are in a hurry, they do not want to learn how to walk first before they start running, as a result they tend to steal from their masters. So that long before they were *freed*, some have bought state-of-the-art cars, some pay for shop rents for up to five years in advance while some even go as far as building mansions. The most painful aspect is that they have the tacit support of their parents. That is why some people insist on blood-oath. You will have to assure me therefore that this is not going to be the case with your son, strong-head or not,' Chief Osungwa finally puffed to an end.

'God forbid,' Abraham responded, clicking his thumb and middle finger in a snap to emphasize his point, having first swung it round his head, 'I have not raised any thief for a child and if he steals to bring home to me I will kill him with my bare hands first. I am glad though, that you will not insist on a blood-oath, it is not the road that children of God should tread with their eyes open.'

'Good. What other bad behaviour does your son have apart from strong-head? I ask because I don't want anybody that will come here and spoil my children.'

Akunne, who had listened to the conversation up to this point without saying anything, intervened. 'Omifukwu I think you should take this job of being ThankGod's mentor without trepidation. I guarantee him one hundred percent. What all of us should be doing at this time is to give thanks to God that he is still young enough to be molded.'

'If you are sure Ozo Akunne then I raise my hand in surrender.'

Having settled the matter amicably, they then veered into Nigerian people's favourite pastime: vigorously dissecting the problem with Nigeria and proffering unsolicited solutions. It had always formed the bedrock of discussions among gatherings of Nigerians, small or big, rich or poor, with everyone volunteering their own particular brand of solution. Solutions, that would supposedly usher in equitable distribution of the country's vast wealth; banish poverty; enthrone democratic rule devoid of ethnic politics and finally bury the *curse* to the Nation's route to development that was corruption. But it had also, always, been a headache-inducing exercise with no discernible profit, an effort in futility, for no one ever heard these myriad of solutions never mind using them to re-chart Nigeria into a beneficial-for-all-country.

After they had shouted themselves hoarse, Ozo Akunne sighed and mournfully asked 'Who is to say how Nigeria's problem could be solved, even the white man has given up.'

'*Mba, mba, mba*. No, no, no. Ozo Akunne, please don't even start that one, which white man are you talking about? Did they not start it?'

'Omifukwu, *o gii k'inekwudi ifenkea?* I say, what are you talking about? Let me ask you, is it the white man that loots our treasury and takes bribes, left, right and centre, leaving the masses in perpetual poverty? Is it the white man that had consistently enthroned mediocrity thereby thwarting the chances of this great country, the giant of Africa, from advancing forward? Eh? Answer me. The problem with our people is that we like deceiving ourselves: forever pointing accusing fingers at unseen persons as the source of our problems, while refusing to look inwards. *Biko*, please, tell *umuaka* to bring more drinks for me, my throat is suddenly parched,' Akunne concluded his shoulder regally stiffer, with anger.

Abraham waited for Chief Osungwa to stop bellowing for the said drinks before wading into the conversation. 'I think Ozo Akunne is right. But the question is the Nigerian citizenry that are being led, what are they doing? The collective will of the grassroots had been known to topple governments the world over, as history had it. But in the case of Nigerian grassroots, they have been weakened by hunger and deprivation to the extent that they will sell their mothers just so as to eat one square meal every two days. Nobody wants to change the status quo. I believe that individualism and greed among us has this very strangle-grip round the neck of Nigeria. Until *the* fingers are pried open and Nigeria released the Nation will remain a lost cause along with her people. So who will do it I ask you?'

'*Oyi anyi* Abraham, Ozo Akunne, I am very disappointed with the two of you.'

'You are free to be disappointed as much as you want,' Akunne interrupted Chief Osungwa.

'I am not finished yet,' Chief Osungwa inserted quickly as if Akunne was trying to displace him in a queue.

'What I am saying is that the white man accuses us of looting our treasury, taking bribes, being corrupt, and so on and so forth, yet when we carry the said loot to them they accept it and put it in their bank. Now what do you have to say about that?'

Chief Osungwa gleefully asked as he was quite sure that he had floored his opponents. *Let him see how they are going to navigate themselves out of this one,* he grinned, slyly, while adjusting his bulk. He sat up straighter and tucked in his wrapper well between his loins, and looked down—they were still in the belly of the leather couch—expectantly at his guests.

'I did not say that I have all the answers to our problems, and to hide our money in the white man's bank is very bad certainly, but are you saying that if they stopped taking our money out to hide in the white man's bank and the white man stopped accepting to hide the said money, that all our problems will be solved?' Akunne asked tilting his head to one side for a better view of Chief Osungwa.

'No, but it is a start,' Chief Osungwa said, rubbing his palms together, as he warmed up for the final onslaught, 'the white man is the proverbial two-faced man that went to the land of the spirits and aided them to kill a man then doubled back to aid the dead man's kinsmen to bury him, all the while pretending to be heart-broken by his death. That is why I say let the white man remove his dirty hand from our pot of soup for it is beginning to look like the hand of a monkey.'

They all roared into laughter, the mirth brought on by imagining the monkey-like hand of the white man rooting about in the black man's pot of soup before it was exposed for what it was.

The now three friends continued their banter till Akunne and Abraham begged to take their leave for the night was no longer young. As they got up to leave, the electricity went off, and darkness enveloped them like a black shroud. Abraham sighed and then muttered, '*Oji achia nu*'—this is the outcome of blackman's leadership.

Ozo Akunne sighed without saying anything.

Chief Omifukwus' voice rang out calling *umuaka* to bring a lamp which he then used to lead his guests to the car. As each was negotiating the dimly lit stairs, their thoughts were on the electricity outage in Nigeria—one problem that seemed to have seemingly defied solutions.

*   *   *

Abraham returned to Oyi the next day and later that evening informed his household about the agreement he had struck with Chief Osungwa about ThankGod's future. ThankGod objected immediately to being a trader as he would prefer to be an electrician. But Abraham was not ready to condone any more of that nonsense and to show his anger he pinched ThankGod's mouth sharply, shutting him up.

'If you have any sense in your head at all, you buckle down and try to make something out of your life. You may be young today but you will not remain young forever and time has not been known to wait for anybody,' Abraham vented before chasing ThankGod out of his sight.

*   *   *

Chief Osungwas' *talk* to ThankGod on the day he arrived further lent reinforcement to ThankGod's decision to adopt a positive attitude to life which he had earlier reached. On arrival that day his master without mincing words went straight to the point.

'ThankGod!' he bellowed.

'Yesa,' ThankGod meekly answered walking briskly into his master's presence.

'I heard that you do not hear with your ears?' Chief Osungwa asked while piercing him with his protruding eyes, 'but I want to tell you that you are not here for me to cure your deafness but for you to learn a trade that will help you in life. If you want to hear you hear if you do not want to hear, you go the way of the proverbial hard-of-hearing fowl that had her ears opened for her in a pot of soup. Do you hear me?'

'Yesa.'

'Good, go in and join your mates.'

Chief Osungwa had then nodded him, dismissively, out of the living room and turned to natter with his new friend Abraham.

'Take heart *Oyi anyi* Abraham.' Chief Osungwa had intoned, 'he will come around, you know? At this age they tend to be confused, but you have come to the right place, hard work will straighten him.'

Abraham conceded with a nod. The case of ThankGod he had already left in the hand of God.

*   *   *

I, in turn gained admission to attend Government Girls College, Anambra State, but had to cool my heels for a year in the girl's secondary school in my town while the scholarship that came with my admission was being ratified. The day the letter of the admission finally came I was ecstatic and thanked God with all my strength. My time had come to leave the village for Onitsha to see the world. The drawback, however, was that I had to be dispatched to my big sister, Chinelo's house, for the first one year. Why? I did not know, but leaving was the first step, the rest would follow. So gleefully I packed my worldly belongings including my mother's various and constant admonitions, weeks before my departure date. I was going to live in a Township for five years? Good God!

Away to College

ONITSHA URBAN, ANAMBRA STATE, NIGERIA 1991

Celina had woken Gift up, as she woke up herself, at the crack of dawn and had hustled her to sweep the living room after their morning prayers. She then went outside, washed her face, and collected and inserted a chewing stick into her mouth before hurrying off to her Buka to prepare that morning's breakfast for her customers while thanking God that the rain did not persist. As she marched on she pulled the leg of the chewing stick from time to time to brush her teeth.

Sighting her Buka made Celina narrow her thoughts to her business and how it started all those years ago. She knew that the taste of her bean-cake and pap locally known as *akara and akamu* remained unrivaled and she strove hard to maintain her standard. Waking up with the birds gave her enough time to give quality to the preparations. When she reached the Buka, she settled down to wash and grind the beans that had been soaking overnight to soften the light transparent coating and the bean's flesh for ease of removal and grinding. Then she cut up the onions that she'd add later before starting to grind the beans. But then her mind returned to her earlier thoughts of how it all started; she shook her head and at the same time swiped the flies buzzing around the sliced onions while continuing the rhythm. She

did not know why flies should be awake at this hour. She shook her
head at them as she returned to her thoughts; the business had not
made them rich, no, it only enabled her to aid her husband to put
three square meals everyday into their children's mouths.

She saw herself then: hunched under an umbrella mounted on a
wooden pole that served as a shed with a deep frying pan, two bottles
of groundnut oil, one *mudu* of black-eyed peas or beans for the *akara*,
and one *mudu* of butter-yellow corn for the pap to complete her items
of trade.

She shifted on the small wooden kitchen-stool she sat on so as to
reach a firewood that was smoking. She turned it over, then using the
raffia fan beside her, fanned the smouldering embers back into flame.
Gradually over the years her customer base had increased prompting
her to add other items to complement the *akara* and *akamu*.

Her customers sat on long wooden benches or *forms* while using
slightly lower ones as tables to eat their breakfast which consisted
of *akamu* and *akara*, fried yam, fried Titus fish, *Agidi*, very heavy and
firm baked dough in the name of bread and a splash of peppery
stew. Her customers had told her that with the pepper in their
stomach, they were kept on their toes and could put in many hours
of work.

Her customers could order whatever combination of her specialty,
but she had noticed that that depended on their stations in life and this
meant the type of labourer work they were engaged in. For those that
worked in the building sites, laying foundation with the starchy bread
with *akara* wedged in-between or yam and stew and fish all washed down
with chilled bottle of coke or water was not out of order. While the
office workers—those that work in the pool-betting offices, palmwine
bars, the barbing saloon, bus drivers and their conductors—on the
other hand, would make do with just the lighter *akamu* and *akara* or
yam with stew and fish, as their work was not heavy.

She also had the village school children as clientele. All in all, as
she had noted, the business did not make her rich, but her children
would not starve or be naked. Their wealth would come.

*   *   *

'Gift, my daughter, I will give you this one advice; leave suffering
for your father and me and concentrate on your studies, because
that is the only passport you need for everything: English jobs,
respectability, *ezigbo di*, name it Gift *nwam* and it is yours but first you
need education.'

A variation of this would always surface in our conversations, especially, as I got older and it became apparent that everything academic sat down well with me. I did not mind that really and it was easy to adhere to.

So today, I was going to see the City as it was told to start that education that would bring in all the goodies. I would travel with my pa, first by foot through the winding village road that would burst abruptly onto the town's major road to board one of the *tuke tuke* buses. These buses would take us to Onitsha on the express road from Otuocha. I had been on the express road before with ThankGod to watch cars fly past: the lucky cars that were going to the City of Onitsha. However, on these previous visits, it was not only the flying cars that ply the road but also old *Gwongworos*, overloaded with goods, belching and farting on their way to Onitsha too. I never let on that we had ventured this far to anybody that would have invited; '*nwa iyefu kwa nu efu biko nu,*' comment. This child you will go astray please, and this accompanied by a major ear-twisting.

My stomach was full with anticipation so I couldn't eat my breakfast. Instead I went to ready my things and when we left, I meekly treaded subdued steps behind my father. When we reached my mother's Buka she came out and hugged me and I thought I saw tears shining in her eyes, but I was not sure: my mother was a stone, water could not be found easily anywhere in her, it must be from my own eyes. I held her tightly to garner strength and more comfort that would accompany and stay with me while away from home. Finally my ma broke the tight embrace and looked at me, 'Remember all that we talked about, eh, *ilue ijisie ike n'akwukwo gi, inu ivem nekwu?* When you reach there pay attention to your schoolwork, do you hear me? And do not forget to pray. Anyway, Chinelo *nia n'egekwia nti inu gie; noo ada nnegi k'obu, inulia?* Chinelo is there, always listen to her, she is your senior sister, do you hear me? It will be well with us.' My father shook his head and interrupted the flow of jumbled advice with, '*Nne* Obumneme *ozugo zia.*'

My mother stopped and then concluded '*ngwa nu jebe zia nu. Papa obum biko natakwa n'oge o.*' My father nodded, stooped down and collected my luggage and at straightening up he tilted his head to our direction and I turned towards it immediately, leading the way as we left, my mother's words swirling round my ears.

But the weight of my heart was such that it was not possible to begin to reflect about all that my mother had been drumming into my head since the day she gave birth to me but moreso after I turned twelve and my breast from nowhere sprouted followed by my monthly period. However, I had abandoned all line of thought to concentrate on matching my father's footsteps. I was supposed to be tall for my age, but even with my father's considerate stride, I could not match his steps, and that was including of the fact that he was carrying my things packed in a brand new 'Ghana must go' bag that was tucked under his armpit. My father told me that the bag had acquired its name when Ghanaians, on the directive of Nigerian federal government, in the early eighties left the country, and had used the said bag to pack their belongings. Since then the name had stuck.

When we burst out on the major road that would take us to Onitsha we had to wait awhile for our transport. When it eventually came I was acutely disappointed as we had to board one of those *tuke tuke* buses to Onitsha urban! I did not know what made me think that it'd be a different transport. We squeezed in and the bus rattled off at such speed that made the trees and the road and everything flying by cloud my vision. Finally I closed my eyes to stop it from swimming and making me dizzy.

When we arrived, Onitsha was doused from a downpour. But in spite of the rain I was deeply impressed with Onitsha. It was a big city; bigger than my fevered mind could have conjured having Oyi town landscape as the framework to draw from. The roads were paved, tarred and glistening, proper gutters on hand to carry away the floods. There was electricity in every compound as I had been told by ThankGod.

When we arrived at *Oseokwordu* motor-park, my big sister Chinelo was already there, waiting for us. We transferred to a smaller *tuke tuke* bus enroute to Fegge, where she lived. My head kept swiveling round and round as we traveled: I needed to take in so much in so little time. But we kept going, then the landscape started changing until I noticed that we were moving towards a poorer neighbourhood, but it did not matter, this was Onitsha.

My sister's place, as we moved along the dimly lit corridor towards the back, was in a compound housing about twelve families. Inside their own living room, which was carved out from their one room residence with a curtain serving as a wall, stood a high table with assorted bric-a-brac; an old radio stood on one side and what turned out later to be a broken, black and white television stood proudly on the centre of the table with a white *atumakasa*—knitted table cover, sitting on its head. Two dining-table chairs faced the table while an old sofa that must have been picked from a skip, because it couldn't be described, and at the danger of disintegrating, graced the end of the living room facing the television.

I steered clear of the sofa and sat on one of the high chairs but jumped up immediately from the squeaking noise. Grasping the back of the chair I shook it vigorously, peered at the flat bum-holding surface before I start down again. My weight transferred to my legs so that the nails holding the chairs in places but more out than in would not impale me, as well as, to ensure that the chair would not collapse on account of my relaxing fully.

I looked around in amazement: *was this where my sister lived with her family of seven? No wonder my ma and pa always sent food items and even money to her.*

*   *   *

After the meal my pa rested a while before announcing that he would be on his way back to Oyi and left amidst cries of, 'when are we coming to visit the village, grandpa? Greet our grandma for us o,' chorused Chinelo's children. We all trouped outside to see him off before we returned to the compound.

As I had time now to look around properly I observed that the building's entrance continued all the way to the back with the rooms occupied by different families in a kind of *face me I face you* way ending into an open space as the backyard. The whole compound was enclosed within a high wall. You could still see into the next compound if you were so inclined, but you had to jump up and down to do so.

I also noted that the backyard served as the playground for the numerous children from various families of the compound. My sister and husband, Ikemefuna Odinkenme, had managed to bring five children into the world between them; the oldest was eight years old.

As soon as she had put away my luggage, Chinelo took me round for full introduction to the other families that lived in the compound and to the communal facilities. One bucket-toilet system and a bathroom housed in one hut of a building separated by a high-wall in between the two facilities for privacy, served all the families of the compound. The said wall did not reach the unceiled roof, probably for ventilation purposes; after bathing, one must go away with a faint odour of urine and feaces clinging fleetingly on your body. However, this bathroom cum toilet building was situated at one end of the compound cum playground while the building housing the kitchen, was at the other side.

Beside the kitchen stood the public water tap where families fetched water to store in their individual reservoirs. Chinelo informed me that the tap ran only on alternate three days hence the need for storage. The surroundings of the tap were designated for laundry, washing of cooking utensils and any or every other thing done with water, including bathing of children. Having the tap, though in alternate three days, was still better than going to the stream miles away in the village.

The kitchen building was an open plan with one entrance and a tiny window facing it. Families staked out their spaces with their dwarf cupboards, the food press, kerosene stoves and small plastic buckets that served as waste-bin. They might all look alike but everybody knew their property, I came to realize, when I had settled in. When families cooked, they brought their water and kitchen stools and positioned themselves in front of their stoves. Some did not even own kerosene stoves; rather, they had tripod stands made of steel. To cook, they lit stacked firewood underneath the tripod and seemed oblivious of the tear-inducing smoke issuing from their corner.

I had wondered how these people could stay in the kitchen and have conversations with each other seemingly unaware that tears were streaming down their faces. I asked sister Chinelo, she smiled and then said 'You get used to the smoke Gift. What are a few tears now and then among neighbours?' Then she patted my head as she concluded, 'Don't worry you'll get used to it.' I didn't think so but if she said so, I'd really want to see how that could be.

In the village we cooked with firewood alright, but our mother's kitchen was well ventilated so that smoke was carried away immediately by the wind. Here, apart from the entrance, the other opening which was intended as a window could barely pass a hen, a slight hen at that.

I was surprised however, that as I continued to live with my sister, I lost my reservations about the din in the kitchen. Everything just blended as part of one's daily activities. I stopped resenting those who cooked with firewood. It was funny how your body adjusted to a situation, especially if you decided not to consider it an issue anymore. Amazing.

*   *   *

On my first day at the school, I had woken up at about 4.30am to follow mama Onyibo to the vegetables market, and then from there to my sister's shed at Ozudaa mammy market which she shared with mama Onyibo and two others before returning home to shout my nieces and nephews as well as mama Onyibo's children into readiness for school. It was a battle racing to finish these chores as I was really not so adept with it. Afterwards, I took care of my own needs before leaving for school.

On this first day we were on mufti as our uniform would be collected that day and so I tushed up in what I considered my smartest outfit. But by the time I got to the school premises I was sweating profusely with a round wet patch sitting uncomfortably under my armpits.

I went and sat down on a tree stump under a leafy Dogonyaro tree by the school gate to catch my breath and at the same time study my new school where I would spend the next five years.

It was not bad at all. In fact I could even venture to call it 'abroad' based on my snatched television watching episodes at Eziamaka's house, where the houses were in smart rows with neatly trimmed flowers. When I had sufficiently rested and my breathing normalized I went in search of the Principal's office. As I went deeper into the compound I became confused as to which building housed it. When I rounded a corner and saw three girls holding hands and whispering I was relieved and veered towards them to make my inquiry. They looked at me, up and down, and then continued with their interrupted gist like I had not spoken.

I was taken aback, to say the least, and for whatever reason I could not name, felt inadequate and inferior immediately. I looked about wildly for an escape route then shot off and barged through one of the open doors into a large square room with desks and chairs in rows. Realizing that it was empty I went further in and sat down to lick my wounds while still keeping the girls in my line of vision.

'Did they just snub me or what?' Oh . . . that hurt, deep. And it baffled me. Were these girls not my equal? And for all of us to be here, we must all be brainy. Maybe there were some shortcomings that I had not been aware of. So I tried to take stock.

First I looked closely at my nails: clean. My face? Scrubbed. My sandals? Brand new Cortina made by the famous Bata itself; I had coveted them for so long and they were bought exclusively for this school by sister Chinelo, so they could not be the offender. My hair? Neatly plaited. My armpits? Smell free; doused with a healthy dose of FA deodorizing spray. My dress? Very clean and ironed to an inch of its life. It must be lurking somewhere. Maybe because my dress was third-hand and compared to what I saw on those girls, I could be a vagrant's grand-aunty! My mind latched on to that fast. It must be the reason.

Those girls looked very neat and well-appointed: groomed, comported and restrained all in a self-assured kind of way: like 'ladies'.

But it occurred to me that their action did not in fact conform to any ladylike mannerism. 'Look at them,' I bleated. *Their parents must be rich*, I thought dryly. It must come from something I did not have. And what else could it be but money?

'Is it really money?' I dared to voice my fear. I peeked again at the girls and decided that it probably was not only money. I then vowed that whatever conferred that type of confidence and poise on these girls I must have and if money was part of it I was not averse to having that either!

The incident made me self-conscious and subsequently I took extra care with my daily grooming. Even though I had concluded that money was at the centre of that it would do no harm to look clean all the same. So every morning I scrubbed my body thoroughly with Lux soap; doused my armpits. My uniform was crisp and I ensured that it was not stained by the charcoal used to fire the heavy metal contraption that was the iron. The iron was a novelty to me when I first saw it. That was before I realized that it was ancient and should have been consigned to the storage of a museum the day I went to visit one of 'those girls' and saw an electric iron in use. Now that was something!

*   *   *

I became rather popular in the school, which was a surprise considering how it started off, and even managed to count 'those girls' as my friends. Amazing! It must be my quick mind then I reasoned. But my friends were equally quick-minded though they would rather not study at all if it were up to them. In fact they did not study except when exam came, and then they'd indulge in a massive crash programme: studying day and night and engaging in all sorts of trickery to keep awake. Some went as far as steeping their legs in cold water in a bucket underneath their study desks. Some would have heavy books like the dictionary centered on their heads while some drank and ate endless supplies of coffee and kolanut. So what could it be then that attracted these girls to me? I continued to wrack my brain. I have always considered myself amiable and outgoing, willing to help, so long as it was not an inconvenience and I was not afraid to say so if it was. Maybe that was it. But then I remembered one of my friends, Faith, telling me one time that I brought sunshine with me always. I liked that. Maybe that was it.

*   *   *

As soon as Chinelo returned from the market that evening, she dropped her basket and made straight for the backyard of the compound: she had to attack a big basin of washing that she had soaked for three days going. The tap should be running today, she thought. It had better, it was supposed to be their turn.

She got to the tap, which was running, washed her face with cold water from it and sighed: the joy from such simple things. Then she sat down on a stool, pulled the basin between her legs and started washing the clothes. It had not been easy, a very tough job juggling two careers while managing her family at the same time. This was not what she had envisaged when she married and joined her husband who was in the firewood business in Onitsha. Leaving the village to live with her husband was like going to Heaven. That was then.

Gift's arrival was a great relief: a live-in helper in the person of her own sister. How time flies, she smiled, look at Gift, a big girl now in secondary school. 'Gift of yesterday,' Chinelo murmured and shook her head in wonder. She remembered that Gift was only about four or so when she got married and left to live in Onitsha. She got up to fetch water with a second basin for rinsing.

Having clothes soaked for sometime had a way of loosening all the hidden dirts. She suspected that she'd have to rinse them two or three times. With the tap running that day, calculated to a T when she soaked the clothes, it would not be a problem, however.

As she rhythmically pummeled the dirty clothes, she rummaged through her mind lining up the process that had brought her husband and herself this far. Not that it was an enviable far, but it could have been worse.

When she had arrived in Onitsha, green from the village, she had plunged into married life with her two feet: cooking, cleaning and generally keeping house for her husband. He sold firewood at Ochanja market. Every morning she saw him off, attended morning mass at a nearby parish then sat back to await his return with all her house-keeping functions performed inbetween.

One morning, turning back to step into the verandah from seeing her husband off, she had bumped into mama Ejima, mother of twins, their next-door neighbour, who must have been lying in wait to accost her. This conclusion was reached, based on the one-sided conversation that had ensued, Chinelo had surmised later, when she had had time to review the *chanced* meeting.

'*O'nima chodu i'figa alu, ko nkua di gi n'ele k'iga eji zua umuaka gi, eh?*
Are you not going to look for what to do, is it from this firewood your
husband sells that you will train your children from? had been mama
Ejima's answer to Chinelo's good morning. Chinelo did not know
what to say for mama Ejima was not her age-mate and so would not
be looking to cause quarrel. But she did not waste time in thinking
further so she quickly genuflected in thanks and ran into their one
room to worry.

What could she do? She had asked herself. She had not voiced the
question out to herself before now, but it must have been somewhere
in her mind waiting to be plucked out. It was as if mama Ejima had
broken a dam, for she was then assailed with questions upon questions
about what to do, day in, day out.

Chinelo considered herself a half-illiterate in the sense that she
had only finished primary school and attended secondary school in
the next village, where they had to trek for two hours to and fro, all
of three months, just long enough to attract a husband. As soon as
that happened, the whole family concluded that there was no need
to continue. So she was not trained to be anything, neither was she
fully educated to be of use to anybody. If she had sat for her junior
WAEC at least she could work as an office clerk in a pool-betting office
at a minimum. She could not follow in her mother's footsteps and
set up an *akara* and *akamu* joint, that business was like pure water
business in this area: everybody seemed to be doing it; you'd wonder
who bought from whom. In fact every business you could think of
had been effectively overpopulated by her neighbours from the
compound, the street and the general neighbourhood. Then one
day while returning from morning mass she observed what led to the
start of her own business enterprise; numerous men were clustered at
Ogbo Nmanu junction, and on enquiry she was told that they were *ndi
ana m'acholu*—laborers for hire

So today like her mother, she sold food from a street corner to
early morning day-labourers who must come out as early as 5am to find
work. But in her own case, she sold boiled rice, beans and yam with
tomato stew and a choice of fried ice-fish, round-about—cow intestine,
kpomo—cow hide, and *shaki*—cow tripe. She used a wheelbarrow to
display the foods. There was no buka of any sort, because the local
government council would not allow it. Even with the wheelbarrow, you
had to be on the permanent lookout for them and if they caught you,
it'd amount to the proverbial washing of hand to crack palm-kernel
for the chicken, because they'd fleece you of all you'd made that day
plus more. And you dared not ask for receipt.

So with the threat of the council people on her shoulder, in a corner of Ogbonmanu junction Chinelo sold her wares under the stars of heaven, where her customers stood, wolfed down their breakfast before rushing off to be employed by anybody that needed labourers for the day.

If any one of them was not selected by 10 am, it meant that that day had passed for nothing. But it also meant that her food business ended at about the same time so she had learnt to cook only enough. She would then quickly return to the house to pack her wheelbarrow along with her utensils then rush off to Ozudaa mammy market where she sold fresh vegetables consisting of *ugu*, waterleaf, *okazi*, green and palm nut.

Both businesses took a lot out of her for it demanded that she started her day as early as 4am, but because she could not be in the two places at the same time she devised a way. She'd give her neighbour, mama Onyibo, the money that she would use to buy and transport her share of the vegetables to the stall in the market which they shared.

When she initially approached mama Onyibo, she had proposed to pay her a fee for the help, but mama Onyibo told her to forget it: according to her nobody knew who'd rub each other's back tomorrow. Since she must buy these vegetables for her own stall she might as well do it for her.

Chinelo, in turn, then ensured that mama Onyibo's children prepared and left for school with her own children after feeding them every morning. She also took along enough food, from her leftovers, for mama Onyibo and herself, when she went to join her in the market later in the morning.

Chinelo had since realized that people who were at the lowest echelon of the ladder of life could either live in co-operation and harmony, which would go a long way to cushion the effects of poverty, or live and die alone. Their two-woman co-operative suited them fine. Now with Gift's presence, and envisaged help, she'd be immensely relieved. But it was not as if she was complaining, they were happy and it would get better, and that she knew.

*   *   *

I absorbed as much *culture* as I could from my friends who had it to offer. I did not envy them their lifestyle anymore, having made up my mind to be like them somehow; traipsing from one country to another, looking like princesses who never had to do a day's work in their life. I could not do anything about money, but I could polish myself I reasoned, so I attuned to that with vigour. I sailed through my junior school and the exams in flying colours and, as was usual, I always went home each vacation to spend the holidays with our parents.

*   *   *

I passed nine O Level subjects and gained admission to study Political Science and Economics at the University of Lagos. I remember that day so vividly: the day I got my admission letter, the day that the rays of the sun shed their burning fierceness, the hue glowingly clothing my village in magnificent radiance. I was nearly suffocated by happiness. But when I came to my senses it became a mixed feeling: how could one consider something beyond one's reach a blessing? Though everybody was happy for me I knew that it would amount to an uphill task for me to go to University—an impossibility. My father could not afford to pay for my University education.

But it was done. My father declared that, 'even if it means borrowing money', as this was his only child that went this far in education, he must see to the end of it. And true to his words he followed it up. I went to Onitsha with him to visit his friend, Ozo Akunne Odiari, and the next thing I knew I was in the University.

...He *found me*

I struggled and finally felt my thoughts snaking reluctantly back to the present with the panoramic views gliding away, fading into nothingness. When I felt sufficiently grounded in the present I got up and dragged myself towards the bathroom. As I brushed my teeth I tried to make sense of this Osahon's visit. I did not know the Osahon I had encountered when I returned from Italy. Now he was back. I sighed deeply. I think I'd rather hold on to the hope that this trip must be traced to money so all that about *wiping the hurt in my soul* was just nonsense and as such it'd also be easier for me to handle him. I just needed to be sure I was ready for the battle, because he was not going to suck me dry again.

But on second thought, what of our Supermarket, the biggest in West Africa? Should he not have increased and multiplied with the wealth he had amassed or had he lost the whole lot? I gasped out in horror, 'I just hope not.'

'So?' If he had lost the whole lot *nko*, what's my concern there? If he thought for one moment that he could insinuate his way back into our lives he had better squash such a thought, it's not going to happen. Osahon is not going to destroy my life again; I cannot allow that!

Not after I have been given another chance to pluck at destiny afresh. I shook my head, finished brushing my teeth and stepped into the shower. The hot water immediately started its work; soothing my frayed nerves. I gave myself a good wash in an attempt to scrub off the gloom.

Osahon

As soon as Gift banged the door shut in his face, Osahon left. He was not about to prolong the embarrassment, it was not in his nature to stand such shoddy business. As he walked to the bus stop he resolved that the best medicine to this dilemma was to allow Gift a few days to simmer down before he returned; because they had to sort out these things one way or the other. He couldn't be left hanging, now could he? He was her husband for fuck's sake, she had better clue in to that!

Yes, he admired women who had minds of their own and used them to their advantage now and then, but there had to be a time and place to brandish such minds. His Gift was always a softie, very malleable, and she never had such strong *minds*, not when it was about him. She'd come round.

He must concede, though, that the Gift he met today was one hell of a bitch, scary even. For one moment there, he thought she would pounce on him.

'*Shuo!* What was she playing at?' He scratched his head as he examined this new behavior that Gift has acquired. As he contemplated, something like cold water started to flow slowly into his bloodstream dampening his feverish thoughts as he remembered how her eyes had flashed, rather dangerously in a very strange sort of way, like that of a mad fellow. He hoped that she was still alright up there; he needed her to be hale and hearty.

He had heard though, that it was kind of hard-going living out here in these foreign places: what with the white people's tendency to mind their business all the time. You did not even get to share a full-hearted morning with your neighbours with good old natter where you had to enquire about the entire household by name including the goats and chickens! How could anybody not go mad living amongst people that did not talk?

But the kind of fire emanating from Gift's eyes was not like that of a mad person's, it was much more than that. He could not place it. Or was it a case of hell hath no fury . . . ? He squared his shoulders, mentally shrugging off this temporary obstruction to his plans. He knew his Princess, he would wear her down. She was putty in his hands then, she'd be putty in his hands again. All he needed was time, he reasoned. But she had better not give him any aggro when he returned, because then, he would really show her his red eyes. He hadn't made this journey in vain.

Arriving yesternight to this freezer of a country, he smirked, while pushing his balled fists further into his pockets. His plan was to find somewhere to hang out for a day or two and then move in with her. He didn't even wait to buy decent socks to ward off the cold that was stiffening his toes before rushing off this morning, all in a bid to secure a warm and comfortable bed in her house. Now this? Well, delay was not denial, as it was said, and he would not let her rest until he got what he wanted. And he never failed to get what he wanted; she of all people should know that.

When bus 38 thundered into the bus stop bringing Osahon back to reality, he consulted the hand-drawn map and other information given to him by John, the receptionist at the B&B where he lodged last night, to confirm that he was to board bus 39 back to the City Centre. But everybody at the bus stop was boarding this one except him, and they were neatly dressed, like people going to the City, so he boarded the bus too. It did not matter really, he told himself, it was not as if he was in a hurry to anywhere, he needed to clear his mind and think things through anyway.

He was greatly shocked when the nubile young thing sitting next to him smiled at him in greeting. This severely damaged what he had heard about the white people. Even though his trip to Italy then, failed to confirm what he had heard, he had held on tenaciously to the premise that, if it was not the white man of Italy, then it must be the white man of London or the white man of somewhere. It was said that they tended to look through you as if you did not exist. And he had come prepared. Nobody was going to look through him as if he was nothing. He would look that person to death with his wicked eyes. Maybe he should rely less on hearsay going forward.

Slowly, he smiled back and was rewarded with a full-blown grin. Osahon had never considered himself your regular shy guy, just that the trauma of the last one and a half years of his life, coupled with the circumstances of the last one hour had combined to disquiet him. But you were what you were and if opportunity presented itself positively you embraced it wholeheartedly. So he responded with a wide-grin of his own and in his best fake-Oyibo accent he spoke, but firstly, he wanted to know if the bus would get him to O' Connell Street. This asked with a quick peek at his map/instruction to confirm the name. At confirmation by the nubile young thing, he then introduced himself, stretched his legs as much as the space would allow and relaxed visibly to enjoy the company of this fresh-morning-dew whose name was 'Nave'. His current and past problems pushed to the back of his mind. There was time yet to think about Gift and all her shit.

Gift

Having spent so much time, circling my life problems, I realized that I didn't have enough time on my hands afterall and had to end my shower, no matter how soothing. I stepped out and trailed droplets of water into the room as I briskly dried my body. I dressed up quickly but spent a bit of time working on my face to mask my inner turmoil. I stepped back to scrutinize the effect having carefully chosen my clothes. I nodded satisfactorily. I then hurried downstairs, gathered my children and tweaked my window blinds to confirm that Osahon was not skulking around, waiting to pounce, before I crammed all of us into our car and drove off sharply to Blanchardstown hoping to drop them at Erica's. This battle was not a battle you fight empty handed, neither was it a battle you fight with children clinging to your hem. It needed clear head and superior strategy.

*   *   *

I knew Erica would be very surprised to see me and my children on her doorstep so early on a Saturday morning, so to divert her attention and any questions that'd follow I fired a question at her immediately I sighted her.

'Erica, I hope your husband is not home yet because I need you to mind my kids for three hours at least. There is fire on the mountain.'

I knew this would draw Erica's attention away from my agitated demeanor giving me the chance to launch into a convoluted story of sorts to fit the scenario. But a closer look at Erica told me that I need not have bothered. Her face was swollen, her eyes red and she was sniffling like she had a cold or maybe it was from crying, which became apparent the more I stared at her.

'What fire?' she intoned nasally, 'That fire can not compare to what has been burning in this house since yesterday.'

'*Shuo.*' I murmured, 'What is the problem?'

Of all the times to choose to reveal things, Erica certainly chose the wrong time. We had been reunited for over four years now and not so much as a peek into our intimate lives, just like it was in our university days. Now she wanted to draw me into a catastrophe-imbued conversation that I did not have the mindset to listen to. Sure, I know I hadn't looked for whom to tell my own life-story to and had never encouraged intimate tête-à-têtes of any sorts with anybody, least of all Erica, but . . . Erica's voice cut short my uncharitable thoughts.

'Gift, my sister has killed me ooh. Our Refugee Status is being threatened; it may even be cancelled as it is!'

'What are you talking about? Which sister? What Refugee Status? Is your Residency not as a result of being parents of Irish Citizen Child?' I asked thoroughly confused.

'It is a long story,' Erica wailed and to my horror, she burst into this loud cry that startled my son, rubbing her already red-rimmed eyes furiously to stem the torrential tears. At this turn of events I had no choice but to follow her into the house. This *wahala* could not be sorted standing outside and it seemed more serious than the mere fact that Osahon had appeared here in Dublin.

I looked around very well before choosing a seat to draw us down on, I would not cherish being glued onto the chair by stale food, before turning to quietly console Erica. The more I pleaded that she should take it easy with the crying, the more Erica cried. After a while I started fidgeting, yet Erica persisted with the crying and she had not added to her initial exclamation so I was still in the dark about the source of her distress. As it was, I was not sure of what to ask again that'd enlighten me since no answer had been offered to my first question. But, I had to say something because I also had emergencies of my own threatening to engulf me and if Erica was not ready to say more then I had to get going.

'Where is your husband?' I finally asked. Maybe that would elicit some other type of reaction other than crying.

'He traveled down to Cork early this morning to consult a solicitor.'

'In Cork? Good Heavens! What on Earth is going on Erica?'

'I don't know what is chasing after you this early morning Gift so go after it. I can hold on for two hours, maybe then Emma will have some news for me from Cork. We need the special Grace of God to come out of this problem. Please pray for us, ooh Gift my sister, we are dead.' I looked at Erica and knew that I was better off going now; this situation seemed to be more than the naked eye could see and I had other fish to fry. I nodded and stood up before commenting, 'In that case I will go and come back. Are you sure you will be alright? Where is that househelp of yours by the way?'

I frowned looking around. She should have been all over the place by now smarmy and solicitious; overcompensating for not always being home which had me always wonder at the kind of househelp she was, more like Erica's madam, but then Erica seemed blind to her behavior and so I never raised the issue. As it stood, I was not sure that at the rate tears were flowing down Erica's face that she'd be able to cope with all the children as I did not want to return to meet the Gardai or the Social Workers or both taking the children into custody! If Erica's residency was in jeopardy where was the guarantee that they'd not investigate close associates?

'She is part of the problem, oo o my sister, but don't worry go and come I will manage,' Erica said while blowing her nose noisily sending mucus flying all over the place. I sprang up and stepped quickly away from the immediate vicinity of the flying mucus and Erica laughed. She had the impudence to laugh for nearly spraying me with her waste. At least it lightened the situation and made it easier on my conscience for planning to leave my children in the care of somebody who was mourning the loss of her Residency status. Because in whichever direction you want to view it from, it was a big calamity.

I took my daughter, Frances, aside and implored her to be extra vigilant with minding her two siblings, as I would not be in the mood for any long stories when I returned. To ensure a job reasonably done I promised to treat them to a film at the cinema and suggested that they spend their time while I was away deciding on the film they would want to see. Frances blinked twice, peered at me and said, 'Mum, I don't think that will be a good idea. You know we want to watch different things. If you want us quiet today, then give us homework.'

It pained me that in this crises-ridden moment, in this our hour of need, that it was my seven-year old child that had her senses firmly rooted in place. At least somebody's thinking faculty was still functional. I looked at my daughter again and nodded.

'Good thinking girl,' I murmured, 'but what of Lucky?' I must still be confused, otherwise how could I be looking for a solution from Frances?

'We will get him to draw and paint, remember he loves doing that.' Frances looked at me again before asking, 'Are sure you're fine mum?'

'I am fine. Why do you ask?'

She frowned worriedly but said nothing, her eyes on Erica. She probably remembered our earlier crying session and was wondering why all the mums were at it today. Then she reached up and hugged me, stepped back and looked up to continue to search my face: looking for signs to confirm that I was or was not OK. I relaxed my features to normalness. It must have worked for she stepped further back and smiled.

I patted her head as praise for being so smart and reassured her that all would be well. And that my going out was to ensure that it remained so. I went up with her to Erica's children's room to look for schoolbooks and all what not. At least if my own children were busily engaged Erica would have less to stress about. Under twenty minutes later I sailed out.

* * *

Finally on my own, I drove maniacally back to our house, parked the car, then trekked to the bus stop and boarded bus 39 to the City Centre. I knew that my current state of mind would not sustain the kind of concentration I needed to negotiate the narrow roads of Dublin.

At one of the numerous call centres on O'Connell Street I placed a call to my big sister, Chinelo, in Nigeria. I did not want to disturb ThankGod whose wife Faith, an old friend of mine, had just delivered a baby boy two days ago. When Chinelo answered the phone I could discern that she was in a good mood because she was very chatty. But when she launched into a convoluted story about the exploits of the Catholic Women's Organization in the recently concluded Harvest & Bazaar of her Parish I stepped in and blurted out, 'Sister, do you know that Osahon came to see me this morning!'

I could feel the cold fingers of fear crackling through the phone line as my sister went deathly quiet, leaving my information floating interminably. The fingers of fear became a sharp knife that plunged into my lungs, puncturing them, probably, for I could feel something flowing freely down into my stomach, raking the walls sharp-toothedly as it went. My heart started racing: dancing *atilogwu* dance along the way; causing erratic beatings, malfunctioning it seemed, for my system suddenly shut down paralyzing every fiber in my body. I sat there frozen in acute pain. There was something more ominous than Osahon's presence in Ireland I could glean from the fear emanating from my sister. Then I heard something croak.

'Sister, what is the problem, what has happened?'

Discerning the croak as a question I realized it was from me.

'Strange things have been happening for sometime now, but how did he find you?' my sister asked in fear.

'Strange things?' I whispered with dread, 'what strange things?'

'Gift, what happened in Ireland?' The steel but calm voice had effect. Trust sister Chinelo, she was truly her mother's daughter. So calmly I answered,

'I don't know, sister. He came to my house early this morning.' But then I abandoned the calmness and sharply said, 'You must know something, sister. I thought you promised to be on the look out and warn me if anything happens? So what are these strange things you are talking about?' I stopped abruptly realizing that my sister would not care for the tone of voice I was using with her. Her answer confirmed my suspicion.

'I know what I promised Gift. But how was I to know that he could locate you? It has been more than four years remember . . . ?' She stopped and I didn't speak. Then she continued.

'Well, I suppose he is desperate.'

'Desperate for what, sister?'

'In a nutshell, he is finished, everything he has gone, all within three months. I first heard that his house in the village got burnt.'

'Got burnt! My goodness, sister what happened?'

'Nobody could say exactly what led to the fire, but it was put down to faulty electrical wiring or something like that. Then his famous supermarket followed suit.'

'*Chineke e*! God o! What is the meaning of all these, sister? What are you telling me?' I wailed, all plan to speak calmly forgotten.

'Gift calm down, I have not finished. Remember the Igebu family?'

'Yes,' I answered, then decided to qualify my answer to be sure we were speaking of the same family, 'That rich and powerful family that loves to thrive in controversy *abi*? Are they the one burning down his properties? He is definitely way out of his league I must say.'

'I did not say that,' Chinelo pointed out before continuing.

'Anyway, it emerged that Osahon bought the two plots of land where he built his mansion in Benin City from the Uzukobve family. The problem was that the Uzukobve family was dragged to court by the Igebu family over the ownership of the said land. Meanwhile the Igebus took the law into their own hands and evicted Osahon from the plot and property even as the law court was still trying to unravel who the true owners were.'

'Sister, what of his property on the land, are they going to refund him that? Oh sister, what am I going to do?' I added, without waiting for my sister's answer to any of my questions. This was serious trouble. If Osahon had lost all his properties, including the Supermarket, he would look to extract money from me if he perceived that I had it to give. And Osahon was not the type to pay for unnecessary things like insurance.

'I still have not finished. You have to let me tell you what happened here, and maybe it will give us a clue as to his sudden appearance there,' Chinelo said exasperatingly before she continued, 'As I was saying his bank, Proficient International Bank Ltd., was among the banks that died, well a lot of banks always die here all the time. Is it like that over there? Anyway for Proficient, who has been sick for sometime, it was said that they were not able to find any healthy bank that would merge with them in order to meet up with the new directives by the Central Bank. *Eeem* you know about this now Gift? More money for equity or something like that *eeh*? Ok so the bank died with Osahon's millions trapped in there. Even *sef* there was rumour that the Central Bank Governor had promised depositors that they would get their money back, sometime in the shadowy future. But you know how things usually are in this country, who knows when that will be. Besides in the past depositors were only paid N50, 000 not minding what they had in the account so this one the Central Bank Governor is saying *na* talk, when we see *am* we go believe. So my sister this is the situation,' Chinelo finally finished with a sigh.

We kept quiet; I, to digest all I had heard and its implication, on my sister's part, I was not sure of what she was thinking. Only our breathing that indicated our presence.

After sometime she asked, 'Gift are you still there?'

I heard her but I did not speak so she rattled the telephone set and then smacked it, muttering something about Nitel, the national telecommunication company. I suspected that she'd drop the phone next believing that we had been cut off so I said, 'I am still here sister.' Then I followed that with a question that can only be answered by

God, 'What kind of bad-luck is this, eh sister? How could anybody lose all he had in one go; *if no be curse dem curse am?*'

'It is unbelievable, my sister, but people have to pay sometime for what they did in life, you know?'

Then it suddenly occurred to me that Chinelo seemed to know too much. It was not as if she lived in the same neighbourhood with Osahon nor had friends in common. They did not belong to the same social standing, much as ThankGod and I had helped her and her family to move a notch above scratching level. But that would still not by any stretch bring them into Osahon's orbit. Barely recognizing my own voice I conveyed my thoughts to my sister.

'Sister, are you sure about all these informations, how come you know so much?'

Mindful of the fact that my head was pounding furiously and my ears seemed blocked from the racket going on in my head, making me feel disembodied, I strained with much effort to listen to my big sister.

'As luck would have it, his wife's sister belongs to my very own Catholic Women's Organization meeting.'

'In our church?' I squealed, sounding as if the Holy Family Catholic Church, where I used to attend so many years ago when I lived with my sister, belonged to us exclusively.

Chinelo snorted a laugh before answering and she did understand the question perfectly from her answer, 'Our very own church, o my sister. Initially when I found out who she was, the usurper's kin, and how she was blooming all the time, it did not leave a good taste in my mouth, but I also heard that she was reputed to be a very respectful girl: all that wealth did not get into her head and she did not have an inkling about your existence, unlike some girls that would seek married men and out their wives if given the chance and then flaunt the man's wealth like no man's business. Anyway, to answer your question I heard the stories from a distance, you know how gossips fly about in this our meeting, never mind what the association was supposed to stand for.'

'So does her sister still attend the meeting?'

'Not for sometime now. However, I heard she finally had a baby, after series of miscarriage, shortly before the first fire and her sister has not returned to the meeting since, but her circle of friends kept me in the know.'

'Sister, what do you think he wants from me this time around?'

'What did he say to you when he visited?'

'When you say visit, you make it sound as if he was invited,' I grumbled before continuing, 'anyway he said that he "*came to wipe the hurt he put in my soul.*" Have you ever heard such a drivel sister? This time he is making himself out as an angel of mercy or something. Shameless goat!'

'That sounds serious, Gift. On face value, it looks as if he came to reconcile with you, but he must be looking for money. I have to go and look for the sister of that wife of his; she might give us a clue. I will go under the auspices of the CWO,' Chinelo said. But then she must have changed her mind by deciding that enough was enough when she declared, 'I do not need a disguise, if Osahon bit our buttocks without minding the feaces, why should we mind his brain when we bite his head?'

I chuckled then laughed. Nicely surmised. I knew that her maternal instinct had kicked into a combatant mode: like a mother hen protective of her brood. She has always treated me like I was one of her daughters.

'Sister, please one way or the other do let me know, it will give me an insight into what he has up his sleeve and how to deal with him here.'

'What he has up his sleeve you already know, so don't let him con you a second time: only a fool allows the branch of a tree, in the same position, to pierce his eyes a second time.' I knew where she was going and I didn't want to encourage her by either keeping quiet or by arguing so I side-stepped the storm neatly.

'What of my pa and mama, when did you see them last? I really miss them.'

I finished meekly, employing my-last-born-position voice.

'I saw them over a month ago.' Her soothing voice indicated that she had fallen into the trap. I smiled. 'But don't worry about them,' she continued oblivious of my web, 'I will go home next weekend to rejoice with them about ThankGod's news. Imagine! ThankGod, a married man and now a father? Mmmh, this God is a great God.' I snorted but did not want to be drawn into the analysis of the greatness of our God or His ability to redirect us humans since I had yet to find my way back into His good books as to enjoy His abundant mercies, so I said instead, 'I will try and speak with them now before I go back home, but remember not a word about this. We do not need to worry them prematurely.'

'I know. Take care of yourselves and your children. Try not to worry, and trust in our God. He will win this war for us.'

Nothing shakes Chinelo's trust in God but whether HE would fight for a sinner like me remained to be seen.

I rang off, paid my bill and left. But I did not want to go home yet to face Erica and all the unpleasantness she'd be ready to divulge by now. So I decided to window shop, to further calm myself down. As I made to cross the street towards Clery's, a gentle breeze floated past carrying with it the sweet smell and massaging fragrances of various fresh hand-made soaps from Lush so I turned back to follow the smell. Halfway down, I changed my mind and went into Café Aspire on top of Arnotts Shopping Arcade instead. There, I ordered a cup of coffee and a plate of naked salad, nothing but leaves, and nursed both of them for almost an hour, while lost in thought. Finally I concluded that it was of no use, whatever Osahon wanted this time. I did not have it, and you do not give what you don't have. But not having any way of fathoming the extent to which this appearance would affect my life yet again, I wearily and very reluctantly left for home.

PART TWO

1995 Rising dream ...

LAGOS, NIGERIA

Eeei this world sef; *okwanu onye bitee aka ofu ife.* In this our world, it was he who lived long that would see things: 'So me Gift will now be a university undergraduate *biko nu?*' I nodded to myself as if to affirm not only the novelty of that to any onlooker, but to attest also to the fact that I represent a living example of impossibility. These types of thoughts couldn't help but bubble up to the surface each time I engaged in the little things that reminded me of the next stage in my life, like now. I looked around before I asserted defiantly, 'And I am going to show the world; let them just watch and see that the height you climb in life is as a result of pure hard work.' After the speech I raised my eyes up to the clouds and smiled to God before quickly looking down for a well-aimed jump across an open gutter upsetting the flies who buzzed angrily before settling back down, to pick my way gingerly to the *okirika*—the second hand clothes—section of Ochanja market.

How could anyone explain this magic; university education is not a small thing *obia buluzia for nwa nwogbenye di kam. Chineke a idi egwu*—let alone for a daughter of a poor man like me. This God, you are a wonder. I shook my head again but this time at God's infinite power to surprise.

But just because my family constantly strung my path with words of wisdom from the good Lord Himself, so that I did not trip on the fowler's snares that littered life, did not mean that I would not enjoy myself. No, I must allow myself to not only pass through the university but the university must pass through me, I have to turn out a well-rounded person and not a local champion, you know.

And that was what brought me to the *Okirika* section of Ochanja market. For starters, I could not arrive in the school looking like the village bumpkin. No need to advertise oneself. So I must acquire clothings that befitted the university ambience, whatever that represented. Being a Jambite, first year undergraduate, fresh from secondary school, eager faced, ready to taste the forbidden fruit of freedom and all it had to offer in the citadel of knowledge called University, must be masked by all means, at least in appearance.

In anticipation, I had already spent two agonizing weeks scouring the *Okirika* market sorting through the traders' heaps until I was satisfied, or till the limit of my pocket quenched the thirst for acquisition. So this trip today was to pay for and collect what I had selected on my previous visit. As I dodged rubbish after rubbish, hand after hand and even abuse from sour traders, I felt this thrill run through my body again as I remembered that I would also now be away from the indulging eyes of my family for the first time. To do as I liked! I was now a grown up, all of eighteen years.

It was expected that the life I had led so far, the knowledge and wisdom I had acquired as a member of the Ofoedu family, as a child of God, guided by the map of life generously steeped in the ways of the Lord, would guide my outlook and decisions even as I was away from my family and familiar settings. That was every parent's wish, that was every teenager's taciturn agreement and they all usually came to a compromise and it worked out more often than not. Well . . . I knew what was expected from me and I would not disappoint myself and my family. As I entered the market proper it started as usual; calls from different traders seeking customers.

'Ah *wetin* fine girl like you *dey* find for this dirty market e? *oya* come take am for my shed no need to go further, you hear?!'

'Come now *na* me you dey find!'

'Fine girl this way,' as the trader was saying that he turned to berate others, '*abeg* make *una* leave am for me, *abi* na that *una* nonsense clothes fine girl like her go buy, or *una* no dey see well again?'

'Follow me abeg, *na* me get *wetin* you *dey* find!'

These entire summonses in various forms, from various quarters, were followed by tugging and patting of different parts of my body but my hand mostly. I beat them off while I meandered to the part of the market I wanted, remembering to hang on to my meager savings buried deep in my handbag before pickpockets dealt me a mortal blow.

* * *

On D-day, Chinelo, in the company of my father who had arrived the previous day from the village to witness this momentous day in history, saw me off to the Lagos motor park. When the Peugeot 504 stationwagon drove off for Lagos, I waved till my arms ached, though not as much as my heart. It was a terrible wrench and to a place so far away. But I knew that I would make it. It was the beginnings of my dream come true, so I must not only survive, but survive with excellence.

The journey was short and long at the same time and was not made easy by the terrible heat and rancid smell from the boot of the stationwagon. Some woman had dried bush-meat in the boot of the car and had exchanged hot words with the well-dressed man in the front seat who had the audacity to ask whether she was sure the meat had not gone bad, otherwise why was it stinking so. Since that question was asked, our car had heated further up with hot words.

I had to hide behind the book I was reading to avoid taking sides as a furious row ensued, not just between the woman and the man, but between the members of the invisible camp that has been born, for and against, adding further to the heat. I almost felt sorry for the man, but it was a bit too much on his part to have asked such a question. Would it make the smell go away? No. 'So of what use was the question?' I had muttered in annoyance.

The driver was oblivious to the racket swirling around him, his feet firmly planted on the accelerator, as if the devil himself was after us.

After a while the quarrel changed target. Now it was the driver's turn to receive abuse: he was driving too fast. At a stage one woman, sitting directly behind him spat on his head after she had tried, to no avail, to ascertain whether he was paid to deliver our blood to his occult group.

To the driver's credit, he never reacted to the abuses, the shouting and the spitting; he just made himself a stone wall of silence. I took his cue and ignored the melee, praying that nothing untoward should happen, the raucousness and the speed were bad enough.

When, after five hours, we finally drove into Iddo motor park, the Lagos terminus for all forms of transport arriving from the Eastern part of Nigeria, I heaved a great sigh of relief while looking around. I noted that this motor park seemed to house lesser gods in public transportation. I did not see any sign of luxurious buses; the likes of Ekene Dili Chukwu, Izuchukwu Transport Ltd., Ifesinachi, ABC Line, etc, they must since have carved out their own terminus I concluded.

Our driver parked the car, and we all, for the first time breathed a sigh of relief in unison, grateful to God for delivering us from the hands of the devil. For after the lengthy abuse, which later turned into entreaties, the driver had continued to ignore the troublesome passengers, one woman at the back tentatively started a song for God's intervention but the response was unbelievably lukewarm attesting to the extent of our fears because to not respond to something that had to do with God in Nigeria, in the midst of a nightmare? Totally uncharacteristic! It was left for all of us individually then to seek God's intervention and this was carried out with vigor fuelled by fear, fiery prayer missiles collided as they sought their way to heaven. Meanwhile those of us, very few I assure you, with our forced quiet demeanor clutched our hearts in our hands literally—we did not find solace in quarreling nor could we pray in the steamy cauldron.

I thanked God gently and came down, my legs tingling from the cramped position they had endured. Then I looked around and became instantly and thoroughly confused. I thought that I had been living in a city for the last five years? Apparently not.

Why were there so many people? Milling about, pushing and shoving as they went. And to where? As I stood there gaping around like a fool, I was being nudged gently on and before I knew what was happening, I had been dragged along by the human traffic before I realized it and noted also that my luggage was not with me and that I was not sure of the direction we were headed. I had to turn back immediately!

But that I found a bit of a struggle, for to go against the human traffic was not like eating pepper-soup by any stretch of the imagination. However, I continued doggedly. Finally arriving back at the motor park, I secured a space on a bench and sat down to catch my breath and my bearings. What an adventure. And I had barely arrived!

I collected my worldly belongings from a fiery and tough-talking park attendant who dressed me down for not only leaving my luggage for thieves to plunder but creating the added work of looking after it for him. I thanked him and apologized all at the same time and then sat back down to beat off entreaties from load-carriers who were bent on carrying my luggage even at half-price or less. It must be a very dull day for them if it had come to that, irrespective of the entire bustling park. But employing them constituted a risk of its own as it has been known that some of them would make away with peoples loads and as I wasn't about to lose mine to anybody, I ignored them but somehow they must have smelt my newness for they refused to leave, trapping me in the semi-circle they had formed around me. I did not know how to proceed from there really. Finally Onyema, the fiery park attendant, as he had told me his name was, took time off his busy schedule and came to my rescue. Firmly he shooed the load-carriers away and then berated me further, 'this one *wey* you just *tanda* there like wood you no no say *na* Lagos you dey so? In Lagos you have to shine your eyes well well oo if you wan survive.' I kept nodding my head positively and when he finished I thanked him. Finally he directed me to Unilag, short for University of Lagos.

I had never seen such a collection of imposing handsome buildings in one place flashing past as the *tuke tuke* bus I boarded to Unilag wove in and out of traffic through Oyingbo market to Yaba where Unilag was located. The scenery, however, was marred here and there by fly-infested heaps of rubbish sitting in front of and beside tall elegant buildings.

There was not enough space in the boot of our *tuke tuke* so my luggages were stuck here and there, some of them under my feet, making me to sit with my legs bunched up and my knees squashing my chin. Lagos *na wah*! I mused. When I was as comfortable as could be expected, I looked around to realize that most of the passengers were sitting in similar positions—with their luggage stuffed where their legs should have been. But nobody seemed to mind. Barely settled in I was shocked out of my reverie by the shout of 'campus gate!' from the bus-conductor, causing me to smack my neighbour's mouth with my elbow in my haste, who, in turn erupted into a stream of abuses in Yoruba language. Though I suspected that the woman was not of the Yoruba stock by her looks, it seemed that everybody spoke Yoruba in Lagos. Well, it must be as in "when in Rome behave like the Romans," saying.

I pacified my neighbour and cautiously but hurriedly picked my way out of and jumped down from the bus and happily collected my luggages passed down so fast by the conductor that before my fingers clasped the last of the bags, the bus had disappeared in a swirl of dust. Aaah . . . Lagos!

I shook my head in wonder. I had heard so much about Lagos. So this is it? And I am here, in Lagos itself? Wonders shall never cease to happen! I was not disappointed or daunted at all. I was deliriously happy. This is my kind of city definitely; fast-paced, mad, beautiful, smelly rubbish and all.

I dragged my luggage along and crossed the road to the campus side and went in through a gigantic gate that had, "Welcome to the University Of Lagos, Akoka, Yaba," mounted on top of it, in the form of an arch with the university crest sitting dignified in the middle of it. As soon as I crossed the gate, I felt goose-bumps all over my body. My head swelled up making me woozy. But this was a feeling of happiness, I discerned, for I had crossed the gate of one of the finest institutions of learning in my great country, Nigeria, not as a visitor but as a student. I was ever going to remain one of the alumni of Unilag. I closed my eyes and while standing still, raised the name of God in praise and exaltation: thanking him for this day. I had arrived!

When I got closer to the administrative building I stopped, to scan round and take stock of the situation. I was supposed to look up my hostel of residence at the Registrar's office, but I did not intend to ask anybody, remembering my ordeal that long time ago in Government College. Once was enough. To my relief and happiness, there were signages with names of places and streets and where they were to be found.

I followed the sign to the Registrar's office and found myself in a big building with a cavernous innard and rumbling with activities. Everybody must have arrived at the same time! Valiantly I fought my way to the glass-fronted Notice Board. I could barely contain my glee as it turned out I was in the famous Moremi Hall! Wow! When I had announced to my friends from my secondary school that I had passed University of Lagos, they promptly told me to ensure that I was in Moremi Hall, period. It was simply the only place to be. The chicks who resided there were said to look like they were hand-picked. I had decided there and then that I needed to know more about Unilag and Moremi Hall, for they were well outside my forte. The research involved getting my friends to ask their other friends, who had ever been to or passed through Lagos, to gather as much information as they could about Unilag.

The information had come in fast and furious. Everybody had something to say about Unilag. It was a very hot university both academically and otherwise. It was the otherwise aspect that I was interested in. I was told that the chicks in Moremi Hall spoke through their noses: to imitate *oyibo* accents of British extract no less, otherwise referred to as *phone.* It seemed that they were not aware of American accent. This was partly because of lack of role models, not enough students came all the way from America as to carve out an influence, I was told.

Those chicks that could not speak the *phone* kept trying till they perfected the art, it was a *do or die affair*, no compromise, otherwise you were then a regular ordinary student, which was uninteresting.

In Moremi Hall, almost everybody's parents were rich to the teeth, supposedly. It had been rumoured, however, that some of these *rich* chicks in reality were reputed to sell their bodies to men to maintain Moremi lifestyle. That did not worry me, I was from a good stock and one did not learn how to be left-handed in old age.

I had also been told that some of these chicks in Moremi Hall were supposed to be living fabulous lives: breakfast in London, lunch in Paris and dinner in Amsterdam. They supposedly jet off by Thursdays to be with their families, lovers, sugar-daddies, whoever, in London, Paris, Austria, Switzerland, Italy, name it and still attend lectures, come Monday morning sharp, their purses bulging with foreign currencies!

'Oh my goodness!' I had screamed with delight, rubbing my palms, already itching to touch the foreign currencies, no less. I couldn't wait to see things for myself and I came prepared, what with all my trips to the *Okirika* market. You have to keep the facade.

Finally my researchers mentioned the *Aristocrats*: the big-boys with serious money to burn. Some of them look like shit, nothing to write home about, but all in all, they have the cash which was what mattered . . . . mmm. It kept you in style.

Well, I would just have to have my eyes peeled and mind unfettered to see how it played out. On the final lap of my search for Moremi Hall it started drizzling, just to cap the day.

I entered Moremi Hall and shook water off myself not unlike a wet chicken. I had aimed to enter regally, to make a mark, but fate had intervened. While trying to make myself presentable I observed the traffic that disappeared into a big door that opened and closed. I looked closely and concluded that that must be what I had read about called a lift. Great. Carefully I followed the next batch of traffic and stepped in along with my luggages. My heart pounded but I had to be careful not to announce my ignorance. I could never live it down. So, though my bones were rattling, my teeth shaking and my intestines knotted, I presented a very calm front. Wasn't Celina my mother? No indication at all that I might spray my lift neighbour with the remnants of my breakfast any moment, at the rate the lift was making the contents of my stomach rest on the upper section of my gullet, threatening to erupt into my mouth.

When it finally lurched to a stop on my floor, the third floor, I stumbled out even as I wondered how it knew to stop me there, for I never got the chance to find out what you did when you entered a lift. I rested my forehead on the cold aluminium panel next to the door of the lift, which had immediately closed and rattled away, as soon I was disgorged along with a few others whom I didn't even notice before I was enveloped by a mist. Wearily I closed my eyes to calm down fully. When I finally opened my eyes, it dawned on me with a sharp twist in my already tender gut that the lift had left with my things!

'Christ in heaven,' I muttered shakily, 'who is going to go back into that thing?' I knew for sure that there was no way I would be found in that contraption again, not while I was still alive.

Gloomily, I cast about and soon noticed the security post. I made straight to the uniformed Baba lolling on a pink plastic chair and without prompting narrated my predicament. Baba happened to be the porter in charge of Moremi Hall, third floor. He tutted in sympathy while nodding knowingly.

'It happens all the time, you know? Don't mind, we will find your bags. Which room were you assigned to?' Baba waited then continued, probably not expecting any answer from the distressed girl.

'Do you know yet? Because then I can check the register for you?'

'It is Room 325,' I offered tentatively. Baba nodded, as if he knew something about Room 325 but would not tell. Well, I was not in the mood for any guessing games, and not with Baba! So I ignored Baba's *knowing* nod.

Twenty minutes later, my luggage retrieved, I once more lugged them along in search of my room. The lift mercifully had waited for Baba and me to collect my luggages this time and while we were at it, Baba threw a few lessons into the bargain. I had a lot to learn.

Exhausted, wet, irritable and disjointed, combined with the previously inhaled dust at the bus stop threatening to clog my throat, my mood had changed from ecstatic to bad and I was not too far from busting into tears if care was not taken, by the time I finally stumbled into my assigned room.

Imagine my shock then to discover that somebody was already in the room, seemingly unaffected by anything. I looked at her from the tail of my eyes and saw a short girl of about 5ft 4", with every inch of her person glowing. She was well groomed. Not a thing out of place and expensive too! Who was she?

Then my heart sank with a sickening realization. Am I going to live in the same room with one of them chicks? One of the famed Moremi chicks? I would have preferred to relate with them from a very safe distance. Yes, I loved glamour, money and all it could afford, but I would most certainly not want to live in the same room with any *pro* on the sly! Wouldn't we all be tarred with the same brush?

Imagine being branded a prostitute? 'God forbid!' I sniffed under my breath.

I peeked at the chick again, and noticed that everything she wore was coordinated to match: the navy blue flowers on her culottes and top went with her slip-on while the white background matched the strap of her wrist watch! She was the epitome of cool and collected, an altogether chick, though a brief one.

In any case, this chick was relaxed, reclining on the bed in the inner corner of the room reading the latest copy of Vogue magazine. I sighed, banged the door shut and slumped on the remainder of the two six-spring beds in the room, then turned to my roommate. She has to be my roommate, who else could she be, and said sarcastically,

'Did you arrive yesterday before the doors of this great institution were opened to us lesser mortals or what?'

I was taken aback by the intensity of my resentment. I was not prone to such anger in a flash like that but this girl was the height of it. How could she be so calm and she chose the better corner!

The chick in question lowered the Vogue magazine to glance at Gift before raising her brows in a question mark. Her scrutiny was met by the sheer beauty of a vision before her. So she let her eyes roam up and then down the tall slender girl. Her body seemed sculptured, upholding heavy but firm breasts, straining, unsupported by anything but a narrow ribcage and a waist that flared out and terminated into an upturned buttocks and this whole miracle was finished off with a very long legs; an epitome of femaleness on legs. Not being a tall person, height had always intrigued her especially when it was bestowed on a woman.

This lady looked interesting; you don't see this kind of perfection in one single person, but such rude manners? She exhaled quietly as she advised herself to better watch it, for it looked like this harridan could bite. She and her friend Erica may need to activate Plan B quickly afterall. She had no time for nonsense. She then followed her thoughts with words.

'I don't know the source of your discomfort and anger and I don't particularly care. But let me give you three pieces of good advice for the future: First, do not vent your frustration on the first person you see unless you had sought for and were invited to do so. Secondly, it is always good to create an impression when you meet people for the first time. What kind of impression you create is up to you. What you have done is uncouth and smacks of lack of good breeding. Finally, we have four years to spend in this room. I am working on the assumption that you are my roommate, but if you want nasty I will give you nasty.'

She then re-opened her Vogue and ignored Gift.

I was flabbergasted by the pure British *phone* that spewed from the *tiger-lady*'s mouth. All my years in Government College were spent polishing my spoken English with the accompanying *phone* but I did not realize that I was learning from learners! It just dawned on me that all my friends then had learnt their English accent by association—acquired in the course of their numerous travels and making foreign friends. This girl did not sound like them in any way. She must have been born into that *kind of life* accent, it had to be. She spoke like how Her Majesty, the Queen of England herself, would speak.

I stood up, straightening myself to my full height of 5ft 9", extended my arms, palms facing up in a conciliatory gesture and said,

'In that case, let's start afresh then, my name is Gift Nkiruka Virginia Ofoedu from Oyi town, in Anambra State. I will be studying Political Science and Economics.'

My change of attitude sprang from quick guilt at attacking my unsuspecting roommate who did not add to or subtract from my earlier misadventures. And to think that I had vowed, not too long ago, to not disgrace myself again or give anybody cause to.

My roommate stood up and stretching her own arms in an embrace-leading kind of way; the two arms straightened out at shoulder level but with the two palms facing each other across the length of the stretch, her eyes twinkling, in a victory shine, she murmured, 'Well . . . in that case, my name is Ifeoma Philomena Iwuije. I will be studying Economics and I am from Nnewi Town. But don't ever call me Philomena, because then I will kill you.'

'You can afford to say that because you were not the one saddled with Virginia.' We smiled tentatively and then laughed as we embraced. When Ifeoma had stood up for our formal introduction, this powerful presence stood up with her and took up every available space in the room, pulsating. One was forced to immediately focus on her. Her confidence was that huge.

We spent the rest of that day and half the night talking: discovering and learning new things from each other, teaching, admonishing, vowing and promising to remain steadfast to the friendship. Eventually we succumbed to sleep. I was relieved that Ifeoma was a good girl, in my estimation, judging from her revelations, because I honestly did not have the desire or the energy to wage any war. She just did not suffer fools gladly, that's all.

Later, with our morning ablutions behind us, we left for the academic blocks together to join in the orientation classes for the first years which preceded registration. As the days flew by, we became inseparable, except for when we were in our different classes, though being in the same Faculty of Social Sciences we had many elective courses together.

As our friendship blossomed, over the days and the weeks, we came to realize that we both had a lot in common: We were the last children in our families, pampered within the means available to the respective families; were perennially bugged, we discovered, to always go for confessions; diligently do our Easter Duties: dying to self through denying our body what it most craved during the Lenten period backed up by fasting; should always be in a position to receive Holy Communion every Sunday at least; this was supposed to proclaim our state of Grace; to always seek for the strength to overcome temptations from the Good Lord. Yes, we were both of Catholic faith.

Ifeoma told me that she was a British citizen born and brought up in the Knightsbridge area of London. So I was proved right in my earlier summation: Ifeoma most definitely did not learn her accent.

She also told me that she had only ever been to Nigeria on two occasions before now. One summer holiday period, when their parents felt that they had to know their roots and so they were shipped to Nigeria for four weeks. The second time was when her paternal grandmother, Oduenyi Philomena Iwuije died; they had stormed her village then, she said, for her burial. Baffled, I asked, 'You must have liked what you saw then to make you come back?'

'The first three days, during our first visit were horrible, but I like challenges. If all the people I saw, lived and survived in the scorching heat and relentless dust why not me? Then as time went on I had this brainwave to study for my first degree in Nigeria and so here I am.'

'And your parents did not object?' I asked, my confusion heightening. I mean why should anybody living abroad want to come back to Nigeria for university education? Talk of Brain-Drain syndrome in reversal. Well, not exactly, I had no name for my friend's brand of decision and therefore gave up on any guesswork. Instead I listened to her answer.

'My parents have this tendency to overanalyse issues that we come to them with leaning more on the flaws of it than the good and that tells you two things, that the idea may not work and that they would not support you. Based on their negative findings against the idea, more often than not we end up dropping the issue looking like it was at our own volition though you were left with that sneaky feeling that they made you. My parents are both professors lecturing in the university in case you are wondering. So when I mentioned my interest of studying in Nigeria and it was not analyzed to death I knew that it was OK and that was it for me then.'

I shook my head, 'Well in a way most parents are alike that, they are either trying to dissuade you or steering you, unsuspected by you, to what they perceived would benefit you, but to come to Nigeria for your university is baffling, however, since you're here there must be some merit in it somewhere.'

As our warts and all continued to tumble out, I went on to inform Ifeoma that I had never left the shores of Oyi for anywhere beyond the shores of Onitsha Urban before now which compared to Lagos should remove the word urban from its name immediately before somebody took it to task on that account.

Despite our parent's good intentions we realized in a way that we would be considered very worldly, at least for people within our age range. What do parents know anyway? We smirked. It came to pass that we had tasted life or what we considered life then: going to parties, drinking alcohol, gossiping non-stop, reading teen magazines and aping the stars and models judiciously. We then concurred that we had breezed through the greater part of our teenage years unscathed. And now, poised to enter adulthood, were too old to be trapped into any undesirable situations that we could not control.

*   *   *

Our orientation classes over and registration done with, I settled down to campus life with my very desirably formed alliance. So though in our various ways we could be said to be worldly, it was apparent that Ifeoma had definitely lived a more charmed life in my estimation and so I positioned myself to absorb more *culture* from her and in turn, tutor her in her areas of shortcomings. We propped each other along and united we smoothened out any rough edges encountered along the way together.

Over a month later our routine had assumed a steady pattern: wake up in the morning, go for morning lectures and then go down to any of the canteens in and around the school for breakfast. Ifeoma had vowed that she'd not be found dead eating refectory food. We would then go back to lectures till mid-afternoon, snack in any of the tuck-shops dotted all over the campus, finish our lectures and then go back to the hostel. Much later we would go out for dinner. If we were up to it afterwards, we would go to the library for reading and researching. Or stay back in the room and gossip, exchange information and generally laze about.

Six weeks into the term, I came back one afternoon from my lectures and met Erica coming out of our room.

'Hi Erica,' I greeted breezily ready to move on. Erica was Ifeoma's friend from wherever. I had not asked her about Erica because at first encounter it looked as if Erica did not particularly like me, so I in turn did not waste any time cluttering my brain with useless information about her. The greatest injustice you could do to yourself was to want somebody who did not want you. Who needed that?

'Aaa ha! Acada, you no go let the library rest?' was Erica's response.

Look at this girl oh? Between Erica and myself who spent more time in the library? I steamed, but let it go, shrugged and went into our room. Erica can go to hell. 'Acada indeed,' I fumed under my breath, banged the door shut, clattered my books on my reading table and opened and reached for a bottle of chilled coca cola in our mini-fridge. Everybody in this campus pretended not to read so as to fain surprise at passing very well without having had to read. Geniuses.

'Who is fooling who?' I snorted and followed that with a long hiss.

Ifeoma looked up and laughed out loud. Erica rubbed me the wrong way and it gladdened Ifeoma's heart to see me riled. I was far too serene, she had complained and had advised me, repeatedly, to thaw and take life easy; otherwise my icy-regal-attitude may harm my chances of catching an *Aristocrat* if care was not taken. But I did not mind her suppositions. *Aristocrats* or not, appearances must be maintained. Any serious *Aristocrat* should be able to crack the shell to get to the pearl.

'You saw Erica then?' Ifeoma finally asked.

'Where did you say you met that one from *sef*?' I asked surprised, surprised because Ifeoma had seemed not to notice the undercurrent that simmered between Erica and me all this while.

'I never said where I met her; incidentally I actually met her in this school.'

'Pardon me? What do you mean by "in this school?" When could that have been?'

'Take it easy Gift. I gave her a ride from the campus gate the morning that the school resumed and we became friends when we realized that we were in the same hostel and in first year too.'

'You mean, you met her only hours before we did?' I asked in amazement.

'Yes.'

'Why then does she behave as if you had known each other forever? As if I was trying to come between what had been established of old?'

'When we met earlier that day, before you blew in like a cyclone, we had agreed that she could share this room with me. We had put all sorts of plan in place. Even mentioned it to old Baba, the porter, hinting at something being in it for him if need be, to move the girl with the name 'Gift' out. We had assumed that you must be one of those Bible-carrying gals, you know? The Scripture Union babes. With a name like Gift and Virginia for that matter we did not expect anything less.' Ifeoma took the coke from me, tilted her head back, had a long swig, shook the bottle and finished the content before continuing.

'It irked Erica when I stalled with our Plan B after I met you as you did not fit the bill we had in mind, but not wanting to sever her friendship with me she turned her anger on you, seeing you as an usurper and all.'

I looked at Ifeoma and asked, 'You mean the two of you would have gotten me out of this room just like that?' I snapped my fingers to show the ease and then followed it with a supposition, 'I am sure that you would have met with some opposition somewhere along the line though, afterall I wasn't part of the deal and we are talking about me here.'

'But of course, and without a jot of remorse my dear if you had turned out otherwise. As for *meeting with opposition* as you put it, forget it. I have come to realize in my short time in this country, that there's nothing you wanted that you cannot have, as long as you have the wherewithal and are committed to the project. Some people will even offer to become your foot-runner to make it faster for you.'

I sat down. 'So what exactly does she want? And what do you have to give that is making her want to edge me out so much?'

'Don't go naïve on me Gift, people read situations differently; she probably felt that her association with me would lift her a notch or two on the ladder of life, but my friendship with you, she believed, may put *sand sand for her Garri* judging by our closeness. You are guileless Gift, but not everybody is like you.'

I looked at my friend and felt that I was neither going to pursue Erica's purposes and intentions at this time nor engage in the analysis of my *guileless-nature* for now. I would take Erica up on her stupid assumptions next time; life is too short for unnecessary frictions.

'But how come you didn't tell me about this before now?'

'I was waiting for you to ask.'

'Really?'

Ifeoma shrugged but said nothing. So I turned my back on her while sitting on my bed thinking, but why did she not tell me? What exactly did her not telling me imply? What made her keep such information? It was not like it was that important but why should I not know?

'Gi, I am sorry, it just never occurred to me that you would care. Besides you and Erica do not see eye to eye so I did not want to add to the aggravation.'

Imagine plotting to oust me even before I had arrived! Oh well . . . I turned and glared at her before accepting her apology.

Ifeoma then looked at her wrist-watch and shrieked, 'If we don't hurry now, we'll be late for G.S 101 and we both knew how stuffy Dr. Ndukwe could get about " . . . you make me loose my trend of thought when you gals saunter in at will." She mimicked the esteemed Doc.

That doused my curiosity and I jumped up and was out the door in a flash, stay-at-home clothes and all, closely behind Ifeoma.

                                *   *   *

We plowed through our weekdays which were an endless round of lectures, but no weekend passed us unsung. Ifeoma had this knack of sniffing out the poshest of parties around and I seamlessly blended in as if to the manor born. It was amazing what we got up to. As our feet got stronger and stronger as bona fide undergraduates I felt that the time had come for me to begin to streamline my future so I sought out and became a member of the Students Union Governing Body as I wanted to see first hand how politics was conducted. I also joined the university's debating society. The art of speaking, sparring and aiming to outsmart your political opponent must be mastered and this was the time to begin. I had to imbue myself with the defining culture of my chosen career not just in dressing and *phone*. Ifeoma in jest called me Senator Gift. But I was passionate about my desire to be a civil servant and a spokesperson for the women of Nigeria in general and my part of the country in particular and from there launch my bid for a seat in the Senate.

The term was almost coming to an end. Still, I had not lost my virginity and it was not from lack of guys *chasing* me. Was I going to die an unconsummated old maid? When I confided my fears to Ifeoma she asked, 'Don't you feel anything at all for men?'

'I do feel some stirrings when we neck and grope but I feel that it should be more than a stirring, if I take what I knew as standard, right?'

'Well, if you are sure, then wait for the right guy. You have to be able to enjoy it otherwise what would be the point of doing it at all?'

'Then I will increase my search, I mean I have to know what it's all about.'

Ifeoma laughed and called me *ashawo,* but then she got serious and advised 'You have to be careful not to create a reputation as an *easy chick* like some of our sisters in this hall. You will never live it down.'

'Ah, have a heart Ifeoma, I was only trying to unburden my virginity here not bed-hop. And even that I could not manage, well you know me,' I conceded.

'Of course I do. I was only trying to be the voice of reason here. You live in Nigeria and have to contend with the archaic ways of your men without having to add another dimension to it.'

'I know, it is our Igbo brothers that are the culprits. They bed every willing maiden, but when ready to marry, they go down to their village to acquire a *changa*—brand new. Since I am not going to marry an Igbo man, thank you very much, to hell with anybody's *spin.*'

Ifeoma wrinkled her nose at her friend's vehemence then said, 'I even heard that in some villages the bride to be would be required to list the number of men she had slept with prior to meeting her husband. Yuck.' She sniffed before continuing, 'I mean in this day and age? What nonsense. I would walk out on the bloody man and his whole tribe if I had to be subjected to such barbarism.' She snorted to emphasize her anger and disgust.

'I must say that it is the Edo people that do that, not the Igbos. But what if you love the guy, can you walk away from him just like that?' I ventured.

'You and this love *sef,* if the man loves me, will he want to put me through such a barbaric ordeal?' Ifeoma countered, 'Love is a two way process as I understand it. It must be a hundred percent from both of us. If he has been busy sowing his wild oats why should they expect me to come and list the men I have been with because he wants to marry me? No chance my dear.'

'Professor Philomena.' And that immediately earned me a smack. I chuckled and got up to flick her on the bed like she was a featherweight while I strained to get a better look at myself in the mirror.

I straightened up and enquired of Ifeoma who probably had decided not to get up, 'Are we ever going to Maidugiri to visit that Edna friend of yours?'

'You bet we will. We have to *taste* Hausa men *now*. They are reputed to hold masters degree in pampering women I heard.'

'But I also heard that their men are not circumcised.'

'Then we will have the opportunity to put the speculation to rest by separating facts from fiction,' Ifeoma joked.

'Imagine losing my virginity to an uncircumcised Hausa man!'

'You *sef*, were you not just talking about love a few minutes ago? Or is your love limited to only men from your village?'

'Not necessarily. It was just a thought.'

'Well, we will have to be careful though, there are so many diseases flying around.'

'I should be telling you that Ifeoma, remember I am still a virgin.'

'You don't know what you are missing girl. For all we know, your vagina has rusted from lack of use.'

'Don't rub it in. I will get there yet, and then we can compare notes.'

'In that case I won't hold my breath my dear Gift, at the rate you are going I might die waiting!'

The first term of the University's academic year came to an end in the third quarter of December and I left for Oyi but not before going for confession at the university chapel, just to maintain my state of grace. Our campus chapel and Lagos in general are much more liberal: You went to mass in trousers, long or short, spaghetti sleeves and even mini-dresses. In St. Alphonsus you had to cover your hair with a scarf, barely letting your brow breathe. The sleeves of your blouse must also cover your arms well and you dared not enter the church premises in mini. Any infraction would see the warden walk you out supported by the nodding of the *guardians of morality* whose sensibilities were offended even before God's. That is if Fr. Obidi did not twist your ears first.

I left for my village the following day. I was excited about seeing my people and my village. I just hoped that ThankGod would be home too. I had not seen him in a long time.

Oyi Town, Anambra State, Nigeria

1995

I alighted from the rickety bus that brought me home and started trekking. With the eyes of a returning city dweller, I surveyed Oyi town, as I walked and was surprised to note that it had not changed, if anything it looked smaller and I was very surprised that I had actually missed it. Amazing.

Yes, I had wanted to run from it, put so much distance that could not be bridged whatsoever. My dream for cities was unfettered then. It was where people that made it dwelled. Destined to be amongst them, I had dreamt, I had visualized, yearned, ached, and then I left. It was rapturous, first to college, then to University. But now I was shocked to realize that somehow having left, I always desired to return. For as soon as I left, nostalgia latched onto my heart and took residence firmly. Every footpath, no matter how craggy, narrow and thorny with its sharp-toothed stones beneath your feet, with intent to disable, became elevated to this highway that led to mysterious havens of dazzling proportion. The village's mornings resplendent with freezing dews, perched on tall grasses, juggling to drench the most were forgotten while giant elephant-grasses determined to blind, if not cut you into tiny shreds, receded into oblivion. The chirping of the birds, the creaking of the crickets and the rustling of the lizards were magnified into heavenly melodies that defined my well-being and lured me to sleep, in the day and in the night. Then I would yearn to return to this luscious kingdom that I left behind, the yearning so keen that it hurt.

Granted, the atmosphere of my village had always been very calming; here you were at one with nature, with her protective cloak shielding you from the buffetings of the world. It was home. And I loved it. Then I would come back and the reality would show up harshly. The minusculeness of my village starkly apparent, suffocatingly so, snapping at me from all sides. I would constantly juggle for space with everything till I left.

But it was my home, a significant part of my life and therefore not to be discarded at will but rather incorporated as part of what defined me as I went along. But it must also be taken in small, small doses this time, not to be soaked in like before; I didn't want that, it was no longer enough. I had come to realize that I was a city kind of girl, no less.

As I crested the corner that would bring me to our compound, my heart took on a life of its own and started flipping with the anticipated joy of seeing my father again after such a long time, a whole three months. And when I sighted him, in his palmwine shack, hunched over in a snoozing mode, my heart constricted with love. Living far away in Lagos my pa could no longer pinch in a visit like he used to do, ooh I missed him so.

As I got closer I dropped my luggage and ran the rest of the way, decorum thrown to the wind.

My noise must have woken my pa up for suddenly; he stood up turned, saw me and grinned as he opened his arms wide to stop the loose cannon that was me. I flew into his open arms and exclaimed, 'Oh papa! Oh papa. How are you?'

'My mother, you are home?' he exclaimed while looking me up and down with pride. 'Welcome. Good, good.' He finally got to answer my, 'how are you?' question while adding, 'these old bones are still rattling and as you can see; I am as fit as fiddle,' to the equation. He disentangled himself to show off his fitness.

'How was school?' he asked, 'Did you have a good trip? What of your friend Ifeoma, has she traveled back to Great Britain? We were not sure of when to expect you. All your letters did not say, or maybe Fr. Obidi did not read it well to us. I was discussing with your mother only yesterday . . . .' He trailed off and then requested, 'Move back let me take a good look at you again.'

He was beside himself with joy, I could see, and I smiled indulgently while obliging him. I was quite sure that he still saw me as that four-year old, tramping his palmwine rounds with him. I took his hand firmly and we walked deeper into the compound.

Celina had overheard Abraham's sonorous voice while weeding her pepper shrub and was curious as to what had woken him up, so she came out to investigate. She took a step closer and asking nobody in particular said, 'Is that not our Gift?' I dropped my pa's hand to envelop her in a hug laughing out loud.

'Who else can it be mama?' I asked, still laughing. I led them into the livingroom so that they could ask and I could answer all their questions. Their beloved Gift was back from the University in Lagos!

*   *   *

After I ate and had sufficiently rested, my mother informed me that my friends Eliza and Eziamaka were home for Christmas and had earlier came to look for me. I smiled wryly to myself; my mother informing me that my friends called on me? It was a good thing to be considered an adult. I remembered that my mother did not approve of my having too many friends, if at all. If I didn't hang on to these friends with my all, she'd have pried them off. According to her, having too many friends causes confusion and inconsistency in one's life as you're tugged left, right and centre between them, your decisions informed and tinged by diverse opinions that you could do without. It seemed I was now considered old enough to make decisions and good choices based on the bag of home-grown wisdom hanging on my shoulder without fear of being tugged out of sync by *friends*.

I got ready and left to visit said friends, but I also used the opportunity to sneak off into the forest to smoke. Though Ifeoma said she smoked at home I could not imagine the reaction of my parents to such brazen behaviour and I was not ready to find out yet.

I had always spent my holidays in the village with my friends whose education continued in the next village where they attended *girls*, but then after WAEC, the girls had gone their different ways to learn various trades. Eliza left for Warri to train as a seamstress in her father's footsteps, Baba Eliza, our famed village designer; Eziamaka for Nkpor to learn secretarial training; while Nkemdilim had married and gone to join her husband, who lived in Nnewi, but she was also home for the Christmas.

I was the only one to have made it all the way to the university among my set. So I intended to unfurl the world of the university, step

by step, for them through my eyes. Shrugging I continued with my
smoking, hunched over a tree stump, my back shielded by a big tree.
I planned to use this reunion opportunity to start a youth political
awareness club. Puffing away, I plotted: as a united front, we may get
the local government to do one or two things for the village. I had
seen first hand in the university that lobbying worked.

*   *   *

When I got to Eliza's house others were already there helping
her father to hem, attach buttons and stitch his clients' Christmas
orders, as we used to do back in the day. As we sewed, we reminisced;
remembering the various church activities as members of Catholic
Girls Organization; the trudging up and down the worn footpath to the
mission house for the endless catechism classes. Going to the village
stream to fetch water and while at it tuck in one or two odd swims even
as we knew that our ears would be twisted for *sleeping* at the stream.
I regaled them about life as an undergraduate and about Lagos and
Lagosians. They in unison prayed that they would all soon enter their
husband's house safely to start the cycle of life all over again. I begged
to differ at this junction; unlike them, I intended to finish what I
had started plus more. Become a Civil Servant by working for the
Department of Women's Affairs aiming for the highest position there,
like Perm. Sec., or a commissioner or a minister. But my ultimate aim,
I informed them was to be a Senator.

My friends cheered me on. They did not doubt my ability to
achieve all I had outlined. I was always the little madam that knew
where she was headed. Now who, but I, was in the university? If I said I
was aiming for the Senate President that is what I was going to be. But
they entreated me not to forget them then, as they would expect to be
the ones that would handle all the attendant contracts.

I stayed out as late as I wanted before leaving for home. It was
no longer like before when I was forbidden by my parents to join my
friends in the moonlight games or stay out late; late being 5 o'clock
in the evening! At the height of our *oga* game and *kpum boo ololo*,
hide and seek, and the swell game yet to commence. As I passed the
so-called village protector, the *Iyioba* shrine, and took a left that'd bring
me home I ran into mama Kodi. I was not happy about this, as mama
Kodi had the tendency to say hurtful things, even if not true, without
a second thought. As she passed true to type she said, 'Gift go and
marry! I say go and marry! I hope you are not allowing them between
your legs? They would take it and run without marriage you know?

Do not let your beauty deceive you, men want only one thing from women, and it's not our face, I should know.' Abruptly she brushed past me and moved briskly down the lane, on her way. I stood there and stared at the receding figure with a frown, clenching and unclenching my fingers to stem the flow of anger. You could boil an egg from the hot air issuing from my nostrils. This definitely sounded malicious, much as mama Kodi tried to make it look like advice. I continued on my way home but mama Kodi's ramblings refused to dissipate. Some queries kept buzzing around in my brain: people were perpetually guarding their reputation, so it seemed. Just so that that image of *good-person* be maintained. But were people that good really? Or bad as the case may be? If perfection was not being sought from people by others, who were themselves not perfect, wouldn't the world be a more tolerant place? But no, everybody wanted everybody to conform to some unwritten code of behaviours which they themselves in turn flouted *behind closed doors*. Hypocrites!

Look at mama Kodi, the village slut. What gave her the nerve to speak to me in that way? What did she know about anything anyway? Villager like her. Village people never minded their business—I should know that by now—except maybe my mother who did not enjoy *idle gossip* as my father would put it.

As I got closer to my father's compound I heard my mother's excited voice and quickened my steps. Who'd get my mother in a flap like that? I rounded the corner and saw ThankGod and I knew—he was the apple of my mother's eyes and my own too. I rushed the last steps and we flew into each others' hands in a tight and drawn-out embrace. It had been too long to be so held by ThankGod. We kept crossing each other on various visits home over the years now and then, but it was never enough. ThankGod would have 'freed' by now but for the misfortune that befell Chief Osungwa. So he had stayed on doing *Oso Afia*.

The rest of my Christmas holidays were spent in the comfort of ThankGod's company. I was transported back to our growing years but without the chores. We had a lot to catch up on and we naturally gravitated to our *Island* of long ago. It gave us privacy to discuss our personal matters.

As we lounged on our tree-bed on one of our trips to the resort, on one occasion towards the end of the holidays, I decided to shift the tempo of our tête-à-tête. I took a final puff and flung the stub of my cigarette into the flowing stream, took a hefty gulp of palmwine and watched his demeanor. As I was about to speak ThankGod's face tightened and a furrow appeared, causing creases across his forehead.

When we were younger it used to make him look like a wizened old man and it also signified that something did not agree with him and he needed clarification. So I waited.

'Gift please, do not let mama know that you smoke.' I wondered why it took until now for him to mention this *aberration*. Women did not smoke, simple.

'Is it only mama? What of papa?' I countered.

'Well, papa is a man, he may understand.' I nodded as if in agreement before adding, 'I do not have any intentions of letting either of them know, anyway. I love them too, you know, and would not want to hurt them knowingly.'

'Really? If you mean it you should not be smoking at all.' I nodded again. He was being his very deep-self at the moment so I did not want to rile him. But as he spoke I knew that I might as well not have bothered for his teeth were already sunk deeply into the meat.

'But why did you choose to smoke in the first place? Do you want to be one of those *kinds* of girls?'

'What *kinds* of girls?'

'The "what a man can do woman can do better" type.'

'I have not become your *kind* of girl or anything like that. I am only trying to have fun as any healthy eighteen years old in the university would.'

'Indeed. While you are at it, do not develop hard edges around your mouth and squinting creases around your eyes, it would give you a washed out look like an ageing prostitute. Then men would run from you.'

'Why does everything have to start and end with men as if women were solely made for their comfort?'

'It depends on how you want to look at it. If a girl has to leave her parents house to live with her husband and family, change her name to his, cook and keep house for him, have his children and generally subsume herself in her husband, I do not know what you will call that.' At this juncture he threw a scathing look carelessly at me as if to say contend with this and let me see how.

'Will a man be able to do all that without a woman?' I waded in throwing caution to the winds.

'To an extent no.'

'Good. So it should be a mutual relationship not a subsuming one for anybody.'

'Suit yourself Gift. It is a man's world. I did not make the rules. I was only trying to let you know that if you become too equal with men, they don't usually like it, you may end up being alone.' He peered at me suspiciously, 'Or is this part of your career image as "women leader" as you told me long ago?'

'ThankGod I could live with a woman, there is that choice, you know?' I retorted irritatingly. ThankGod could be so annoying when he chose to and now seemed like one of those times. Where did he pick up all this patriarchal mumbo jumbo from?

He shook his head and rubbed the creases on his forehead before giving me a wounded look. We sat there seething individually but he had not finished.

'Gift are you telling me that you are into *that* too?'

'Yes I was into *that too*.' I spoke witheringly. How had it managed to degenerate like this? I was hoping for a nice warm conversation with my brother where I'd slip in this aspect of my life unsuspectingly, but it was not to be so I shrugged and blundered on, 'I am yet to explore the other option though.' As if that would explain everything.

'What do you mean? Are you telling me that you don't like having sex with men or what? Christ! What kind of conversation is this Gift? Have you gone mad? What will people say?' He stopped to survey me from top to bottom, looking for a physical flaw, I guess, that would justify my decision, and not finding any apparently, he decided to continue anyway.

'Are you telling me that this your beauty will be a waste? Nothing to show for it? You want to live and shrivel into this hard-faced-bitter woman, disillusioned from life for going against the natural order of things, all out of your own volition? Come on Gift, you must do better than that.' While speaking, he had his eyes trained on my eyes as if he wanted to be sure that I was not playing with him. After a while he looked away, he must have seen what he did not want to see in my eyes. He looked pained.

'ThankGod, lesbians are not "hard-faced-shriveled up bitter chicks" and they do not need a man to live a fulfilled life. They can have children if they want without a man you know. And for your information I am not a lesbian just that I have not had the opportunity to compare heterosexual sex to that of lesbian sex so as to know.'

'Don't be naïve Gift, you either are or you are not, you cannot sit on the fence waiting to jump to the side that tastes sweeter.' He stopped suddenly and frowned, 'Come on, are you saying that you are still a virgin?'

'Yes.'

'Oh good, but does that mean . . .' he stopped looked at me and then said, 'Then you must be one of those types.'

'I am not.'

'Anyway, you are my little sister and I love you with all my heart, but I will advise you as an older brother and as a man to please work more on the side of being normal, it would gladden everybody's heart.'

My fragile patience, cracked at this point so I jumped down from the tree-bed and snapped, 'Please let's go. If you ThankGod judge me like this what will others do? You that are my blood and family and my best friend.'

'It is not a matter of being your family and best friend, Gift. Society and nature have certain expectations from you. If you go against it, *na you go take your head carry am.* That is all I am saying. It is not as if I am going to ostracize you or anything like that. In fact all of us in the family would be looked upon by the whole village as weird. It may even affect my chances of asking anybody's hand in marriage. So my dear sister you do not flaunt your *deficiency* from nature, you hide it.'

'So I am going to live a lie so as to conform to the expectations of your society.'

'Before *nko?*' ThankGod shouted jumping down himself, before adding,

'Are you saying that in this whole village since the time of our great-grandfathers or grandmothers, as the case may be, that nobody had been created with such genetic inclinations except you? My dear sister don't delude yourself, you could choose not to practice lesbianism, nature or not.'

'I expected you to understand, but I can see that you are being goat-headed today,' I shouted at him more incensed than I realized. My hands were shaking.

'I have since grown up Gift, maybe you should.'

That stung so much that I marched off leaving him there, tears lurking behind my lashes, blinding me as I stumbled home. I hated ThankGod so much just now. Where was his loyalty? I shed part of my anger on the grasses as I trampled them mercilessly hastening as far away as I could from that *treacherous* brother of mine.

But by the time I got to the clearing at the forked road that led to our village I had made up my mind to find myself by myself and only discuss such sensitive matters with people who were *open-minded.* I had always thought that ThankGod was, I could have been fooled. When I had considerably calmed down, I realized that my *hatred* for ThankGod had toned down, so I waited for him to catch up with me so that we could make up. Everybody was entitled to their opinion and ThankGod was only looking out for me really.

Later that evening after we had had our supper, I opted to go for a stroll, not wanting to witness our parents pained disappointed

faces. ThankGod had confided in me earlier about what he intended
to discuss with them after dinner. In the dying light outside I tried
to etch the features of the village into my mind's landscape. I would
need them for comfort as I started the second term in the university.

ThankGod had told me on his first night home that his master
would not give him any money for his 'freedom' but not wanting to
spoil Christmas for our parents he deferred the news until now.

Everybody in the family knew that Chief Osungwa had had a series
of misfortunes for sometime now, but they had lived in the hope that
something would happen to change things positively. Chief Osungwa
himself did not find what was happening easy. Previously rich people
seemed not to know how to adjust to poverty, so they continued to
deceive themselves in maintaining the façade and in Chief Osungwa's
case his gigantic-house was a millstone. I shook my head. Chief
Osungwa certainly had his problems but my immediate concern was
with my parents whose expectations would be crushed; that ThankGod
would, after six years of service, leave with nothing. Whoever thought
life was fair was a fool.

*   *   *

However, before I left for Lagos the next day during my mother's
admonishing farewell chat I remembered mama Kodi and mentioned
her whereupon my mother told me to always treat her with respect
no matter what because she was no longer doing anything with clear
eyes, meaning that she was a little mad and that sometimes things may
not seem as they looked. It was my snickered murmur of 'indeed' that
made her tell me that 'mama Kodi was among those that sent their
children to Gabon during the Nigerian/Biafran civil war to avoid
kwashiorkor and death and then after the war some of the children
that went came back, but some did not and hers were among those
that never returned. Nobody could explain exactly what happened to
her three sons. And like that was not enough her husband threw her
out and married another woman. In the wake of the calamities her
mind left her and it was painful to watch, but her family rallied round
and took her back and fought the madness gallantly.'

'Ha, mama how do you fight madness?'

'Well you can't just fold your arms and watch. Her family took
her to one of those *kwen*—believer—Churches in a neighboring town
where she lived for almost six years and you know those churches can
tear madness out of any brain with the amount of flogging they give
them.'

'But mama are you sure she was really cured?'

'No, but you should have seen her at the time then you'll know to take every blessing gratefully.'

'But . . . it's like she has no control when it came to men?'

'No, that behavior, in her mad state, was fuelled by the belief that she could replace her lost children.'

No wonder the people of the village were always kind to her including my mother, despite her sluttish and spiteful ways. It never even occurred to me to ask. I felt like crying.

*   *   *

I left for Lagos and once again immersed myself in the campus life, both academic and social. I was beginning to attain a certain level of maturity as befitting a nineteen-year old. I had calmed down considerably which suited me fine. The need to grab fun from every angle had gradually started to seep out of me. I had come to realize that you did not guzzle life in one go; you sipped it gently for ease of digestion and nourishment—otherwise it'd choke you to death.

Everything about my life was as I would have wished, save for the fact that I was still a virgin and boyfriendless. But there was nothing wrong with being a virgin at nineteen; it was not a disease afterall. Then towards the last week to the end of the academic year, my destiny took a turn: Ifeoma and I were invited by Erica, who was in the English/Literature department, to their famous annual Literary Party at Anthill. There, I met Osahon and all my life perspectives took a drastic overhaul: I fell in love.

At Last!

LAGOS, NIGERIA

JUNE 1997

It was a miracle. And to think that it was at a literary event! The English/
Literature department's yuppie *do* was usually said to be a cool affair,
held to enhance would-be-writers' artistic abilities by way of Reading
and Acting their works. It was said, however, that immediately after
the readings, everything and anything literary was quickly consigned
to the back burner and a wicked party ensued.

We had heard and hungered to attend, but our hunger was
dampened when we heard it was for a certain class of elites: select final
years; accomplished lecturers that were still in their prime, not the old
farts; select final years from the other three esteemed universities in
the country and a very few elite third years in Unilag. Everybody on
the list must be confirmed *ajebutter* but with a certain IQ level, it was
not enough to speak through your nose, you must be intelligent to
boot! When you hear of select, it was select—about four persons per
group. So you should count yourself lucky if you were invited. We did
not have any chance.

When Erica vowed to not only be at the party—first year or not—and
in the company of her two friends, we deemed it an impossibly up-hill
task, but she did it. How? I did not ask, it was enough that we would
attend, to the envy of the uninvited gals in our hall of residence.

The attraction was that with the cornucopia of invitees including the *externals*, meaning from the three other esteemed universities; University of Nigeria, University of Ibadan and University of Ife, the fertile ground would be greatly enhanced, affording increased scope to search for eligible guys to be turned into boyfriends and or possible future husbands.

* * *

The day of the party had dawned with the face of the sky looking very subdued; pregnant with rain, but we did not give a hoot. Rain or not the *do* must go on. In fact, the cooling effects of the rain should be desirable, it was bound to lend a certain atmosphere to the whole show.

That evening, nobody seeing the three elegantly appointed ladies amble into Anthill would imagine them to be undergraduates never mind first years. We took our seats, settled down and watched as events unfolded. The artists went about their readings and mimings, sometimes acting their pieces with all the nuances and airs that befitted future Nobel Laureates! In between, I used the tail of my eyes to *scan* the audience for a qualifying dude.

With soothing music at interludes, while the scene changes and set adjustments were undertaken, the show took quite a long while—well it had to, afterall that was what it was all about. If it were not for the other anticipated agenda, it would have been an enjoyable educative night, but the afterwards overshadowed the before.

As the end loomed sluggishly, there was a subtle shift in the aura of the atmosphere; it became alive but at the same time condensed with anticipation. Then it was over and everybody was ushered into another hall where nibblings and wines awaited.

When we returned to the Reading Hall, it had transformed; the bright lights were now red and blue coloured giving the hall a subtle romantic hue. From somewhere Bob Marley's *Turn the Lights Low* streamed delicately in to massage and coerce our tautened nerves. The *afterwards* had just commenced. All the snooty and artistic carry-ons were dropped along with the brochure.

Guys and chicks of the literary world milled and mingled, sipping their drinks while sizing up appropriate partners to share the evening with. We were advised early on that to ensure a thorough enjoyment of Anthill we should be wise to get there early for *scanning*; while the bright lights were on to choose and discard as the case may be, the men we intended to tangle with during the afterwards. For with the lights off, everything would be in shadows. Ifeoma had added that in a situation like this; it was always good to leave one's options free, you know, bury the till-death-do-us-part motive. I had concurred, whole-heartedly. Erica demurred. She had a different agenda.

She was seriously looking for a husband, whatever for at this stage in our lives baffled us. Ifeoma wanted a new boyfriend. She was tired of the current one, who lived and breathed her, "it was suffocating," she had claimed. I was tired of being a bat, you know, not a bird and not an animal. So this would afford me the opportunity to look for a boyfriend and so find out once and for all what my sexuality was exactly. I had previously thought of just doing *it* with any half-decent guy but had chickened out at the last moment. I wanted to be able to relax in the *sanctity* of a relationship.

Dancing *blues,* partners glued together as one dancing to a slow music, was something to look forward to in Anthill readings! The literary undertone was a camouflage though it made it more titillating. I took a discrete look to ensure that my targeted man was still in my line of vision. People were already seriously engaged!

As I turned back to my friends, Erica's head tilted to the side, our agreed sign to split up so as to enhance our chances of being *toasted.* I shrugged on my invisible *attraction-garb* and gravitated towards my *scanned* target. As I floated on, I felt a feather-tap on my left shoulder. I faltered and turned to behold this very imposing guy towering over me. Wow, that was quite something, because I could count on one hand the number of guys that usually towered over me. This guy must be over 6ft! But I was not sure I had seen him during *scanning.* This was a worrying fact. What if he turned out to not be good-looking? I stared back at the shadow of my earlier target that was oblivious of my approach. This was dilemma on four legs. But quickly, I made up my mind to take a chance with the giant. It was not as if I had a date with the target I was rooting for; it was also a chance thing. So I smiled warmly up to the giant. So long as there was no bad whiff from his breath, he would be alright—afterall, the beauty of a man was his pocket not his face.

'I have watched you for a while but did not want to intrude while your friends were about,' the giant said in a deep voice that started a sort of vibratory massage on my body.

'Oh,' I said, while getting seriously worried, confused at what was happening to me.

'Well, I am glad you are alone now 'cos then I can claim you for myself.'

'Really?'

'Yes, really. Didn't you know that you were destined to be mine?' he said while pausing to look deeply into my eyes. I was sure that the pause and subsequent probe of my eyes were for effect; he could not see a thing. He persisted with his questions, however.

'Don't you know that? Didn't you feel it when I approached?'

How could I have landed a mad man? I thought puzzled. I know I could feel him, but so what? What was this talk? Very soon he'd tell me that it had been prophesied, and then I'd slap him for spoiling my night.

'Please do not start your *manifesto* like that, it's off-putting.'

'I am not *tuning* you baby, I am telling you God's own truth as I see it.'

'Then tone it down before it kills the joy of today OK?' He shook his head as if I had failed to see what he knew.

'May I dance with you then? My name is Osahon.'

I shrugged and said nothing, but followed him anyway like he had a magnet pulling me.

He gently led me to the dancefloor which happened to be everywhere; the chairs used for the readings having been removed. He opened his arms and I stepped into them as if it was meant for me. He then enveloped me in a tender-hug while I rested my head on his shoulders before sighing. However, I advised myself to take it easy and see how it proceeded; it would not do to be so taken. 'So what's your name?' he murmured into my hair.

'Gift.'

He nodded as we swayed to the music.

Halfway through the third dance, I became aware that I was being skillfully maneuvered out of the hall. I was definitely not going to protest. I was a big girl now, ready for anything, this should be the start.

An hour later we were still busy smooching inside Osahon's old Jalopy well hidden under a tree. When I came up for air again, I took in my surroundings and marveled at how we got there. I remembered taking the steps and when we crested the small hill leading away from Anthill, but that was all. It must be the wine; it had mellowed my perception faculty but had awakened my feelings faculty. My nerves were on fire; tingling from head to toe. It was no longer the *stirring* I had complained about, this was something else, zooming all over my body through the veins. I welcomed it heartily. I would have swallowed Osahon given half the chance; it was the only way to keep him to myself forever. He did things to me.

I was mortified when Osahon gently pulled me away from him. It must be from all these abstinences I reasoned, or else, how could anybody explain to me why I would not let a guy I had just met drink water and safely put the cup down. But this guy certainly knew what he was doing. An expert if ever there was one. And we were only at the kissing and fumbling stage!

Osahon urged me to tidy up; for he could no longer restrain himself. When we were both ready, he escorted me to the front of my hostel. It was 3.30am. Before we parted, he pulled me to himself and enveloped me once more in his arms and refused to let go. While we were still melted in each other, he cupped my face with both palms and murmured, 'I will love you forever, my gift from the gods. I respected your wish tonight; otherwise I would have ravaged you. You unleash the animal in me, my Princess.' For lack of what to say I nodded. I would have preferred to have been ravaged but had made the mistake of telling him to not do anything, at least for that night, no matter what and was disappointed that he kept his promise. I thanked him and then raced down the short stairs from the car port and disappeared into Moremi Hall with the promise of seeing him the next day.

I danced up the stairs to my floor giving the lift a wide berth: I was still raw from that long ago ordeal. I pranced into my room, removed my shoes and gave Ifeoma who was removing her makeup—she had obviously just come in herself—a very crushing hug and a kiss on her forehead, cleanser and all. I did a jig, ballet; *atilogwu* and flamenco all in one go. Ifeoma turned to look at me with a curious frown on her brow.

'Oh, Ifeoma, your tale about sex never did include love. It did not capture the *feelings*. I am absolutely mad about Osahon.'

'Easy Gift, I only described the act of sex, and the intensity that went with it. I am not an expert on the love/feelings aspect. And who the hell is Osahon? Have you done it finally then?' Ifeoma stopped to rub her eyes as if to clear cobwebs from it and then pleaded.

'Gift please sit down; you are making me dizzy following your mad-prancing.'

'Fifi,' ignoring her pleading I continued, 'I am in love with a capital L. Don't ask me to describe the feelings because I can't, but I will try to see if you will understand. There is this something that wells up inside me, weakening and then strengthening as well as spreading a message of goodwill all over my body. It makes me desire to be nice to everybody including Erica. In fact I am going to let her know that I will not obstruct her ambition to leech on to you. I will advise her though, to not approach friendships with ulterior motives, such friendship would not go far.'

'Mmmh Gift, Erica will not take kindly to that. Better tread softly there.'

'You think I don't know that?' I retorted before continuing, 'Anyway that is by the way. As I was saying before you rudely interrupted the flow, the campus environment has suddenly taken on a beautiful shade: I imagine the streets are lined with twinkling lights, the trees, with healthy branches and luscious green leaves, standing in neat rows.'

'But those are already like that.'

'Please don't interrupt me. The birds chirrup lustily with joy and the toilet ends do not smell anymore.'

At this point I jumped onto Ifeoma's bed and sat down with drawn knees and my arms hugging them so that I could look into my friend's face while happiness cascaded like waterfall over me.

'Do you know? I imagine that the intensity of the sun rays will no longer be as hot on the skin, more like the effects of the moon,' I said as I stared at Ifeoma without seeing her.

'I am going to assume that you have not gone mad,' was Ifeoma's contribution while looking wide-eyed at me; searching for madness in my eyes probably.

'I feel like I am floating. I did not even feel the pinch on my little toes from those wicked purple shoes that I wore tonight,' I sighed before announcing.

'I'm in love at last Ifeoma and it suits me. I am at peace with myself. It is the effect Osahon has on me.'

'Mmmh,' Ifeoma snorted, 'Was it not at about 11pm last night that we all got separated?' she asked, but I did not respond so she continued, 'That will make it four hours ago. How could this guy have wrought such a massive change in the way your eyes perceive objects as well as in your views of physical inconveniences! Who is this Osahon, by the way? Do we know him from anywhere?'

'Ifeoma, have you ever fallen in love?' I asked before branching off. 'You snooty aristocrat, his father does not have to be somebody for me to fall in love with him you know, so don't start.' I was not dampened however.

'Wow Gift, has it reached that stage? He must be a pauper if you are already on the defensive, but remember that you're the one that wanted wealth not me. To answer your first question, yes, I have been in love. In fact several times, but it certainly did not elicit this strange imaginings of yours in me.'

'There you are,' I shouted gloatingly, 'you must have been falling in lust all these while then. Let me tell you Ifeoma, love will keep you awake; it will make you want to shed tears of happiness unbidden. You will radiate with bliss, in harmony with your being and others. Can you see it?' I asked as I flung out my hands wide to give Ifeoma a proper view of the joy and happiness and bliss emanating from my love-infused body.

'So you have done it then?' Ifeoma ventured.

'We have not done *it* yet,' I responded and Ifeoma nodded, widening her eyes before commenting.

'Oh. How come?'

'I told him I'd rather not go all the way with him for now. Much as I'm in need of being disvirgined, I would not want to send the wrong message out, you know, to be seen as cheap. Besides, I think it should be approached with decorum and not while my bum is sticking up in the air, in an old car. And do you know, even in the heat of things, he kept his words. A perfect gentleman.'

'Are you sure that he is in love with you then?'

'Oh, Fifi, need you ask? He told me so severally. In fact he intends to marry me!'

'You don't say? What a smooth operator! But I am surprised that even as you were oozing willingness, he was able to restrain himself. This somehow negates the notion of smooth operators. Or was there other motive? I suppose time will tell. If I were you though, I will enjoy every drop of what he has to offer before the bubble bursts.'

'Oh, you don't need to tell me girl, I will do just that, watch me.'

*   *   *

The relationship took off with a bang. I rolled around the campus in a daze unaware of my surroundings. I was always coming or going with Osahon. All the four corners of the campus had been worn out with our presence. Every corner converted into a love zone. He shared his life dreams and ambitions of becoming a supermarket Chieftain, to be known the length and breadth of Benin City and beyond. It was a niche begging for investment he claimed and he hoped to cash in before it was flooded: *you no say Naija people sabi rush* into any newly introduced business, until they killed off that sector with over-flooding.

I, in turn shared my own dreams of being a civil servant, and then gradually working my way to become a Perm. Secretary, a

Commissioner or a Minister with the ultimate aim of a seat in the Senate. Women issues foremost on my agenda, of course.

We both marveled at the coincidence of wanting to be in the limelight. But it wasn't coincidence, it was destiny, he had informed me. So we pooled our dreams and they became one; we would work hard and make money which would free us from the daily drudgery. To cap it all, when I became a Senator, Osahon's way would be paved as a Government contractor!

*   *   *

Two weeks later, Osahon went back to Benin City where he lived. I did not get it. 'How could he leave?' I asked nobody in particular. But Ifeoma elected to answer anyway. 'Because he should be at work or is he a student in Unilag by any chance?' I ignored her.

I pined, I whined, my heart was constricted with pain, with love. Now that he was gone, my friends became my friends again. I regaled them with the minutest of details. I could see in their eyes that they were tempted to become envious, or wished they were the ones in love, but they were truly happy for me, I could see that too, even Erica.

While Gift was busy prattling, Ifeoma watched her and wondered. So a Nigerian man could love and be this devoted, consider his woman's interests, opinions and feelings in every decision he took, never letting her frown, carrying her like she was an egg? Her sister would cuff her ears for lying if she described Osahon's behaviour towards Gift as it would negate their long-held notion that Nigerian men loom larger than life in the lives of their women who must bow and scrape if they hope to hold on to them.

*   *   *

Then he came back. And it was a very intense reunion that left both of us in tenth heaven. I had agreed within myself that this was the weekend! I was going to finally allow Osahon to open the parcel; we had pinched around the edges for too long, though he never questioned my reasons for saying no. Aside from the apprehension of giving up my virginity, I was really in a jitter: It was generally an unaccepted reality that most campus guys sought one thing from us gals and once eaten, that's it; the intensity would reduce, and if care was not taken, trail off to nothing. The guys meanwhile would move on to plunder the next willing maiden. While the chicks mourned.

Much as I was not looking for a husband I would not wish for a very short-term relationship either. Ifeoma's style of love them and leave them, which I had promptly adopted myself, no longer applied where this Osahon guy was concerned. He was just too much.

As I rushed down the steps, I tried to think of what it would feel like to not be a virgin anymore.

'Goodness me! Who would believe it?' I muttered 'That I, one of the hottest chicks on campus, was still a virgin.' Of course in the village and amongst my friends it was the state to be in: you keep it for the *him*. And before university, I did not mind all that, but seeing that everybody was having fun I felt very deprived. And I do not like being deprived. For what!

I joined Osahon and after our ritual long-time-no-see kiss, we drove off to town to our regular *slaughter-house* as they were nicknamed: all the small small *mushroom* hotels that dotted Unilag for *emergencies*. We paid for and took the key to our regular room in Angelina Inn, "home away from home," it claimed.

We were well-known in Angelina Inn, now counted as regulars. It never reduced the cost of the room, though. And I did not mind footing the room bill for our lovingities. It did not matter. It should not matter.

We settled in and Osahon brought out a bottle of red wine to accompany the Mr. Bigs Chicken Marigold and chips we had bought enroute. I sat on his lap as we munched and drank. One thing led to the other and we abandoned the eating completely, and this time I did not demur so Osahon abandoned himself to the work at hand and stopped searching my face for any objection nuance.

*   *   *

Osahon was elated: at last he was going to *chop* this thing; the chick had hoarded the something for too long, haba! The thought of it set him on fire. This Gift was something else. But even in the heat of passion, he did not lose sight of a certain unexpected fact: She was a virgin!

'Shit!' he hissed, temporarily motionless. He looked at her and she looked back, her eyes glazed. His mind was awhirl; different emotions chasing each other but he said nothing more, just stared at her. Seeing his dilemma I moved my hips, nudging him in and he murmured again, 'Shit. Shit,' before ramming home completely. All the way in, up to the beginning of my chest.

When we finally stopped, to catch a rest, I knew that this was an experience I would never forget till I leave this earth. Yes.

As my thoughts wandered, I remembered Mrs. Igwenagu, my Biology mistress back in secondary school and her deflowering ranting speech that went on and on; to keep our knickers on our waist, where they belonged. It was supposed to be our only saving grace. I could see where she was going to then, now!

Different strokes for different people. If you heard Glory, Erica's roommate, narrating the loss of her virginity, you would have died of fright from the mere thought of doing it. It would always pay to seek experience and knowledge yourself; other people own would not suffice.

Osahon pulled Gift close to him enfolding her, to ensure that she would not disappear, and closed his eyes. Was this chick for real? What was she keeping *that* for? Now he had to be the one to open the container first! He shivered. Was this good or bad? Certainly not what he would have chosen to do with his eyes wide open, but . . . Whatever the case, he'd never let her out of his sight. She had what other girls he'd been with did not have, could not have. He'd never get tired of her; his elegant princess, his own princess. When they had variously returned, fully, from the orgasmic journey, he turned to her and sang her a tribute:

> 'Heavenly Gift . . .
> Beautiful Angel . . .
> If ever one existed . . .
> My elegant Princess
> 1ˢᵗ year in Unilag!
> And for fucks sake
> She had not been *opened* by any . . .
> Could somebody out there pinch me awake?'

After the silly song, with no noticeable rhyme, Osahon vowed to me while kneeling down that he would love me forever. This was becoming a ritual. I lapped it all up while inwardly congratulating myself for holding on, the reward was worth it in every ramification, it seemed.

Except for going out to stretch our limbs and to buy this and that to keep up our energies, we were cocooned in Angelina Inn throughout that weekend. And it was a wonder that we were alive to tell the story. I could not get enough of sex and Osahon could not get enough of me. What an exhilarating experience. I had to make sure that I was not denied again, ever.

Sunday morning dawned uninvited and we had to leave early to indulge our favourite pastime: Visiting Mega Plaza, the biggest Departmental Supermarket in Victoria Island, Lagos, and in Nigeria for that matter, if it was safe to claim that. Mega Plaza was the stuff that dreams were built on. It occupied four floors in a large expanse of land. Each floor, sectioned according to stocks; different brands vying for attention. The clothing, shoes, bags and accessories departments, home unit departments, childrens department, foods department, electronics section, etc., were well and tastefully displayed. Mega Plaza housed anything you could think of, expensive anything though; it was not for every rat and lizard.

Each time we entered Mega Plaza, we became physically transformed, our dreams highly enhanced to the extent that we could see it. We could see us owning just such a place but domiciled in Benin City. Mega Plaza inspired us to an unimaginable level; it gave shape to our dream. We would usually browse till bone-tired. But that Sunday, we cut our browsing short, it was the wrong day, Osahon had to leave.

*   *   *

Osahon had told me that he'd give me a wide berth so that I'd concentrate on my studies and he kept his promise, but after my exams, two days before the commencement of the long holidays, he did not turn up as arranged and I couldn't reach him on his cell phone. It was an absolute nightmare and caused untold heartache to us trio.

I was beside myself with worry when I discovered that I did not know Osahon beyond his appearing in my school as and when he wanted, which was often. I did not have his address either except for his mobile phone number. The funny thing was that even the mobile phone was a gift to him from me; to enable us communicate with ease. My repeated calls went straight into voice messages. This calamity was thoroughly analyzed amongst us three and it was finally concluded that I should send a text to him informing him that I would not leave for my village until he got in touch.

I did. And he saved me that agony of staying behind alone in school by calling the next morning. He had been struck down by malaria right after he left Lagos and by Monday morning was admitted to a nearby clinic two streets away from his street. He had only just begun to take in his surroundings. He was very sorry to have marred my beautiful

face with worry lines. I cut him short, got his details, bade my friend's
goodbye and happy long-vacation and flew to Benin City.

It was easy for me to locate Osahon's abode. It was not, however,
an environment that I would have chosen to live in, my being from
a poor home notwithstanding, I mused as I walked down the street
towards his apartment block, skirting open fly-infested gutters. But to
hell, Osahon resided here, that was good enough for me.

I took care of him. He did not look like he was at death's door as
he claimed, but with a constitution like his, it would take more than
malaria to make him look like death-warmed-over. We also had pure
and undiluted fun. Osahon's sparsely furnished room and parlour
set-up was like a corner in paradise. It was made for love. He may have
been ill but we managed to make love at least thrice a day excluding
the nightcaps. I took him to Onitsha, to introduce him to my big sister
Chinelo the next day and regretted that move instantly. Chinelo was
aghast at my insistence that I leave with him. In fact she was appalled
and extremely disappointed in me and said so. I took her aside and
told her that this was 1997 and so what was the haranguing for? How
was I ever going to get married? I had asked her. Chinelo shook her
head sadly before telling me that 'living with a man is not a passage
to marriage if with your education you did not know that then may
God help you'. However, reluctantly she gave in, her mouth clenched
tightly shut in a very disagreeable way, like our mother's, but she kept
her peace.

*   *   *

Osahon was proud of his catch in me, and boy, was he besotted.
He took me everywhere: to all the 'happening places' in Benin City;
to his friends; and finally to show his parents. I was greatly surprised,
for Osahon's parents were well to do. So why was their son living in
penury? I hoped to find out later, though Osahon would more readily
die than allow any information to fall out of his mouth, I had come
to notice. After one week of living decadently in Benin City, I left for
my village.

As soon as I arrived there, I knew that I had made the second
major mistake: the serenity that was my village vanished, replaced by
restlessness. The tranquility became stifling instead. I was thrown into
turmoil: itching to share the beauty but with my lover not my family.
I was no longer content to haunt my old terrain alone; something
bigger than the cricket had been trapped in its hole. I had to do
something before I went mad.

One morning I woke up and informed my parents that I would rather spend the rest of my holidays with sister Chinelo; it was not right that I had neglected her since starting university, she deserved all the help I could give her, I pleaded. My parents agreed and I left.

*   *   *

At returning, I unpacked only all that I was given to give her—cocoyam, palm oil, vegetables—ora, bitterleaf, arigbe—mint, ugbogulu—pumpkin, and the spice ogili for making the ora and bitterleaf soups. I repacked my bag and the next morning I left, amidst Chinelo's objections, for Osahon's place and called in to my sister's once in a while. This was madness Chinelo had told me but she was helpless, finally she offered to pray that I work it out of my system, because it was no longer funny.

*   *   *

When the long vacation came to an end, I returned to school reluctantly to start the first term of my second year. Everything was as it should be. I went about my registration and subsequently for lectures with Ifeoma while we regaled each other with all the antics we had got into during the holidays.

Ifeoma had fallen head-over-heals with a Jamaican rock musician named Prince. I could not fit the image so presented in my head; a rock musician of Jamaican descent and Ifeoma. I peered at Ifeoma who certainly did not look the part of a girlfriend to a budding rock star. She was going to be a financial wheeler-dealer. In fact she was one already as far as I could tell.

But love was a strange thing; it struck swift and precise and you were lost. So now it's Ifeoma's turn to prattle nonsense, though she still had her senses intact, she claimed.

The fact that she got close enough to a Jamaican and a musician at that was enough to tell me that she was not with her senses. Erica moaned and moaned, she was yet to snag anybody.

We had advised her but she wouldn't listen: to remove the *quest for a husband demeanor* from her face. Guys have ways of sniffing out those women that came to trap them and run with the wind at their back. The husband-seeking-pungent-odour emanating from her was of suffocating proportion, even we that were her female friends could *hear* the rancid whiff miles away. She should relax and take things easy.

'Are you not only twenty-one Erica?' We had both queried in unison at one stage. Why did she even want to get hitched so early in life anyway? Erica never seemed to listen to us in any case. Her attitude had always been that of 'what do we know' kind. And true true we didn't know beyond the fact that she was on our floor, was Ifeoma's friend and was from Rivers State.

Before the month came to an end I realized that I had fallen pregnant.

Completely and utterly stunned I stood still to digest this fact when I had finally acknowledged that my monthly cycle was late and did not look like it was going to show up. This was not in the script. Afterwards I kept asking myself "what are you going to do Gift?" interspersed by a dash to the bathroom to check for any hint at all of blood. Nothing. At one point I started using a sanitary towel in case, and the terror of what I couldn't even begin to imagine aided to induce phantom menstrual pain all of which lent their weight to my continual deceit of myself. However after two weeks of sleeplessness and much soul searching I conceded that it was time to pinch at what the future had in stock for me by taking the news to Osahon. But first I assured myself that I was not in any way going to face the unpleasant drawback of becoming pregnant before I was married and settled in my husband's home; or before I had made 'something' out of my life; or before I had brought light to my family, alone. I reached this belief based on my summation of the quality of my relationship with Osahon. I mean we were practically married and so the real marriage—which would be the natural step seeing that I was now expecting—would be a matter of formality and that, I believe, would appease any objecting mouth.

I frowned as more thoughts inveigled in, well . . . I would overcome this, I noted to assure myself. I got up and went to scrutinize my face in the mirror: to see if the pregnancy was causing changes already. Seeing nothing I went about to prepare for lectures alone. Ifeoma had left an hour ago.

As I walked along the *twinkling* streets of the campus to my Pol-Science 207 lecture, I adjusted my blouse: flattening it. It was making my flat stomach stick out like that of a pregnant woman. I had to smile at that thought, I am a pregnant woman, though no soul had been confided that to yet. I continued with my thoughts as I went.

I had seen with my own eyes how some young girls, who ate the forbidden fruit before their time had ruined their lives, became nothing and were looked down on. Their innocence, their childhood, their ideals shattered into nothingness. They were forced to grow up overnight; with another life to wean, to nurture. Their own life consigned to the back burner. It was no fun. Even though they caused that to happen to them, they felt cheated, the responsibility was too much, they were still children, they felt lost, but they had made their bed, life must go on.

I remembered when our friend Azukaego's big sister, Ugboaku, got pregnant and my mother had told me to reduce my visits to their house.

'But mama, I have to play with my friend and her mother asked us to look after Ugboaku; she is always crying,' I remembered piping at the time. Characteristic of my mother: a pump and plain person, she told me that that was medicine after death; they should have guided her before the harm was done. It was mind-baffling then but what was at stake became clearer as I got older. The effort it took to wheedle a visit approval from my mother killed the relationship. I stopped going and Azukaego stopped visiting too. Then she was sent to live with her grandmother in another village and I had not seen her since. It was probably to safeguard her reputation from the reverberating effect of her sister's action. All sorts of things could accrue from that singular mistake of Ugboaku's; the girls of the family might now be considered too loose for wives and their mother a failure in one of her gender roles.

But my case was different from Ugboaku's of course; I was twenty already, I had positioned myself on the ladder to my goals. I had tasted life. I was in love. I was going to marry the love of my life and it would be alright, it had to be. Osahon loved me to pieces and had sworn to love me forever, I hugged myself while remembering our last night together but that was quickly replaced by the thoughts of what the outcome of my trip to the village would be via Benin.

Then I espied Aloysius, the third year Economics student that had been pestering me for friendship, and had to veer off my route. I would be late at this rate but I had to. 'Aloysius did not just get it', I muttered, 'I have been spoken for.' Skirting the buildings, I peered left and then right before making a dash to my department. All this cloak and dagger!

*   *   *

Since this my situation, known only to me at this stage, Ifeoma's complaint that she could not understand me anymore, had to be shrugged off. But as I was getting ready for that trip to Benin she accosted me.

'Why Gift, didn't you just return from Benin City barely a week now?' At my shrug she moved in for the kill with, 'Is that how you are going to be a Senator or what?'

I just smiled and shook my head. I was not ready for Ifeoma and told her so, which exasperated her. I finished packing my bag and left in a cloud of perfume. Halfway down the stairs I came back up and confided in her, but did not give her enough time to digest the information before I left again, her mouth still half-open.

*　　*　　*

When Osahon saw Gift, he was happy; he had not stopped being amazed at her beauty and her impulsiveness both of which suited him well. They embraced and he held her for a long time studying her face before he led her to the inner office of their 'supermarket' to ascertain her reason for this trip. He was amazed at her smooth lie of wanting to see his face—she did that all the time, visiting to see his face, but this time there was something in her eyes which betrayed her; she was not telling the truth. His Princess was an open book, but he let her be, she'd tell him.

*　　*　　*

I saw the doubt flit past Osahon's face at my reason for the visit, but said nothing. After our dinner of boiled spaghetti with egg-stew, and then safely ensconced in his arms, I told him.

My blood turned into ice when Osahon went very quiet and stayed that way for a very long time, staring at me intensely. I could see, however, that he was not focused on me at all. At a point I became visibly agitated. What was going on here? Did I get it all wrong? I was not sure he ever said anything about children. But if you wanted to love and be with somebody forever, which translated meant marriage, did it not include having children? Finally, he focused on me and asked.

'What do you want to do, Princess?' Strange question but not off the wall as such.

'Get married, I guess.' Was this how proposals were done? I wasn't sure but . . .

'Would that make you happy, really happy at this time?'

'Very much or don't you think so?' He didn't respond right away. I held my breath. Finally he sighed.

'Then marriage it will be. But remember our dreams. We have to work twice harder to achieve those goals, now that there is a third person in the equation.'

I let out the air stagnating in my lungs, my equilibrium now restored I sighed, happily snuggling closer. Was that what was disturbing him? He shouldn't worry and I went ahead to reassure him.

'Babes, you did not grow up in poverty, I did. If anything, I should be the one to warn you about keeping steadfastly to our dreams.'

'Okay. When do you want me to meet your parents then, or should I go with you on this trip?'

'No babes, let me see them first. I will let you know when.'

Much later, we went to bed and Osahon had held me, tightly, all night. Something was on his mind and it was not about the third arm of the equation. Yes, Osahon had always been a man of few words but this was unusually quiet even for him. But he did not really squirm about our marriage and that was what was important to me at the time.

In the morning I left for my village. Osahon had visibly cheered up and I was mightily relieved. He must have worked out what was eating him last night. That was very close there! What if he had dragged his feet? What would I have told my God? I shivered but not from cold, for the rays were already strong on the skin, so early in the morning. But whatever his fears, we'd learn to confront as one, I comforted myself as I left.

*   *   *

I was brought down a notch or two, from my euphoric haven, when I told my parents. I knew nobody was going to raise a band to sing my praises but their reaction was too extreme. The news made them *slump* with shock while looking at me dejectedly, then askance, then with anger. I could see the various emotions flitting across their faces especially my mother's. Unable to hold her anger anymore, she had erupted.

'You wild animal, do you have to go this far only to throw it all away? If you wanted to make babies, why did you not marry right after secondary? What have you done? Where is the pride I saw in your eyes when you marched out of this house to go to that university of yours? Eh? Where is it?' She stopped but the force of her anger did not. Then she barked,

'Look at me Gift.'

My head snapped up, eyes boring into her.

'Do you envy me? Do you ever wish that you were in my shoes? Do you? Do you? Answer me. Of course you don't. Let me tell you something you did not know: People in my position do not inspire dreams. But it is every parent's dream that their offspring fare better than them, much better. You held such promises Gift. You held such promises. Yes you did. You were on the road to greatness. And now . . . . Now, now . . . Nothing.' She then looked at me and asked, 'Why Gift? Why?' Her voice laden with so much sorrow and her eyes glistened with unshed tears. I looked away. I should not see my strong mother in her weakness. It was not a good sight. And I caused it! When I looked away she turned to her husband and implored, 'Abraham, where did we go wrong eh tell me, what did we do wrong? What . . . eh . . . what? Please talk to your mother, talk to your mother now to stop this nonsense, she has to stop this nonsense!'

Stop me!

What is mother saying? I looked at my father, who had not uttered a word, for clarification. He looked away. I did not get it.

Stop me?

Should they not be tripping in haste to marry me off before I started showing? But I was too scared to ask. The emotion floating about with the dust mote was too thick, too raw.

*　　*　　*

Abraham had looked away from his daughter before allowing his painful thoughts to reflect on his already tired face. He tried to put his hand on where it all went wrong. He had barely paid off the loan he took from his friend, Akunne, for her school fees. He had made the journey to Onitsha with so much pride, so much hope. Akunne was happy for him and gladly lent him the money without a murmur, never asking how and when it'd be paid, but proudly informed him that his destiny had begun to rise after so many years of rubbing around the edges of life and he would not begrudge him. Now they were back to the starting line, but with a twist. Abraham shook his head, he heard his wife, but he would not talk, he couldn't.

*　　*　　*

'We are in love mama and Osahon is going to marry me. Love does not choose its time. Do not condemn me papa.' I implored daring to raise my eyes to search his face—my friend. My mother hissed and stood up and started to advance towards me.

'Shut up. I say shut up. If you were born well, you will not open that you rotten mouth to talk rubbish.' I shrank back when she continued to close in on me about to pounce, probably to beat that love out of me. But then she stopped and spat at me, supporting it with a snap of her fingers, first swung round her head for potency. '*Tufiakwa gi bu nwaa!* You are a goat Gift that is what you are, a goat,' she rained on me before retreating to her seat. At least I was now a home animal, no longer a wild one, I thought as I sat there stupefied by sadness.

Love! Abraham's mind latched on to that. Children of nowadays put too much stock on love and it made them take all sorts of risks. But then when push came to shove it never seemed to carry them far. He just prayed that the young man would be a desirable son-in-law; nobody would mistreat his mother and get away with it!

He took a long forlorn look at Celina, his beautiful and enduring wife, the love of his life, the glue that held the family together and knew that her heart had been broken. She might be strong but not where her hope of leaving poverty behind was pinned. Her eyes were emitting sparks ready to consume anything on her way as she looked at their daughter. How could he ever hope to pacify her? She had hoped so much on Gift giving the family a voice. She had looked so much to the day she would be called the mother of a graduate. Every imaginable gain that could accrue from that would be ashes in her mouth now. He sighed, cleared his throat and very wearily implored, 'Cee, it is enough. We do not throw away a recalcitrant child with the bath water.' He then turned to me.

'And you, where is this man of yours, is he from around here?'

'No, Papa. I wanted to see you first before bringing him home. He is from Irue in Edo State. I know you will feel disappointed now, but you will see, everything will work out fine. I will not disappoint you. You will see.' I was babbling but I couldn't stop: the relief that everything was going to be alright was overwhelming. I looked at my mother, and saw that her own forgiveness would be long in coming. I had wounded her personally, but that was because she did not see it the way Osahon and I had mapped out everything. If she had, she'd not be so sad. But she'd be happy for me later, that I know. Things have always worked out for me.

*   *   *

Chinelo's tough negotiation brought my parents round and they grudgingly consented and so Osahon and his family would be here any minute for the first step in the marriage process: the knocking on the door or introduction.

I watched as ThankGod came out from Obumneme's room and went about setting out the chairs under the palmfrond-roofed canopy and played back his reluctant reactions before Chinelo had stepped in.

ThankGod was of the opinion that I should give birth and leave the child with Chinelo, our big sister, and continue with my studies. And to make his suggestion more palatable he added that I was pretty enough and therefore, should be able to snare a husband any time. And then he soured it with, 'But what do you want with a husband anyway? Were you not spouting, not too long ago, that women can live without men?' At that point our mother scraped the wooden form she was sitting on backwards and got up, eyed all of us malevolently and hissed out, 'what won't I hear from you children?' before marching out of the *meeting*.

When the effect of her *hiss* had dissipated and the atmosphere had settled down somehow, I reminded ThankGod that at the time we had had that conversation, I had not met Osahon and had not fallen in love.

'Indeed,' was all he muttered before storming out too.

My big brother, Obumneme, did not, as was his nature, frown fiercely like the others at my decision. His words to me were, 'You have always been a wise girl, our Gift, be sure that you know what you are doing.' I had assured him that it was a forever thing and that he should not worry.

Chinelo had taken me aside and asked, 'Our Gift, what is this all about? I know I was privy to your traipsing with that Osahon boy, but has it come to this?'

'Sister, it has. I love him and will do anything to be with him, always.'

'Don't talk like that my dear sister; he is mere human.'

'I know sister, but it is just how I feel.'

'What about him?'

'Same.'

'But . . .'

'Please sister, wish me well. I am no longer a child, you were married at a much younger age than I am now, what is the issue here?'

'The issue here is that of all of us your star is shining the brightest and is set to light our path. You have made us think and gloat about not only producing a graduate, but the circle of poverty enclosing the family for generations will be broken. You have made us dream impossible dreams. We were beginning to see the semblance of the proverbial light at the end of the tunnel through your stride. Don't squash our dreams, Gift, it'd be wrong.' She breathed out heavily then changed tactic.

'Have you thought of papa?' At the mention of my pa, I had got up and went and hugged my sister. 'Sister it will be alright please, help me to talk to mama.' She had nodded, and I added, 'It is not as if am dead you know, everything will be alright.'

'Amen,' Chinelo had intoned.

I was right, it was not a funeral. Why were they all carrying long faces around? None of them could see beyond the present so why had they all turned into an out—of-control soothsayer all of a sudden? But then sister Chinelo stepped in and and all the arguments ended.

... Happiness

BENIN CITY, EDO STATE, NIGERIA

Knowing that it was not going to be a big ceremony, I had invited only Ifeoma and Faith, out of all my friends, for the occasion. Others would just have to wait for the wedding, which was supposed to be the grand-daddy of all weddings! Besides, I wanted to afford them both, most especially Ifeoma, who had promised to arrive a day earlier, the opportunity to see a proper village.

Ifeoma's arrival was announced by the bleating of the goats, the squawking of the chickens, the rustling of the lizards, etc., etc., all protesting the disturbances of the tranquility while fleeing for dear life from the car that brought her. When I heard the commotion, I ran out to see Ifeoma with an elated grin on her face amidst the cacophony of noises.

She came down from the car grinning from ear to ear in awe, while refusing to take cognizance of the pain in her neck as a result of rotating it from left to right and then forward to backward in an attempt to take in the scenery all at once. She was happy. Now, this was what one could call a real village; so natural, unspoilt, uneven lush trees, clean air, very calming. This was more like the village of her dream, long formulated from reading Chinua Achebe's *Things Fall Apart*. A village she could not identify in her own hometown, Nnewi, which was more of a bustling commercial city. She was already enthralled with this place and couldn't wait to sink her teeth into exploring. No wonder Gift was such a serene person.

I stood still observing my friend, noting her face that was suffused with joy. She was virtually glowing! I wondered what could be the cause, for Ifeoma was not given to outward display of emotions easily, but that could wait, I would be told in due course.

Noticing me, Ifeoma walked towards me still full of smiles, we hugged and I shook my head in amusement as I took her, along with her luggage, to our room. 'So you made it in one piece?' I asked.

'Oh Gift,' she enthused, still slightly thrown off balance, 'your village is a paradise on earth.' I shook my head again and smiled. If I did not know her very well, I would have declared that she was actually jealous.

'You want to trade places then?'

'I may just,' she teased before continuing, 'but seriously Gift, I envy you. I should have visited sooner if I half suspected this.'

'Well, you are here now so enjoy,' I said, still amused as we settled her many luggages.

When we reappeared, I took her round for introduction. My family was happy to finally see my *Oyibo* friend. They knew Ifeoma was black, of course, but preferred to refer to her as *Oyibo*. My mother had fretted, when I mentioned that Ifeoma would be coming to stay for the ceremony, about what to cook for her but most importantly, where to quarter her as "*obu onye ocha*"—she is a white person.

Introduction over, Ifeoma promptly requested a tour of the village, especially to all the secret groves. I had laughed at Ifeoma's enthusiasm; it seemed I had promoted my village too much. Nonetheless, I promised to set her mind at rest as soon as we had both changed into befitting clothing for the tour.

My mother was not too impressed with me: brandishing my growing tummy around the village like that, but I could not be deterred. I was not going to hide because I was pregnant, moreso now that I was getting married, where was the shame then? My mother was a complex woman; you'd never fathom her thoughts. Just what she wanted from me I did not have a clue.

We left in a cloud of her frown and subsequent hiss. Mothers, perennially worrying about image.

'Where do they draw a line to stop and let go?' I mumbled as we took the turn that'd lead us out of the village. But Ifeoma assured me that it must be the same world over, even her mother, with all her *acada*, harangued her all the time.

We tramped the thickets, passed the village stream and went deeper into the dense forest with Ifeoma stopping now and then to exclaim over one thing or the other: a snail going about its business was an object of thirty minutes of intense scrutiny and exclamation; a centipede impeded our journey for over twenty minutes since we had to skirt the route; when we encountered a deer, Ifeoma nearly dropped her camcorder in ecstasy; a bold monkey snatched her yellow cap off her head and put it on its own head, and then crowned Ifeoma's joy by pelting us with unripe mangoes, as thank you, for a photography session. Finally, we reached our *resort* of old. Ifeoma changed into her swim gear and jumped into the serene flowing stream and then jumped right out, her scream reverberating in the wilderness; a green snake was also cooling itself in the stream, afterall it was scorching hot. I shooed it away before we swam lazily in the flowing river. It was a very refreshing experience, she claimed. It should be, after all the excitement she had whipped up. When we got tired of swimming, we waded out and Ifeoma promptly climbed the famous tree-bed, curving her spine accordingly while pretending to sleep. It was as if she was trying to relive my childhood as I had told her.

As the sun began its journey to the other side of the earth, we assembled our things and sauntered back home with Ifeoma lugging a basket laden with all sorts of fruits, from the garden of Eden, according to her: pawpaw, mango, *udala*, pear—a variety that Ifeoma had never seen in her life but was willing to accept my word that it was very tasty when eaten together with roasted corn on the cob. When we got home and had divested ourselves of the cornucopia of fruits we retired under the shade of the old but leafy German-Mango tree beside my father's palmwine shed and started on the next level of treat: drinking palmwine. My mother got busy roasting the corn with the pear for us. Ifeoma, who had only ever seen palmwine from a distance, during her grandfather's burial, fell in love with the delicious natural brew which we used to wash down the pear and corn.

Later, my mother brought us tasty *Onugbu* soup made with plenty of dried cat-fish and chunky bush meat accompanied by *nni akpu*—pounded cassava. The *nni akpu*, Ifeoma claimed, floated down her throat unhindered, with the leaves, the fishes and bush-meat guiding it.

Ifeoma belched, massaged her stomach and noted that she had over-eaten as she picked her teeth, but that it was a very contented kind of over-eating. In all these, she made sure to capture everything with her camcorder and camera accompanied by running commentary.

After the heavy dinner and more palmwine, Ifeoma looked really tired so I nudged her to find out whether she'd want to go to bed. But my mother overheard us and advised that we should sleep outside for a while to catch some breeze. She then swept a portion of the compound and spread raffia-palm mats, made more comfortable with her wrappers, then invited us to lie down. Having filled ourselves to the gills we were gently nudged into sleep by the breeze.

*　　　*　　　*

When Ifeoma opened her eyes, what she considered to be some minutes later, it was dawn and somebody had covered them with another set of wrappers. She couldn't believe it. She had looked forward for so long to visiting Gift. Even though she had envisaged it would be entertaining, she had had some misgivings about village-life without any of the modern comforts she was accustomed to, especially when Gift informed her that they did not have electricity and they slept on mud beds! But she did not, in her wildest imagination, expect to enjoy herself this much.

Seeing the village and all it had to offer firsthand was something! Gift's family were contented and clean people. She was, however, surprised at how Gift had managed to rise above her station considering this extremely humble beginning. She also could not see how this place had not dulled her desire to amount to something by its calmness. Instead she had not only emerged from this cushioned cocoon but aimed so high: a Senator! No less. A very tall ambition, but then she was a staunch believer in hard work herself and in Gift's case she appeared poised to scale the wall while aiming at the moon.

She brought her thoughts down to her immediate need which was a cup of pure unadulterated coffee. She looked around, was not sure of how to start the fire, did not see anything that could help her to do so even if she could, so she burrowed deeper into the wrapper and flipped her ear open for anybody that would stir.

*　　　*　　　*

When Faith arrived later that morning, Ifeoma offered to take her on *tour de village* as she herself was yet to satiate the hunger of something different and that way would continue to feed her imagination. Gift was not willing to tackle the forest yet again, but then she had to go with them for fear that they may get lost and derail the ceremony.

Ifeoma observed that ThankGod, whom Gift had failed to tell them was a very handsome guy, had followed Faith with the tail of his eyes all through. The gang had drowned out her observation with laughter. But then, the future had always remained an uncharted route for us humans. What do we know!

*   *   *

The arrival of the in-laws increased the tempo of activity in the compound and put paid to our larking about.

Osahon came with his parents and a handful of relatives to *knock* at my father's door to intimate him and his inner kinsmen of his desire to marry me. They brought 'kolanut' made up of all sorts of drinks, including Schnapps, used for pouring libations to the ancestors, as well as native kolanuts. During the breaking of the kolanut supplications would be sent to the ancestors for protection and the fruitful union of the two families. The drinks and the kolanuts were presented to my father and his kinsmen while the *women* presents of Abada wrapper, crate of minerals and malt drinks were for my mother. Marriage in my place was usually a four-stage ceremony; the knocking, paying of bride price, wine-carrying and the church wedding—for Christians.

But on this visit, the first two stages would be combined because Osahon and I had pleaded that we be allowed to do that as well as skip the last two to when we had made enough money for them. My father accepted our request and thereafter the traditionally mandatory bride-price of 24 Naira was paid, part of which was given back to Osahon because marriage is a relationship that should endure, he was not buying me.

To be honest, I was disappointed. I had wanted a big traditional wine-carrying and a bigger church wedding, but I swallowed my wish. All that would come later. Osahon had promised that when we made it, we would return in style and show the villagers how a wedding should be conducted.

The two families, now related by marriage, continued to make merry far into the evening. After much eating and drinking, it was time for the in-laws to leave with their bride, for the *Imalu uno*—the bride to know her husband's place, so I got ready and left with my husband and his family, now mine.

There's this ceremony, according to the custom of my husband's people, that would be conducted at his place and was considered very critical to the longevity of the marriage. It involved telling your in-laws how many men you had slept with before your husband. I smiled. For me it was nothing. Osahon's mum had explained that after the bride had been made welcome, she would be installed on a high chair and handed a full ear of corn. She would then be required to pluck out as many kernels of the corn as was required to represent the number of men she had slept with before her husband, one corn-kernel, one man, simple. I remembered the day I had the conversation with Ifeoma, not knowing that it would be my lot to marry a man from Bini and shook my head.

Some marriages had been annulled where the groom and his family could not stomach the number of men who had gone through their bride. Should that be the case they would simply return the disgraced bride to her family along with an instant refund of the bride price.

I had slept only with one man—Osahon—so I had no problem there, well . . . I had to discount my shenanigans with other girls while in secondary school, and prayed hard that my in-laws and indeed Osahon would have no inkling of that which seemed so shadowy now.

I was however very uneasy about my womanly skills: cooking, cleaning and generally keeping house, those were among the bedrock of a marriage, after children. I knew I was not cut out for such chores and Osahon had not exhibited any interest in my culinary skills so far. I remembered him telling me early on, 'You are my Princess, meant to be pampered, and no slaving away in the kitchen for you. Ok?' I had hid a smile while wondering if his stomach was consulted before that decision was taken. I conceded though that he never seemed to want to eat anyway, and when he did, we always went out. But then I was not exactly his wife at the time, I reminded myself. Marriage tended to change men's perspective about issues. But I would just have to peel my eyes for any changes and adjust immediately. Osahon was a prize that should be treasured. There should not be any strain at all in this marriage. I would make sure of that!

After the knocking on the door cum bride price ceremony I changed into another outfit from my meager marriage trousseau and as I was getting ready to leave with my new family my mother came into the room with her shoulders slumped, subdued with sadness. My heart immediately softened towards her. She rummaged in her clothes basket and left immediately without saying a word. But my mind had already fastened on her demeanor and my thoughts wandered un-gauged: my mother had always been a complex woman, few of words but many in action. But this time it looked like something bigger than the cricket had been caught in its trap: she was thoroughly put out by the whole affair. She did not find it funny at all, especially the aspect of postponing the church wedding. Her view was that we should do everything low-key and settle down. 'What would stop you children from having this marriage blessed in the eyes of God? There will always be occasions for big parties in future,' she had remonstrated.

I had succeeded in calming her down by promising that we would not wait for long before organizing the wedding. I would have settled for a 'morning mass' wedding to ease my mother's bewilderment but Osahon adamantly refused. 'How can I do that to you, Princess? Don't you know how much I love you? I will take you down the aisle in style and show the world what you mean to me.' He had sealed that talk with a melting kiss and I felt that he had said it all. What more was there to add? My mother would have to bear it a little while longer.

It was my father who had me worried; ever the voluble one he became silent. I had wounded him deeply, too, I knew and so would have to find a way to smoothen out those ridges on their foreheads. But I knew what to do? I must hold fast to my mapped out track and follow its scraggy route to greatness. That would make things right. I had no intention of failing them. Osahon and all that came with it was a temporary distraction.

*　*　*

The ceremony in Osahon's place did not go as planned as he announced, to the consternation of his family, that I was a virgin when he met me and that was that. And so we left for Benin City that evening. I was not even required to showcase my *womanly skills* before Osahon whisked me away.

Osahon's father who had been itching to get me on my own, finally succeeded and took me aside before we left, for words of advice.

'Gift, my daughter, my son Osahon has always had his eyes permanently fixed beyond the skies, please try and have yours fixed on our earth, that way you'll be living here on earth which I assure you is a sure way to a happier life together.'

I had thanked him and joined Osahon in his jalopy which he swung out of the compound in a cloud of dust, his face thunderous, scrunched in a fierce lightning scowl. Like he had eaten raw cocoyam!

I had discerned that my husband was not happy with his father's *words of advice* to me and so allowed him to simmer for some minutes before turning to him.

'Babes, what's the problem?' But really I did not want to know.

'That man rubs me the wrong way, I swear. He interferes too much with my affairs and that I do not like. But I thought I had outgrown the resentment.'

After that outburst we drove on in silence, each mauling whatever seemed appropriate thoughts, as we flew along the smooth nylon-tar road to Benin City.

Suddenly Osahon grinned which cleared his clouded face then declared,

'I hope my dad is not going to resurrect his old meddlesome ways through you? Better not let him, whatever he may have told you.'

'Are you fishing?' I asked laughingly.

'No, I am not.'

'Good because I am not letting on.'

He nodded humming along with the music on the FM 2 Radio, his anger forgotten completely. Osahon should be any woman's dream. How does he do it: not holding onto grudges for long? Well I thank God because it implied that we were going to have a swell life together, as it seemed we were alike in more ways than I had previously believed. I switched my mind back to where it was before: being assigned yet another *saving* job. I wondered if I had been created for the singular purpose of helping to elevate people's lives. I could live with that, just that I had not been given a blueprint and a timeframe for when to start and how to do the job.

*   *   *

We arrived in Benin City and crawled through the traffic till we reached our neighbourhood more than an hour later. Osahon parked the car at the end of the street and we ferried our things from there to our one room and parlor abode. I dropped the only luggage Osahon allowed me to carry to yawn and stretch tiredness out of my body. It had been a long day and this would be my first day as a married woman, living officially in my husband's home in the eyes of tradition, if not the church.

As I surveyed the dusty parlour, I reminded myself that I must leave for Lagos within the week to continue with my studies and *shame the devil*. Everybody concerned would see me in action and their fears would be laid to rest once and for all.

That did not include the idea of leaving Osahon, which was not appealing at all. Being with him was life itself; a whirlwind of unending fun-packed activities. Osahon never let me frown. He carried me like I was a very fragile object. He was always there for me. What he could not say in words he covered with action. What more could a girl ask for? It was going to be a marriage made in heaven; I could already feel that in my bones.

Oh ...

BENIN CITY, EDO STATE, NIGERIA

I woke up one morning and the one week I had allotted to the practicals of married life had melted away. It seemed like a day, but if indeed it was up to a week, then it was a week which I would not forget in a hurry.

When we had finished unpacking that day, Osahon made it clear that he was going to be in charge and told me to put my legs up and relax, while he cooked and cleaned. Look at Osahon, so macho, so nonchalant, yet so domesticated. Such talents did not mix well, not in a man, anyway, and in Osahon? So out-of-place, yet ... Though it had continued to baffle me, I felt blessed all the same and gloried in it. This was living!

I, however, advised myself to go easy on a particular treat of his; fish pepper-soup. He had consistently made this favourite delicacy of his for me since our return. But the pepper in the sauce was extremely hot; so scorching that it unsettled my stomach and the baby, who kicked furiously in protest with every mouthful. When I asked him to take it easy with the pepper, he pulled a very long and heavy face, so I quickly retracted my suggestion and demurely ate up, but became very adept at eating only the fish and sneaked the sauce into the sink. He probably thought that it was an attempt on my part to turn up my nose at his cooking! Indeed.

The following Sunday I left for Lagos. It was so heart wrenching, but it had to be done. You don't achieve a dream by truncating the process. That morning Osahon took me to the motor park and delayed the taxi from leaving, holding me tightly. The driver had to intervene before he released me. I simply sobbed, my neighbour in the cab patted me gently telling me to stop crying but warned me to be wary of a man that clung to a woman; it was not a normal behaviour. I nodded and cleaned my eyes, putting down her warning to jealousy, while trying hard to think of a way to live without my husband.

Ifeoma, who was all for get-Gift-back-to-school effort, was waiting for me beside the Lagos motor park with a car-hire Mercedes Benz and we drove off immediately to the campus. I settled down and our usual lifestyle was resumed but with some changes.

I was no longer the life and soul of parties. My numerous beaus drastically reduced, initially to a trickle and then to nothing. That was to be expected. It would not be a viable venture to *toast* a married woman, a pregnant married woman at that, when there were single and willing babes all over the place.

Apart from attending my lectures and reading occasionally, my thoughts were filled with Osahon and half of the time I was on the phone where we whispered sweet nothings to each other. In fact, I was sure that Osahon felt my absence more, for he was always moaning that I should come home. But I was not going to give up all I had held dear and had pursued vigorously without a fight, most especially seeing the effect my treachery had had on my family. I would hold on and very tightly too until I had transferred to the University of Benin, Uniben, as we planned. Though it was very tough to resist Osahon I hung in there, practically on my fingernails.

Then one morning I woke with a scream on my lips. There was this sharp pain that held me captive. I could not even locate the position of the pain; it was all over my stomach. Ifeoma jumped in brandishing her first aid experience but to no avail, however, after sometime, the pain subsided and I managed to calm down. I got dressed and took the longest journey of my life to the campus medical centre. There, I was treated to the best of their ability—they were not equipped for my kind of illness, pregnancy.

By the time we returned from our afternoon lecture, I was once more engulfed by pain and I took to my bed for the rest of the day. Ifeoma was not equipped to handle a pregnant and tearful roommate but she stayed with me anyway, scrubbing away my tears and dampening my forehead with a cold-cloth to bring down my temperature. I got much better and slept through the night. The next morning I was up and about and even went for my lectures without any pain.

The pains came back later in the evening and were joined by cramps and nausea that always ended with vomiting. I couldn't take a step without vomiting and this baffled the three of us. Was this how it usually was with other women? Or was something wrong with the baby or me? When I was not asking myself questions that I could not answer, I was on the phone with Osahon sobbing my heart out. Osahon who could not bear my anguish any longer came down to Lagos by the end of that week.

*   *   *

Within three days of his arrival, he had processed to defer my schooling for the time being and took me home to Ifeoma's chagrin. 'You are a very stubborn girl, Gift,' she had told me in her best British accent when we had an altercation initially about my pregnancy and plan to marry Osahon. I did not think the comment deserved an answer so I ignored her but she had continued unchecked.

'Who would believe that one shack with Osahon got you addicted to sex! Then marriage and now this.' It had amazed me that with Ifeoma's know-how as I put it, she neither saw what I saw in Osahon, nor what we had together. So I had tried to enlighten her.

'Look Ifeoma you had to let me be. It is not about sex you know! In case you have not noticed, our hearts have fused together, we are in l-o-v-e,' I spelt it out then put it together LOVE before continuing, 'we are one and I cannot bear to be away from him.'

She had looked at me then and shook her head wearily. Then patiently, as if speaking to a child, she said, 'You claim to be in love with Osahon, not that there is anything wrong with that, just that my friend has turned into somebody else. You live and breathe Osahon, and that cannot be healthy. And what do I know about love, you ask?' She smiled at the question, probably thinking of her Prince, before continuing, 'I know about love, but maybe the percentage or the quality of my knowledge is lower, I don't know, though I cannot see how, and in any case, I'd rather remain at my threshold than tip over to yours and if as you say, that your soul is entwined with Osahon's, believe me Gift that is quite scary.' I didn't comment. What was the point? She got it quite right, except the scary part but then I do not see with her eyes.

*   *   *

Osahon settled me in and took care of me. I would be okay one week, then in pain the next. The gynecologist we consulted said it was nothing. It was my first pregnancy and was bound to act up; I should get on with it. Osahon advised me to forget about going back to school until after the birth or at least until I was no longer sick on an hourly basis. It was a welcome relief to me and I visibly brightened at that very suggestion. I was in too much pain to do any reading anyway.

*   *   *

School vacated and Ifeoma flew into Benin City to see me before traveling home to London. She was taken aback when she saw me and came closer to study me before commenting 'You are visibly glowing Gi, are you not supposed to be sick with pregnancy or something?'

I collapsed into a giggle but managed to answer her, 'Ah, Ifeoma, if I did not know you very well I would say that you're jealous. Pregnancy is not a sickness I will have you know. I was just not carrying it well while in school, that's all.'

'Shouldn't you come back then now that you've got yourself back to form?'

'Fifi, let's not go through all that again. I have only four months to go then I will be back before you can snap your fingers.'

'Oh yeah.'

She sniggered.

'How about our friend Erica?' I asked changing the course of the conversation.

'She's fine and has snared herself one *Ofe nmanu* man like that. It is looking serious by the day as she is in a hurry to settle down.'

'A Yoruba man and soon to be married? Congratulate her for me oh.' Then I turned to Ifeoma properly, now that we were on the subject of marriage.

'I assume you're not looking to settle down yet even for your Rasta?'

'And do what then? Cook, clean, shag, a few brats and . . .'

'Spare me the litany, please,' I cut her off with a laugh.

'I thought love had struck by way of Rasta, but obviously not. Whenever it does happen, I will not fail to remind you of all these abominations you're spouting now.'

'Please do.'

Ifeoma had stayed as long as she could before she flew back to Lagos.

*   *   *

Osahon and I had settled into a semi-married life since my leave of absence. Our shared dream of being *somebody* in life was thus brought forward: to set up our one-in-town supermarket, the largest in the country, dwarfing even Mega Plaza, that'd cater for the *who is who* of Benin City. We would then pursue our other dreams unfettered by such things as economic-lack—that is enjoying a high unfettered lifestyle.

Osahon already had a small provision store which was not making money by any standard, as far as I could see, which wasn't far at all. But then how could it? It was an excuse of a shop. One could count the stock in the shop on one hand and still have some fingers to spare. It was located in a slum and needed revamping to even live up to the standard of the neighbourhood! In short, we would have to relocate the shop. For now though, we would simply upgrade it, while we marshalled out our plans. Big supermarkets were not built in a day.

To jumpstart this dream, or more appropriately; to clear the bushes covering the ground where we would later lay the foundation stones for our dream, I gave him my life savings of one hundred and fifty thousand Naira to plow into the provision business. This saving was from monies given to me as gifts by various *Aristocrats*. I did not have any misgivings about giving the money to Osahon; afterall we were now two-in-one, therefore, should share things as one.

After this major investment, it became even more of an uphill task for the shop to bring in money, which was baffling. If I ever had cause to blame unseen hands for my misfortunes in life, which I never had to resort to before, now would be very appropriate to claim that somebody somewhere had done *juju* for us so that we would not progress.

What seemed to amaze me, however, and kept my spirits up was Osahon. He was always cheerful; never for one moment sagging from the weight of life and its intrigues. He told me when I mooted my worries to relax.

'Gift my Princess, our time will come. We should not lose sight of that and then miss it. We must be positioned. And you do not do that with long-face, complaints and hissing, you embrace all with warmth; good times, bad times, all of them, but always keep your eyes on the ball.'

Good words, right attitude, but the burden of our debt was mounting, and the weight was on my shoulders. My family may have been poor but I had never felt the pressure of it. Nobody discussed finances with me and I never lacked as far as my poverty-jaundiced eyes saw. My dream of amounting to somebody in life was not born out of desperation. It was more of an aspiration to change my life to something better than what my parents had. What I had done so far in my estimation was on the mark, it would make my life better not worse. And back home we had always been a happy family which shows that happiness was not dependent on the size of your pocket. But here as Osahon's wife somehow, I was beginning to experience desperation and it was not sitting well on my shoulders at all. However, I decided to bear it, tucked myself in well and calmly continued to serve our customers day in day out whenever I could make it to the shop.

After a particularly nasty day, when people kept streaming into the shop willing to buy, but went away empty-handed from lack of stock, I resolved to take Osahon up on the state of affairs.

'What kind of provision store sells pure-water and Okin biscuits?' I snapped while gnashing my teeth angrily. I would see an end to this nonsense this night. Was this how we were going to build a mega-supermarket?

Delicately, so as to not imply what I did not mean, I questioned Osahon about what he did with the money I gave him. He cheerfully informed me that he had used it to offset his old debts: rents, for the shop and for the apartment, to my dismay. I thought all men were born with good business acumen. I swallowed the consternation however, and ventured, 'But you should have put the money in our business and pay them from the proceeds, babes,' the babes added to soften my tone; I was straining to not strangle him.

'Mmmh Princess, you don't know anything. Do you know that both my landlords were planning to have me murdered? I had to get them out of my hair pronto. That money was really God sent.'

'Oh.' My mouth was a perfect O. I closed it, and then opened it again.

'I did not know that,' was all I could mutter. I looked closely at him; he certainly did not resemble somebody that had survived imminent death.

I remembered though, that I did not object when he wined and dined me or when he bought me various pieces of jewelries now and then. Things I did not need or want, not now anyway. I had my suspicions about where the funding for them came from. I also noted that Osahon may not have had a lot of things but the few he had were very expensive things, designers all. He derived joy from spending money on good quality things, not unlike me but . . .

I finally came to the conclusion that my husband was a spendthrift who was not versed in any money-making activities. But did it have to include squandering our jump-start investment funds? He should have enough business sense to not do that. After a while, I advised myself to ignore my fears, which Osahon had managed to make to seem irrational, as always. But I couldn't help prodding my thought further.

Was this what his father meant then? When he took me aside on the day of our marriage? Well, things must have to sort themselves out somehow, because I would concentrate on my plans going forward; hurry up and go back to school, graduate and get a job. All I had to do for now, it would seem would be to borrow a leaf from my husband; not worry, or if I must, worry less. It should be able to help me adjust, and then see how things turned out.

As it stood, my cup was overflowing already with my growing stomach, therefore I was not about to develop high-blood pressure from poverty worries on top of that. I had also come to realize that I should not shoot a man's pride down with my penny-pinching attitude and words. You did not do that. A man's pride, especially when that man was your husband, should always be held up in reverence, and accorded great amount of respect too! Rich or poor. This wisdom was imparted by Chinelo when I took my worries to her.

It then occurred to me that I was the one dragging our happiness backwards with 'long-face,' if I could borrow his words. But it also seemed that he had a way of choosing his words that cut me to the soul, therefore dragging up a different and inappropriate emotion for me. His desire to live the good life and the way he went about describing how it should be made me feel responsible for our lack. Or maybe I should change my thought process in that regard which usually informed my state of unhappiness. Osahon was the head of this household; therefore, it was up to him to worry about our financial well-being.

*   *   *

Close to my due date I relocated to Oyi to stay with my parents so that my mother could help with the baby as well as ensure that we were properly fed, but I didn't let them know this. During my stay in the village, Osahon was always there urging me to make haste and return as he did not want me out of his life for one second nor to stay in a house that did not have me in it. When our baby was born Osahon named her GodKnows, after some uncle of his, but to be sure that our daughter would not lug about a name like that I insisted and Frances was included as her name. When she was two months old, we packed up and departed for Benin with Osahon in his old and faithful jalopy.

...AGAIN!

Two months after our return to Benin city, I found out I was pregnant again! I couldn't imagine how that had happened. Well, I could imagine how it happened, but this I would assure you now would not augur well with our current circumstances at all. A four—month old baby, another on the way, a spendthrift of a husband, a long-face-carrying-wife, all in a penury-infested household destined for destitution? Not good.

When I told Osahon of my suspicion he looked at me, his eyes wide, in apparent confusion. When what I said had soaked into him, made sense to him, he looked at me in disbelief. Then when it must have reached saturation point, he exploded. It then occurred to me when he roared that that must be what was usually referred to as *blowing a fuse*, for he simply went crazy, unhinged, and then ripped into me nice and smooth.

'How could any one person be so stupid and dense?' He had asked the room baffled.

'Look at me, Gift.'

I did, raising doleful eyes to stare at him obediently.

'Do I look like a fool to you?'

I shook my head negatively.

'Am I standing on my head?'

I frowned.

'Then let me tell you something; I did not bargain for this, do you hear me, I did not. And if you think that you are going to stunt my life, my style, think again . . . .' On and on and on he rumbled. My skin lacerated with each whiplash of words, while some pincers, held by the devil itself, grabbed my heart and squeezed at the lash of every word. Sadness and sorrow were dripping like sweat off my brows. How did it manage to reach this stage so fast?

I stood there uncertain, my head positioned to continue to receive the severe words but gradually my ears went numb, then froze completely shutting the words out. I stopped hearing what he was saying or rather, I could hear him alright but could no longer make out the words, could not absorb them anymore. I was that hurt and dazed; wounded beyond words. This was not my Osahon.

Then suddenly some words penetrated: ' . . . do yourself a favour woman . . . abort that burden you are carrying. There is a limit to how much a man can take and I will not be forced to continue to suffer unnecessarily.'

He suddenly stopped, flung his blazing eyes about as if looking for something, then proceeded to go round the room in circles while firmly clamping his two ears with his palms; as if trying to block out sounds or words.

I was quite sure that I had not uttered a word since the very one that brought on the explosion. I looked around myself to ascertain that somehow a neighbour had not come into our apartment to explore the source of the uproar, the volume of which I was sure broadcasted in the whole compound. The walls demarcating the rooms were not designed with the tenant's privacy in mind. But when I didn't see anybody I returned my gaze to my husband who had stopped his madness-inspired-circular-movement. He peered at me as if seeing me for the first time then quickly veered towards the door that led out of the apartment, nearly bringing the house down when he flung it shut behind him.

Immediately he left, I sat down to try and recover from my own shock. I hugged myself as guilt descended and wrapped itself like the vampire's heavy cloak round my shoulders. I could feel my life-blood being sucked out but I still managed to claw firmly to my senses, to deter my thinking faculty from following suit. How could I be so stupid? I berated. Could I not even be trusted to do the simplest of things like not getting pregnant so soon? My husband had endured so much yet here I was adding to it. I understood his problems perfectly well. Having been born in a rich household and having been rich previously had conspired to make it hard on him: it was not easy, under the circumstances, to adjust to this penny-pinching business which was what our family economic life had been!

'What am I going to do?' I asked myself but nothing came to mind. 'There must be something that I should be able to do to ease his pain,' I wailed wishing that Ifeoma was there for me to confide in but quickly wished the wish away. Ifeoma was no good. She'd simply ask me to walk away. She did not understand. I sat very still, I needed to concentrate and it would come to me. My life was Osahon, I could not do without him and I would give my last breath to make money and make him happy. He had given me love and happiness, but what had I given him in return? Burden and pressure that's what!

I waited for him to come home. He did not. I could not settle down, my husband had never stormed out in anger before, in fact my husband had never been angry with me before, talkless of storming out. I was not sure of what to do. After a while, I bundled Frances up and put a few things together and went to consult my sister who had been in the business of marriage long enough.

*   *   *

Though dusk had descended, Chinelo went ahead and spread her washing on the clothesline in front of their compound, using wooden clothespins to hold them from being blown away. When she sighted Gift alighting from a bus her face lit up with smiles, but then she had a rethink; why was Gift in a public transport and where was Osahon? She then took a closer look at Gift's face and knew that trouble had finally descended on paradise; for her face was very heavy, crowded by sadness, one could fry *akara* from the intensity of the misery.

Chinelo took Frances from me and led me inside. When I had found a nail-free part of the chair to settle down properly, I looked up into my sister's eyes and realized that she was waiting for me to come out with whatever it was. In a very tiny voice I said, 'Sister, it is Osahon.'

'Ehee, what about him?'

'He left.'

'What do you mean by "he left?"' she mimicked before rephrasing the question.

'Left for where and why?'

'I don't know, sister.'

'That I cannot accept from you Gift. What do you mean by "you don't know?" Have you not seen me quarrel with Ikemefuna, my husband, before?'

I nodded.

'And have you not seen us make up?'

I nodded again.

'Then you have to do better than "you don't know."

I let out my breath and sighed.

'I told him I suspected that I was pregnant and he didn't like that. He really scared me, sister, and after shouting at me for ages he left and that was in the afternoon. I haven't seen him since and do not know how to or even where to look for him.'

Chinelo smiled with understanding. Then she asked in a laughter-laden voice. 'Is that all? Don't worry. If you were a man struggling to make ends meet, you would understand why he was angry. But I want you to know that he was not angry at you Gift. He was angry at his impotence: his inability to provide for his family the way he would want. He was angry at seeing you suffer when you are supposed to be pampered as befits a Princess. Look at you, do you think it gives him joy to see your mouth down at the sides from worry? No! Don't take it to heart, he is being a man.'

Chinelo looked at me as if what she'd say next would not be as palatable. I held her gaze.

'I must use this opportunity to point out though, that your husband Osahon is not living in this our world you know. Osahon your husband has his eyes up!' Chinelo indicated the sky by flicking her brows up. 'And when things like this happen it tends to bring him down to earth, he does not like it. Stay here tonight and go home in the morning. He will be there.'

I nodded; I had no intention of staying there.

Chinelo's children rushed in and nearly knocked me off the chair in their haste to hug me.

'Aunty Gift, we have not seen you since? Where is uncle?' Chinwe, the eldest, asked on behalf of the gang.

I smiled, even as a replica of misery personified. I still marveled at how much the children had grown. Look at them, not too long ago I was cleaning their snouts and dragging them to school. This life self; very soon, they would start talking about love and wanting to be allowed to make their own choices! 'Your uncle is fine. He did not come with us today.' I finally found my voice and responded to their question.

'So you will not stay long then?'

'Yes, we will leave as soon as we've had dinner, how . . .' but they had scooped the baby before I could finish and hooted out, allowing us to peacefully continue our heavy-natter. Chinelo's face was in a scowl because I had mentioned that I would leave but she'd just have to un-scowl it. I must be there when my husband returned. I decided to drop the bombshell now that the coast is clear.

'Sister, I am not sure I should not be worried, he wanted me to have an abortion!'

'What! Now that is serious. Very serious. What kinds of life were you living with Osahon that could have led to that kind of talk, eh Gift?' I couldn't respond because on my part I wasn't sure of what I had to do with Osahon's talk but I didn't ask. Besides Chinelo was only starting on her sermon. 'Osahon surely is not the first neither will he be the last to live in lack. Besides, the two of you have barely started life. What made him think that your life will not change tomorrow for the better? What am I saying? Why must your life change at all before you could have children in succession? Please tell that man I said he should not toy with such words, it is not good for the ears, or better still I would come with you to tell him so myself.' She stopped and looked at my scowling face pointedly, to indicate that she couldn't care less before continuing. 'And you Gift', this time she had her two fingers wagging at me menacingly, 'you have been brought up on life's ups and downs and therefore should be able to discern good from bad. You should not allow life's inconveniences to distort and distract you from the truth. Life is sacred; one should not indiscriminately take it away because it is going to stunt your lifestyle!'

I sighed. My sister was just like our mother. What did I do to deserve this rebuke, as if I was colluding with Osahon?

'Sister I am not planning to have any abortion, but what am I going to tell him when he returns? He is really in pain, sister, and it looks as if I am compounding our problems. What if he never came back, how am I going to cope? How am I going to bring up two children on my own? How?'

'What is right is right, problems or not. But it will not come to that, I assure you. Osahon is just being a normal man; when problem *full ground remain*, they tend to get confused and say things that are out of tune, but he will rally round. It was a good thing he stormed out, he could use that opportunity of being alone to think things through.' When Chinelo stopped this time I thought she had finally finished and was about to sigh with relief when I looked at her mouth and saw that some words were still lurking there. I quickly stifled my relief. I'd rather wait. She was, however, reluctant to let out the words, weighing them, or rather the effect of them more like, then she spoke.

'You used to be prayerful Gift or have you lost your faith married to Osahon?' She didn't give me a chance to reply before she launched on. 'Well if you have, the time has come to find it because I can see that it has been relegated to an ice chamber. Pray about it and leave it in the hands of God, He will know what to do.'

'I know sister just that I don't think that He would really listen to me. I have not been close to Him for a long time now.'

'If you are in a marriage where your husband is demanding that you abort a child, a child that two of you made, you are not even in contact with Him, talkless of relating with Him. However, it is not late, it is never late to seek His face, to seek His presence and protection for your family. Always remember He is a faithful God, He will never fail to answer you when you call Him in truth and in spirit.'

I felt that my sister must have looked into the turmoil in my soul or maybe it was mirrored on my face because when she continued, she had tempered her voice with sympathy. 'I did not mean to sound unconcerned, and I am sorry if it came out like that, but that is the only way I know. Look at my family, we are not rich but we are OK, we are healthy, we eat three square meals a day and our children are all in school. I am aware that it is not much by today's standard but what more can we ask for? If Osahon is truly your husband, he will not abandon you because you became pregnant again so soon, he will rally round I tell you.'

I kept my counsel, and got up to busy myself with the task of putting dinner together, but Chinelo took over, asking me to go and sit down and rest. More like to think over her words to me.

After we ate I gathered my things and my sleeping daughter and left for home in trepidation, refusing Chinelo's plea to stay the night. I would not want to cause Osahon further worry when he returned to meet an empty house.

*   *   *

But Osahon did not come back that night and I did not sleep a wink either, keeping my ears very alert for the sound of his return. With the first ray of dawn I got up to get us ready to face a new day. By mid-morning I could not stand the quietness of the apartment anymore and Frances had chosen that period to take to sleeping instead of her favourite pastime of crying. She probably had smelt the fear emanating from me. I worried.

Believing that being in the shop would make him happier at his return I took Frances, stuck a note on the door, and we left for the shop before I lost it completely by worrying.

It was at sunset, while listlessly serving a trickle of customers, that I saw him treading his way from across the street. The immediate emotion that coursed through me was that of relief, and then I trained me eyes to his face, searching out his mood, gauging it. When he continued to walk into the store, bearing down straight to where I was, I abandoned the customers and fled into the inner office. I had failed to read his demeanor and remembering the age old adage that when you wake up in the morning to find yourself being pursued by a chicken, it would do you a world of good to run as if the devil itself were after you for you did not know whether the chicken had grown teeth overnight.

Osahon's behaviour in the last twenty-four hours was unusual, maybe he had come back to beat me up or something worse! As I sat on a stool behind Frances' cot, she was snoozing peacefully in there, I shivered. I wished I were a child at that very moment, shielded from the worries of life.

*   *   *

Osahon saw Gift run into the inner office and smiled to himself. But he refrained from following her immediately. Instead he finished serving the customers she had abandoned then went into the inner office himself where he took one look at his wife and enveloped her in a very deep and tight embrace. Her legs must have buckled and gave way, Osahon thought when she collapsed on him.

'Princess, I was wrong and I want you to know that I will never repeat last night again, ever. You have brought me joy, if not wealth, and I should not take my frustrations out on you. I'm sorry, okay?'

Osahons' first utterance lifted the Dracula's cloak from my shoulders, all the lacerations on my skin closed up and my heart was released and instantly the smooth flow of my life was restored. The combined weight of the ailment had firmly and consistently tried to strangle me, all night long and into the first quarter of the day. Now it was over. I beamed and clung to him, my lifeline. Osahon freed his right hand, bent down and lifted our sleeping daughter, to include her in the family reunion hug.

'Both of you have brought joy into my life. Princess, I want you to know from this day that you are my life, I will love you forever and therefore will cherish any child you give me.' He looked at me with so serious a face before continuing, 'I have always advocated for us to not lose sight of the bigger picture and I nearly messed it up myself.' I was not sure I saw the picture, but I was not about to bring any attention to my ignorance at this time.

'Who am I to sneer at God's gift because of material wealth? I think this was a test from God and mark my words Princess, this child will be a blessing to us. It is a sign of the good things to come. Therefore, be it a boy or a girl we will name it Blessing,' he declared solemnly.

'Certainly babes,' I concurred then added, 'You know that I love you with my whole being and my life would mean nothing without you. I really am sorry for inadvertently causing you untold heartache and would reverse it if I could. I would do anything for you, you know? And . . .' Osahon placed his forefinger on my lips, sealing it and blocking my words, then he returned the baby back to her cot, kicked the door that led to the shop closed with his leg and calmly undressed me. When I was completely naked he stopped. He moved back and gazed at my body with desire gleaming in his eyes. I was already quivering. I could never get enough of Osahon, nor him me. Gently he took me.

But that was pure ephemeral, flickered into my mind immediately after. The reality was that Osahon had no money and the concept of saving was alien to him while his money-making ideas were very wild and absurd. No wonder he was poor. He had told me that he had money before but was swindled out of it. Granted, he showed signs of having lived in affluence before, but that was before. This was now and I could not see how we would cope. For me there was no problem. Osahon was the problem here. He would never take a bus when there was cab and did not see why we should not go out and have fun on weekends. My Osahon liked to wear quality apparels and all that went with it because as a big boy he had to impress. As long as we had money at hand, then it would be spent. He was probably trying not to fall into the *okpaku elieli* debacle which alleged that though a millionaire, died from starvation and as he was laid-in-state, it was claimed that his lips were dry, scaly and stuck together in an upward curl in protest to being starved to death. *Now what kind of a foolish man was that?* I mused, while imagining the kind of frenzy that would engulf his kinsmen who'd spend the better part of their remaining lives squabbling over the wealth left by the dead man.

At least the stingy Igbo man made his money himself. He just did not like to eat, that's all. Osahon did not like to make money, or to be fair, he did not know how to make money but had a Masters Degree in spending, while I, Gift, had acquired a PhD in worrying and complaining about our lack. As my thoughts started to spiral out of line I reined them and reiterated again as I had done months ago; to leave all that worry to Osahon. If he so desired to live in splendor he should go and look for the money, full stop. I had enough worry on my plate.

*   *   *

After the disappearance incident, our lives returned back to normal, of sorts, limping along as our days blended into weeks and then months, but they had acquired a subtle undercurrent which I could not place. But if I could acknowledge it, only to myself mind you, I would say that Osahon had become a little distant, very subtle, a very thin subtle. It was not there, yet it was. I could feel it shimmer just beneath the surface, very faint, hovering. At the same time he seemed his most caring self as if nothing awkward was in the offing but . . .

It started with his nightmares right after the storming out incident. Osahon would turn and thrash about in his sleep which would progress to jumbled-mumbled whisperings with sweat pouring off his body like a broken dam. It was greatly unsettling to me and initially I would wake him up to inquire about the cause of these nightmares. He was genuinely surprised and baffled by my question the first time.

My persistent questioning did not elicit any change in his denials or the consistency of the nightmares. Finally one day the dance step changed style: at questioning him after a particularly vicious thrashing about, he *twisted* the scenario and wagging his finger at me accused me of trying to cover-up the fact that I was the one that had been engaging in the nocturnal thrashings, jumbled-mumblings and whisperings. Since he was certainly not having any nightmares, it must be me, he concluded. I did not have any problems accepting his accusation if only he did not make it sound so ominous, with devious connotations: you know the kind of activity that could only be engaged in by witches and sorcerers and in the dead of night. He could not, however, explain the sweating aspect of the bizarre situation when I pointed that out, whereupon he suggested that it must be from the heat that had been roasting us alive.

'How could sweat not pour off my body?' he had countered. Then followed it by alluding to our impoverished position; 'If only we could afford to buy quality air-conditioning units, it'd help to tone down the temperature of the room to an acceptable cool, then we would not be having this conversation in the middle of the night when people, who knew what they are doing, are sleeping in cool comfortable atmospheres.' I was securely enveloped in his arms during this impassioned speech about other peoples' atmosphere, so the message sank in smoothly. He kissed my forehead and assured me to not worry, he would take it in his stride. I should just concentrate on the baby in my womb and the one outside my womb.

* * *

With the birth of our baby Osahon's nightmares intensified! Sometimes he would fall off the bed during his thrashings and would only wake up when I had exhausted myself trying to lift him onto the bed. Such times he would calmly get up, climb back into the bed and slept off without acknowledging me.

When Ifeoma came to visit, I sobbed out the whole story to her. I needed a shoulder to unburden what I had bottled up for too long. After the heaving sobs I felt physically lighter even though I knew that Ifeoma's brand of advice would not be suitable but rather her than my family. Without mincing words, of course, she informed me that Osahon belonged to the breed of men she referred to as *back-of-men*—shadows, pathetic, and that I should not allow him to twist my mind. I told her off and we had a good shouting match and thereafter stiffly made desultory conversations.

* * *

Ifeoma had not planned at sleeping over in Benin because she would be leaving for London the next night as she had informed Gift on arrival, but now she did not know how to leave in view of their current altercation. She fidgeted and Gift ignored her because you don't come into people's house and insult their husband, friend or not, and expect to get away with it easily. Finally, Ifeoma got up having made a decision; she gave Gift a cheque, to be paid back to her at an unspecified future but with the advice that it was only meant for her and the children alone. Then in an anger-laden voice she added vehemently, 'Nightmares or not, Osahon should go and make himself useful somewhere instead of keeping you awake on top of your numerous stresses.'

I shook my head while sighing inwardly after this display of support from my friend who had consistently failed or refused to see what really existed between Osahon and me. But I did not berate or enlighten her this time, I was getting rather tired of doing that. So we sat there with animosity air floating around us. After a while Ifeoma left.

* * *

Ifeoma went outside, flagged down a cab and went to see Chinelo instead, just to cool down. There, she took the children for a walk as

she did not know what to discuss with Chinelo. The walk turned into
a treat outing for the children and a sort of a balm for Ifeoma. By
the time they returned a considerable time had passed and she bade
Chinelo and her family a good evening. And went back to see Gift.

When I answered to Ifeoma's knock, I could see relief on her face
and so knew that at least she was no longer as mad with me; I offered a
ghost of a reconciliatory smile and then voiced a tiny apology that tore
away the remnants of our quarrel and we fell into our old routine, but
strenuously steered clear of Osahon talk.

Airborne the next morning, Ifeoma gave vent to her thoughts, to see
if she'd appreciate this type of love between Gift and her husband. After
a while she gave up, she couldn't. 'Osahon should go fuck himself,' she
swore. Nightmares indeed! Gift should see him for what he was—a loser
and a leech. Grudgingly though, she admitted that he must really love
Gift. Look at the way he was always hanging around her with dewy eyes.
And let's face it, what was there to leech out of Gift materially? If only
he had it in him to give his family some semblance of material comfort.
Instead, at the rate he was going, he'd end up sending Gift to an early
grave. And the poor girl was always at pains to get her to understand,
when she couldn't, she told her that if she found love the way she did
she'd understand. But Ifeoma made sure to convey it plainly to her
that she had bought a double-vision-lenses just so as to make sure she
steered clear of such love, thank you very much. They had both laughed
then and the tension had gradually eased away.

So in all honesty Ifeoma did not trust Gift not to give the money to
that husband of hers. She seethed a while on that before reaching the
conclusion that it didn't really matter, afterall what was her business
in their affair? Actually she would not really mind if she did give the
money to Osahon. What was mere money between friends, not to
talk of between spouses, and she had it to give anyway. If it would
help to launch them onto the road to financial recovery, she would
gladly give more, they could always pay her back, when and if they so
wished. Look at her, she mused, if she, several times removed from
Gift's heart could think like this, how much more two people deeply
in love like those two. She must hand it to them. The pair was well and
truly drawn to each other and whatever reservations she had on the
other aspects of their life; she could not deny their love for each other.
She promised herself to endeavour to keep in touch with them all the
time, even after graduating, which was less than six months away. This
was because for some reason her gut instinct refused to be eased on
Osahon. She kept imagining that there must be more, yet to unfold.
But what could that be? What was it his father had said that day of

their so-called marriage? She tried to remember what Gift had told her, but it failed to come up so she gave up. She loved her Jamaican Prince to distraction, but would she be willing to stick with him if he was this nonsense at being a man like Osahon?

She floundered a bit on this then abandoned it, rearranged herself and shut her eyes for a snooze.

*   *   *

The state of affairs during the night in the Iguedia household remained unchanged. No! Not unchanged, I quickly amended. How could I possibly make such a mistake? Was I subconsciously trying to mask the reality of our night-life? Surely not! Anyway, Osahon had continued to remain the perfect and loving husband during the day; carrying on cheerfully and I had got addicted to all the attention he always lavished on me. I just prayed that I would not get pregnant so soon again, after all said and done.

But nonetheless, we had carried on until one day Osahon came home from the shop looking even more tired and dejected causing my heart and my mood to nosedive but I didn't say anything to him, rather I held myself and got busier with his dinner. I had learned to adjust my level of consciousness on his demeanor as gleaned from scanning his face immediately I encountered him—seeking for signs, anything at all, and adjusting accordingly!

Uncharacteristically, Osahon went straight into the room without a glance or a word to me, strange that, and then came back out armed with the plastic bucket and our sponge and soap holder enroute to the communal bathroom. Because of the queue in the morning time, he had opted to bath when he returned in the evenings, but hello young man your Princess was sitting right in front of you, but no he went out with no backward glance.

We ate but with minimal communication and, as was customary, afterwards made ourselves comfortable on the couch in front of our 21" black and white television with me ensconced in the crook of his arms. This act usually renewed and restored my confidence in our togetherness. He kissed my forehead after I had settled in, and pulled me close to his heart with his eyes boring into mine. I stretched my left arm and cradled his face with his eyes still deeply holding mine. We held each other like that for some time, then he broke the silence and told me that he had found a solution to our financial problems but that he was yet to find a way to put it to me. I closed my eyes briefly, opened them and looked deeply into his eyes.

'Tell me, babes.'

There was no point in our pinching a package that would be opened eventually. He might as well get it over and done with.

'Would you at least consider the proposition?'

I looked at him with fear in my eyes; was he planning for us to engage in armed robbery operation or what? But if it was that then it wouldn't be that difficult to propose because for some reason it seemed like everybody's favourite pastime these days. So it must be something much more sinister that needed to be discussed with such solemnity. I looked at him again. But even though I had continued to search my darling's face I was still clueless as his face had remained inscrutable so I went ahead and answered his question in the affirmative. Somehow, however, I started feeling that whatever it was was not going to be palatable because at my yes answer to his solicitation he had looked away and started drumming his fingers on his lap. I waited and waited then from nowhere salty water dropped on the back of my left hand that I had placed face down on his thigh to help me lean further in to my husband's face so as to not miss out on this solution. I followed the course of the water up and it ended in Osahon's eyes—they were dripping tears. I was not alarmed, if anything, I felt that things finally were coming to a head, so I moved in fully well and held him tightly to show my solidarity and support for this would-be solution while having the presence of mind to think that it must be one hell of a solution if it was taking so long to come forth. At last I decided to hasten things up, Osahon apparently lacked the courage.

'Babes, it could not be that bad you know? We are not the poorest people on earth by far. I am not a demanding woman as you know and I will walk the ends of the earth for you. Please stop crying, you are breaking my heart.'

Osahon did not stop his silent cry and we remained like that for what seemed like hours, then he quietly told me. I heard him alright, but I could not have, right? Certainly not! I shifted my position to take a closer look at my husband and then said.

'Pardon me, what did you say?'

'Could we go to Italy and work for some time?'

I was not born yesterday and having grown up in Nigeria I knew "what going to Italy to work" meant and therefore that the 'we' meant me. But I could not explain what or how I felt. In fact I did not have any feelings whatsoever. My only coherent thought was that this proposed solution out of our financial doldrums was a very nasty one. He undressed me gently and throughout that night we made love on the couch, on the floor and everywhere, sleeping in bits and pieces, until about two am when his nightmares usually started. That night it was the most violent to date.

After that night, Osahon never mentioned the proposed financial solution again. Neither did I. We carried on with our lives as if nothing was ever said, but if you looked closely enough, you'd see the proposal floating around in the room and parlour and in the shop with the dust motes. It was always there with us, between us and around us. It had been invoked and thus had come to stay, we could not escape it. One night, after a particularly explosive love-making, I slipped into a deep sleep. But I was woken by a commotion; our children were awake, lending a supporting hand to their father's thrashing and crying with their own. I lay on the bed immobilized. Eventually, when the children's cries reached a crescendo, I got up and fed them. As for Osahon, I did not have a solution.

I wasn't so surprised therefore, when I said yes to my husband's crazy request he had made more than a month before; a yes that plunged me thereafter into a life of darkness, devoid of feelings and thoughts.

Two months later with my last child only four months old, I was air-borne to Italy with my husband, in pursuit of a dream.

…He Found me

The bus swerved and veered sharply in front of Blanchardstown Shopping Centre and after much toing and froing, the driver finally parked and we all disembarked en-masse. I came down carefully, while gripping the rails with my hands and the walls of the bus, with my shoulder, so as to not tumble from the stairs. This driver did not seem like he minded about his passengers not leaving with all their body parts intact.

When I came down and out of the bus I decided to head to Marks and Spencer to purchase ice-cream and other goodies that children tended to like before going home. As I whizzed through the aisles throwing things into my shopping basket I remembered Erica and her troubles. It shocked me to realize that I had not spared a moment for my friend's problem, whatever it was. I had selfishly wallowed in mine.

But I had to shrug off the feeling, every man to his own; I just hoped that she had heard from her husband and that some sort of arrangement has been made as to how to sort out their problem.

I went home first to drop off some of the things I bought and took the rest over to Erica's. When I got out of my car I looked around before climbing the stairs scanning for unseen foes while hoping that Erica's frame of mind had changed for the better. Because if I so much as espied a tear lurking around her eyes I myself would out bawl her and I did not want to ever do that sort of thing in front of Erica.

The house was deathly quiet as I got closer. This was strange; with five children in there? No way! I hurried up and pressed the buzzer;

whatever it was I'd know sooner than later. Frances opened the door. I studied her face looking for any telltale sign of anything in the offing and seeing nothing I stepped in and closed the door amidst my daughter's shout of welcome.

Erica was sitting on a corner of the sofa in the livingroom facing the telly but lost in thought. I cleared my throat to attract her attention, she looked up and muttered.

'Oh. It's you,' followed by a sigh. I didn't think the question needed any response so I didn't respond but went and sat down beside her and whispered, 'Any news from Emmanuel yet?'

'Yes.' And nothing more.

'And?'

A heavier sigh, this time accompanied by much shifting and flicking off unseen lint from her blouse and still nothing.

'Look Erica, I am not trying to pry. If you don't feel like talking about it, that's alright with me.'

'Gift, it's not that. I am sorry. I was just thinking about man's inhumanity to man.' She quoted and then lapsed back into silence. This was heavy. Erica being philosophical was a rare event. I wondered at the nature of this their problem. Suddenly she moaned in this terrible voice: laden with sorrow and hurt, 'My own sister eh?' while banging on her chest with her fisted hand. I winced but said nothing. After a while Erica continued.

'I know that I have become hardened after what happened to us, but to upstage me knowing that it would destroy my life and probably my marriage? That was pure absolute wickedness. It is a wicked wickedness.'

'Erica what are you talking about. You are an only child or do you mean a cousin?' When she didn't respond I added, 'Maybe I should go now and come back when you are ready to make sense.'

'No. No. Stay. Do you want a cup of tea?'

Tea?

'Yes, please.'

Erica stood up and drifted towards her kitchen leaving me with thoughts darting from A to Z that finally zeroed into the present: what has happened to the children? Including Frances that opened the door for me, it seemed like they had disappeared. Mystifying. I stood up and went in search of them. They were huddled in the children's room variously engaged but in a very unnatural atmosphere, silence. Erica's condition must have put the fear of God in them, I thought, as I shared out the goodies I brought for them but refrained from speaking to them. Better to not break the spell. When I finished, I

went back down to the livingroom. I needed the quietness to be able
to take in this version of wicked wickedness Erica was talking about.

Erica rejoined me bearing a tray loaded with all sorts of biscuits
in addition to the pot of tea. Something really was wrong. It was not
enough that she had offered me tea but she had accompanied it with
edibles. Erica, with her Araldite fists?

She put the tray down and served both of us and then without
bidding the whole story came tumbling out unhindered and I sat
there rooted. I did not interrupt her. I couldn't have. Erica would
not have heard me anyway. And it was such a bizarre story that I did
not even know what to ask. But then I remembered what she had said
about her househelp being part of the problem and not seeing any
connection to what she had just told me I asked her,

'But Erica where is Benita now and what is her role in this saga?'

'Benita is my sister's daughter and her role was continual flouting
of our authorities in this house including insulting my husband at will
and beating my children, abandoning them at will to go off to God
knows wherever which led to my telling her and my sister, her mother,
that I have had enough and was going to send her back to Nigeria, but
before I could finish drawing in a deep breath my sister arrived and
messed up my life and took her daughter and left.' I shook my head
with tiredness at having to wean Erica off the notion that she had a
sister. But I had to try again.

'Erica you don't have a sister, remember?'

'I have a sister, Gift.'

Life was complicated enough so I left well alone; if Erica said she
had a sister then it must be that she had one which our years and years
of knowing each other did not afford me the opportunity of being
aware of, or maybe Ifeoma knew, otherwise this her problem had
twisted her brain somehow. I nodded and decided that I had better
start looking to maintain my own sanity, starting with not probing
Erica further.

I commiserated with her as much as I could before driving home
with my children and a promise to call her later. As I drove home, I
mulled over Erica's narration. How could a sister, one's own blood
sister, according to Erica do her in? There must be merit in the saying
that one would live to grow grey hairs if not killed by those who knew
them from Adam, as in blood kin. Erica's problem being a case in
hand. That said sister could travel all the way from Nigeria, her anger
not dissipated by the distance, boarded and descended from various
buses to *Justice* and still had the energy to tell them that the story
upon which her sister's Refugee Status was based on, was false. And

not only that, she went ahead to prove her claims by showing them all the necessary documents she had procured for Erica, from Oluwole master forgers, copies of which were sent through DHL from Nigeria then, to back up her claims.

My God! This simply was beyond comprehension if true. A thoroughbred wickedness, with a capital W; the stuff that populated the world of nightmares. I shivered and then remembered and quickly wired off a prayer on Erica's behalf as she had requested, this was in case she was really telling the truth. The prayer point being; that *Justice* would not cancel their Refugee Status, but if they did that the solicitor her husband went to consult in Cork would be able to file for another Residency Status on their behalf based, this time, on having Irish Citizen Children. And also hoping that God still listened to people like me. Out of curiosity I had managed to ask Erica why she did not withdraw from the asylum process when she had her first child as she had advised me to do during my own asylum process. Her response was that right after her first interview, before she had even delivered, they were granted Refugee Status, which was a very big surprise to them. Because according to her the story they told was so silly and laughable that they did not expect anything out of it. It was supposed to act as a door opener, yet they were granted the Status. Believing that it didn't really matter then, afterall, Residency Status was what they wanted ultimately and Residency Status was what they got, even though based on a flimsy cock and bull story. So they did nothing and now the shit, as they say, had hit the fan.

When we got home, I tried to recapture as much of our Saturday that had been lost as I could and by the Sunday night somehow, I had succeeded in putting Osahon and his problems behind my back and our lives assumed a tentative normality. I expected him to show his hand soon enough because I could vouch that he didn't come to Ireland to say hello. But until he did I would have to hunker down and grasp at peace and stability.

*   *   *

However, for some reason, as the hours stretched into days, I gradually became edgy instead of relaxing, jumping at every sound and haranguing my children at the littlest of anything. At work I was on autopilot. Coffee became my best friend since Una, my good friend, had retreated after asking me, not once, not twice even, what was going on, without getting any satisfactory answer. She then resorted to sending hurt and doleful look towards *her so-called friend*.

When nothing whatsoever was forthcoming from me, the look turned to frost, adding another passenger to my already brimming canoe.

But how could I tell Una what was going on when I myself did not know. Or should I start by telling her the genesis of what *really* led to my self-imposed exile to Ireland? With the hope that she'd comprehend and then be able to come up with a solution? I don't think so! The few that knew about that were enough.

I did not know how the rift had degenerated so fast and wanted to mend it but did not know how. When Una and I first met in far away Donegal, she was already aware that I was a single mother of three so I had merely added that I was separated from my husband which when added to the stress of childbirth had taken its toll and led to my emotional collapse. That was enough then for Una and for myself. Who knew that Osahon would one day find his way to Ireland? Imagine what Una's reaction would be if I inflicted her with the whole saga? Talk of digging your own grave.

*   *   *

After three days I couldn't stand Una's averted eyes, pursed-lips, squared-shoulders, stiffened-back and clipped 'hi Gift' and any other class of hurt-related demeanors she could drag up and in the process dispelling any lingering hope of our usual tête-à-tête. The unseen pressure was closing in on me from all angles and I really needed an ally. So I called a truce.

During lunch break I made my way to Una's desk hoping that we could go out for lunch together as we were used to doing before she started bringing in packed lunch! I stood in front of her but when no invitation was issued to sit I did so anyway and told Una as much as I could manage mindful of the landmines.

'My husband came calling.'

Una looked at me unimpressed. Probably thinking "yeah and you think I'd be swayed by . . ." Then suddenly my words must have hit the mark for she reacted.

'What! What did you just say?'

'Osahon came to see me on Saturday.'

'Is that not your husband's name . . .' At my confirming nod she went, 'Oh my word! You silly girl, why didn't you say something?'

Some of my fear and anger at my friend's cold shoulder disappeared with that sentence.

'Una, I was overwhelmed. I mean how do you begin to deal with a man that abandoned you for over five years with two children and pregnant with the third?' At least half-truth was better than lying. The strain having been uprooted, though not burnt yet, we got ready and left for our lunch break to go and kill the rest of the gist.

'He's angling to re-enter our lives, so he said,' I threw that on the table as soon as we reached our table in our corner in Café @ Sol, 'but I won't put any stock on that.' I concluded as the fuss of our settling down subsided.

Una nodded looking distracted. Gift's ex sudden appearance or not Una still felt that she hadn't gotten a fair treatment from Gift, if she could hold on to such an explosive information for so long, four days! What else? After mulling over the situation she decided to voice her feelings out.

'Gift, I was there with you during the rough times, now that there is a hint of silver lining on your . . .'

If only you knew the definition of bad times Una my dear, I thought, but I had to cut my friend off. There was no point allowing her to go further on that vein.

'It is not like that, Una. What I failed to let on, because it was still too raw on my soul then, was that Osahon hurt me beyond words. So his sudden appearance threw me and I needed time to grapple with the situation alone and it's still not clear to me yet. Do forgive me.' Una nodded as I saw the naked pain of betrayal that was previously etched in my friend's eyes dissipate, but was immediately replaced by a deeper hurt, for me. With misted eyes she hugged me, our friendship restored, I needn't say anymore, she understood.

'The temerity of him, telling me all that drat about giving *us* a chance,' I spit out getting back to my narration.

'What the feck . . .' Una jumped in then stopped, quickly reversing out from that route. Altercations between husband and wife, even an ex, should always be waded into with cautious steps. They may bind up against you later for taking sides.

'Mnnn-mnnh. Can't you find a little space somewhere in your heart to lodge his request, think it over and see . . .'

'And see what. Look Una, no way! I said there is no way in hell I'll give that goat any chance unless over my dead body.'

Una winced.

'Was it that bad?'

'Beyond your wildest imagination Una, do you know that Lucky was a result of rape. He beat me black and blue and then raped me before throwing me out.'

Before my very eyes Una started shaking, and then followed that with tears. I was mystified.

'Una are you alright?'

She nodded.

'What is the problem then?'

She shook her head before adding, 'This your Osahon I really don't know what to make of him. Don't you think that you . . . that you should . . .' she shook her head again then asked instead, 'so what are you going to do?'

I nodded. White man, as cautious as ever.

'It's a bit hazy and complicated at the moment. But I am waiting; he will tell me what he is after.'

'Look Gift, I will respect your privacy and back off anytime you feel I am interfering too much but until then I will advise you to consult a solicitor immediately. They will help to straighten out the complication.'

'Una I'm really sorry for not being forthright with you initially, but I'd rather wait for him to make the first move.' I held Una's gaze until she nodded. I didn't want her to feel that her suggestion was not good enough.

'You are making it sound like a game of chess.'

'It is more complicated than a game of chess.' I sighed. 'But when the time is right we will go for a solicitor.' The 'we' was deliberate and it got the result.

Una beamed her trademark bright and winsome smile and I knew that I had been forgiven. I felt a little relieved to have shared my burden with somebody closer to home. Ifeoma lived too far away to be a comfort. With a cleaner air enclosing us, we dug into Una's homemade Bacon and Egg Roll tempered with the café's soup of the day.

*   *   *

As usual I picked up my children from their after-school care place on my way home from work. I was honestly relieved and felt happier. We had our dinner and everybody was sorted out and then we loitered in front of the telly waiting to go to bed. Then the doorbell went. I opened the door and then simply slammed it shut; refusing to open it to Osahon's persistent ringing thereafter. My children surrounded me with round question-mark-eyes and a slight frown of fear on their faces. But I did not waver.

PART THREE

...In the wilderness

ROME, ITALY
1998

When the Alitalia flight carrying us from Nigeria touched down at
the Leonardo da Vinci International Airport Rome, my heart skidded
alongside the tyres on the runway, and then plummeted straight
down into the pit of my stomach, with every jolt of the plane giving it
extra momentum. The stone that was my heart must have dislodged
and then split the bile sac enroute, for some bitter liquid started
spreading, quickly filling up my stomach; and then started crawling
up my throat at the same time, the acidic foul smelling fumes of the
liquid took up every space in my nostrils. I was going to choke to
death! But inspite of this knowledge, I clamped my hand firmly to
my mouth, while struggling to get a lee way against the human traffic
filling the aisle to disembark the plane as I made my way to the toilet.
No way was I going to engage in an unbecoming behaviour in public
and embarrass myself.

The banging on the door of the toilet brought me back down to
earth. I had lost count of time. I must have fainted. Or did I? I wasn't
sure of anything anymore. I rinsed my mouth, splashed water on my
face and scrambled out to encounter the green eyes of the air hostess
with the name tag, Heidi. Throughout the duration of the flight,
Heidi was kind to me, sidling down to enquire about my needs. She

must have seen the fear in my eyes; suspected the real reason behind this trip. But how could she? Was she a witch? A mind reader? At that I advised myself to better be careful and tuck my thoughts firmly into my heart to avoid spilling them, unwittingly, to a non-caring stranger. I remembered hearing somewhere that in 'abroad' nobody cared. But should strangers care anyway? I smiled at Heidi to reassure her that I was alright, on the outside, at least. Heidi smiled back, in sympathy, for she must have suspected that this lady, trying so very hard to hold herself together all this while was not alright by any standard with which alright was measured. But she did not pry—rather, she smiled deeply, this time in sisterhood, I believe, then took my hand firmly and escorted me towards the exit where two other hostesses smiled me down and out of the plane to join my husband, Osahon, who was looking visibly worried.

'Babes, I looked back and you were gone, what happened?'

'I felt sick. It must be from the lurching of the plane when it landed.'

'Oh my Princess, I knew you would be tired' He pulled me to his firm chest and held me tightly, before continuing, 'but don't worry, we will soon get to our hotel, then you will have a hot bath and rest, okay.'

Still enclosed in his embrace, I nodded. My head felt woozy and my legs weak, probably attributable to my earlier retching, but I did not want to give way to tiredness. Having drawn a little bit of strength, I stepped back from his chest and held his hand as we headed towards baggage reclaim.

As we walked, I did not bother to take in the beauty of the airport, rather with my head down I cast my mind back to how things were. I knew that Osahon loved me but was it possible to posit that it had slightly increased? Had he become even more protective of me? I had caught him several times, during the last month, looking at me with what I would call a mixture of hurt, nostalgia, desperation and sometimes even anger; as if he had lost something he could never recover again. I had asked him why once, and his reply was that he was deeply sad, his heart broken from knowing that I was willing to take up this job because I loved him. I had felt then that his answer did not say it all, because as our departure date crept closer, I was forced to acknowledge the reality that I was going to live apart from him for a while—to do a certain kind of job! I could also feel him drawing away, more and more into himself. He did not need to reveal the extent of his thoughts, I knew. And I could feel his desperation rising each dawn.

In a two-equals-one relationship equation like ours, heartbeats are one, you react to any problem facing either one of you as if it's yours exclusively; there was just no logical explanation to capture the essence of love. However, I had him promise to carve this sacrifice on his soul for ease of reference, because it was not an easy decision for me to make. I could not even explain why I had accepted. All I knew was that my heart splintered into minuscule pieces each time Osahon was in pain. I was so determined to take that pain away that I did not stop to examine the finer details of how the job would be carried out or of any danger to myself at the time. Now at every opportunity the reality of what I would be doing in the next year would rise like nausea threatening to choke, to engulf me. But I fought it, like a wounded lioness. Finally I was rewarded: I succeeded with locking down my feeling and thinking faculties, my reality and sanity. Remembering that the proceeds would pave the way to the actualization of our shared dreams helped greatly. Then envisioning how it'd be afterwards not only strengthened me but tipped the scale.

Osahon's suggestion that we rest for two weeks in Rome before we leave for Torino to start my new life was quite handy, I used part of the time to work on my sanity and reality. Only then did I relax to enjoy our brief spell. The next twelve months was a long time, long enough to berate myself.

Every morning thereafter, armed with the tourist guide pamphlets, Subway, Tram and Bus timetables, we started touring the City of Rome and all it had to offer with a vengeance, partly to know the city and partly to keep our minds off the weight of the bottom-line that was the reality of the trip. We got confused and then lost several times, what with all houses looking the same; the same matchbox glued to the next, every street the exact replica of the one before and we could not read the maps. Finally we took our fate in our own hands; drew our own map with specific landmarks, as we saw it, to guide our tentative steps with the consolation that in abroad people did not get lost just like that.

It was then that I noticed the bitter cold that was trying to slice through my skin to get to my blood and freeze it and render me immobile. I gave up on my lips: dried, cracked and puckered, even the healthy dose of Vaseline, which I fiercely applied continuously, did not help, rather it made them peel, exposing tender reddish skin for more mauling by the icy winds. They were beyond repair! My fingers could neither bend nor straighten from the cold even after holding steaming cups of tea. Our love-making was reduced to a half-hearted fumbling as neither of us wanted any part of our body exposed to the killer cold. Sometimes it was sunny but we had learnt to not be deceived by that; for you did not feel any heat from the rays of the supposed sun at all, as if it was meant to only just brighten the city. It was a marvel how God managed it; the terrible heat in Nigeria and the extreme cold in Rome.

I had not been abroad before and neither had Osahon. Yes, we had seen *Oyibo* in ones and twos in Nigeria. Yes, we were quite outnumbered on the plane. But we were not prepared for the sea of white faces, milling all over the place, the cacophony of voices that would reach crescendos, in very strange singsong flow of words with unending flailing of hands. It was unbelievable, very contrary to my expectations. Were *Oyibos* not supposed to be a tribe of silent people, moving about very fast, faces down, just so as to not encounter any eye? Mmh. These people certainly went about seeking out eyes, shouting greetings, smiling, touching, embracing, pounding a back here, and patting a head there; a very happy and very noisy people. Like the Yorubas back home in Lagos.

My other preoccupation had not given me the opportunity to imagine what Rome would be like. Sure it'd be a metropolitan city with diverse number of people, different tongues, cultures and worldviews, mingling to achieve their purposes in life but inspite of this knowledge there was no actual mental picture. But on reconnecting with the world after my thought lock-down I was struck right away by the stark differences in the colour of the people and in how everything was orderly, somehow. The cars, the trams, the buses, the human traffic, etc., etc., behaved themselves, the traffic rules obeyed by the vehicles, and the people were not being threatened to be run over by the buses, *okadas* and human traffic as was characteristic of Lagos. But Rome, like Lagos, looked like where pickpockets and all sorts of thievery would thrive. And I made this assumption because some scallywag had tried to sell off gold jewelry to us and you do not do that with goods whose genealogy was intact especially when said scallywag was hiding the gold inside his folded palms while his eyes whirled surreptitiously around to note that the police was not after him. In these respects both countries are jungles in their different ways with Darwin's survival of the fittest as the backdrop.

Both of us being born Catholics we convinced ourselves, in an unspoken unanimity, to visit St. Peter's Basilica first, even when we knew that we should not; knowing that you had committed to do a certain unsavory thing what would you be looking for in the house of God? It didn't make sense, but we went anyway and in there were rendered speechless. We beheld heaven! I had reared back shivering with fear and anticipation; I was frightened as I stood before the glorious house of God literally. I looked around furtively expecting an Angel to step out at any moment to drag us on our ears to God for proper admonition. When nothing of that sort happened I overcame my fear and relaxed, opened my eyes very wide and gradually the vista insinuated itself into my being.

The Basilica was beautiful, glorious and magnificent, standing proudly on a large expanse of obedient space referred to by our guide as the square. As we continued to imbibe the scenery before us, I became self-conscious and uncertain all of a sudden again and had to look away crestfallen. How could I be here? I had no right knowing my intentions thereafter. Osahon must have felt my thoughts for he held out his arms and clasped mine firmly as a sliver of tears silently glided down my face trying to outrace the beating of my heart. Osahon let me cry. When the tears ceased, he wiped my face, kissed my brows and then led us into the bowels of the Cathedral proper at the heel of newer other tourists, as we had got separated from our specific group. Our hearts were too heavy then and had made our legs weak so we could not keep up with them. When you're heavily burdened, you can not mix well with those that are lightly burdened or even unyoked as everything about you seems to drag or lag. We brought up the rear, threading tentatively, while inching deeper and deeper into the Cathedral. But even though we were surrounded by the thronging faithfuls, we felt alone. And as the day wore on, we got separated completely from all groups and ended up spending the rest of the day inside the Basilica with her serene hue enfolding us. We forgot to eat while moving from place to place in a daze, our bruised hearts lulled by the interval tolling of bells, the soft singing from the hidden choir? And the cooing of pigeons or was it the doves, as part of the surrounding aura. It was a peaceful place, this heaven.

At twilight, we stumbled back to the hotel and were glad to find our friend, Enzio, on duty. Gladly, we allowed him to take charge of us, happy to accept whatever he ordered for us from room service. The Bolognese sauce that accompanied the spaghetti was unforgettable to affirm Enzio's claim of spaghetti Bolognese being the hotel's specialty. It was not that I saw myself as a veteran or anything of the sort where sauces were concerned, but it must have represented the best as Bolognese sauces went. I had never tasted anything like that before. In Nigeria we ate our spaghetti with regular tomato stew tempered with fried egg or corn beef. Well, maybe posh people of Nigeria eat their spaghetti the Italian way; having traveled well in their time. If only I was in Italy for pleasure I could have broadened my cooking skills, which would be an invaluable addition to my womanly-skills. Oh well.

As the days merged into one another, flying past, we became more and more adept at using the Tram, the Metro and even the buses; the pushing, shoving and jostling to board any of these transportations was minimal and at least they waited tamely while you took your time to board with all the members of your body intact and fully seated with you inside. This was unlike what we were used to in Nigerian cities where only one-half of your body may have boarded before the driver screeched off. It would seem that the conductor's job was to curse you for not being fast enough thus making them to not only lose the next customer, but made them to not leave fast enough to avoid the menace that was the traffic-control officer, who would have sidled up for his share of the day's earnings. All these delivered not minding that you were still hanging somewhere with the members of your body draped variously on the other passengers; who in turn would lend their voices to the prevailing rumpus, shouting either at you or at the conductor or the driver. It was a wonder that people living in Nigerian cities were sane at all, as they had so much to contend with!

I also realized that my earlier summation was not correct for the people were really not as friendly as I had previously thought; a conclusion I had reached based on the boisterous nature of the natives. Or had they perceived the reason for our mission in Italy or what? Whatever. Of immediate importance for us initially was to get directions from them which had proved somehow an impossible task made worse by Osahons' pointing, flinging and gesticulating of hands in an attempt to convey our queries to the Italians. Once they had ascertained that we could not speak the language, it became a game for them; they would calmly wait for us to finish the question, with mispronounced names and all, then assail us with their own hand-flinging, head-shaking and barrage of words before moving away, sometimes laughingly pointing us to a false lead. Very frustrating. But that did not deter us as I had since suspected that our continued city-trawling was to keep well away from our thoughts, thoughts that'd end up demanding the meaning of the step I was about to take, some sort of justification for my decision, so this traipsing somehow occupied us.

Finally we heeded Enzio's urgings to visit the Colosseum; the international symbol of Rome, because according to him, it was one of those things one should not fail to see and be proud of. Though the Colosseum stood proudly, overwhelming, reminding you of Rome's reputed sporting supremacy in the distant past, it was also a crumbling old ruin, a disappointment. I could not physically see beyond that. So I surmised that maybe seeing the St. Peter's Basilica first had eclipsed the effect of the Colosseum, or maybe we had viewed it with the wrong eyes, the eyes of an outsider. Whatever it was, the Colosseum only evoked emotions that old ruins could evoke in a stranger. Nothing.

Enzio had failed to realize that we were not Romans and therefore could not be expected to feel pride about Rome's National Monument however colossal. The feelings of pride in anybody must spring from ownership; belongingness could elicit such emotions as pride when you view ruins.

During our wanderings, we concluded that white man must like eating; because for every third or fourth house on the various streets, there was bound to be one type of food joint or the other; cafés, restaurants, fast food outlets, etc. We did our best to sample different kinds of food as we went along, savouring the various gourmets on offer. We also observed that for every meal you start with bread; long or short, hard or soft accompanied by soup, before you progressed to the main meal proper. However, you could buy only soup or bread without bothering with any other food, or as it caught your fancy. Of course at this stage we had long since acquired the habit of eating this particular snack called crisp, very popular. We devoured bars of chocolates, munching away as if there was no tomorrow. We had also acquired the habit of holding hands and kissing as we took every inch of step. It was a magical life and we savoured every minute. In the afternoons, the whole city was practically shut down for siesta, very strange, but who are we to defy tradition, we took siesta at the appointed time dutifully, to awake refreshed, and then back on the prowl, unrestrained, to the various Via Veneto's, shopping malls, and having coffees in tiny cups. We had quickly adapted to white-man lifestyle, we believed. It was more than these of course, but while in Rome you behaved like the Romans.

When the two weeks we allotted ourselves were up, we were ready for business. We bought our train tickets and I with reservations and niggling doubts, like a lamb being led to the alter of sacrifice, followed my husband Osahon to Torino, our final destination, where I was going to pluck money from the streets, literally!

Torino

DECEMBER, 1998

As we drove away from the train station in Okere's Opel Corsa, the scenery became more expanses but busyness sparser telling that Torino was not like Rome. However these observations could not distract me from a more distressing thought; for arriving at the train station, we were met by Okere. I was distressed because Okere was Osahon's childhood friend and I was not aware that Osahon knew anybody in Italy, never mind having him pick us up. And this was not the case of not having my ears close to the ground as befitting a woman, as my mother was wont to say. Osahon did not mention, as a matter of fact, that he had discussed this *thing* with anybody. That went to show how much attention I was paying to the success of this business venture. Of course, I knew that somebody would have to help us at some stage but not somebody that close to home surely? I mulled over that and decided that my best bet should be to adopt a 'wait and see' attitude.

Okere whisked us away swiftly from the city to the outskirts and finally to his abode in a housing estate. He must be doing well, I noted; new car, spacious 3-bed house in what I concluded must be a good neighbourhood. He obviously had squashed the bug of poverty that seemed to have stricken Osahon and myself. I was still worried about who I was supposed to be, since Osahon did not introduce me to Okere as anything other than "meet Gift". When we were led into the living room, I sank gratefully into the couch and watched my husband, looking for details to hold on to, little, little things about him to sear into my consciousness. He was not what you would call a handsome man, never had been, but he commanded attention with his 6 ft 4" all-man height, well-toned muscles, with very interesting eyes, flared nose as a proper African, and wide mouth endowed with full lips. I bored my eyes into him as I needed to file everything to call up for comfort when I would be lonely, for loneliness was an affliction that would strike me very soon. Was I supposed to strike up friendship with my fellow sisters-in-the-game or what? What kind of friends would I make? What kind of women would they be? After working all night—assuming they worked all night—would they dare to show their faces in civilized places in daylight? They must have their lives in compartments definitely, whipping each part up to suit the time and occasion. There was no thought concerning this job that was comforting which was why I had refused to think, but it seemed that all the reprieves I got trudging Rome had deserted me as we got closer to the D-day.

Okere introduced his wife Oya and their two children to us and then invited us to feel at home and, as if to lend credence to that invitation, Oya asked me to join her in the kitchen. I scrambled up immediately and followed her, happy to be in another woman's company, leaving Osahon to talk with Okere, while the children clambered upstairs as instructed by their father. In the kitchen I pulled out a chair and sat down not wanting to speak first; I did not want to put the wrong foot out.

*   *   *

Oya, pretending to be busy observed Gift from under her lashes, taking in her physical composition; sophisticated, very reserved and hot. But a wife? She shuddered from the thought. *Na wah*! She swallowed to make sure that her thoughts did not tinge her voice before she addressed Gift.

'I have lunch ready and will be glad if you can serve it with me.'

Gift shrugged her consent and got up to help gather all that would be needed to serve said lunch.

As they continued to work to serve the food, Oya could not contain herself anymore as curiosity had wrought havoc to her composure. The calm demeanor she had put in place cracked and she blurted, 'I understood that you want to *work* for your husband?' The word work had never been made to sound so repulsive. *What was Osahon playing at?* I fumed inwardly. These were his friends from his village, at least the man according to him. If they were in on our secret how could I ever hope to raise up my head in my husband's village? Even with money! He should have chosen a total stranger to put us through this business. I was furious, but calmly I nodded and then asked, 'What does it really involve, do you know?'

There I had asked the first question, thus acknowledging that I was really going through with it. My question seemed to stop Oya in her tracks and she stared into space. Finally she moved and sat down beside me and held out her hands. I placed mine in them and then she looked up directly into my eyes and said, 'I want you to know that marriage is like a package, when you open your own what you see is what you have been given, but how you manage the content in the package, your husband, the children that will come and yourself is up to you.' Oya stopped speaking and looked away as if unsure of what to say next, but then she returned her gaze to my face and continued, 'You know, if you have been living in Italy you will know that all sorts of things happen, but one thing you should be aware of is that it is a rough, vicious trade. You are a beautiful woman and if I am not mistaken you will not have it easy and I do not have any word to convey it to you properly, you can only experience it and everybody's experiences vary. But if you keep your head, you will succeed. My husband has contacts that will help to set you up properly, all said and done, the main problem you may have, however, will be from your husband. Be careful. If you ever need help come to me and if I can I will help.'

Rough and vicious? This was a dimension that I had not considered. What exactly did she mean by that? Not wanting her to switch to another topic I quickly asked, 'Vicious?'

Oya smiled wryly and answered, 'Yes, vicious. It is not your regular kind of job, you know? It is very competitive and the customers are not exactly saints but hard-nosed set of people who are ready to extract beyond their money's worth, at least in this country. It is a business where you need a strong heart to survive.' She drew in a long slow breath, released my hands and continued, 'I am not trying to scare you, I just do not want you to be taken unaware, being new to the game and the country, but it has its good sides supposedly. If you are lucky you will meet the nicer ones and you will make money fast, but I would advise you to push for your own 'office' instead of standing on the street. But that shouldn't worry Madam Mary will see to that, she will do you well.' This time Oya got up and went to one of the units and brought down drinking glasses and water jugs indicating that for now our *discussion* was over.

I decided then that I had better stick to the temporary policy I had in place; close my mind to everything until the time came. I did not need this information now, it might just push me to want to apply some thoughts to this venture and I had refused to do just that. As for my husband being my "main problem," as she put it, I'd not even dwell on that either.

However, I concluded that Oya would not be interested in what my thoughts and future strategies were but would expect an appropriate reply to her advice instead, so I made my own short speech in return.

'Thank you Oya, my sister, it comforts me to know that I have somebody to call my own and to come to. You may not know it, but I feel much better now and I am happy that you pointed out these things to me. I will be careful and will not hesitate to come to you if need be.'

Oya waved away my thanks and carried plates down from the upper shelves of the unit. I got up and took them from her and set them on the dining table as I struggled to beat down the rough, vicious and hard-nosed images that started to crowd in.

After we had eaten and cleared the table Oya called her children down to eat which they did in the kitchen, while in the livingroom, Okere immediately launched into the *talk* right away.

'Depending on the amount of money you are looking to make, a year maximum should do it as you no *dey* owe anybody for sponsorship *na im* be say you are your own master, the only thing be say you go need to pay for 'protection' and a 'stand." I looked at my husband expecting him to say something; ask questions that would elucidate the job details but he did not, or rather, he did but not what I expected.

'I think I understand what you mean Okere but we will work all of that out with Madam Mary as you said.'

Okay. So they had been talking? I couldn't help but wonder at what would have happened if I had made this journey alone as I had initially wanted. Would I have coped? It was good that Osahon had insisted on accompanying me.

Osahon and Okere maintained a steady stream of conversation; starting from their naughty days in primary school, through the wild time of secondary school and gradually working their way up to the present while I pretended to be deep in thought so as not to be drawn into any sort of conversation. When I resurfaced, it was over two hours later and Osahon was shaking me awake. I had slept off. I stumbled up to the room we were shown earlier with Osahon behind me. I managed to change into my nightdress, burrowed deeply into the sleeping cover and dropped off into another dreamless sleep.

*   *   *

Madam Mary's house was large and rambling and she lived alone. How depressing. The particular room where we were received for the 'business meeting' was tastefully decorated; the floral-patterned curtains were easy on the eyes and matched the buttery-cream soft leather sofas. The centre glass table was not cluttered with only a bowl of fruit adorning it. The mid-day sunshine, streaming in, made everything bright and cheerful, all this I noted while observing and cataloguing our host, my would-be madam. She was seated on a very high chair, more like a throne, and looked down on us imperiously. Her face must have been beautiful once but was now overshadowed by a double chin currently layered with Fashion Fair 'maximum coverage' pancake and her eyes made up with the black kohl of Nefertiti fame. Women blessed with-good pair of boobs and not-so-good pairs usually did a good job of flaunting them, but Madam Mary must have a hell of a job trying to 'unflaunt' hers with corsets and all, for she was over-abundantly blessed. When she had finished assessing her guests, she waved us to sit down and stood up herself.

She was a very tall lady with the upper part of her body supported by a pair of long k-legs that were encased in a bum-moulding jeans skirt that tapered off to reveal sparrow-ankles. Her bum was like that of a sugar-ant. She must have been in love with gold jewelry for she had quite a fair amount in its purest carat sense on her. Her hair-do defied all descriptions.

In a deep sonorous voice befitting her bearing Madam Mary asked Okere to bring 'beverages' for us and her usual for her. I looked at Okere with the tail of my eyes. Did he know this woman beyond a handshake? "Bring my usual?" But reminding myself that I was just a JJC in the entire scenario, I moved deeper into the sofa to watch events.

Our 'beverages' turned out to be assorted bottles of hot and soft drinks accompanied by deeply fried 'local' chicken thighs stacked high in a deep bowl while her 'usual' was a concoction of an indeterminate something in a frosty glass.

We dug into the beverages and after a while madam declared the meeting open with her first sentence which was more of an attack. I was not surprised for she had been shooting baleful darts at me since we arrived. Now the reason was laid bare. And I could see that she was a fearless woman.

'She is beautiful!' was the opening bark. Then she qualified the bark, 'I did not bargain for that o, neither will I be asked to bear responsibility of any trouble that will come. But if you insist then she will have to pay $500 monthly to enable me provide extra 'eyes' for her.'

Osahon appeared taken aback by Madam Mary's vehemence judging by his croaky voice when he managed to squeeze out, 'Could you tell us exactly what it is all about,' but noting the change in Madam's demeanor he quickly inserted, 'not that we are questioning your fee, it's just that we will want to understand what is what, because we are new in this business.'

Madam Mary visibly relaxed her ruffled features and then went on to enlighten us by declaring that, 'The business is simple: all she has to do is make up her mind that she is going to do it and the rest is history.' I felt that Madam Mary had not said anything new since this meeting commenced. I had always thought that in the man/woman relationship scenario, being beautiful was considered one of the good assets for any woman, but maybe in the business of prostitution it was not. But I would really be grateful if this Madam would be more forthcoming with needed information. Finally I summoned up courage, bravely looked Madam Mary squarely in the eyeballs, smiled and said, 'Madam please tell me all you think I need to know and I will try not to get myself into any trouble at all.'

Madam Mary did not erupt to my surprise, she smiled instead then said, 'My daughter, *na* your cunning go do the trick, *dem* rules go confuse you. But don't worry, we go work *am* out, me and you, trust me.' She moved her bum this way and that way on her throne as if to release tension from the tight skirt, drank from her indeterminate-looking drink, delicately patted her lips with a tiny purple lacy handkerchief and continued as if she had solved all my problems, 'This lady will need double protection from the police, from the Mafia and from her fellow girls, but that should not worry you now that we have all agreed.' The next sentence, I felt, was addressed to me but with her eyes, 'Once the word is out that she is my girl, nobody will dare to misbehave.' She bared her teeth in Osahon's direction, to remind him not to be stingy with protection money, I suppose, before she continued, 'However, I want you to appreciate my partnership here and I will not entertain any nonsense from you, young man.' This said with her jowl quivering at Osahon. She then smiled, folded her hand across her enormous bosom and waited for any of us to contradict her. We didn't.

Osahon quickly adjusted his face suitably and apologized for giving the wrong impression, and promised to make the payments later.

But it seemed she hadn't finished with Osahon yet for she boomed, 'I don't deal with "later",' then turning to Okere barked, 'Where you find this one bring *sef*,' and then swinging back to Osahon continued, 'Look here mister, if you are here to do business with me, then seal am right away, you fit no enter this house again.' She pierced him again with her heavily kholed lids, then notified us while pointing at me, 'This madam will be on apprentice for now, so the fee is upfront and for three months as she is not expected to make money as she *dey* learn. I no *dey* protect for credit and won't start now. I have my reputation!'

Osahon's eyes immediately bulged, became glacial, shiny and dark, not unlike Madam Mary's and I knew why: we did not have up to $1,500 to pay upfront after our 'honeymoon.' Okere quickly intervened, brought out his wallet, counted out the money and paid up.

'Mmmh,' Madam Mary snorted.

Afterwards, we thanked Madam Mary profusely and as we made our way gingerly to the front door we heard her querulous demand.

'Where you *dey* go, you?'

We turned and I could feel the men stare at her with trepidation. I felt nothing. Madam indicated that I should stay back because she expected me to start work later that night. But Osahon pleaded that he needed to sort some things out with me before 'we' could commence. Maybe it was the way he looked or something else she must have glimpsed, because Madam Mary smiled and said that she understood perfectly well how these things were but that we should not take too long. Then she advised Osahon that for his own interest he should go home and allow the woman to make a success of the job. Osahon assured her that he would be traveling back in two day's time.

When we had successfully left Madam's presence, Okere apologized on behalf of Madam Mary. 'You guys have to understand that in her line of business people would shaft you at the slightest opportunity and in her case she did not have it easy when she first arrived, so I heard. She has come a long way from then, but you can never be too careful. As I told you earlier, it is good to have her on your side. She may be expensive but through her you will deal with the crème de la crème of our fine Torino society and make it in no time.'

We nodded in unison as if previously agreed to accept anything we were told even if we did not agree. So rearranging our faces to that of 'feeling sorry' for Madam Mary, in view of what she went through, hoping, on my part, to elicit more information from Okere about my new boss, we nodded in unison. But it obviously didn't work. Okere did not say anything more. We went out and boarded his car and he drove away.

Since nothing was forthcoming, I discarded that demeanor and withdrew into my own thoughts, as soon as we hit the road while the men continued, rather more verbosely from where they left off last night. The adrenalin released while in Madam's presence must have loosened their tongues. Three days later Osahon left.

Osahon left for Nigeria and took along with him my essence; leaving me bereft and lonely. He was the one that made my world spin vibrantly afterall. But I knew that I should move on; it was not about my state of being, it was about making a success of this venture, so I'd have to subsume myself for now. Quietly, I resolved that even if it took the last breath in me, I'd do all that was within my power to elevate our lives to what they should be. So "rough" and "vicious" beware. I shook my head sadly at realizing that I was only trying to encourage myself, the fact was, I was afraid.

Oya's welcoming smiles of previous days vanished as she peered at me with unenthusiastic eyes when I returned with Okere from dropping Osahon at the train station for his onward journey to Nigeria. As I sat down on the sofa, I did a swift calculation and concluded that we had not been in Oya's company for more than thirty minutes at a time since our arrival three days ago. Therefore, I could not have done anything during this very short period of time to offend her without my being aware of it. Maybe it was because I had not been helping her around the house? But she should understand that we would have time for that later, for now all arrangements had to be concluded quickly so that Osahon could leave and allow me to work. But Oya's clouded face and reluctant demeanor extended till late in the evening making me uneasy. I had tried to be alone with her, helped to cook and clean, even put her children to bed which was quite exhausting, still . . .

I had assumed that we would be friends afterall, silly me. The arrangement with the Okeres was that I would live with them long enough to make money, pay off our indebtedness to them, then find and move into my own place. This I envisaged would take me up to three months or more to achieve. What with my 'apprenticeship' and all. Oya's current behaviour did not portend a very warm stay, but what could I do? Swallow and grin, that's what.

I was in the kitchen trying hard to get some food through my dry throat when I heard Okere drive out. Quick like lightning Oya came into the kitchen and informed me right away that she was not in support of my living with them: 'You sharp-eyed girls will not think twice about messing with other people's husband. Not that I expect it of you, but one never knows, and I am not willing to find out. I offered to help if you need me, but I did not offer to house you and I will be happier to help if you do not live in my house. So you make arrangements and move out immediately. Tomorrow will be too far. Okere need not know about this conversation and it is for your own good.'

The proverbial *it never rains but pours* sprang into my mind. This was certainly a deluge. And look at me thinking that mere housework was the issue here! I sighed heavily, tilted my head backwards resting it on the high-backed dining chair, and closed my eyes. This was the first unforeseen clog in the family's wheel of fortune.

What was I going to do? I thought I had acquired a family in Oya and Okere but obviously I knew nothing. *Oya, aren't you the sly one,* I thought. But who could blame her for taking such a stand? If one really dug into her words, they made sense. She had to protect her territory and who better to do it than her? Men do not see things the way women do or maybe they do but pretend not to anyway, for ulterior motives. I understood the route Oya was walking.

But of what use was this insight to me?

I should be more concerned about being without a roof over my head. Who would help me in this strange city? I told Oya that I'd heard her and would try and move out as soon as I could gather myself together.

As if summoned, Madam Mary called, thus nipping my potential threat of homelessness. My internship was about to start. I packed my luggage and left for Madam Mary's. She had a client who needed my services instantly.

*   *   *

My first day on the job did not start well at all, not by any standard. There was no customer awaiting my attention. After repeating basically the same words of two days ago she dispatched me off to the street to ply my trade.

I arrived at my place of work and was amazed at the number of girls on the street already. Some clustered together, others standing on their own. They were all scantily dressed! Smoke from their cigarettes fogging the already foggy night. I located a patch further away from the girls and took possession while shivering from the cold and at the same time trying to keep a *sharp-eyed* lookout for customers. I tried to search the inner recesses of my mind to see if I could pull out anything at all that would aid me on how to snag a customer. When I couldn't, I gave up and resolved to approach any car that stopped by me and try to convince whoever that I was equal to any task, *Pretty Woman* style.

I was freezing to death, even in my multi-layered clothing, and not sure that my mouth, which by now had clamped together, could open to enable me to solicit for custom. Then out of nowhere, somebody approached but certainly not a man. It was one of my co-workers and on getting closer she stretched out her leg and raked both of mine up. It was too swift to describe. As I went down, it occurred to me that I must have became weightless in the period that I stood out there, otherwise why was I floating? Before I could pry my lips loose to emit any sort of sound, the rest of the girls descended on me. They kicked, slapped, bit and shouted at me.

I lay there, senseless with pain, but I made sure that my face and head were hidden from both the torrent of vitriolic abuse and the fierce kicking. When the kicking subsided, I curled up and held tenaciously to dear life, not daring to even as much as open my eyes.

What did I do? I hadn't snagged any customer yet and hardly spoke to any living soul since securing my 'office'.

Then I heard one of the girls hiss.

'Who made you think that you can show your ugly face here?'

Then I knew.

My so-called beauty was already at work here, and my confusion at Madam Mary's tirade against it became even more confusing. But one thing was clear to me: these girls were afraid of me, afraid of my beauty, of my taking their customers away from them, but was this not a free-for-all kind of work?

I stood up shakily and looked at the girls crowded around me, and said, 'My name is Gift and I would want to use this opportunity to thank you girls for your warm welcome.'

One of them broke through the rank, stuck her face into mine and hissed, 'We want you out of here now! And if you know what is good for you, then do just that. You hear me?' She clapped, highly incensed.

I didn't say a word.

'We don't want you here, you are bad luck,' she stated. Then she moved further into my face, if that was possible, as she continued, 'Who you dey work for *sef*?' With her hand akimbo on her waist, her extended right foot tapping to an unknown music, she waited, her head now slanted to the side, for my answer.

'Sisters, please do not take offence. I need to work. I need to earn money. Please don't send me away. I have come from a far place, please,' I groveled.

'Who you dey work for, you fool?' she asked again, this time impatiently.

'Na Madam Mary,' I answered reluctantly, reverting to Pidgin English, apparently the lingua franca here.

'Na she say make you come here?' she wanted to know.

'Yes,' was all I was able to mumble, hoping that Madam Mary's 'protection' extended to these particular girls: they did not look like that sort of thing worked on them.

The girls moved away and conferred among themselves, briefly, in low tones, and then the same girl came back.

'If Madam Mary say make you work here, you work here but nobody go help you. If you want help, join our association and then we can talk, but not tonight. Make you no tell Madam Mary anything ooh, we no wan her wahala.'

I was relieved. But join an association? Association of what? Prostitutes? These people are not serious.

Meanwhile, what was I going to do that night since they had ordered that I go away? So I asked, and the reply came, 'If *na* Madam Mary send you true true, make you work, but we go check am, as we no like am when people think say *dem* go just *tanda* for our patch anyhow. We can be harsh you know?' cracked the wiry one that had raked me down, their spokesperson of sorts, while the other girls looked on stonily, nodding in agreement. I thanked them profusely for their generosity, and limped to a corner to nurse my wounds and watch events from there.

One by one, most of the girls left with their patrons and eventually, it was down to me and the wiry one, whose name I had come to learn was Ofure. Not that anybody did the honours, I overhead when Ofure engaged briefly in a conversation with the girl standing next to me.

As we waited, Ofure stalked about, smacking her heels impatiently on the pavement in frustration. She should have been on the move by now, I surmised. Maybe her customers did not want any business today or maybe they took other girls from other patches. Who knows? Though a truce had been called, I did not want to incur Ofure's wrath, so any time she stormed past me, I would vigorously rub on my bloodied top, inspect my shoes, and scratch my neck that'd make me turn the other way, all in a bid to avoid looking at her.

'If my customer comes and you dare to raise as much as your eyelash, I will bite you,' she suddenly barked, very close to my ear. I jumped, taken aback. Bite me *ke*? And how did she get so close without my being aware? Dangerous chick, this.

'Let me know when they arrive and I will disappear,' I offered, wondering why she did not speak in their trademark Pidgin-English now.

'Oh you will know alright. They are my biggest customers.'

'Just so that we don't misunderstand each other, wink immediately you sight them,' I suggested, and then wondered if winking was such a good idea in a dark place like this, but I kept my peace.

As it happened Ofure's clients came in a convoy of cars and demanded that I come with them. Ofure did not like this, but I smiled in my mind: he who paid the piper called the tune. Her chest rose and fell in anger, like a toad's after a fast run, but I couldn't care less. I was on my way to earn my first money. Now I'd know exactly what really transpired.

As we sat, side by side, in the back of the car, she hissed from the side of her mouth. 'No one messes with my customers or else . . .' she swallowed the rest of the threat but I couldn't care less. One on one I was sure that I would break her skinny frame.

*   *   *

I was disappointed at not rendering any service; so as to, at least, get that out of the way, but having consoled myself that tomorrow is another day, I got up from the bed where I had slept with my customer, dressed up and crept out on to the short corridor across the room only to discover that I had bumped into the dining room of the house. On espying Ofure, I quickly retreated and ducked, flattening myself against the wall: I needed to get my wits, the false bravery in the car, full of Ofure's customers, had deserted me this morning. I hadn't unraveled Ofure's threat of last night yet and I never did get enough time to fine tune the details of exactly what would happen as she had left that bit hanging. But it was too late; Ofure had seen me and pounced.

'Did you steal from him?'

'I beg your pardon?'

'I said, did you steal from him or have you gone deaf, eh?'

'Look here Ofure, I may have chosen to be a prostitute but I must have you know that I am not a thief.'

'Big deal. How am I to know that?' she taunted.

Fiam!

Something swished past and my handbag was gone. And before I could digest what had just happened, it was being upturned by Ofure on the dining table, madly searching for something. I was very furious and with what I considered a poisonous voice demanded, 'May I be told what is going on here exactly and has been going on since last night? Do I know you before now Ofure? Why have you taken it upon yourself to take me out, *dem* send you?' Not getting any reply from Ofure who was still very busy, I sat down on one of the dining chairs and continued but this time mumbling to myself instead, bitterly.

Ofure found what she was looking for and waved it gleefully at me.

'No be you talk say you no be thief? *Na wetin* be this? Where you get this kin money, eh? Answer me. Where? Miss English.'

Ofure was seriously in frenzy and the reason eluded me yet so I sat there and watched her prancing about.

Then quietly, after she had calmed down, I asked, 'Ofure what is really going on? Since we met, you have engineered my being beaten up and have continued to threaten me for one thing or the other. As it is, we happen to be on the same patch, would it not be better if you give me a list of the rules and regulations and save us all these frothing all the time?'

Ofure squealed with laughter.

'You know, you are a strange one. Written rules and regulations indeed, how did you come about this amount of money *jare?*'

'My client gave it to me.'

'How come?'

I sighed. I might as well explain if I hoped to get anything out of this one.

'When we arrived last night, he went straight to bed and asked me to undress and join him. I did only to realize that he has slept off. This morning when he woke up, he was annoyed about something I must have done or did not do. But he was rather rushed, on his way out though he peeled out some notes and dropped them on me, then asked me to keep my Wednesdays free from now on.'

'Just like that?'

I nodded.

'So you did nothing, yet he gave you so much, is that what you are telling me?'

I nodded again.

Ofure looked me up and down, sighed, nodded, and then commented dryly. 'Your body good *sha*, maybe *na im* make *am*. Now you must not allow him to over sleep again, never, and keep your

Wednesdays free as he said. You have just acquired your own regular patron.'

'What is this stealing business all about?'

'How much are you paying your sponsor?'

'$500 dollars a month, excluding rent.'

'What! What do you mean? Are you sure you're a regular *ashawo* with a controller?' she screamed at me. This Ofure girl is crazy, that's the only conclusion I could reach; any and everything sets her off.

'You are paying your sponsor $500 a month for protection!?' Ofure rubbed at her eyes, as if to clear them of cobwebs, looked closely at me then asked, 'Where you *sef* come from?' But she continued immediately without waiting for my answer, so the $60,000 regular fee to free yourself no do you *abi*, na *im* make you add this $6,000 protection, as *jara eh*?' Ofure looked baffled, shaped her mouth to say something but then stopped, shook her head as her demeanor changed which also affected the direction of our discussion as she said, 'Anyway, to be able to raise your sponsor's money in no time, you must steal from your customers, but not the regulars, because they know you and would come back and break your neck.'

I nodded. I had no intentions of stealing from anybody, but the dictum that no knowledge was a waste made me probe further.

'How do I steal from them?'

'*Dey* no *de* teach person how to steal my friend, which kind person you be *sef*?' As if she didn't just finish shouting at me, she asked, 'Where do you live? Because we have to be on our way, in case you haven't noticed, this place is not our personal mansion.'

I knew I had not asked enough questions but it seemed that prickly Ofure did not want to talk anymore.

'I stay with Madam Mary for now.'

'That is not a wise thing to do. You must do quick and move otherwise you will not be able to save any money for yourself until you have paid off all your debt first!'

'That is alright with me for now. I needed to get my bearings.'

'Suit yourself,' she threw at me as she gathered her things ready to leave.

I did same and on our way to board the tram to the city asked, 'How do we charge for a session?'

'Oh fuck. Are you a researcher?'

'No.'

'It's $20 per come, converted from Lira,' she conceded with a chuckle.

'And he must pay before he comes, otherwise you'll have to whistle for your money *Oyibo* no *dey waste time to come,* what he needed is just your hole, for say five minutes. Sometimes you may only need to massage them with your hand and they come. The important thing is to get them to come and as fast as you can. If it takes him longer to come, you collect another $20.'

'OK. OK. But why pay for a room in a hotel just for a five minutes job?'

'Who told you that? You are full of weird ideas, this girl. If you are charging $20 per five minute how much will it cost to travel to the hotel alone? A*bi* your *pussy na* gold? You have to be sharp in this business girl. I don't know what you came to Italy to do but if you are going to work this work, then you have to accept that you are on the street prostitute in what they call the 'red light district' to service drive-by clients in the night and sometimes during the day if you want to. You hear me? Here, we do it here—on the street corner, or in the customers' car.' Ofure eyed me sternly as if to deter me from contesting *our* job description.

Ofure's method of teaching, though irritating, was straight to the point. No-holds-barred-style. But then in this profession, should she not be? I hoped I would not turn out like her too. Just then the tram arrived and we agreed to meet later in the evening at Café Noir on Bundesling Veneto, so that we could talk some more before walking down to our patch.

Before I boarded the tram, she advised me to always keep away from her when at the patch, at least for now, and to manage to snare as many customers as I could. Because, I would be living in a fool's paradise if I thought that what I collected last night was the norm, it was not. Last night was special.

She also informed me that I must accompany her next Sunday to the Adigi Women's Social Club to register. That way, she would be free to tell me as much as I wanted to know. I nodded my thanks, boarded the tram and waved to my comrade. I nodded, feeling that I had made my first friend of sorts as well as a teacher thrown in. I settled in on my seat to enable me ruminate over all that I had been told as the tram clattered off

Madam Mary

When I got home, Madam Mary took one look at me and fell about laughing. It felt very strange to be an object of laughter, especially when you were hurt. What could be amusing? I knew I was not looking my best, but . . . . I didn't have long to wonder.

'I can see that you have been initiated,' Madam Mary managed to splutter.

I still did not think that it was a thing to laugh about. If Madam Mary knew that they were going to *initiate* me by way of being beating to an inch of my life, why was I paying protection money to include those girls then? I dared not let my face reflect my thoughts though. The thought of being homeless kept me in check. Also not knowing whether I was expected to answer, I kept quiet and stared at my madam.

'Come and have a bath, I have drawn one for you.'

'Ooh.'

My spirit lifted, then fell as certain implication insinuated itself. Was I going to service Madam Mary? I shrugged off the thought.

Madam Mary, oblivious of my nasty thought apparently, showed me the bathroom and left. I laughed out in relief. Madam Mary's size was very daunting and in addition did not arouse any sexual feeling at all. And that brought me up short immediately. Was I supposed to enjoy sex with my customers or what? I thought very deeply about it before concluding that maybe I was not supposed to, besides it was business, you don't mix business with pleasure.

I undressed and sank into the bath. Scented steams rose and titillated my senses, it was magical. It eased all the tensions and tiredness from my weary bones and nerves. This madam *sabi* enjoy life *jare*.

*   *   *

I entered the kitchen to be enveloped by the aroma of food, reminding me that I had not had anything to eat since leaving Oya's place yesterday evening. Madam Mary invited me to sit down and help myself to the food which I did without waiting for a second bidding. As I was contemplating what to say to her, she spoke.

'I wanted them to toughen you up; you looked too demure and unworldly for this job. I needed you to understand the rudiments the hard way. To be able to stand up for yourself.'

'I suppose you're right,' I concurred grimly, and then commented, 'But you could have hinted, you know, they nearly killed me.'

'Don't be dramatic, dear. I knew they will not hurt you badly and you did not die afterall.'

'Did you really ask them to beat me up?'

'I didn't need to. Being on their patch, just like that, would work them up and it's very important that we get that out of the way, but from now onwards it is plain sailing.'

I pursed my lips. Everything seemed to be plain sailing to Madam Mary.

'Thank you,' however, was all I could mutter. Plain sailing. Of course! How could it not be? She was not the one that was battered to a pulp out there, was she? Neither did she have to shiver in the cold waiting to be paid $20 per five minutes per come. That suddenly brought the problem of 'service and pay' dilemma back and how to even determine what was to be paid. But there were issues that must be solved to enable me to calculate how much I would aim to make and how long it would take me to make it. Thank God I did not have a 'real' madam to be paid off first; otherwise it would take me forever to make any money for us.

Fresh worries reared in immediately; how many men do I have to service to make any reasonable money? Just how many! This business was not a joke oh. I would have to sit down and do the arithmetic. I sighed, *well, I had come, I had come, there's no going back* I thought as I ate, finally, hopelessly reinstating my vow about not thinking. That'd be the best route to go, honest.

I peeked at Madam Mary and realized that she must have a story to tell herself and wished that I knew what it was. That may help me to see the job as plain sailing, like she kept saying.

'What is the matter child?'

'Nothing Madam, I was indulging my thought that's all.'

I was startled by her reaction; like she was stung by a wicked scorpion.

'Eh! Please oh, don't do that, you hear me? Don't you ever do that, ever! Otherwise you *go* mad oh, it will destroy you, *na* me tell you. Do not think, period.' As she spoke, she had the lobe of one of her ears in between her thumb and the forefinger of her left hand, while the forefinger of her right hand was being wagged at me in an up and down movement all geared towards emphasis. Then she put the two hands on her hips before delivering the final missile, legs apart, 'Not in any circumstances, you hear me, not in any circumstances must you think, you must not think period. Instead look for wetin go help you outsmart your clients and on how to stay alive, that should occupy you just fine. Why, is not a question that should be answered now and may never get to be answered anyway. And thinking brings about all sorts of whys, so forget it. Bury it deep inside your mind. That was *wetin* help me survive and today I made it. *Abi* no be so?' she concluded with a query. I was sure that the question was not meant to be answered by me, do I know her worth? So I kept quiet.

'Try and get some sleep, my dear, you need all your strength,' Madam flung at me enroute to the living room, as if I had suddenly angered her. Hurriedly I finished my meal and headed to my room, not wanting her to meet me again out there. As soon as I sat on the bed, I became tired again. And I should be; had I not been on my toes all night long?

*   *   *

Madam Mary marched into her living-room, mixed her usual: a combination of Amarula and passion fruit, generously sprinkled with Vermouth and Mateuse Rose, topped with ice cubes, with olives buried here and there. The concoction calmed her nerves, which were easily rattled these days. And it was way better than doing drugs any day, she believed. In any case, she needed to enjoy her money with all her senses intact. With the drink in hand, she strolled to her favourite rocker, sat down and tuned her mind to the mystery that was Gift.

She had wondered over and over again why she came. What was the young man to her? She hoped that the girl knew what she was doing. She'd probably make it, but she needed to be pointed in the right direction, so that she could save a bit on the side. That shifty-eyed young man looked like he was going to suck her dry before he freed her.

However, that *na* Gift personal problem, any advice beside money making one would be lost on her now. But money no be everything but she wasn't sure that Gift would be interest in the sense *wey* follow that talk. She, Madam Mary, was a living example.

Look at her, she had money and all that it could buy, including worthwhile investments in properties and shares in Nigeria and Italy. She had taken innumerable chieftaincy titles in her village. Everybody respected her on the surface based on what they could get from her. She had continued to regret not marrying and having children: that would have given her succour. She did not think them important then, now it was too late, it seemed. It looked like she would spend her old age alone and that was not a pleasant prospect.

There was some glimmer of hope though; she was just biding her time to visit that scientist or whatever he called himself, to see how he would plant a baby inside her womb, as he claimed that he could do. And while at it, she'd have to ask for two at once. If that happened, she would retire immediately, return to her village and devote her time to raising her children.

Mary did not want to indulge her thoughts, she never allowed it, but her thoughts had refused to be caged these days. It was easier in the early days. Then, she was riding the waves. Now she had to indulge them, otherwise they'd drive her crazy. How could anyone remain sane in this madness of a business anyway?

She was born Rosemary Ifemnacho Odiatu, the only girl and the last child of Nwilo and Oliaku Odiatu. Her father was a lazy man but she loved him nonetheless, which was strange, a hard worker like herself, who could not stand layabouts. Her mother as long as she had known her, had risen with the roosters and returned with the hens. She had worked her fingers to the bones and was glad to hand over her daughter to somebody without question; somebody who was supposed to give her a better life.

Rosemary's arrival in Italy was like finding herself in heaven with wonder shinning out of her bulging bright eyes. She came as a housemaid to a supposed rich and industrious family. She shook her head as her memory laid into her.

Her whole family had gathered to wave her off, at their village Eke market, since they could not afford to travel to the big Onitsha

Township where they would enter luxurious bus to Lagos for the flight to Italy. She had skipped alongside her *rescuer* at the envy of her mates; if it was possible to use the word skip where she was concerned: she was tall and gangly as a teenager with her two legs knocking together in a K at the knee. But she was endowed with heavy breasts, considered a blessing for the suckling of the young ones.

At fifteen, she was matured in look if not in wisdom. Her father would have had her married off then, but her mother insisted that they should wait until she was eighteen at least, that way, she may be lucky to get a better offer than what they had received so far.

Besides, her mother had further argued, that she had borne the burden of poverty enough to cover her children's share, especially her only daughter. She would not, therefore, send her to where hunger go kill am. So when the offer came to send her to Italy, her mother grabbed it with both hands.

The offer for the position of a housemaid came in the form of a lady who came one hot afternoon. The lady was welcomed warmly, because she was referred to them by one of their townsmen living in Onitsha. The offer however was problematic; they were divided, with father and brothers saying no and mother and daughter saying yes. Eventually, however, she was happily handed over to the stranger. It was a decision that had haunted her mother and subsequently hounded her to her grave!

On arrival, supposedly to the illustrious family's house, Rosemary had set to and scrubbed the living daylights out of the house, top to bottom. She could not however, for the life of her unspawned children, determine why the family needed a maid. There was not a speck of dirt lurking anyway in the house. Everything was sparkling and spotless. But she did not mind, she had to show her handiwork, her skills as an accomplished housemaid having been cooking and cleaning from the womb.

Three days passed, yet she had not set eyes on any member of the industrious rich family. She had seen only her *rescuer* and another well-fed woman, at a distance. And they were constantly engaged in a lot of whispering. But Rosemary was undaunted. She was confident in her abilities.

After one week of eating, sleeping, cleaning and re-cleaning, nothing had happened. Her hands itched for real dirt. She missed her family terribly and wished that they could be magically dropped with her to live off the excesses of this household. Then the joys of her good fortune would be shared with her family and her happiness would be complete.

The whispering must have yielded results because she was put to work on the eight day of her arrival to Italy, but for another kind of work, a work that was so far removed from maidship. She worked out of an apartment with three rooms shared by three other girls, one person, one room. And for the next four years, she had spent her life lying on her back with her legs permanently raised and spread wide to accommodate the strings of men that passed through her. Fat and thin, ugly and handsome, drunk and sober, mad and sane.

Rosemary had protested at learning what her new job was, but she was beaten into a swollen pulp, bruised and broken, to extract submission. They forcefully cut a tiny bit of her pubic hair for juju rites, then told her that they had put her under oath and so she should never reveal her benefactors' names to anybody and to do her job without giving them troubles, otherwise, she would not only go mad, but her family would bear the brunt of her disobedience . . .

But what made the matter worst was that she did not see the colour of the money that was paid for her services, not to talk of spending it. She was given just enough to buy food. Her rent had been taken care of, so it seemed, for nobody spoke to her about anything of that sort or of any sort of anything in actual fact. She was sent to and was treated by a particular doctor and no other when she had the itchings in her vagina which was often. It was one of the banes of that work.

She was also sent there when she got pregnant—four times because her clients would rather not use raincoat, so as to enjoy their spending better. Her continued protests to her benefactors were in vain; she was told to be grateful and could leave as soon as she had paid her benefactor's debt of $25,000 that was incurred on her behalf.

To a fifteen year old, who had lived all her life in a rural village, the name of the money alone was enough to frighten her, never mind the amount. But was she not employed to be paid? What debt were they talking about and how did that happen? Did she choose to come here and do this work? Why should she be the one to pay them for doing this kind of dirty devil-work? Nobody answered her questions, for nobody stayed long enough to listen to her. Finally, through her other inmates she found out what that money they were talking about meant in Nigerian money, and she took to her bed with high fever, it was N975,000 @ N39 per dollar. Her inmates helpfully rounded it up for her, to ease the pronouncing, and that was how the word one million came to meet her.

If you had never been opportuned in your entire life to spend a whole N20 on yourself, imagine being told that you owed one million Naira for accepting to become a housemaid, where on arrival, your job function was arbitrarily changed and on top of that you were now in debt. Her fever increased its fierceness, but finally she got well. And she made it alive. She did not succumb to death from diseases or depression or madness, and that was quite a feat.

Through the other girls in the half-prison like place they lived in she learnt how to do small runs on the side for herself and as a result was able to save a little money. Over the years she gradually untangled the web. It took exactly four years but finally she was free. And it was only when she resurfaced from the sewer that she learnt she had been sold to the well-fed lady that was engaged in the extensive whisperings when she first arrived in Italy. She was called Madam Gold.

She celebrated her twenty years on earth and one year of freedom, but though she was only twenty she had the mind of a foolish fifty year-old. She had grown up alright, but her mental faculties and worldviews were all warped. If not, how could she have refused her mother's tearful entreaties not to return to Italy now that she had saved herself?

It was hell loosened on earth when she went home. She would have held her tongue but she could not, she was still a child at heart so she sobbed the whole story out as soon as she was surrounded by her family. It was like a funeral, a second funeral actually.

For five years after she left and her family did not hear anything about her they started looking for her. The search took them to the person that referred the *rescuer* to them, but it was of no use because the man said that it was his wife's market stall-mate that knew the contact for the *rescuer.* However they were told that the said stall-mate became widowed not long after Rosemary left for Italy and had to relocate to her home village and nobody could remember now the name of this village.

Dead end.

And so they had lost the only daughter of the family. Then she came back with strange stories. But since she had escaped, what then did she want to go back for? She was asked in unison.

No. She must go back.

If she did it to make money for somebody else why should she not do it to make money for them all? Afterall, the damage had been done. The logic had sounded very good to her at the time and so she did not give anybody the chance to convince her otherwise.

There was no dissenting voice this time; her family was united in their refusal for her to leave. She was the only one in her corner, but she did not care. Those who were against would come round when the money started to roll in she believed.

Her mother, the chief of the against, refused to be swayed by anything and over time became a recluse and remained so till she lost her mind and floated through life in a daze, finally succumbing to death by drowning. Rosemary, now, could identify with her mother's pain and misery, but not then. Oliaku blamed herself till she could no longer see any other part of herself to be blamed. If she had allowed her daughter to be married off then, as suggested by her husband, this would not have happened. If this, if that, if, if, until she lost it. She refused to partake in the flow of milk and honey from her daughter's exploits in Italy. She estranged herself from her family and then herself from herself.

Rosemary made money. Real money. She did not forget her people, her brothers were all settled, properly, as befitted the relations of a moneybag. With time her father re-married and took chieftaincy titles. It was of no use beating yourself up he reasoned. His wife had several names for him when she was still able, but who could have known the future? Who was to know how things would turn out by that singular decision to give their daughter a better opportunity? Was it not she, Oliaku, that spearheaded the journey? Or was it because he was not the type of person that would continually beat anybody up with "did I not say no to this and that," that made her include him in her mad ramblings? In this world one had to learn to adjust as you go along, was the only advice he gave her.

When the rays of the sun fell into her eyes forcing her to blink, Rosemary realized that a substantial amount of time had passed. Her tears had flowed freely and into her drink which she had wedged in between her breasts as if purposely poised to collect the tears.

She was a sad and a lonely woman.

She had missed out on a certain kind of life in her hey days and now was not any better, either.

There you go Rosie, we thought you had worked out how to beat your thoughts, eh?

These people had been speaking to her for sometime now for no reason and uninvited. Sometimes she was also forgetful and it was becoming embarrassing. Was she going to end up like her mother? Was there madness in her family? Not that she had heard, but such things were usually hidden from children and now nobody would bother to tell her anything. She hoped she would remember to ask her brothers, when next she spoke with them while continuing to pray fervently so that God would not allow such a bad thing to happen to her and so stop her from enjoying her money.

She would have to speak to Gift sometime, to ask her whether she was quite sure about this job she chose to do. Or maybe it'd be better instead to allow her to bleed whatever made her come to Italy out of her bloodstream, hopefully she'd come round to that quick as this business destroys the soul even if *na* you say you *wan* do the business. Yes, now she knew some of the ladies that came willingly to make money for themselves, so even though they had sponsors, ultimately when they freed, they worked for themselves happily buying expensive gold jewelries, wrappers, cars and building houses in Nigeria. But if you like telling yourself the truth, to break it down to simple ABC then choosing to be a prostitute is not really a decision made with a complete mind. But who'd tell who.

She got up, downed her drink, even with the tears and then tiptoed into the room to check on Gift. She was snoring gently, looking rather exhausted. Rosemary smiled, it was only a day's work my dear girl; this was just the first day!

Osahon's Hand!

Osahon heaved a great sigh of freedom, as he wriggled his bum here and then there trying to catch an itch on the cheek of his buttocks that tended towards his left thigh. He couldn't reach it. *This seat is fucking tight.*

'Christ,' he mumbled in frustration as he still couldn't reach the itch, which at this stage had started toying with his control element. He thrust his bum forward and then backward with his thighs clenched firmly on the seat hoping to affect the itch in the process. It worked.

Then his mind returned to his earlier thoughts that were quenched by the itch.

'So it is over?' he asked.

'The fucking show, finally, has hit the road,' he continued out loud, before sighing again, and then released a flurry of air from a huge yawn, shifted his bulk once more, and noisily kicked out his legs. The Lebanese man, seated on his right hand side, eyed him irritably. Osahon eyed him back fiercely. He was not ready for any nonsense from anybody. Then he mouthed, 'enemies of progress' at the Lebanese before turning his back on him to signal at the stewardess passing by his section of his need for a stiff drink. He could feel the Lebanese man's glare on his back but he couldn't be bothered. What did he know? Silly baboon. He and his whole family, for that matter, could go to hell. What he needed badly was to quench his thirst; he had been under enormous pressure lately. He had never had to work so hard in his entire life.

'Christ,' he muttered again, before twisting round and craning his neck, in an attempt to see the back of the plane, in search of the stewardess.

'Is she brewing this drink herself or what?'

This miss had better hurry up with that stuff before he got angry, his throat badly needed to be warmed, besides the success of his trip called for a celebration, it was not easy setting the bloody fucking business up.

No man! It was not. He thumped the armrest, to the chagrin of the Lebanese. Osahon looked at him and snorted insolently. The man quickly turned away in case anything was going to fly out of the nose, but nothing did. Osahon laughed, this yeye Lebanese man should not annoy him here, make him no think say *na* Naija we *dey* so where they *don* commandeer all printing and paper businesses *sotay* we, *wey* be the original sons of the soil, we *wey* get Nigeria, no fit enter the business *sef.* Even to enter better position for their company *nko?* W*hosai, na* their brothers *wey* no sabi anything them go for their village bring. As *dem* manage get visa enter Naija pass me. Na only the work *wey* no get category, *wey* no reach to pay minimum wage *na* there them put our people, packed in sweltering steamy ovens called factories. Printing business *na* multi-million Naira sector for mouth only; where the money *dey?* Nowhere, *na* so these *wayo* people go just *dey* repatriate the money anyhow. Why *dem* still allow them enter Naija I no know. I suppose all of them dey chop from the same plate. He glared at the man who quickly looked away. No place *wey dey* no fit enter for Naija even before any Nigerian, imagine that. I swear if this man misbehaves I go rib am with my elbow.

His drink arrived at that moment signaling the start of good things and while sipping it, he thought back on how his life would progress henceforth. Gift, his lovely Gift, had given him a new lease on life. He never dreamt that it would be that easy, but there you are, the power of love! Never to be underestimated. He did not even have to work so hard really at persuading her. He had snaffled and waffled by way of nightmares and then bam, rammed it into her throat and the rest became easy game. However, he must not fail to see Baba Ojei as soon as he got home to burn the *oath* and seal the deal permanently. Then she'd make money for him for life. 'Oh sweet fuck, Osahon you have arrived in a big way trust me!' he told himself.

He had realized that Gift's beauty should not be wasted on mere wifely duties. It must be put to better use. This was pure celestial revelation. It was such a good thing that she was so in love with him.

Always eager to please him, willing to try anything, anything at all that would make him happy. That had worked in his favour eventually. Though it did not look like that initially, because, at the time, he had failed to see the advantage. His Gift's love for him was her undoing, because pitted against the backdrop of mule—contractual prostitutes—who may be recalcitrant, kicking and spitting all the way to Italy, Gift won hands down. In any case, he did not want a contractual relationship with a *mule* as that would have a timeframe. He needed to be kept in luxury for life or not at all.

But women could be stupid atimes; imagine, just when he thought he had sunk his claws, deeply into Gift, wham! She set about unraveling the whole knot. His future empire crashing with her sudden announcement that she was pregnant and looked like it might stay in coma with another pregnancy in tow. How could she do that to him? How could any one woman be so stupid, so determined to thwart his life's plan. It took him exactly two years and four months to disentangle himself. Yeah, two fucking years and four fucking months!

But he did it. And now he would position himself to become a Mega Big Boy and nothing, nothing at all would stop it. Baba Ojei would hand him the key and he would throw it into the deep blue ocean, then Gift would mint money for him forever.

The droning of the plane turned into a balm on Osahon's distressed thought after his drink and gradually, it lulled him to sleep, to the thankful relief of the Lebanese. He slept long and deep and when their flight landed at Muritala Mohammed Airport Lagos, seven hours later, he woke quite refreshed. As he marched down the plane jauntily, full of confidence, he marveled at how the thought of money calmed him. There was nothing that gave cast-iron confidence to a man than knowing that the balance in his account was fat and would keep growing. Well, his wealth was about to start flowing in but his confidence as a man of means had already seeped into his blood and there was no looking back. In Benin City, he would take his deserved place. Yes. Now his dented image was going to be restored and he could now also back up his bragging.

Who would stop my destiny, eh? Who? Tell me? He looked about fiercely as if in search of the culprit that would truncate his carefully laid out destiny. Not seeing anybody in that mould, he headed to the taxi rank where he took one to Iddo motor park for the final leg of his trip home to Benin City.

To ensure a precise and clean severity of chord with Gift, he decided to move forward only, no glancing back and so his first action towards this resolve was to dispatch their two daughters to his in-laws.

His mother, who was looking after them up to now, would have to give them up; more grandchildren would come when he was properly married. But he had to devise how to go about dissuading her to relinquish them. That woman was always on his case, what was wrong with her *self*? Always interfering. Anything that had to do with him she held on to tenaciously but she had to learn to let go, the way his old man did years ago. Yeah, that's it man, release!

Then he smiled, softening his nasty thoughts towards his mother, remembering all the years she had stuck out for him and smiled. He supposed mothers were meant to worry. His own mother's case therefore should not be different, he should just learn not be so hard on her, but, first things first.

In League with the Spirits

Baba Ojei threw the shot of *kaikai,* native Gin, into the back of his throat, swallowed hard, causing his Adams' apple to jig up and down, as if to attest to the fieriness of the drink. He shook his head vigorously, blew out his cheeks and smacked his lips noisily before banging the gin shot on the wooden stool, upsetting a lot of rubbish, dusts and flies. As the *kaikai* drinking ceremony was being enacted, Osahon sneered, looking on unimpressed. His thoughts that were reflected starkly on his face implied that Baba Ojei should not go that route, man, if his plan was to weasel out money from him, he had better bury those antics because they wouldn't work. Did he not understand that this was just the beginning? Or was it because he was privy to his trip abroad? He had better take it easy and make sure that his concoctions would be able to 'bind' Gift well as to make her remit all her earnings direct to him as they flowed in with no argument. That's it man, no be all these stunts *wey* him *dey* do.

When Baba Ojei spoke, Osahon was miles away and did not hear him. Baba Ojei cleared his throat and spoke again.

'My *pikin, e* no *dey* good make you *comot* your mind when you *dey* for before spirit, you fit go miss something *sef,* that go *dey* very costly. But me, I *dey altat,* so not to worry I go hear them.'

Osahon felt like laughing but held himself, principally because he had friends who had been using Baba Ojei for a long time, so he did not have to be told about the efficacy of his *tie-tie.* He had seen the results. Otherwise he would have dismissed Baba as a charlatan.

Miss something from the spirit indeed.

Why should he not miss it? Is he a native doctor? Did Baba Ojei see him, Osahon, in the school where he learnt his trade? But he kept those thoughts to himself, instead he asked,

'Baba Ojei, have we not passed this very stage wey you dey talk so?'

'I know my *pikin,* but you never know; they may want to add somethings.'

'Did they add anything then?'

'Not yet.'

'Not yet? Are they planning to?'

'Did you bring the paper?' Baba asked, staring directly at Osahon, changing the direction of the conversation, which he did all the time and which annoyed Osahon each time.

'No worry yourself,' Baba consoled, 'make we do our own, the spirit go do their own. If they need us dem go tell me.'

'More like it Baba,' Osahon breathed in relief. For a moment there he thought that the plan had gone awry.

This Baba Ojei sef!

As it happened, Osahon found his whole day spent at Baba Ojei's shack. For without announcement Baba went into a trance and stayed in the spirit-world for over three human-world hours. Osahon did not find that funny because Baba did not intimate him on the procedures and as a result he was left at a loose end with nothing to do and he was afraid of losing concentration again. Not necessarily for the chance of failing to hear the spirits, but more from not wanting to be harmed.

Yeah man, a risky situation there!

As he looked around, it occurred to him that he was not sure if the spirits were familiar with the routes as they went about distributing curses or whatever they went about distributing. And this Baba Ojei's cluttered shack might prove hazardous. What if one of the spirits stumbled and dropped unintended curse on him? He gathered himself, to see if he could make himself smaller to escape notice. What would be the point of being a millionaire then if he was not well enough to enjoy it? Or worse still, he might even be dead?

'Osanobua!' Osahon muttered, shivering from the thought of the imagined unknown effects of the unknown curses on him. But then he realized that he must stay calm for he did not know how long he would be in Baba's shack. He had to stay to conclude his business which was interrupted by the trance and he dared not approach Baba, so such thoughts would only make matters worse. He must occupy himself somehow and wait. He looked around one more time before he lit up a cigarette. If Baba Ojei could drink his shit in here why could he not smoke? He drew the first smoke deep into his lungs and held it, savouring the joy as a cough tickled his throat and he was forced to release the trapped smoke quickly. He coughed and coughed, finally he stubbed out the cigarette as tears started streaming down his face. He got up and stumbled outside for fresh air. This Baba Ojei *na* dangerous man o; even as he *dey* for Spirit world so, he still *dey* control *wetin dey* happen here? He fished frantically in his pocket for the 'paper' and was relieved to find it still there. He gulped in more fresh air and it helped to clear his head and calm him down. Sufficiently recovered he considered resuming the smoking briefly but thought against it. So he stood outside, folded his arms against his chest, with the 'paper' clutched firmly in his right palm and watched Baba Ojei from a distance.

When Baba Ojei eventually re-surfaced, he looked particularly pained, his forehead deeply furrowed and his shaggy brows pointing negatively. He must have seen something that did not agree with him out there Osahon concluded. Well, so long as it did not have anything to do with him personally, he could not care less. He looked furtively at Baba and, to quickly establish that Baba Ojei's gloomy face did not have anything to do with him he went back in to the shack and guardedly asked,'Baba Ojei, is anything the matter?'

'It is done,' Baba Ojei intoned glumly.

'Good,' Osahon said his face splitting into a wide grin, he stretched his hand to shake Baba Ojei's for a job well done having transferred the 'paper' to the left hand when suddenly the 'paper' burst into flame and he screamed, dropping it.

This 'paper' was the whole reason why he went to Italy with Gift at Baba Ojei's express instruction. To ensure that Gift wrote the contract, so agreed with the contracting party in whatever circumstances, with her own hand and sign it. Then he, Osahon would bring it home and he Baba Ojei would take it from there. Now it had turned to ashes. Osahon folded down on the nearest seat like a piece of rag, a picture of despair, despondently gazing at Baba Ojei, his two cheeks in his two palms supported by his elbows on his knees.

Baba Ojei ignored Osahon completely and went about his business quietly; scraping the ashes of the burnt 'paper' into a leaf, which he had warmed over the fireplace, to make it more malleable, folding it neatly he tied it firmly with a dirty red rag before strolling regally to Osahon and pushed the package at him as he reeled out strings of instructions.

' . . . Rub this on your woman's forehead as she dey look you, with her eyes wide open, make she no blink ooh! Then *na im* be say the deal don seal *kpatakpata;* no shaking, no change, *na* so ego be forever,' Baba finished gravely.

'It got burnt Baba,' Osahon croaked, but then he noted Baba Ojei's nonchalant attitude to the burnt paper—this made him begin to rally round but to be sure he asked, 'Are you sure everything is still alright?'

'Everything still *dey* as *e* supposes be.'

Baba Ojei's face was always like a closed book, you could never read anything from it, but then if he said not to worry, then he should not worry.

'But my woman *dey* Italy now as you know, how I go fit rub this on her forehead and if she come ask me, *wetin* I go tell am say *naim* I dey do?'

This Baba sef, he must think that I'm stupid.

'You go find way, no worry, you go find way. I say *apatunity* go present *imself* to you.'

Osahon nodded. Cleared his throat before saying, 'Ehee Baba, about your money . . .'

'No worry about am, I no say you *nefa getam*, bring am when you do.'

Osahon, greatly relieved, sauntered out of Baba Ojei's ramshackle of a house, a little smile playing around his lips, as he skirted his way towards where he hid his car. He played back the events of the day in his mind and it seemed satisfactory to him, but for Baba Ojei's comment about payment at the last minute. Why was Baba Ojei so willing to let him go just like that? Or was he planning to draw him back with juju? Osahon stopped and thought about this briefly before discarding it, it could not be so. He did not have any reason to worry himself; Baba Ojei was not a small boy, he should know not to be so trusting because not even wild horses could drag him back to this place. He chuckled, then whooped and started walking again.

No chance, man!

Baba had to whistle for his money because he, Osahon, would not willingly give him any.

As he went, he cast about again; looking for signs of affluence, a sign to tie to Baba Ojei's attested reputation, but nothing worthy could be seen. After looking around once more he concluded that Baba's other clients clearly did not pay him. They must be cheating him out of his due too, otherwise how come he was living in a place like this? The bloody man did not even look healthy; were native doctors not reputed to live on fresh supply of goats, chicken, fat yams and all manner of offerings from their customers?

And what did you come with? came from nowhere to attack him and kept at him until it grew into a gargoyle stalking him, resoundingly, round and round, enveloping him. Quickly he scanned the environment to find nothing, he continued on but took the precaution of stepping up his stride, and then he increased the tempo to trotting, now highly spooked. But after a while he slowed down, this was ridiculous, he told himself, but continued in a brisk walk, before finally resuming normal steps, having assured himself that he was alone. Calming down, he defended the accusation with, 'I'm not a regular customer to this sort of thing, man. What do you take me for?' That seemed to have upset something somewhere as he found himself picking up speed again. This Baba Ojei is a wicked man oh, but as soon as the thought had left his mind, it seemed to collide with him and he stumbled and fell into the side bush upsetting a horde of flies feeding on a dead something. Osahon was very upset by this turn of event, how could a big boy like him be falling about in the bush because of a stupid stupid native doctor? He resolved to go back and warn Baba Ojei from tampering with his dignity. But he couldn't seem to find a good footing to help hoist himself up. It was most baffling. Finally he wrenched his foot out of something that was holding it tearing his trouser. This incensed him so much that the force of it was able to help him get up. He turned back towards Baba Ojei's hut for the warning, but suddenly he noticed that the grasses around him were getting taller by the minute and gazing at him with bad eyes.

He turned towards the grasses and screamed, 'What is this, you enemies of progress?'

He then kicked out at them and fell. He scrambled up and fell again. When he got up this time he turned round towards his car and employing the fullness of his long legs ran off.

By the last quarter of the new month, Osahon went back to Torino having got Gift to send him the money needed for the trip. While there, he successfully rubbed the ashes on Gift's forehead while she was wide awake and staring at him, her two eyes open. And the beauty of it all was that she never suspected a thing. What a coup!

This Baba Ojei *na* something else.

A true wizard!

*   *   *

Fuelled by the belief that he was now set for life, Osahon became even more puffed up and arrogant than could be attributed to him previously. *Oh man, so there's money in this ashawo business and I didn't even know. Look at what I have made in six weeks!*

Shit man!

'How come I didn't start before now?' he asked, then remembered bitterly that Gift was busy making babies.

'Stupid woman. Imagine how much money I would have made by now,' he ground out in fury, gnashing his teeth. Women! They never get their priorities right. They should thank their God that we men are around to guide them.

'Fools!'

He spat angrily. Anyway, it's good that he had taken all the necessary steps to seal every foreseeable loophole, now he'd just settle into his life as a bachelor once more. He had to be careful though and make the right noises at the right time especially when it came to those stupid in-laws of his trying to make trouble for him. He was not about to rock his boat that had barely set sail.

Over the two months following his return from Italy, Osahon saw his life change; spending money like it was water. This money that had insulted him for so long, he had in abundance now and this was just the beginning. It was his turn to insult money from now onwards and nothing would deter him, not even Baba Ojei and his array of fetishes. An-upwardly-mobile millionaire like him deterred by what?

'Watch out, man!' he mouthed to no one. Then he noticed that people were staring at him strangely and bared his teeth at them.

He was becoming increasingly pissed with the attitude of people in this neighborhood; people did not respect their elders these days. Yeah, he deserved every respect accrued to his elder status conferred by money. But no, they tended to look through him, like he's nothing. He thought about it as he progressed towards his dry cleaners and came up with a satisfying reason: he had lived in the neighbourhood for too long, that's what. Wasn't it said that a prophet was not respected in his own village? Written in God's own book!

Yeah.

But nobody was going to mess with him. He'd move out of the shit hole of a place soon.

On the Street

When I arrived at Bundesling Veneto later that evening, as we agreed, there was no Ofure so I loitered about for a while, walking up and down to ward off the cold before finally going into Café Noir for coffee. Ofure came shortly after and ordered coffee too. When her coffee arrived, she fished for and brought out a small flask from her cavernous handbag and poured something out of it into her cup. I proffered my cup and she obliged, but told me in no uncertain terms to get my own flask with, 'This our work no *sabi* friendship o make you just know.'

I shrugged while mentally adding 'flask' to my list of what was needed. We downed our brandy-laden coffee and left immediately.

As we walked towards the roundabout that would take us to our patch, on turning right at the junction, I asked Ofure why she had to put so much make-up on. She eyed me but said nothing. After we had covered a little more distance she asked, 'You didn't bring any of that with you?'

'No, I can always buy what I need. It is the quantity you put on I have problems with.'

'Well it's because the more you apply the more men you attract.'

'With lipstick, eye-shadow and eye-pencil? Ofure please . . .'

'You *sef,* you think say *na* ordinary makeup be this? Abeg no make me laugh. You better ask your mother to bring you some *cooked* ones otherwise you'll die with nothing much to show for your sufferings, mark my words.'

I didn't see where Ofure was going immediately, and then it clicked, 'Like visit the native doctor and all that?'

Ofure did not deem the question answerable.

'Just try as much as your instinct leads you. The rest would be unraveled but that is after you have joined the club.'

'Thanks,' I mumbled. As we crested the junction, Ofure pushed me ahead and told me to pretend we didn't come together.

By the time we finished our shift and were trouping home in twos and threes in the wee hours of the morning, I knew that I'd really have to prepare for this job, otherwise I would not last the week. That I did not want to think was a good policy to have, it did help to numb the mind and keep the pain at bay, but, that did not preclude stocking up on the job requirements; like failing to have any condoms on the first night of full operation. I missed that completely and that must not repeat again. It was quite a struggle, throughout that night, to get my customers to not enter without condom. Most of them abused me for not having it and left in disgust, while some I was able to satisfy with my hands. But as a result of my unintended stupidity, I did not have much money to show for the night's labour in the biting cold. But fair was fair, I did not blame my clients. It was my duty to look after my life, why should the responsibility be foisted on another person, a predatory other at that? So on that first day of full operation it was still like a game for me, but then the last customer refused to leave and forced his way in. Hell!

I returned home and went straight into my room without saying much to Madam Mary. I made to lie down on my bed but then shot up immediately like a bullet; I couldn't lie on my bed with such a dirty body! But I couldn't sit down either so I stood in one corner of my room as various thoughts scuttled by but none settled so that I could dwell on it. Nothing. After a while I went and stood in front of the standing mirror in the room and surveyed myself. What do you see when you debase yourself? What were you supposed to see? Because I did not see anything. But there was something. So I took a bath but the something was still there. I still couldn't lie on my bed so I went in and sat on the toilet seat. As I sat there one thought finally settled and I could think about it, I could feel it; it was the thought that alerted me to the fact the something I was scrubbing earlier was not on my skin, it was not physical, it is in my soul. Realization brought pain to my eyes and the pain started trickling down as tears. I sat there on the toilet seat hunched over; a befitting place to be, as my life-force was being emptied out from my soul through my eyes. I lost count of how long I sat there, the minutes just ticked by regardless. Finally I got up and went to lie down, the aversion not to be on the bed had left me as I had come to grasp that physical dirt can never be compared to spiritual dirt. Which must be why I had advised myself not to think in the first place, why everybody I had met so far in this business had told me to close my mind to thoughts; because thinking would destroy me. That was the last time I allowed myself to think.

I switched to autopilot and got on with the job, swigging from my flask whenever I could to ward off the cold and aid the mind in clamping down on my thoughts.

Until the day that the man with the big dick arrived. Apparently the others knew him and would rather not deal with him to his annoyance. Seeing a new face, he made straight for me, good, the more the better, I reasoned. But when he pulled down his pants, I gasped and stepped back, his something was massive, turgid and nodding like Agama lizard! I knew that there was no way I was going to accommodate him. So I immediately offered to give his money back and a free massage thrown in, but the man would not hear of it and tore into me mercilessly. The worst part was that he *refused* to come as was customary—in a matter of minutes. He spent over five minutes digging and afterwards paid only $15 extra. I did not even have the energy to protest the payment and I couldn't think of what to do either. I could now clearly see why my co-workers had resorted to stealing! I should have stolen the bastard's wallet, imagine paying $15 extra with that equipment of his! But I wasn't going to stoop that low. And I also knew that I had to find a better way of doing this job—this roadside style would only earn me pittance and I didn't come to Italy for that.

*   *   *

The Sunday finally came and I accompanied Ofure and joined the club, paid the registration fee as well as the stipulated monthly due and was consequently declared a bona fide member of Adigi Socials, as it was fondly referred to by members. Then, gradually Ofure unfurled the secrets of the business which I absorbed especially those informations that would greatly enhance my chances at maximizing my turnover. I was intrigued by some of the things Ofure said and astonished that they actually believed them. Like getting native doctors concoction that would be used with lipsticks, placed under the tongue, in eyebrow liner, in the face powder, body cream and there were some creams that could be rubbed on the edges of the vagina. All aimed at not only increasing the number of customers but also to induce them

to part with more money. What the client couldn't part with by juju or
wiles, was appropriated by way of stealing. No hard feelings there, it's
all part of the game.

*   *   *

I was just a notch above being tipsy, on duty, off duty, awake
or sleeping. I had no choice I told myself. This was not a business
you do with clear-eyes. But even in my situation I still saw and have
great sympathy for the wild-eyed, dazed pre-teen girls that worked as
sexual-slaves in the various patches and brothels scattered all over the
city. They were barely out of their nappies. So how did they get to Italy?
Could it really ever be so bad that anybody would debase a child's life?
Ofure had informed me early on, when I muted my resentment to
such child abuse, that most of the parents of those children were paid
to part with them. I thought over the idea of accepting money for
any child of mine to become a sexual object to these jerks. It didn't
present a pleasant picture, which I banished immediately. What was
I doing veering into such a tangent? Courting madness or what? I
should mind my business and those images and thoughts would mind
theirs. But I did not need a mental picture; they were with me here
in reality dodging my every step. In all these, money remained the
currency, the singular most important factor to the oppressed and the
oppressor.

Every day blended into the next and then Osahon announced
that he was coming to see me. I didn't want him to, I didn't want
to see his eyes, or give him the chance to look into my soul during
this period, but he insisted and so I sent the money and gave him
my address, having moved out of Madam Mary's against her advice.
I believed she had some nut loose somewhere and I didn't want her
motherly intents, but I still paid protection money duly.

One mid-morning, bleary-eyed from my nocturnal activities, I
answered the door to Osahon's knock. As soon as he had divested
himself of his light luggage, he launched into the reason for the trip.
So though I was staring at him, I was practically asleep and didn't
hear a word of his explanation and plans but was vaguely aware
that he touched my forehead. He must have been smoothening the
permanent frown that I believed had been etched on it ever since.

Osahon must have put me to bed sometime, for when I woke up, I
was on the bed and he was smoking and drinking while seated beside
the bed. He recounted his reason for this trip again: He had arranged
with one Emeka Onwuajoka, the CEO of Mekus La Moda Couture,

a high-range fashion aficionado, whose boutique was making waves
on the famous Allen Avenue, Ikeja, Lagos. He was always in Italy and
would call on me to collect whatever money I had made having given
Osahon the Naira equivalent in Nigeria.

Osahon also came with tonnes of condoms as he was not sure they
had very strong and effective ones in Italy. After ascertaining that I
had not allowed any of my clients to relieve himself without one, he
relaxed and we had a good two days.

He declined to visit the Okere's after I narrated Oya's turncoat
and told me to stay away from them and not to pay the $1,500 we owed
them, if that was how they wanted to play it. I had already paid that, a
debt was a debt, and you honour yours no matter.

He also came with the architectural drawings showing plans of
our Supermarket and that of our home. He was, according to him,
negotiating for the land and as soon as he had acquired them would
commence work immediately.

'You see my Princess, from my calculation, by this time next year,
you'll be home,' he had finished in a flourish. When it was time for
him to leave for Nigeria, I clung to him and refused to let go. He held
me tightly, cooing to me, massaging the tension on my neck and back;
coercing them to relax and murmured non-stop, endearingly in my
ears. He reminded me to be careful and stay away from troublemakers
and ensured that I used condoms all the time. He gave me a new
mobile phone number which he said was dedicated for me to reach
him 24hrs and told me to avoid unnecessary friendship with anybody
whatsoever. Then he left and I launched myself back into our business.
It would soon be over.

Initially I continued to telephone Osahon, all the time, but
realized afterwards, that it was not doing me any good. Most times after
speaking with him for hours on-end with Osahon pleading, cajoling,
I would end up not going to work for two days, crying my eyes out,
at such times because I had opened a window that questioned my
purpose. Then our dream would dramatically transform to reality
before my very eyes, I'd square my jaw and plow on.

Ofure thought that I was a fool and told me so, when she found
me, on the second day absent from work, at home sobbing. 'How could
you stay at home crying, wasting precious time? Since you came in the
first place, you might as well come to terms with it and make yourself
useful,' she had chided, 'Or did you think that I, Ofure, did not have
any reason to cry? Wake up girl,' she had added in conclusion. After
that session, I called Osahon less and handed over my earnings to Mr.
Onwuajoka as arranged, to shorten my going home days. Osahon on

his part called me sparingly: only when it was absolutely necessary, to give me progress reports on our building, and to put more pressure on me to work harder.

'It would hasten your return, Princess,' he'd tell me. Which in turn justified his taking money in advance from Mr. Onwuajoka, much more than I could manage. This made me more desperate and daring. So as I had earlier decided I got Madam Mary to use her connections to get me a room in a hotel from where I did the work. I employed the services of a hotel staff that discreetly spread the word. After that I started getting quality patrons which increased my turnover greatly—I gave them what they wanted and they give me what I wanted. Ofure was aghast at my brazenness, but standing on the street did not only put you in a certain category of prostitution, you did not make as much with the added risk of being harmed faster. Ofure disagreed and warned me consistently that it was I who was courting danger, but I did not want to go into much argument with Ofure. What I got paid for in one night, I could not have earned in a week on the road. It wasn't as if the road was safe, there were incessant and indiscriminate raids by the *polizia*. Didn't Ofure herself tell me about how the person I was using her patch was shot dead before her very eyes and nothing came of it. Risk was everywhere in life, even in the air we breathe in. I'd just have to be extra careful.

It was during my daring forays that I learnt so much about the deep and dangerous carnal instincts of the human breed. Not being vast in knowledge before this time I could not compare, but the world of sex seemed comparable to the pit of hell. Customers would ask to be chained to bedposts, to be flogged, to have group-sex and some even wanted it through the anus! What depraved and degrading acts. I stuck to what I knew and what would not hurt me, but if anybody wanted to be flogged, I flogged him, it was his body. It also dawned on me that there was no gentleness in prostitution, having been beaten up severally to attest to that and none of us could do anything about it. Let's face it, who would you go to for help? And these customers knew it. And this was part of why I took up a room in a hotel believing that it'd reduce the percentage of danger.

However it wasn't all gloomy, sometimes some of my clients would pay and be content to just talk. At such times I listened and gave advice as much as I could grasp the problem. It was always almost based on the wives suspected infidelity; uninterested in their advances; always busy with children; refusal to engage in adventurous sex, especially anal sex. I would promptly inform any such client at this juncture that that also was a no-go area for me. They would sulk and I would coerce them back to good humour with other tricks.

One day a new client burst into tears after I had tried to get him to do his thing and be on his way.

'My penis does not stand anymore!' he wailed and his wife was threatening fire and brimstone about going into their neighbour's bed if he did not do something about it and quick too. *Now what?* I thought. I had been turned to a shrink that must provide solutions too? But then I reasoned that humans were the same all over the world, all they needed was a little comforting in times of distress. And it usually worked except that this very client did not hear a word I said, he was busy bemoaning his fate. Eventually I was able to catch his attention and then explained to him what I saw was his problem: he worked too hard and too long daily, so much so that the last thing on his mind at getting home was sex, but the wife would not hear of that, which put pressure on the very member of him that the wife needed most. So I advised him to take his wife on vacation without the children, that would give him a chance to not only rest but to recover his stamina. It must have worked because he came back a month later full of smiles and the ones I counted as my regular patrons increased by one . . .

*   *   *

One day, Ofure announced that it'd be too dangerous to work, at least for the next three or four days.

'And why is that?'

'You have closed your eyes and ears to what is happening around you, but I will tell you, our governor and his wife are around.'

I looked at Ofure and shook my head why would the presence of a governor and his wife make the atmosphere unconducive to our work?

'What do you mean?' I asked for clarification.

'Godspower is in town.'

'Ofure either you tell me what this is all about in full sentences or you don't.'

'The governor of my state is in town. And usually the *polizia*, in collusion with him and our ambassador, raids indiscriminately for illegal immigrants for deportation.'

'Why do the *polizia* need his collusion to deport illegal immigrants?'

'Don't mind me; I was just laying my anger anywhere. Anyway our governor, in support of his wife's pet project, 'Operation Self-Sufficient,' needs people.'

'Mmmh, Ofure, would you stop going round and get to the matter?'

'Apparently, it has been said that most girls from my part of our country see prostitution as a lucrative job and flock to Italy to rake in the money. The Italian government is not happy with this development but cannot stamp out the inflow or chase us back to Nigeria. This project therefore, is God sent, because if they send us back and we become actively engaged, they'd clean up their streets of prostitutes or at least reduce the numbers, afterall no be only Naija girls *dey* do *ashawo* for Italy.'

'Mmmh.'

'Is that your only contribution?' Ofure asked irritably.

'Well, at least the girls so repatriated are going to get jobs, which apparently was lacking before now. But what kind of a job do they have in mind?'

'*Na* their mama *dem* go put for that their job so.'

'It is not a good job?'

'Fashion designing my foot. Which *kin yeye* money you go make for fashion designing. *Na* we go design clothes *wey* the governor wife go wear? After them *don* carry all our money *commot*, na who *dem* think say *dem dey* deceive? God punish them there. Bastards!'

'Ofure take am easy, d*em* never catch you yet. Maybe you should go home and try the fashion designing thing; you may just make it, you never know. Eeh . . . but if all of you go back and then train as fashion designers, who will buy from who?'

'*Abeg* make I hear, they want take idea turn us into Obioma tailors more like. Yeye people, who dey even listen to that nonsense. Armed robbers.' I had to laugh; Ofure was really consumed by her anger and hatred. But who wouldn't be, what our government does with our money was a mystery. The amount of millions of dollars flying over the heads of the poor through news reports could leave you permanently in a daze if you paid heed to it, yet nothing could be pointed at as achievements. There was no space big enough to put in the unemployment figure on account of it being high, no job creation—well, this fashion designing business of Ofure's governor's wife could . . . I stopped this is Nigeria we were talking about; government projects have a way of being derailed, and after millions had been spent.

And so we laid low for three days and truly there were extensive raids even at the official reception party for the governor. I even heard that some people went home voluntarily. I wasn't concerned with that. I had bigger plans which could not be found in fashion designing. We resumed duty when the coast cleared and the months continued to fly by.

*   *   *

I dragged myself up from my bed and groaned, my eyes were still glued shut, but I could hear Ofure's rustling in the kitchenette, probably busy boiling hot water with which she hoped to alleviate my pains. I was brutally raped, front and back, and none of them used a condom, subjecting me to the most horrendous pain anybody could ever inflict on another. Ofure's constant warnings had come to pass. She had pursed her lips, frowned and had hissed non-stop since arriving to nurse me. After the attack I had hid in the darkness beside a building shivering and unable to call a cab being naked. But even in the death defying jump I undertook to escape my tormentors, I had held tenaciously to my handbag filled to the brim with Lira. They paid me and in excess too before the ordeal. I should have suspected foul play. I could not even remember how I managed to call Oya who came and took me to my place.

When I had sufficiently recovered, I knew that my quest in Italy was over but first I had to have tests carried out, to confirm that I had not contracted HIV/Aids or got pregnant. It took ages but then both tests came back negative and I was elated. I went to Madam Mary and told her that the time had come for me to go home. I had been in Italy for fifteen months, three months over our estimated limit and had made two and a half times more money than we estimated. She beamed with joy and hastily went into her room, came back with an envelope and thrust it to me. It contained every single dollar I had paid as protection money. She then told me to consider it her contribution towards a good life back home. She also informed me that she would be going home as soon as she got pregnant. I was happy for her.

PART FOUR

Oyi Town, Anambra State, Nigeria

2000

It started to rain towards sundown. It was a welcome relief; the heat coming down from the sun and the one rising from the bowels of the baked earth had been so severe that the villagers were moving about listlessly, expecting to be set on fire at any moment. Roosters had lost their strength to crow and the lizards were found lying flat underneath dry leaves, panting with their tongues sticking out like they were begging for drops of water. The mother hens took leave from their ceaseless scratching for food to hide under the pepper shrub. The whole village had lost its vibrancy, coated in red dust and dry leaves and the relentless rays. So the pellets of rain were a soothing balm to the patched earth and souls. The earth drank greedily to her heart's content before allowing *idei*—flood, to stream down the footpaths while the souls were set free.

I sat on a kitchen stool in front of my mother's chicken and goat shed neither feeling the heat nor the rain when it came. Since returning from Benin City that afternoon I had not uttered a word to anybody, not even to my father. I overheard him advise patience.

'She will tell us at her own time,' he had added, as if he was privy to my decisions. It must be worrying for both of them yet I did not move. So I sat there and reflected while vowing not to allow madness to envelop me, as I had to be sane to salvage what was left of my life now that I had been cut adrift. I'd been back from Italy three days, two of which I had spent wandering the streets of God knows where all because of Osahon. My trip to Benin City was to see my husband. To let him stare me in the eyes and tell me why he was delaying about my return. We were soul mates. You did not cut off parts of your own body. No you don't. That was what I knew. What I had believed. What had kept me going. But he did. He cut and flung me off callously to bleed slowly to death.

My parents were surprised when I came back, too quickly for somebody who had been living away from her husband for so long, but were also deeply shocked, before impotent rage enveloped them. I was bruised all over, my clothes torn in places and muddied. I looked half-mad.

'What, in the name of our Lord Jesus Christ, is going on here?' my father had demanded, but I waved to calm them down, then went outside and sat in my current position.

*   *   *

Abraham and Celina had heard snatches of rumours from time to time that Gift may be living in Italy. Of course, everybody knew what it meant to live in Italy. But their daughter was not living in Italy, she could not be. They were quite sure that she told them when she appeared suddenly with her husband then that she was going to live and work in England. When Osahon came back three weeks later, he brought letters, pictures and many presents as well as their two granddaughters. They were overjoyed and hungry for news. Osahon and the children had stayed the whole day, and then he left, alone!

They were happy to have the children even though they had wondered why Osahon's mother, Ivene, had decided to relinquish them. What had changed her mind? It had strained the relationship between the two families when Celina had earlier insisted the children would be better off staying with her, but Ivene had objected and had kept them.

Now the mystery had deepened with Gift's return, and she had not uttered a word so far.

But all the mysteries must be explained to her today, Celina suddenly vowed to Abraham. She was no longer going to "exercise patience".

When it started raining and Gift was still sitting outside like a statue, Celina told Abraham that the joke had gone too far and stormed out to confront her daughter.

*   *   *

'*Chinekem e e eh. Alu emekwanu mu ooo!*' My God e e eh. Calamity has befallen me o o oh! Celina screamed, while flailing her hands in supplication to the unseen God.

'*Onye gee som wee kwue no o.* Who will advocate for me? My daughter has gone mad o o oh!' she continued to wail.

The scream brought Abraham out to behold his wife running in circles round the daughter who was laughing, her head tilted back, face raised up to the sky, rain drenched, uncaring, as if she had truly gone mad.

'May I have peace and quiet in this compound,' he roared.

On hearing his voice, Celina stopped and then sprang into action, with the agility of a monkey, 'Are you speaking of peace and quiet, eh? Can you not see what my eyes are seeing?' Abraham tried and was able to hold Celina's two hands together before speaking firmly, 'Celina hold yourself together now!' That poured cold water on Celina and she started crying quietly. Abraham released his wife's hand and turned to Gift.

'Gift my daughter, what is it?'

The pain in my father's voice clawed its way into the inner recesses of my mind and I stopped laughing, brought my head down and turned to look at my parents, my face still wreathed with a serene smile. My father nodded at his accomplishment, he then held out his hands to me. I grasped them and got up from the very low kitchen stool wincing with pain as my waist protested from being subjected to such a position for hours. Sandwiched between my parents, we turned to proceed towards the house, away from the torrential rain, and our neighbour, Akego, who must have decided to come and investigate after her repeated o *nnidi mee?* What has happened? went unanswered. As we passed her, my mother told her to go back in and she would see her later. Akego nodded and turned to shuffle back to her hut on her arthritic toes, she must have forgotten her walking stick in her hurry.

They settled me on a wooden chair, and then both sat on the mud bed cum couch facing and staring at me despondently. I stared back at them with my heart bleeding and my mouth heavy: I was going to shatter their lives. But first I skirted with lighter issues by announcing that I had not gone mad, rather had been freed! My parents did not want to hazard any guess as to what I meant, they were tired of guessing, this, I gleaned from their look. So I decided to get it over and done with.

By the time I had gone half-way through my story, my mother's tears had drenched her completely and my father could barely restrain his anger but found solace in grinding his teeth instead. I told them that I loved Osahon as they no doubt were aware of, but the attempt to ensure that he would be with me till *death do us part* made me foolish and blind. I did not want anything, as small as money issue, to blight our love. So I went to Italy and worked as a prostitute. My parents turned to look at each other after this pronunciation, then returned their gaze on me speechless, but ensured that they did not crack a muscle to show what they felt about such wisdom, I guessed. They had waited so long for information that at this point they did not want to antagonize or berate me yet. As they sat there in their soaked clothes, the story unraveling was getting weirder.

*   *   *

How could it not be, Abraham thought bitterly; Osahon became rich, arrogant and pompous overnight, forgot them and his children. Their repeated efforts at seeing him, to enquire about their daughter, were rebuffed and when seen at all was full of empty promises of coming back with her on his next trip to London! Short of arresting him with the police, which they had attempted, but did not have the wherewithal to carry through, what else could they do but to continue to place it before God, asking him to intervene? Especially when the policeman at the station informed them that there was hardly anything they could do, having been told by Osahon and naively confirmed by her parents that the said lady went off to London on her on volition and had sent pictures and letters since leaving. The officer even went as far as admonishing them for causing trouble for their son-in-law who had had the bad luck of marrying a wife that went abroad and refused to come back. Were they not ashamed of themselves for spawning such a she-devil who could abandon her husband and children like that?!

Of course, when you're a poor person dragging issues with a deep pocket before a police officer, forget it, you'd be better off seeking other means to solve your problem, you could not win.

Besides, the police officer further nailed the case against them when he asked whether they expected the police to involve the Interpol just to go after a recalcitrant wife. 'This is a domestic affair, in case you don't know.' And to drive it home, he further chided them to stop wasting tax-payers' money and police time unnecessarily. In conclusion he had advised that Osahon should marry another wife if the present one continued to refuse to come back.

*   *   *

While Abraham was ruminating about their failed attempt at bringing Osahon to book, Celina could only stare at her daughter: remembering the countless decades of rosary she had prayed, supplicating Mother Mary to intercede on her behalf and put in a word to her son, Jesus Christ our Savior, and now this? Well, one could hardly blame the Hosts of Heaven for her daughter's misdeeds. At least she was alive to tell the story and would have plenty of time to atone for this abomination.

However, the story took a different twist when Gift informed them what she found out in Benin City; that Osahon had married another wife who was pregnant for him, thus bringing to the fore the horrors of what their daughter went through and now for nothing.

Abraham looked at his wife and shook his head 'no' when he noted the change in her demeanor at this turn of events, imploring with his eyes for her not to interfere yet.

When I had arrived Osahon's house that evening and rang the bell at the gate his Hausa security man through the intercom informed me that 'Oga and madam go *hasipiti*, but oga e go *kwom* back now now.'

I had then informed him that I would want to wait for oga, whereupon the *aboki* demanded to know who I was, 'as *ebi* say oga don marry, 'im sisters no dey *kwom* for house again, so which one you be eh?'

So Osahon my husband has been having girlfriends in my absence and now he is married? Married? To whom? I rallied however, and informed him that "I be oga true sister wey de live abroad."

'Abroad? Haba.'

After that comment the gate was thrown wide open and he invited me in with '*kwom* in sister. Na true, you resemble oga well well.'

Then he instructed me in a conspiratorial tone to be careful of that witch of a housemaid installed by madam when I entered the main house. I had smiled my appreciation while noting that the

word 'abroad' uttered anywhere in Nigeria had never failed to elicit
a positive reaction, at the same time surmising that rivalry between
household paid employees was always simmering beneath the edge of
the surface. It came with the territory, especially in a big household
that needed so many servants to run. I was not sure, however, that
Osahon's household was big enough to qualify, but what did I
know? I dashed the *aboki* N500 and this threw him into a paroxysm
of appreciation, 'may Allah bless you madam, you go marry better
azband madam, *tanki* you madam,' as he kept bowing and invoking all
manner of blessings on me I left him to it and went up the main house
wary as instructed. But the said witch of a housemaid did not display
any witchly conduct, rather she welcomed me in after I had repeated
what I told the guard, she installed me in a vantage position to espy
the arrival of my *brother.*

Nothing could have prepared me for Osahon's behaviour when he
came back. Having been informed at the gate by his *aboki*, apparently,
of the presence of his *sister* from abroad, he had gone berserk: for
he ran into the house ranting and raving, the gist of which was, what
gave me the temerity to come into his home without permission?
Who did I think I was? Meanwhile, he was punctuating his words with
the removal of his wristwatch and neck chains, rings, sunglasses and
ear-studs like he was getting ready for a physical combat.

Having chased the maid out and locked the door he charged at
me, unleashing his anger. He flogged me black and blue with the belt
loosened from his waist. He kicked, he bit and he pummeled me with
wild punches, reducing me to a quivering mess. Finally he raped me
and then proceeded to strangle me.

I heard my parents gasp, their sharp intake of air brought me to my
senses. I stopped my narration and stared into space: flicking through
the pictures. I would not let my parents see the gory details. They
did not need that picture added to their landscape of helplessness.
But it was at that very moment in my ordeal with Osahon that I felt
that I had lost it, that I had gone mad: for from then on, everything
became fuzzy and I remembered nagging myself for failing to wear
Jeans trouser to embark on the journey. That could not possibly be
the thought of a sane person being raped, surely? Then I thought
that I was still in Torino when I had faced similar ordeal. But there
was something different this time, something very wrong. This time I
was being raped with a familiar penis and the voice . . . the voice was
achingly familiar, not the slurring voices of drunk Italian rednecks.
And it was that voice that forced me back from the beckoning abyss.
It reminded me of the good times I had with the owner of that voice:

when we were poor but were in love and were happy. It was the voice that made me pay attention.

But why was he sounding like that; distressed, and then defeated? And why was he crying? What was causing his distress? Should I not be the one crying? Then his words penetrated my consciousness. But they were confusing words: they did not tally with his actions . . . . *Oh Gift. My Princess. My babes. Do you know that I love you so much? Too much . . . Do you know that? You do . . . Don't you? You were the great love of my life. The only one . . . You are my life, my world. Why? Gift why? I couldn't keep you . . . I had to give you up . . . I had to babes . . . You know babes . . . You know that . . . You understood my needs don't you? Yes you do . . . Answer me you fucking cunt!*

I was dumbfounded. The bastard had cracked. He had to be; otherwise he certainly had a way of showing his love! All that feeling he spouted did not spare me from his anger which exploded after uttering the last sentence punctuating every word with ripping and ramming. I was raw with pain, everywhere. Then he screamed my name as he was wracked by waves upon waves of orgasm. I had watched him with half-closed eyes, detached. When he had sufficiently recovered, he looked at me with disgust and then proceeded to choke me. I had then lost consciousness, believing that the end had finally come. And not too soon . . .

I sighed closing that window, knowing that I'd never forget, it had now been seared on my soul, but I also knew that this my parents would never see. I looked at them, still frozen, and continued with my story, it would be better for everybody for the tale to be told once and for all, but with certain pages concealed. So I flicked through and resumed my narration from when I resurfaced from death. I could not feel Osahon's weight on me anymore but I could hear him, this time though his voice had turned menacing and chilling, like the relentless bitter-Italian cold slashing my skin. The voice informed me that he was never in love with me. That the whole idea of dating me was set up for the sole purpose of using me to make money which I stupidly complicated and nearly thwarted by getting pregnant twice! My parents looked at each other but returned their gazes quickly on me. *But you told us that both of you were in love then*, was the interpretation I could give the look but they said nothing and I continued.

I told them that Osahon went further to shred my heart into tiny fragments by noting that even if he was remotely in love with me then, what made me think that he would live with an *ashawo* like me now? Did I not have any shame? Then he informed me that, 'I am now happily married, to the apple of my eyes, and we are expecting our first issue so vamoose from my sight.'

'*Olisa binigwe, oginizi di nkea?* God in heaven, what is this?' my mother exclaimed while my father stared at me with his mouth pursed. I continued. Osahon then advised me to find my own level. He did not know how I managed to come back in the first place, because I was not supposed to return. In any case, he said, now that I had returned against his wishes, my best bet would be to go back and continue with my work, but if I insisted on not obeying him, then I had better ensure that our paths should never cross, because then I would incur his wrath, to the full measure, which he assured me would end in my death. Yes, my death! My parents drew in a sharp breath in unison, but I did not stop.

He then kicked me out of the house with my clothes half-torn and in disarray. And in my haste to dodge further blows, I missed the last step and fell, whereupon, he threw my blouse at me which he must have torn off me in his frenzy as well as my handbag, shouted at me to cover my shameless body and get out of his compound fast while reiterating the death threat.

I scrambled to my feet and ran into the security post at the gate. I did not take Osahon's threat lightly: I had heard and seen what happened to my fellow Nigerians sent to Italy to prostitute for their patrons: madams, pimps, sponsors, or whatever name they bear, who had failed to comply with the agreed contracts. But then, I never likened my position to theirs. I was not like them. I was in a class of my own: in a joint business with my husband. It was never a contract; it was a gesture of love on my part. *More the fool* I thought bitterly.

To suddenly find myself among that group was bloodcurdling, a physical blow to my heart. Nothing seemed to make sense anymore. Osahon had twisted my mind, thither and hither and then back in full circle with his actions and words.

But I was more concerned with the, "You were not meant to come back" part, which had stuck. What did he mean by that? However, I did not stay to find out, rather I hastened and left the compound immediately. If Osahon planned the whole saga, as he claimed, did it mean that there was a blood-oath in existence somewhere? Did he place juju on me? And if he did what did it mean exactly? That comment "you were not meant to come back" must be reviewed but not in his compound. Much as I was terrified by the effect of a rampaging 'blood-oath', I was still clear-headed enough to take to my heels. Osahon had taken dangerous to a new height!

I caught my parents shaking their heads, confounded. I continued anyway. I needed to tell the story, in its entirety, to see if it could relieve the pressure it was exerting on my brain. So I continued.

'As I roamed, so many incidents were flashing before my eyes so fast that, at a point I became very dizzy and had to seek for a resting place in a *buka* filled with clamouring clients.'

I was mildly surprised to note that it was morning. I then sat on the edge of one of the benches facing away from the crowd so as not to attract their attention, just until the ground stopped rushing up to my face. I must have been lost in thought again, because when I paid attention to the hungry 'mob,' it dawned on me that they were in fact arguing about what could be the matter with me.

'. . . Her madness must be new,' someone had pointed out while shaking his head in pity. Another concurred by noting that 'her clothes are still clean, even though some places are torn, she could not have been on the road for long.'

'But look at the state of her feet, it tells a different story, she must have been walking since the madness seized her,' a very sturdy man observed. Another pointed out that my hair was an absolute mess, but that I was beautiful and must have been one of those high flyers when I was still alright. They had carried on discussing me openly, resting on the conviction of my being 'newly mad' as they put it, and so could neither decipher nor understand what they were saying.

I got up instantly and left, my heart racing with panic. It was then that I took a proper look at myself and realized that I looked a mess. I then moved as far away from the buka as I could and tried flagging down a taxi to bring me home.

None of the taxi's stopped until the one that demanded payment of seven thousand Naira upfront. Through him I was able to decode the mystery of where I was, though how I was able to cover such a distance eluded me. I did not argue the price, neither did I blame him for insisting that he be paid upfront: In his line of business stories abound where certain women would offer to pay 'in-kind' when they had reached their destination. Could he use 'in-kind' to pay for petrol, house rent or his children's school fees? Who could do anything with payment 'in-kind' anyway? It had also been said that some of their clients would disappear into a compound, on the pretence that they were going to collect money, and never return.

I counted out the seven thousand Naira as demanded and was about to pay the cabbie, but on second thought decided to give him the whole bundle of ten thousand Naira with me and announce to him that having saved me, he should take the total of what I earned on the 'prowl' that night. This, I pointed out to my shell-shocked parents, was to deter his being tempted to kill me, when we had turned into the lonely dirt road to the village, believing that I had more money on me, as some of the bad eggs were known to do, of which you were aware of. *Nigerians!*

My parents did not know when the story ended; they were that stunned and rigid with anger. Eventually my father collected himself and asked, 'Gift my daughter; did you enter into any blood-oath with or for Osahon?'

I had wondered about this same question myself at Osahon's compound but I firmly shook my head no as I would have remembered if I did. That seemed to calm them before they settled to digest all that they had heard.

After a considerable time had elapsed with my parents still stunned into stupor, I got up to go into my room, to at least change out of my wet clothing, but my mother's wooden voice stopped me.

'People who do not know when rain started to fall on them would not know when it stopped falling on them either. You vehemently refused our pleading and married Osahon. Then while married to him you abandoned the values we had instilled in you. We never had money flowing in this house; we never starved and we had our honor intact. So who sent you to go and debase yourself? Your new found freedom as a big university student, eh? The university that you did not finish. So was it your books that led you astray, eh? All because of what Gift? Money? *Zam nu.* Answer me now. You chose money over morals, over what is right, *okwia*? Inspite of our best efforts you have managed to slap our faces and heaped feaces on our heads, now flies would start to not only congregate, but will follow us around. *Odinma*, alright, now that you have ate what was keeping you awake for so long, maybe you can go to sleep.'

She stopped as suddenly as she had started and I sat back down and started crying . . .

Healing

While in the plane leaving Italy, my thoughts were in tatters: nervous yet hopeful. How was I going to confront Osahon? What would he do when he saw me? All those jitters and apprehension had been put to rest. Now it was over. He simply destroyed me. I tried to steer clear from thinking about him because then this strange carpentry workshop, set up on the crown of my head down to my forehead, would swing into staccato-hammering action. Then a tingling ringing would start in my ears, supported by my mother's words which had calcified into a spiral iron, poking at my ear-drum in an advance-withdraw style, with my father's mute-stare bringing the rear as a dark blanket that'd cover me, suffocating me into unconsciousness. I could now lay claim to knowing the meaning of "in the shadow of death." For it was something that one could ever only understand living it.

My mother, after that speech, and from that day kept away from my path like I would infect her and that was a different pain altogether. My father lost his desire to nap in his shed, preferring instead to gaze into the distance.

As each day continued to turn into another, I noted that I had been too hasty to pronounce my freedom, on the day of the rain, the day I returned from Benin City. I was a long way away from freedom. If anything, I was now in prison proper. I couldn't venture out except in the cloak of darkness, since I heard my mother one day hissing to my father that people were asking after me in that funny way of the village, because they knew that something was smelling but they couldn't say what. In my part of the world, when you marry, you visit your family, only. An overly extended visit was off, something must be wrong if so, especially when it looked like you were hiding. Even if you decided to close your doors to them, they'd come for, 'nne Gift, *odikwa na nma, nkea anaka afurogi izua?* Hope everything is alright, this one that we have not seen you this week?' This week, mind you, may actually be a day, and the visit accompanied by sharp wandering, speculative eyes. All things considered, therefore, I had to really snap out of my frightful situation, I couldn't allow my parents to be the object of the villagers' tongues. And for that singular reason I made the effort to shed my grief.

And luckily, it worked. My darkness started to recede, even though my heart refused to mend: when it shattered, the bits and pieces were too tiny to be pieced together. A broken heart cannot mend except maybe where each piece was found and glued back, one by one, accordingly. Some pieces of mine must have been left behind in Osahon's compound in my haste to escape. So the gap remained open. Mainly because the picture of my last encounter with Osahon had taken root and eclipsed every other thing we had had: casting a dismal, blistering shadow over my whole self and life. If I knew I was going to mourn our love like this I would not have bothered to leave his compound in the first place. I would have implored him to kill me instead.

But I needed to be sane. I had to be sane. So I tried and with the method I had long since perfected in Torino: block the dark thoughts. Lock them up. I won. As the day continued to turn to the next, I knew that it was a good decision. It should be. Didn't it serve me well in Torino?

When other thoughts started filtering in like the one that reminded me that I had two children to think of, I allowed it. And then the gentle spirit of the village like warmed *okwuma*, sheabutter, on a sprained ankle, gradually started seeping in. Healing? That I do not know about. Only time will tell. But it was good to stop giving my father the work of picking up my fainted body all the time. My mother she spoke to me only when it was absolutely necessary, which was very rare. But to me, what really mattered was that I was home and I would not hurt anymore.

However, I saw that I had emerged from the cocoon of pain a different butterfly; a butterfly without any luster—a sad butterfly that crawled, like an ant, instead of shimmering in flight. But I held on tenaciously to life. I must forge on.

* * *

In the second week of my return, I went to my father to seek absolution and information. The long-standing tradition of father and daughter tramping about immediately after the first cock crow, regardless of the dew, to catch the fresh frothing palmwine, for its potency and quality, was reactivated. We both stepped into it like I had never left the village. I remembered my mother then warning my father to not make a drunk out of me, how I valiantly chose to certify my father's palmwine over going to school, though to my knowledge, none of my father's brew had failed to pass the test with or without my expertise! I shook my head sadly and continued to natter gently with my father while sipping the natural brew. I chose to believe that that close relationship, forged all those years, had not been broken by my absence and transgression. But . . .

Stretching my cup for more drinks I looked closely at him and was startled to see that he had aged. It must be the manual labour of having to climb so many palm trees twice daily to tap wine. And the irony of it all was that there was nothing to show for all his efforts, financially.

But he should not look that old at sixty years, even though the recent life expectancy report for Nigerian men was now as low as fifty years, that did not mean that the men should look dried, shriveled, haggard and half-dead even before they get to die. I drank deeply, cleared my throat and asked, 'Papa, what am I going to do about mama?'

I did not look at him.

'Nothing. Your mother is grieving deeply. Give her time.'

I nodded. Then throwing caution to the wind I said, 'Papa I am deeply sorry for what I did to myself and to you and mama, forgive me.'

If I have ever felt remorse for doing anything I shouldn't have done in my entire life, that single "forgive me" carried the whole weight. He closed his eyes and did not answer. I decided to let it go and tried another track. I would come back to that later.

'Papa, do you not think that it is time to retire?' He still kept quiet, his eyes closed. Finally he spoke.

'Retire and do what my daughter? You know it was a good thing that I had this work to look forward to, it kept my mind occupied during your absence.' He kept quiet again, and we became enveloped

by a certain silence, the silence of unsaid things. Eventually my father
cleared his throat.

'I know what you mean, but what can I do?'

'Why don't you employ a climber?'

'You know that I cannot afford that luxury; there is not much
money in this business, especially here in the village where it is sold
for nothing. That is not all, much as I would like to take things easy,
what will happen to your brother and his family? We do what we can
for them you know and I have to be working to do that. I will not allow
your mother to kill herself with work.'

'Why must Obumneme continue to work as a bicycle repairer, can
he not look for something else to do or combine that with farming
even? On top of that he made too many children.' I stopped to take a
deep breath that'd carry the next sentence, 'He drinks a bit too much
too Papa, or don't you think so?' My voice was tinged with irritation.
Obumneme, as far I could glean, was a weakling, that's what, and our
parents were the ones maintaining his weakness by propping him.

'We will just have to continue to help him and his family as long as
we can. As for his drinking, when a man misses the step to the ladder
of life, he is either content with the situation and manages somehow
or he is not, in which case, he turns to something for comfort, to make
him forget. And don't forget also that he is your senior brother.'

I was surprised that my father admitted this much and didn't want
to miss this opportunity so presented so I plunged on.

'But Papa, nobody will accuse you of being rich, yet you did not
acquire that habit.'

'Mmm. I want you to forge ahead; do not allow this missed-step
to trap you. You have transgressed yes, but the cure will not be to
lie down and grovel in shame; you do not stop running till death.
Stopping is to accept defeat. However, you must first seek to reconcile
with our God unfailingly.'

'Alright Papa.' I breathed a sigh of relief but did not want him to
move deeper into that line of talk; it was stirring emotions I'd rather
hold down, preferring to stay on mundane issues.

'Papa, please look for a climber and negotiate with him, I will pay
his salary.'

'You do not have to trouble yourself, my daughter; you have
enough on your plate.'

'Papa, it is not going to be any trouble for me to pay for a climber,
please.'

'No my daughter, you must do something about your life first
before you begin to worry about me. Like I said, we will manage.'

'You have not forgiven me then?'

'Your transgression is not mine to forgive; I can only condemn the action. Make peace with God my daughter; it is His forgiveness you need. It is His forgiveness that is important. I will let you know when I find a climber.'

My father's words silenced me: my fear had been unearthed, exposed. The ring of condemnation and sadness underpinning my father's voice, even though expertly masked, was resounding everywhere, raking my healing wound. My father . . . ! And I knew then that he'd not look for a climber.

That evening my mother returned from her *buka* and, as if in conspiracy with my father, launched her own campaign by asking me what I intended to do now. I blanched from the vehemence in her words as she continued without minding my reaction, 'Or have you decided to live in the village? Because if you have, then you should start making feasible plans to accompany the decision, sitting down at home drinking palmwine is not a job,' she finished and walked away to potter in her pepper shrub—it had become some sort of a safe haven for her these days, maybe so as not to share the same air with me.

For the first time I really wondered at what outsiders would make of my behaviour if they got to know. From the mini-world that was my family I concluded that this was a portion of my life that would be put under lock and key and the key buried in an unmarked grave. Nobody outside would ever get to know. But the tragedy was not in being rejected by everybody but in your joining force to reject yourself, there lies the calamity. So skulking in the village was not an option.

But I couldn't help wondering about the feminists of the world: on what perspective would they base my action? What role did patriarchy play? Did socialization, subjugation and the subordination of women, so imbued in my psyche as a woman in our patriarchal society, stretch their ugly hands, in their various capacities, to push me, convincing me that it was my wifely role to make my husband happy? Work my fingers to the bone, in this case my body. Would they be convinced that I was genuinely in love and wanted to make us both happy, by satisfying a given want—being rich? Or maybe they'd applaud my action, afterall, I made a choice, carried it through regardless of my societally assigned role as a woman. Or they may not, if looked at on the basis of my allowing myself to be exploited in order to retain the love of a man. Now that, the feminists might hold against me.

But if Osahon had been truly in love with me and everything worked out and went according to plan, would it have made it alright?

I felt that not many people would choose to become a prostitute
because of somebody else voluntarily, except stupid people like me,
who do not look before leaping. What if I had prostituted to feed
my children, would it make it understandable and less condemning?
Would it get people's approval? Would it be classed as exploitation of
the weak, vulnerable and gullible? But why am I really worried about
societal approval? Which society in particular am I talking about? In
Ofure's part of our country, parents accept payments from patrons
to allow their daughters to work as prostitutes in Italy. It was a pure
business arrangement and not one daughter felt an iota of shame for
doing the job, not from what I witnessed out there. In fact these girls
vied for who would erect the best mansion, who received titles before
the others, whose car was cooler . . . , *Gift stop deceiving yourself. Your
mother asked you a question, answer it.*

Ok.

Well in all its stark reality, it was an extremely foolish thing that I
did, love or no love.

And now I had seen that my parent's bitterness and anger would
not cease if I continued to live with them, my presence a constant
reminder of how the mighty had fallen, how all their hopes had been
dashed and how I had committed the incomprehensible.

I had accepted that I would never be truly free from what I did,
from Osahon or the memory of him, good and bad, but I had to live
and since I had lifted the burden of deceit, there was no reason to not
try and put my life back on track. But where do I go?

*   *   *

I noted that my father had changed; now contemplative, withdrawn
and not voluble. And I brought that into life. I wanted my father to
forgive, to let him know that I was the sinner and so the cross was
mine to bear, but he had refused to engage in any talk of my lost
years because to forgive he would have to confront what I did and that
he did not want to do. But when I went in to see him on that I lost
my argument so I just sat there shifting uneasily from time to time,
studying his profile hoping to detect an accepting aura. After a while
I said, 'Papa I have learnt a hard and bitter lesson and I would know
to watch myself in future, but there will not be a viable future if I have
to also carry the burden of your unforgiveness as well as knowing that
you are shouldering my sin.'

My father still didn't say anything. It was baffling to me. What had
happened to my father? Finally he spoke.

'Gift my daughter, what we do ultimately affects not just us but all concerned *maka na ofu aka luta nmanu ozue ora onu.* When one finger was soiled by oil it'd soil the rest. You may not know but it is also my cross as a father, but we would not carry our grief forever for what is done is done. The question is where are you going to start from?'

I shivered and stared back at my father. I didn't realize how much of a gully that had developed between us. It hurt. I maintained my pained gaze on him as I responded.

'Papa, I need you, please forgive me.' He steered his face away from mine and stared into the distance. Then he responded to my plea, by clasping my hand but without a word. I grasped his hand firmly, knowing that this was better than nothing.

'Papa, I have enough to manage with, do not worry.' I held his gaze and reluctantly he nodded. There was no way I would ever say a thing like that to my mother, she'd strangle me. Then I added, 'Give me another month, enough time to streamline a plan then I'll leave.'

'What are these your plans exactly?'

So he was now reduced to questioning his own daughter's words? But who wouldn't, in which world does a husband have a business arrangement for his wife to prostitute for him? The mother of his own children! *Alu emegom n'uwa mputa.* I have suffered abomination in this my life. Eeh Osahon! *'Tufiakwa! Ife chukwu ga ekpe n'ipke akalia, o gini?!'* What would come before God for judgment would be numerous! He lifted his palms and rubbed them together, then sitting up straight he sighed. He would not indulge these thoughts today so he inhaled deeply, to dispel the pain constricting his chest.

Seeing the tension build on my father's neck I rubbed at it while murmuring. 'Papa, it is enough. Please papa it is enough.'

Abraham did not respond but continued to ruminate in the same strain of thought. What had got into our children? What were they searching for? Whatever it was, they had unwittingly invited Satan to take hold of their generation. That's what has happened but they should please allow him to pass away peacefully. For what their acts would unleash on the world was yet to unfold.

Gift's rustling brought him back to the present and they resumed their conversation.

'Papa, I want to bring my children back. Sister Chinelo has tried, taking them in even as they could barely feed their own.'

'Eeh, Ikemefuna has been a good in-law to us and a good husband to your sister. Although his hand is not strong, he is a man.' Abraham looked away, but continued as if he did not stop.

'I will go with you to Onitsha. Send a message to your brother ThankGod to meet us there.'

I nodded. Maybe the time had come to begin to trust in the wisdom of the elders. And so we sat there in companionable silence with flies droning in the background. Then I thought, while we were still on the subject of Osahon it wouldn't hurt to know certain things.

'Papa how do I formally divorce a husband who only paid bride price?' Remembering our proposed *one in town* wine-carrying and *grandfather* of all church weddings, after we had supposedly made it, I shook my head sorrowfully. Osahon really must have taken me for a fool. He never really intended to marry me. But I had to shrug off that train of thought; it'd lead nowhere other than unearth other unpleasantness.

'I have discussed that with your mother, we were only waiting for you to get stronger. I will send a message to Osahon's family to receive us. We will go in the company of our kinsmen to hand over the bride price he paid on your head and that will be that; the marriage will be ended. If we do not do that, even if you marry another man, that new marriage will not be valid and any children produced will still belong to Osahon.'

I narrowed my eyes about to argue that I was not really interested in another marriage but stopped. My father did not need further aggravation from me. Instead I said, 'What I want is to be sure that he will not come calling one day and because of one customary reason or the other I would be asked to go back to him.'

'You need a husband. In case you don't know, God did not create us to live alone if we can marry.'

I nodded, there was no point arguing with him, he was already set in his ways. As an afterthought I asked, 'What of our children, if the bride price is returned, what about his relationship with them?'

'It does not, they are his children. When they are grown up and want to relate with him that will be their decision.'

'I pray that he rejects them, because I will not want any of us to see him again.' Then another thought suddenly shot into my mind and I looked sharply at my father, 'Papa, I hope I will not be required to be there?!' My voice rising in panic.

'No, it can be done in the absence of the two of you,' my father reassured me in a calm tone.

'But what if his kinsmen at his instruction refuse to accept the bride price, does it mean I will be tied to him forever?'

'No. In that case we will inform our traditional ruler and his council of elders, they will help us to return the money to Osahon's family through their own traditional ruler. Do not worry my daughter, the case is in our favour; he left the marriage not you.'

*   *   *

We went to Onitsha, met up with ThankGod, and together brought my children back as planned. Frances my first daughter was now two years and eight months old while Blessing was one year and seven months old. I tucked away in my mind, to remember to change Blessing's name: I was not about to be confronted daily by the phony reasoning behind it. The children did not remember me, of course, but I intended to make it up to them from then onwards.

My children now safely with me I settled down to begin to learn about being a mother while making and discarding different plans about where to relocate to. My children appeared happy at having a physical mother living with them. Frances told me that her mother was a picture; this was because my sister Chinelo had continually pointed me out to them from a picture of my graduation from Government College. When they finally saw me in the flesh they took the news calmly and continued with their life as if nothing untoward had happened. I knew that we'd all have to work hard on our relationship. I, to learn to be a mother and them to be children with a mother that was physically present.

Confident that Osahon would not come after us, ThankGod stayed for only one week and left. He updated me on the progress of his furniture and interior design business which he started with the money he had made from *oso-afia* in addition to the small one Chief Osungwa finally gave him. His next plan, he said, would be to relocate to Benin City so as to be closer to the source of raw materials. I did not doubt that he'd succeed. He has always been very artistic and a dab hand at drawing, painting, carving and all what not. Then my brother dropped a bombshell; his plan to marry Faith, my friend from Government College. It took me awhile to recover from the shock. Then what of the economic disparity between our two families? It's not always a good thing for a poor man to marry into a rich family. For women it may be different, but in the case of men, they were usually expected as the head of the household to provide for their family, so if that position was taken out of his hand by marrying into money what would happen to his pride and his expected role? I doubt that the word 'gold-digger' would sit on a man properly. I could not bear to see anybody demean my brother. And more to the point and the source of shock, the sexual dalliance I had had with her in college.

What did it mean to her in the long run? Or was she marrying to appease her family and have children while she was a closet lesbian, having affairs behind her husband's back, my brother?! Should I tell him or confront Faith? What would be the right thing to do?

'I know what you are thinking.'

'You do?'

Of course you don't, I thought.

'Two things; Faith told me about your relationship with her. But like you it was all in the past. And when we marry, we will work together as a team and make our own music; we will not depend on her family.'

I smiled.

'You've turned into a seer now. But is she really willing to give up her luxurious lifestyle for you? They are too rich and she too entrenched in the ways of the rich.'

'I knew the score and am ready to pluck the stars for her. Besides, she is not going to give up on what she was used to, we are on track to make it ourselves. You may not know it but the furnishing business is very lucrative. We are starting in Benin now but our aim is to have branches all over the country and control it from Abuja.'

'You were a stubborn goat then and now a stubborn entrepreneur, I have no doubt you'll make it if you put your mind to it. But . . . You're sure you love her? I know that she has everything in her favour, but do you love her for herself or . . .'

'I won't marry her otherwise: I love her deeply. From the day she walked into our father's compound I have never doubted my love for her. I was never fixated on wealth Gift; you of all people should know that.'

I did not respond, but it hurt. Even my brother? I gazed at him intently, my eyes mirroring the hurt.

'Oooh Gi, I'm so sorry. I didn't mean it that way.'

I nodded. Then implored, 'Please do not tell her about me.'

'It is not my story to tell.'

ThankGod stretched his hand and dragged me down from our tree-bed and hugged me tightly.

'I did not understand why you did what you did for Osahon then, but now that I have Faith in my life maybe I am beginning to have inkling. My feelings for Faith have given me an insight into what must have pushed you, but I must confess that you really went to the extreme Gift. Love should not destroy. It is supposed to be pure and clean. But do not let that bring your spirit down, make your plans and leave this village as soon as you can to strive at starting afresh.'

My eyes watered immediately, but ThankGod wiped the tears and held my face between his palms.

'Don't cry anymore. Come and live in Benin City and I'll help you.'

I nodded, still blinded by my tears. As we walked back home holding hands, I was infused by comfort and strength from his offer of support. I'll hasten and leave for Benin to search for a place of my own, Osahon or not.

*   *   *

My relationship with my mother thawed but then evolved into a kind of uneasy relationship. Granted, we were never deeply close, but after the fragile thread that held us together had cut, I felt that the onus was on me to make the effort to re-tie it. Some mornings, I'd accompany her to her *buka* instead of staying with my father. Initially she ignored me, but then a small vista was opened by my continued presence. Gradually she started responding to my questions, first with nods, then short sentences. Things started looking positive.

It was in the middle of the second month of my return, as I perched on a stool in my mother's buka chatting with her, that my thoughts suddenly swung and dropped certain information into my mind: I should have menstruated about three weeks ago! I nearly fell off the stool prompting my mother to look sharply at me.

'Gift ogini?' I shook my head to indicate nothing while I scrambled back onto the stool. After a while, I got up and told her that I needed to take the children off my father. I left immediately with my mother's gaze on my retreating back.

God . . . what is this? Osahon. Osahon. Osahon. What did I ever do to you? What? Have you not finished with me yet? I wailed desolately in my soul as I stumbled home.

This was the great-grandmother of all problems. An absolute tragedy. How could fate be so callous? What did it want from me? After moaning and beating myself up I settled it in my mind that I would abort the child. Enough was enough. It became a matter of urgency that I relocate immediately.

Later that night I told my parents that I had decided to relocate to Benin City, as ThankGod had promised to help me. They were better off not knowing anything about my new situation. They did not respond, but the next morning they quietly told me that they were in support of my decision to leave the village and would always be there for us, but they felt that it would be better if I left alone and returned for the children when I had secured a job.

My mother then added a child is a gift from God and no matter how much my generation had trivialized it, life was still very sacred and not to be tampered with. I must also realize that I was no longer in a position to attract a man of my choice because not many men would be in a hurry to marry a woman with children, except of course, where he himself was a widower with his own children. In conclusion she advised that it's always better to have children early in life so that one would be able to provide for them with the strength of youth. When she stopped speaking, I could only nod.

She knew!

My father on the other hand did not utter a word. Probably because he was lost as to what his wife was talking about. He looked askance, first at his wife, who had assumed her usual demeanor—frowning with her lips clamped tight and pursed—and then to his daughter who presented a calm demeanor also. He shrugged the so-long-as-we-all-understood-each-other kind of shrug and looked on, and finally, he shrugged on the coat of cool too. We would have cut a hilarious scenario if it was not so serious a problem.

I did not respond to my mother. I did not need to. She was not the one going to be burdened with the pregnancy or tormented for life by living with the outcome either. So she could say whatever she liked, I would not be drawn into any conversation on that. I found it strange though that it was so easy to decide to abort the baby. Maybe it had become that easy because I had so stretched the boundary of iniquity that I had enough room to accommodate just about anything without a twinge of conscience.

In any case, if I did not say it out nobody would accuse me of tampering with God's gift or I could even claim that I miscarried. But could this kind of thing qualify as a gift from God? What kind of bloody gift came like that? I raised my eyes as a challenge to my mother before calmly leaving for a walk. I needed a smoke to clear my head first before I could even begin to think.

When I returned I assured my mother that I'd keep the pregnancy but I'd have to leave the village along with my children as soon as possible as I would not continue to shirk my responsibility to them, so the earlier we all started to live together the better. My mother's response was a shrug, but after a long moment of indecision, which was very rare for her. Voluble she may not be, but she had never been known to be hesitant with words when she had something to say either.

'A child is a child Gift and since the father is still the father of your daughters, you will forget the circumstances of the conception when it is born. I had thought you knew your left from your right but I am not sure anymore or what you are capable of, so it will be to my eternal damnation, if I keep quiet and something happens to that child.'

She stopped and rubbed her palms together, her head bowed in eternal sorrow, I suppose. I looked at her and saw her then protesting vehemently that I should not marry Osahon, that I should graduate first then decide if I really wanted to marry him. At that time she was a stumbling block to my happiness. And look at her now; again trying to shoulder my pain. Mothers, why did they have to take the blame for everything; if their husbands were lazy, or any of their children turned into a layabout, or any daughter became pregnant at home, and so on, it must be their fault somehow. Were they born with guilt wirings in place of veins? I suppose part of their roles to socialize and maintain societal values in their offspring could account for this. She may have been a strong woman but right now she represented a ruin of her old self. I went and enveloped her in a hug as tears started rolling down our faces. I tuned off, the only thing I could do, to be able, to deal with her anguish. She was right then and probably right now but this was a different circumstance. She wouldn't understand.

*   *   *

The next day I left for Onitsha to stock up on provisions and to use the opportunity to visit sister Chinelo, as well as to speak to ThankGod, who had found an outlet in Benin that was located on a very promising site, according to him, and to let him know that I had decided to move to Abuja instead. Then round up by calling Ifeoma. These would keep me occupied for the day as it seemed that my life would never be free of problems. *That's what happens when you leave the well-worn route.* I ignored that while hoping that I'd remember to give Ifeoma the number of my mobile phone, though the logistics of making and receiving calls in my village with the phone required certain skills; it must be in a high altitude to receive signal. I hooked it atop the German-Mango tree, beside my father's palmwine shack. My sister did not think that I'd still remember how to climb a tree, in response to her teasing; I had reminded her that, properly acquired skills did not desert one easily.

When Ifeoma answered at the third ring, I informed her of my decision to settle in Abuja, and jokingly told her that this decision was informed by rumours that people living in Abuja were literally picking money from the streets, by way of government contracts. Ifeoma's response was that being close to the seat of power may trigger my old desire to be a Senator. Maybe I should re-consider the original plan.

'Maybe,' I responded and we carried on discussing various things until I told her that Faith was going to marry ThankGod.

'Aaah, and all of you shouted me down on the day of your marriage when I mentioned ThankGod's eyes on her. Now I am vindicated.'

'No less a prophetess,' I chuckled.

'He'd be a good catch for any woman and he didn't look like a strong head to me then so Faith I must say is a lucky woman. But what of your dalliance with her?'

'She told him'

'What!'

'Yes, she did.'

'Noo. She did? That is love pushing; I like that true love should not conceal what may cause hurt in future, it should be out in the open there and then.'

'I do not support that, not all men can take the truth.'

'So? I believe it is wise to tell all.'

'Mmh. This one you're suddenly an authority on love matters, is there something I should know?'

'Nothing really just mourning what seemed to be slipping through my fingers'

'Prince?'

No answer.

'Alright what about him?'

'I really love him I just wish he'd be less of a . . . I really do not know what I want from him.'

'Since when did you not know what you want from people?'

'He is giving me hard times but please let's talk about something else for now.'

'Ifeomaaah, I hope you remember that Prince is a Jamaican. What can you want from him?'

'That's the problem. Look Gift, let's forget it.'

'Are you sure?'

'At least not today.'

'OK. As I was saying my worry about ThankGod's decision to marry Faith stems from the fact that her family may snub or look down on him. You know how you rich people behave.'

'If he's what you said he is then he'll find a way to cope,' Ifeoma responded calmly.

'I suppose you're right. Anyway I am pregnant,' I rushed out in one breath and waited for Ifeoma's reaction. It was not what I expected when it came.

She burst out laughing!

Could anybody believe that? But then when she didn't stop or could not, I began to see the funny side of the whole bizarre scenario and started laughing myself.

'Oh Gift, Osahon didn't want you and he made sure nobody else would either. If you ask me better make hay while the sun shines, you really do not need to be in your village for that.'

'You are right. The longer I stay the chances are that people will start hearing things. I am surprised they have not yet.'

'Nobody has picked on that your business venture yet because you held such promises and people would be hard put placing you on that kind, but don't push it.'

'You're right.' After we had talked for a while, I bade her goodbye reminding her to call me later in the night to test the phone's ability to receive international calls. I was about to ring off when she said, 'Have you thought of living in London?'

'Everyday but how could that be done?'

'If you want to live in Britain, then we will find a way,' she countered.

'In that case I'll be most delighted to live in Britain if ever it could be arranged.' So we rang off to chew further on this twist in the tale.

*   *   *

Later that evening, I sat near the German-Mango tree, in readiness for Ifeoma's call, with my parents lying not too far away, on a mat, pretending to be asleep, while hoping to catch the conversation between us. They probably didn't believe me about going to live in London this time around, while the proverbial once bitten . . . flitted past and I swallowed a hurt. My parent's attitude towards my goings and comings tied in nicely with the proverbial being wary of blue-bottle if you had been stung by a bee. I sighed, hoping that they'd live long enough for me to make amends for my transgression and regain their trust.

With the agility of a monkey, I flew up the tree and snatched the phone at first ring. Ifeoma was surprised that I answered right away.

'Didn't you say that the phone was hung up on a tree or something?'

'It is, but you forgot that I was almost a monkey.'

'Oh. I had intended this first ring as a forerunner: to give you sufficient time to climb the tree. Anyway, how are you?'

'As fine as could be, considering, and you?'

'Mellow sort of but it is alright.'

We talked far into the night making plans. I could hear my parents snoring happily having confirmed that it was Ifeoma on the phone truly. Ifeoma told me that she had recently purchased a 3-bed-house in Edgeware, North London, for resell, but after renovation she decided to live in it instead and offered for us to stay with her, at least until we were settled and I had got a job. That last bit said with a hint of laughter.

I ignored that but reminded her that I was not trained for any profession as I never did graduate from the university or had she forgotten? The reason for her laughter became apparent when she informed me that lots of people who did not *break any slate* were making it in London, how much more a sharp-eyed chick like me. 'If nothing else,' she had continued, 'you will train as *nurse Eliza,* you know, or Care Assistants, as they are fashionably referred to here, and then, the sky will be your limit. You'd literally be picking pounds sterling like manna by working in old people's home.' We both bursted out laughing at the same time, as we could not imagine me being a *nurse Eliza.* Some people were not cut out for certain professions and we both knew that I definitely was not cut out to be a care assistant. But at least it was there to be considered if push came to shove.

As soon as I felt that Ifeoma's plan could work, after she had detailed it out, I swung into action, and the process of procuring the British Visa was put in motion. First I engaged the services of a lawyer to process a Registration of Business Name which costs about N6, 000. This was towards making me a self-employed businesswoman with my own registered company. I used my sister's residential address as the company's business premises. Next I opened a Business Current Account in First Solid International Bank Nigeria Limited, New Market Road Branch, Onitsha, and then my sister, Chinelo, became the 'sales person' who went to lodge the supposed proceeds of sales daily into the bank account. These *sales* proceeds actually were the money I came back with.

The whole process was to enable me create an impressive statement of account that I would submit, as part of the Visa application requirements, to the Embassy. And having a business current account, as opposed to savings account, would bestow not only a level of seriousness but also credibility on me.

Twice monthly I'd withdraw money from the account to supposedly 'purchase' my items of trade which included; Ladies Fashion Accessories; Designer Clothings; Shoes and Bags Sets, Jewelries and so many small small things that appeal to women. It appeared like a thriving business with the illusion of turnover so created. Because I was not a borrowing customer, I knew that my Bank would not really be concerned about the location of the shop and come calling. Finally, when everything appeared OK, I made a new international passport for myself since Osahon had the one I traveled to Italy with, as well as for my children and everything totaled thirty thousand Naira and took two days.

Having gathered all the required documents, inclusive of Ifeoma's letter of invitation, I set off to Lagos with my children to make the application on the pretence that we were visiting Britain. We arrived in Lagos late in the night and had barely closed our eyes, before we had to set off for the British High Commission on Marina Street, a throbbing heart of Lagos.

I had been advised to be up with the birds if we hoped to see the gate of the Embassy that day, not to talk of entering it. So arriving at the Embassy as early as 5am, smirking that nobody could beat that record, we were in for a surprise; there were hundreds of people already encamped outside the closed gate of the Embassy.

Nonetheless, we joined the tail of the queue which happened to be on another street. As we stood there, frozen with disappointment, I learnt that many of the people on the queue were touts who sleep there overnight and sell their prime position to willing *customers*. I did not think that funny; inflating the number on the queue thus making our destination, the Embassy, so far away all because of what? But when I simmered down, and had had time to ponder it, I had to marvel at people's resourcefulness. How could I have even questioned their ingenuity? They have to find their daily bread somehow, because nobody would do it for them. As we continued to inch forward, snail-like, I felt a tug on my sleeve. I froze instantly and stilled my breath. I had been warned of pick-pockets, but why was this one announcing his presence? A firmer tug and I whirled fiercely to confront a lanky scruffy youngster pulling at the hem of my sleeve.

'Na wetin?' I exploded in Pidgin English.

'Aaah take am easy sister abi you no wan dey front?' he asked calmly, like nothing fazes him.

'Who no go want dey for front?'

'I get space for you and your pikins.'

'Indeed.' The tout ignored my sarcasm. They must have been used to people treating them like that; loathing them but at the same time willing to transact business with them.

'Na N400.00 for all of you.'

'400 what? You dey craze? Come take am now make I see. *Ole.*'

'No bi you get these pikins?'

'Eh? Abi we dey four for your eyes?'

'Haba! You no go pay for the one wey dey your belle so?'

'God punish you. Na so dem dey make money for una place? I go pay N50 *jare.*'

'*Ole ni.* You be thief. Na kobo. Me I no do business like that.'

'Alright. How much last,' I had to backtrack. The idea of moving to the front had taken root and appealed to me nicely, and if I didn't take the offer, somebody else would.

'Na as I talk am before, 400.'

'OK now, go find another person. Me, I go pay N100.'

'Wetin dey worry you sef, fine woman like you, why you wan spoil market for me this early morning? Na wah for you oh. OK, pay N300 last. Make I just manage am like that, I never chop.'

I was getting tired of this early morning haggling that was not going anywhere, so I paid and we moved dramatically nearer to the front of the line, shielding abuses from left and right, as we went. People were not happy to be displaced.

At 8am sharp, a side gate opened and a tall, thin and droopy white man, with receding hairline, came out and, speaking through his nose, informed us that we should not in any way patronize touts. All services, but the visa fees, were free and we should not allow *these people* to rip us off.

I looked at the man and hissed. What was the need of all that long grammar? If they were concerned about the content of people's pockets, or their welfare, as the case maybe, then they should ensure that people were allowed access to the Embassy as they arrive, taking a number and a seat, and the entry gate closed as soon as they have reached the maximum they'd attend to at a given period. Anything less would smack of insincerity.

Shortly after the announcement, the gates were thrown open and we were directed into the bowels of the Embassy according to the line so formed. By the time it got to our turn, it was past 12 noon. I was irritated, sleepy and hungry and in addition I had to manage two strangers in the persons of my two hungry children. I did not pack any food for them, I did not bring enough pampers for them and I prayed that the last ones I used should hold them till we got back to our hotel.

But when they called out our numbers I closed the door to frustration and presented a calm façade as usual. To conceal the extent of my six-months pregnancy, which was really not protruding as such, as well as to look the part of an affluent businesswoman, I had worn an expensive flowing *boubou* or caftan dress made with Swiss lace; a matching Hayes scarf; a Ferragamo set of sandals and handbag, and Swarovski trinkets adorning my ears, neck and wrists with my finger nails well manicured. A discrete dab of High Society perfume to touch up my earlier one heightened my confidence: I hoped I had achieved the look of a wealthy businesswoman.

For whatever reason, the white man that interviewed me for the visa was very pleasant and not very inquisitive as I was told they usually were. I must have disarmed him with the combination of my dressing; a high quality imitation of British accent, perfected long ago; and a calm disposition, while delivering my answers in a measured and assured manner. Our visas were approved, and I was told to collect them the next day. At this point Frances, my first daughter, started whimpering and our interviewer smiled at me then asked us to wait a moment to see if he could arrange for us to collect the visa same day instead of the usual next day, to save me the trouble of ferrying the children up and down. I didn't know what to say to that, such consideration. I sat back down and when he returned, his smile widened, yes we could pay and collect the visas. I thanked him, went as directed and paid the necessary fees and truly, our visas were ready for collection within one hour. I clamped down on my elation, because I had heard it said that visas had been cancelled where recipients showed excessive happiness. They probably surmised that they would not come back. The only emotion I showed was a tiny smile of thank you. The next day, we left for Oyi immediately to share the good news. Later that night I called Ifeoma to tell her of the first victory.

*   *   *

Abraham and Celina had tried not to be too worried about Gift taking her children to Lagos because they had observed she was not very warm towards her daughters; always keeping them at arms length. How would she cope with them alone in Lagos and in this London she was talking about? Even the idea of them going off to live so far away did not appeal to them as they would have preferred them closer so that they could help from time to time. Much as they trusted God, in his infinite wisdom, they were still worried knowing that God's will did not always coincide with human wants; Him preferring to deal with needs, and they were really not sure into which category this desire fell into. Abraham had assured Celina that God would do His best for them in the long run which was key. But she chose to worry anyway.

When the travelers arrived beaming with smiles, Abraham and Celina were very pleased in a mixed kind of way. However, they thanked God in unison—He has done it again.

*   *   *

I held a long discussion with my parents, the long and short of which was that my life abroad this time would be different, promising to strive to stick to the straight and narrow and to be in touch with them. I also gave them Ifeoma's address and telephone number so that they could always reach me through the mobile phone installed up on the tree.

As our people would say, you do not kill a tortoise and dilly dally about eating it, so I scheduled our departure in three days time, for the onward journey to London. On the day, it dawned dull and overcast: the clouds were grey with rain. The whole family gathered to wish us safe journey; my big sister Chinelo had arrived with the last three of her children, the first two were away in the university and couldn't make it; my big brother Obumneme with his wife and two of their children as the first three were grown and had left the house. ThankGod and his intended, Faith were there. I had not told her anything about my lapsed years though we had met and reactivated our friendship. It'd keep for now, let her become a member of the family first before we step up to the secrets-sharing level.

After we had had our night meal, on the eve of our departure, a prayer session went underway led by no other than my big sister Chinelo. The prayer started with songs of praise to get us into the proper frame of mind before Chinelo took it from there. First, my children and I were commended into the able hands of God, and then she asked for a fruitful and holy life in London. Faith looked at me and frowned. I winked at her, sure she was confused—a holy life, no less. As the prayer progressed, I searched my parent's faces and saw that there was no joy on them anymore, not after my plight. I remembered when I left for Onitsha how proud they were and for Lagos—magical. Then *fiam:* nothing. I must tease out that glow again even if it took my last breath and . . . . The prayer ended. I had since forgotten we were praying.

He Found Me

GIFT AND OSAHON

By the second week of his appearance in Dublin, it had become a regular scenario to open the door to the ringing of the doorbell and slam it shut immediately. It was him. But when it became an everyday affair, I knew that the time had come to take action and get to the bottom of the reason for his trip so I took one week off work and got ready. When the doorbell rang this time I thought that he couldn't have chosen a better time; early enough to have missed the children and enough time to fight before they came back. He must be stalking us.

And for somebody who claimed that he came to make up, not one word of 'how about the children?' escaped his lips. I invited him in, waved him to a sofa and sat down myself well away from him. As we continued to look at each other across the room I realized that it was easy to spout hatred from a safe distance. Cad that he was and no matter how much of a bold face I put on it, my soul was still vicely gripped in Osahon's hand, he was the great love of my life. But . . . the time to wrest my soul from him had come, to incise him from that position and that could not be achieved by running.

*   *   *

Osahon sat down on the indicated sofa and mutely looked at Gift, studying her. Ransacking her with his eyes; looking for the changes that must have wrought themselves on her over the years. Finally he sighed inwardly, she had not really changed, he realized, rather she had become even more beautiful. Her skin that had always radiated with life seemed to be at its peak; her boobs were pulsating, begging to be released and gently massaged. All the pores in her body were oozing with sex. Her eyes, the liquid fire, drilled into him, turning his desire for her into a raging storm. She had a hold on him. A hold he could not extricate himself from even after all these years and all that she had done. Ooh Gift. Why? He thought. Wishing that his hands were all over her, right now, bringing them to heights hitherto unknown to both of them.

He looked more closely but did not see what he saw the last time in terms of intense hatred, she looked very subdued. He congratulated himself. He took a chance, secure in his knowledge of his Gift, and it had paid off. He wasn't wrong in his assumptions; time had worked on her in his favour.

*   *   *

'Will it be too much to tell me what you really wanted from me exactly?' I had to ask, he had been in the house for over ten minutes ogling me, without uttering a word. I no longer had time for game playing. He should know that his ploy would not work this time. Did he not expect that my experiences would have had some impact on my worldview and attitude? A pity if he did not. On the other hand, I didn't exactly display any atom of common sense in my previous dealings with him so he should be forgiven if he thought otherwise. However, much as I detested his presence, would love to detest his presence, I had to beat him at his game. But it had to be carefully executed this time around.

'Have you not given any thought to what I told you the last time?' Osahon responded, softly. Her question had thrown him off balance. Had the bitch not heard what he told her the last time? Or did she expect him to continue on that drippy sort of talk? He hoped not! There was a limit to how much one could pretend. Yeah, he used to love her, still did in a way, well . . . He's still in love with her period. No need to deceive himself. But Hell would freeze over first before he would live with her again, not after that her *ashawo* business.

To imagine it, when it was non-existent was hell enough, but to live with her after her consort with all those men? No way man! No way. Not him. Only God knew what she had got up to since then even. He might end up strangling her imagining all those men on top of her. Unthinkable! But he couldn't carry on pretending he had come back to make up with her. It was becoming very tiring and he was tired. Anyway, he would give her another chance to do the right thing, no need to jeopardize his chances by being nasty yet.

*   *   *

I had to strain my ears to hear him, though I heard him alright. What was I supposed to have considered? Give him the opportunity to start afresh with us or what? Or to afford him the chance to "wipe clean the hurt he had put in my soul?" That would be the day. I shook my head and turned to look at him, fully in the eyes, then in a clear measured voice barked, 'Cut the bullshit, Osahon and get to the point. I was not deceived then and I am not deceived now, it would be very stupid of you to think otherwise.'

A flicker of pain swam past Osahon's eyes before he hastily closed them. He knew it, she was too calm. That had always been her nature, but this new calm was too much and it's thwarting his plans. Maybe he didn't have it in him to rouse her anymore, his thought veered, which was rather sad, because, when he used to give it to her then, it usually obliterated her rational senses. Still he had to plough on; chances were that she wanted to be doubly sure of his true intentions before capitulating. Yeah, it must be and he wouldn't blame her. Wolves were everywhere devouring chicks like foxes.

'Look at it this way, Princess, you need a man in your life and our children need their father. Now would it not be wise to put our disagreements and differences in opinion aside and see how to make something good come out of a bad situation? I have put everything behind me and I am imploring you to do the same, for the sake of the love we had for each other and for the sake of our children. Or do you not love me anymore?'

I looked away. What was Osahon getting at? Did he really believe his own words? And what exactly is love? The true meaning of love, to be precise. And it's interesting to note that it was my love for him that was being questioned. Then I looked at him again in a new light as a thought struck me—maybe he did not realize that I was now aware of his current circumstances? In that case I had better set him right.

'Osahon, my dear, number one: if you loved me, in anyway at all, you would not have entertained the thought of making me a prostitute, not to talk of your plan to make it permanent subsequently, according to you; Two, you would not have taken another lover in my place; Three, you would not have beaten and raped me; and four you would not have wanted me dead for going against your plan. So if it will not be too much to ask do stop reiterating my stupidity and get to the point.'

Osahon lifted his shoulders in a nonchalant shrug, as if to say "if that's how you want it, then that's the way it'd be" making me brace myself to hear the sum he would mention. It had to be money, what else could it be? It must be that the amount he wanted was too large hence his need to employ his usual dilly-dally while he plotted; the cunning bastard. Maybe he was honing this scheme with that his nightmares back then? Oh Osahon, you break my heart, you never really loved me. Then I heard.

' . . . seeing that my child is Irish.'

'Pardon me. Could you repeat that, please?' I started trembling with fear and the stench of it was strong, too strong, stinking up everywhere. How did he know that I had another child for him? Silly question. If he was here, he must know everything.

Osahon frowned at Gift. What was she playing dumb for? What was difficult about his request?

'I said that you should fill out the necessary application forms to enable me to take up my residency status as a father of an Irish Citizen Child. You're not wanting me back will not deny me my God-given right. So stop acting stunned, it will not lead you anywhere.'

The force of those words bruised and confused me. Osahon did not want money which I would not give anyway, but this . . . ? Had he gone totally berserk?

'You're a mad fool if you think for one moment that I will do that. I told you when you first appeared that my children were not fathered by you. You probably did not believe me otherwise you would not be here mouthing such rubbish, but it is the truth, for the last time, Osahon you did not father those children! So do me a favour, go and die.'

He got up and took a step towards me, menacingly. I stood up also and backed away, brandishing my mobile phone like a weapon. 'One dial and the Guards will be crawling all over you like flies on rotten fruit. This is not Nigeria you know?'

Osahon stopped and stared at her deflated. Finally he sighed before sitting down. He had only wanted to hold her, to touch her again, his Princess, to fuck her into submission. When did she become so stubborn? His Gift was not like this before. But better not touch her; being thrown into jail would not do it for him, not now. He was desperate for a way forward from the quagmire that he was steeped in and Gift would not complicate it for him, there were better ways.

He wished he had listened to the talk bandied about at home and gone straight to court on arrival. He had heard about the scandalous behaviours of some of our married women that came to Ireland; how they forgot themselves and where they came from. Having boyfriends all over the place, dictating to their husbands; turning them into nannies and househelps; controlling the purse string because the State's welfare payments had conferred some measure of power on them. Some even went as far as throwing their husbands out of the house! He didn't believe it of course then. Maybe so, but not his Gift. Now it had cleared from his eyes, women would always be women: their brains were too small. Then he spent a bit of time wondering about who gave it to Gift now. Did the man know how to please her? What to do to drive her to the brink of madness? He wouldn't know of course, nobody would. There was only one person on God's earth that could do that for Gift, and that's him Osahon, no other. He would want very much to get his hands around whoever's throat, bastard! Twisting his Gift against him.

'You will hear from me definitely, Princess. Don't think you have seen the last of me, because you haven't. I am going to deal with you. Then you will know not to toy with me; it leaves a nasty taste in my mouth.'

I released my breath gently, causing my racing heart to slow down. Slowly I sat down to recover fully. He's actually leaving? Good. There was nothing here for him. But I couldn't resist knowing.

'Osahon,' I called gently, making him look at me with a glimmer of hope dripping from his eyes. It made me smile: it had never occurred to me that he might be mad. Now I knew he was.

'Did you really mean it? To take up your residency and live here with us?'

Of course I knew he wasn't going to but I needed to hear the lies.

Osahon looked at his Princess and something shifted in his brain, he really loved this girl, no matter what. She had touched his soul as none had ever since; his Gift. He remembered being struck, forcefully, by her beauty the day he met her. He had always dated beautiful and rich girls; he could not be bothered with any girl that failed to meet the two criteria. You had a lot to contend with when it came to women and he was not ready to compound that by dating ones that were found wanting in the beauty department and were not loaded with cash.

But his Gift was not rich and he didn't care. She had everything a man could want from a woman, including a warm agreeable disposition and so he forgot about the cash criteria. Nobody who had ever possessed her could keep his hands off her afterwards. She would deplete any man's supply of sperm in record time. Then he was shocked to find her a virgin! Fuck man . . . That he did not find funny. And this stemmed from the fact that his friends in school then used to posit that girls who married as virgins would end up desiring to taste other men. Crazy boys. He didn't believe that nonsense of course, but then he had never had a virgin until Gift, and he would give anything to remain cocooned in her warm pussy forever! Minus other men, and that was the crux of the matter.

Gift was sweet and very obliging, always gazing at him with dewy eyes. Bestowing gentle balmy love. He became instantly jealous of any man that even so much as looked towards her direction, never mind on her. He hid that efficiently from her. How could he not? He did not want to lose her.

But then he came to the stark realization that he could not marry her either, for the sake of his peace of mind and sanity. She would have been his dream of a wife: gracing his intended numerous future dinner parties with her unearthly presence, when he became rich, but his friends' postulation had taken root and refused to be dislodged. It ate away at him slowly. While entangled with the confusion of what to do, from nowhere, she announced that she was pregnant! Now what type of bullshit was that? How was he expected to cope? Saddled with a virgin wife and, God forbid, children even before he had made his millions? Forget it.

Then his money dream of long ago unearthed itself along with a weird plan for its success and insinuated itself into his consciousness.

He shook his head and gazed at Gift sadly. He had hurt her. The only stab he had at heartfelt love and he hurt her. But it couldn't be helped. It was either her or him and he loved himself too much. After the long soul-searching, he realized however, that she deserved the truth if nothing else so he turned to her and answered her question truthfully.

'Yes Princess, but not with you. I can never live with you again Gift,' he said looking at me sorrowfully, 'You'll have to understand that. So can you do it for me?' he pleaded.

'No,' I replied crisply then elaborated, 'I just wanted to confirm the extent of your hatred for me. Your unrelenting desires to suck me dry for any gain. Be assured that I'd rather live with a brood of vipers than with you.'

I stopped but then said, 'If I may ask, where did I go wrong? What did I ever do differently from your average girl that fell in love?'

'Princess, you still don't get it, do you?'

I nodded no.

'Then let me spell it out to you. People like you are not marriage material. There is no way a man will rest easy with you as a wife, looking the way you do, especially a man like me. Would you rather have me breathing down your neck, always sniffing your knickers to see what you're up to thirty hours a day? And as if that was not enough it turned out that you were a virgin! God, Gift, how could you?' He threw the question at me with outrage, before continuing. 'Anyway it was too much Gift. Too much for any one man to carry on his mind. Or do you not know that in time you will want to taste other men, to see what you're missing? Don't you know that? How do you expect me to keep track of your movements then? Tell me.' He stopped and gazed at me like he was really expecting an answer. But I was oblivious of his questions. Spellbound by his revelations, I gazed back at him stupidly. What on earth was he talking about? So my problem did not start by going to work for him as a prostitute! This Osahon was certainly crazy. I was lucky to have escaped with my life . . .

Osahon shuddered and resumed, cutting off my *thankful* thoughts.

'I will go mad not knowing who you have fucked, whose bed you've tumbled out from. It would be a hard, soul-destroying task for me to keep such a track. It would not have worked Gift, so forget it. If you are giving me my Status willingly, please go ahead and do so, no strings, otherwise you wait and see.'

I found my voice. 'So it was my fault to be born beautiful? Then I committed the mortal felony of being a virgin to top that?' Men, how were women ever going to get it right?

'I don't know your point Princess. I have told you why it went so wrong for us, on my part in any case.'

'That's right Osahon, you were very clear. Anyway, Residency Status, on the basis that I knew of, is for parents who gave birth to Irish citizen children Osahon, and you are not.'

'Why do you keep saying that?'

'Because it is the truth. You did not father any of those children, so go away.' What an irony, so Osahon's love for me, my beauty and my being a virgin were the architects of my ruin. I needed to be alone to salve my wounds.

'You will want me to believe that won't you? But let me tell you, that is a pipe dream, you just wait and see.'

'I am waiting,' I whispered in pain. He loved me, still did, but he couldn't live with me because of what I represented. Was this not stuff that induces madness? Shakily I went to open the door for him to leave. I couldn't take any more.

As I made to pass, he got up, stretched his hand and caught my shoulder, when I didn't resist, he drew me, gently, to him and held me against his pounding chest. I knew that it'd not be wise to let him stay a minute longer in the same room with me but I wanted him also. And I wanted my freedom too; he had the key to the door to my freedom. His hold tightened, possessively, and then he rested his chin on my head and deeply sighed.

The so-called fortified walls I had constructed, wobbled and then crumbled, exposing my heart and soul. Why did I ever have the misfortune of falling in love with him? Even with all that had happened, the passage of time, these new revelations, yet, I hungered for his touch, his kiss, for his hands to roam all over my body, stroking me senseless.

Holding Gift, Osahon saw them together back when it all started. When his Gift was his alone. He held her tighter and they swayed in unison to a hidden music, two souls fused as one.

After a long time, he opened his eyes and started to undress me, gently, he was not in frenzy, there was no need to rush, his eyes on mine. I looked back at him with naked hunger.

Osahon drank from the pool that was her eyes. He could never resist Gift. You do not fight yourself. They were one.

When we were both completely naked, he drew me down to the floor, cradling me, still holding my gaze. There was no anger, no hostility, no bitterness, only naked desire flowing between our souls. Gently, with revered tenderness, he entered me and we rose to that crest where only the two of us could ascend. But when we came back, it was as different souls, finally and irrevocably separated, and we both knew it.

Now that I had been freed, I will get ready to fight him. And with everything I have because it's going to be a death fight.

Gift

I was busy in the kitchen applying my newly acquired cake-making skills when I heard a thump and then a bang which alerted me that the post had come. I wiped my hands and ran to get it. I had been apprehensive for some time now, for I did not know the form Osahon's threat would take. When I opened the letter and saw a Solicitor's letterheaded paper, my heart started pounding, but I knew of no reason why anybody would summon me to the courts; Osahon would not be foolish.

Quickly, I scanned the letter and my heart stilled its frantic drumming: I was being summoned to defend myself from Osahon's application.

Ha.

With great relief I walked into the living room and sat down to digest the letter properly. Osahon's affidavit in sum included: That I deserted our marriage; that he was the father of all my children; that he had been denied access to said children for him to play his fatherly role and finally; that I would not support his application to obtain his residency to enable him to settle down and rear his children. Now it was in the open, the tension was over.

I would get ready and face him, however he wanted it. I shook my head as I remembered our love-making on his last call to the house, two months ago. At that time I didn't know whether I would be unhooked from him. But I had pressed on, I had to find out.

Afterwards, I had lain back on the floor when he got up. He had looked down at me askance, and then stretched his hands to pull me up, but I shook my head no, and continued to watch him as he dressed. When he finished he sat down on the sofa, very close to me, and looked down at my nakedness once more, then the shutters started coming down. Both in him and in me. And gradually we became strangers to each other. And when I looked closely into his eyes, I saw him, the other Osahon, staring back at me. And it confirmed my deepest fears: there was another Osahon in existence. Osahon the venomous one, the toxin that had destroyed us; that had cast me adrift in my prime; the Osahon that would not hesitate to maim me, to kill me even.

That Osahon, that I did not know, had taken position regally now, dwarfing the Osahon I knew, that briefly peeked out. My lover. The Osahon that was ready to walk the ends of the earth for me. But no matter, I had seen the two of them now. And so I knew. We may have previously fused together, him and me. We may have been two-in-one, but now we were no more, and I was glad.

It was clear in my mind now: Osahon would always be two-in-one, but it did not have anything to do with the equation I had thought was us. It was them without me. Osahon and Osahon. And as long as the two Osahons existed in one, nobody was safe from him, whichever one. I had got up then, still naked and opened the door to let him out of the house. Now that he had been exorcised from my soul, he must be exorcised from me physically too. Then I would be free, completely. But I had to be careful not to let any of these thoughts show on my face. This was the dangerous Osahon. He could strangle me without thinking twice.

I was enormously relieved when he left without a word, just a menacing scowl scrawled across his face. That worried me, but not too much; I was now free to fight him.

*   *   *

Later in the evening, I called my long-suffering friend, Ifeoma, to relay the latest. Ifeoma informed me that she'd probably be in Dublin during the hearing, hoping to kill two birds with one stone as she put it. The first bird being her promise to Erica for some financial help in view of their current predicaments, but not before seeing her face to face, to hear what it was all about, since I, Gift, could not help beyond the bare essentials Erica gave me before clamming up. The second bird was the opportunity to see Osahon with her own two eyes before she could even begin to accept the possibility that he was in Ireland. Then she would use the opportunity of the encounter to pull out that his tongue that was used to profess love to me and then subsequently rake out his two eyes, if the Guards had not locked her up before then.

'What could he possibly be playing at?' she had asked having dissipated her anger on the 'wretched and shameless fool,' as she now named Osahon.

'Why don't we keep that analysis till you get here? There was no need of pinching a package that would eventually be opened,' I replied. And so we left it at that.

*   *   *

I dismissed any suggestions and subsequent pressure from both Ifeoma and Una to seek legal advice. Una, not understanding my resolute stand gave up in exhaustion but Ifeoma, who knew the gritty details persisted doggedly. After one argument too many I snapped at her.

'Oh Ifeoma, please give me a break for goodness sake. Tell me, did you seriously expect me to jeopardize my hard earned anonymity, delicate and fragile as it were, to consult a solicitor; to expose myself? No Ifeoma, forget it.'

Ifeoma had nodded, as if Gift could see her, and then said, 'OK. So you start all over again when he or any other person that may have known you during your time in Italy resurfaces?'

'Ifeoma, I know where you are coming from, but I'd rather do it my way than jeopardize our future in one swoop, uncertain as it may be.'

'You have to try and do something other than hiding, otherwise you'll never be free as you want to be.'

'I have worked that out a long time ago but Osahon will not determine when for me. Also, I have heard somewhere that one could defend oneself in court without the services of a counsel. That is what I want to pursue for now.'

'Fine Gift. Let's watch and see.'

Embarking on the self-appointed job of responding to Osahon's affidavit, I followed the format of his own affidavit, included in the summons, to prepare my own. I could already taste the massive gain that would accrue from this court saga: unconditional freedom and that spurred me on.

Osahon

Osahon strolled, reluctantly, along Burgh Quay towards O'Connell Bridge, having come down on Hawkins Street with bus 38, into the city from Castleknock, contemplating what he'd now consider his last amicable call on Gift. His stride was reluctant because he couldn't return to his room in the Bed and Breakfast on Bachelors Walk yet, not until after a certain time. A very stupid rule! As far as he knew, if you had paid for a room in a hotel, you had paid for a room, and you could stay indoors throughout if you wanted to without any disturbances.

But no.

Whiteman had to come up with something in between: Bed and Breakfast; where once it's morning and you've had your breakie, according to the silly proprietress, you were hustled out immediately and would only be allowed back in again in the evening.

A room you had paid for!

Look at him stamping around unnecessarily, like a loafer, and it was not agreeable to him, especially not in the cold. He didn't have any problem with the arrangement at first, then he had a burning mission and breaking down Gift's defences was his priority.

And today, the refreshing sex he had with her was exceptional. It was a healing balm on his bruised ego. But now the stark reality of his situation had hit with a blast, like the searing heat of the sun back home or more appropriately the cold that was currently determined to turn him into a statue as well as nipping the previous euphoria of his ill-conceived mission. Now that his burning mission had been aborted:

no house, no Residency Status, no money, what was he supposed to do? Just what did the bloody Gift expect him to do? Go away and bury his head in shame? She had better forget such nonsense, it won't happen. No chance!

He continued cursing and walking until he came to the big confusing junction with traffic lights all over the place and moved slowly to his left to stand in front of the tall building with Heineken written on it to survey his surroundings while attempting to establish his bearings. He wasn't about to get himself lost. After a while, he followed the crowd to cross O'Connell Bridge towards what he worked out should be O'Connell Street itself. Halfway over the bridge he stopped and went closer to the rail to stare at the water flowing underneath while he thought about his predicament. A lesser man than himself would have thought of flinging himself into the dirty water to end it all, but not him. He was made of sterner stuff.

Yeah. But what should he do? After much thought, he was able to pin-point the exact genesis of his problem in Ireland. Yeah, it started with that defector Okere, his so-called friend. Where was his hand of friendship now? He remembered clearly how helpful he was when he Okere, told him that Gift was residing in Ireland. Without any prodding he had supplied him with her address and then invited him to stay with them when he arrived in Ireland.

Didn't he call him immediately on arrival? And Okere had the guts to tell him Osahon Osanobua Iguedia, that he was not welcome to stay in his house, for no reason. For no reason at all. How could anybody change so fast? It must be the handiwork of that stuck-up bitch of his, Oya, with her bum like that of sugar-ant and face like squirrel. Where did Okere even see that one to marry sef? Stupid people. Anyway they suited each other and it's no skin off his nose.

But why? What had he ever done to that local woman Oya? He barely knew the bloody bitch! Or maybe it was his own Gift that turned Oya against him? Wait till he got his hands on her again, then she'd know how to differentiate the male tortoise from the female one.

He stood on the bridge for a while with the wind battering him and the cold calcifying his bones towards making him a statue. Finally, he decided to abandon his revenge plan and sort out the immediate problem of cold first. He'd have to be alive and well to exact vengeance.

He turned sharply and collided with a make-shift stall, arrayed with all sorts of coral beads, bangles, earrings, necklaces, woolen scarves and hats—pathetic junks really. Just what kind of market was that supposed to be *sef?*

'Oi! Big feller, you mind yerself now, will ya,' bellowed a cold-hardened, wiry fellow, with a big mug of something hot in his hand, Osahon had observed with envy.

He apologized profusely while helping to right the stall and to pick up items that had fallen. He hoped that the man made enough money from these junks to justify the amount of cold he absorbed staying out here. Personally he couldn't imagine himself doing this kind of business. He had forgotten his laughable shop of early days.

'Sorry man. I didn't mean to upset your market.'

'You're alright there, son.'

Osahon noted that the man's mouth looked like it's in the mood for talk so he moved closer and introduced himself.

'My name is Osahon from Africa.'

'I can see that. But where exactly are you from. Africa is a big continent you know?'

Oh yeah? A man of knowledge then. Since being here it seemed that it made the Irish extra happy to lump all black people into one cauldron called Africa and when they bothered to and found out you're from Nigeria, their smile slipped a notch down the scale.

'I am from Nigeria.'

'Ahaa. Nigeria.' The man shook his head and then asked, 'Why are all of you running away from your own country and flooding our Ireland? What is the problem there? I thought they said that the country is rich with all sorts of natural resources including oil?'

Osahon was amused. This little man, eking out a living on a roadside, was well informed.

'You're right there brother, but our wealth is in the hands of a few and the many had to find other means to survive. It is a country riddled with corruption where the leaders only care about their pockets and the rest skulk about singing their leaders praises for crumbs. But mind you if I get the chance to be in office I will do the same.'

'Oh.' The man's face went into shock, his brows practically on his hairline. He shook his head, and that seemed to loosen his voice again. 'Why?'

'Because everybody does it, so why not?'

'But somebody has to stop it.'

'Sure, but it won't be me.'

The trader shook his head, again. Strange fellow, but at least honest.

'So what are you doing in Ireland then?' the trader asked, while his thoughts zeroed in on the question he couldn't ask . . . *to seek asylum and continue to rip off the State, like your people.*

'I only came to look for my wife.'

'You don't say.' The trader drank from his hot mug with Osahon swallowing along with him. The trader licked his lips and a little smile appeared on one corner of his mouth. *That was what all of you men from Nigeria say.* But he didn't voice that out either, rather he asked, 'How come you're looking for her, didn't you know when she left?'

'It is a long story old-boy and the cold is killing me.'

The man eyed him up and down, as if to ascertain that he was actually dying from cold, then advised him, 'Better get yerself into Penneys, before you truly catch your death.' He pointed in the general direction of Penneys while telling him that Eason bookshop should serve as a landmark, he then invited him back afterwards so that they could get to the root of Nigeria's problems.

Osahon thanked his new friend, promised to take him up on his invitation and walked away to find Penneys. Nigeria's problem could not be solved so easily, not with the I-don't-care-kind of citizens she had, and he was not about to waste his time thinking about it, not to talk of discussing it with a man who could not know anything about it and even if he did, what did he care?

He found and went into Penneys and was directed to the first floor where they have the men's sections. He took two fleece tops, five-a-pair thick socks, a big sweater, a workman's jacket, a woolen hat, a pair of fleece hand gloves and topped it all with a fleece scarf. He went into the men's changing room and dressed in his new outfit. He had become too big for the jacket having worn the two fleece tops at once. But he was not about to let go so he forced himself into it. That, however, made hand movements a bit awkward, so he came out of the changing room and swapped the jacket for a much bigger size and went back into the changing room. He studied himself critically in the mirror, after putting the jacket on, and concluded that he looked more like a boxer with expanded chest and bulging biceps, but then he shrugged, it wasn't so bad really, and it'd keep the cold out, which was the purpose of the whole business. He came out of the changing room and stepped gingerly on to the escalator, wondering how come he didn't see it going up. When he reached the ground floor he realized that it was because he went up through another route. He stepped outside, this time ready for the cold. As he walked on, he realized that he didn't pay . . . but . . . nobody had accosted him on the way out actually. This Penneys *sef*, was that how they do business? He continued on his way anyhow. He's sure that they wouldn't miss the paltry forty-eight euros the clothes had totaled. Too bad, was his conclusion as he turned left towards the big Post Office.

But then he retraced his steps and went into Supermacs for lunch, the cold had drained his body of all nutrients and he was feeling rather empty. He took a long time to study the menu and eventually chose two lunch boxes comprising of six pieces of chicken and lots of chips and two drinks with a choice of sauces. He chose garlic sauce. When he finished his meal he was heartily satisfied but he went over to the smoothie section to see what it was all about. He ended up with a concoction of cranberry juice, kiwi, banana, strawberry, apple all on a yoghurt base. When he had satiated himself, he vowed that he must get himself back to his former glory; nothing could beat living the life of the rich where he could afford to buy whatever he wanted. He stayed in Supermacs for some time reading newspapers left by previous customers before he felt that it was time to go and start on his second mission: to find out what Nigerian husbands who were looking for their wives do.

*   *   *

As he made to turn into Henry Street a black guy thrust a hand-bill at him and instinctively he collected the flyer. It advertised Chinese Acupuncture treatment for pile. How are they going to achieve that? He mused. Stick the needle in the anus? Aaah. He shivered. Remembering his quest, he sidled back to the flyer-sharing man. He was black; he may know a thing or two. He may even be a Nigerian. He was and he did know more than Osahon envisaged.

Osahon spent the rest of the day with him, helping him to give out the flyers, and during that time his new friend, Ezra, told him all that he needed to know and do and he took it from there the next day.

*   *   *

Very early the next morning he checked out of the B&B and took bus 4 going to St. Vincent's Hospital but dropped on Lower Mount Street at the Office of the Refugee Applications Commissioner where he sought Asylum; this being the first step towards being declared a Refugee if he was lucky. As luck would have it, he was assigned to a hostel smack in the city centre.

He unpacked his belongings and hung his clothes in the wardrobe allotted to him, wary of sharing a room with a slight man on the next bed who claimed to be from Russia. Do Russians seek asylum too? Aren't they Europeans? He didn't care for the answer though so he didn't dwell on it.

The next day, the new Asylum Seekers in the hostel were directed to *Welfare*, where they collected cheques to cover their clothing and two weeks allowance. As he was told, Osahon went to the General Post Office and turned the cheque into cash immediately, 188.20 Euros complete. He went back to Penneys and bought two Jeans trousers to compliment what he had and various inner wears. He never knew that a country could be so generous. This time he paid as a compliment to the generosity of Ireland.

Through his friend Ezra he got a job distributing flyers too, for different companies advertising everything under the sun.

He also got a second job which started from as early as 7am in the morning till about 9.30am, distributing free morning newspapers and then later in the evenings, running himself ragged selling Evening Herald. At the end of the first week, limping back to his hostel very tired, he decided there and then that that Evening Herald madness of a job would have to go, that business of running after cars in traffic to sell the fucking paper was not his cup of tea, very shameful and undignified, he'd leave that for the likes of Ezra, he had the height for it. He had never envisaged, in his whole life, that he'd ever be distributing newspapers and hand-bills on the road! What would his fellow Big-Boys back home say about that? He shuddered, but then chided himself that it was only for a short while and it was for a purpose, besides nobody would see him. But selling the Evening Herald must go, otherwise he wouldn't survive.

He saved diligently and after about two months he was able to engage the services of a solicitor to start his legal proceedings against Gift. If she wouldn't give him his due amicably then he must wrest it from her. And as the weeks went by he became more relaxed and actually started to enjoy his stay in Ireland.

PART FIVE

...In search of a new beginning

LONDON, GREAT BRITAIN

MARCH 2001

Where I come from it is said that the beginning of crying is usually very difficult but once you get into it the rest is history. So my stab at starting afresh was by trying to put oceans between me and Osahon and that jump-started the crying bit while "the rest is history" aspect included little little things like raising two children, plus one in the making, and striving to live as anonymously as was possible.

And so the first step towards operation "beginning of crying" was now underway as the air hostess helped me to shepherd my children into the British Airways plane that would take us to London from Lagos at 10.05pm. It was an uneventful journey until the announcement heralding our landing was made. This caused relief adrenaline to shoot through my system, but it also unwittingly activated the tension that brought a tiny tremor to my hands and heart and a sigh that forced its escape through my lips. The baby kicked furiously in protest to the change in the weather conditions in the womb, but being me, as usual, I was stoic.

I tried to dissuade my mind from spreading the unwarranted notion that we may not be let in at the port of entry to the other parts of my body to no avail. I tried to swamp it with other thoughts, no way, so I switched to action thoughts like hoping that Ifeoma would be

waiting for us at the arrival lounge as promised, though being so early
in the morning, I wouldn't hold it against her if she didn't. But then
that presented another worry, would we be able to find our way to
her place on our own? Debating about what to do if she wasn't there
occupied me and the immigration control came and went without
a hitch. And Ifeoma was standing calmly in the arrival hall when we
emerged, looking as impeccably appointed as ever. She ran towards
us and we hugged fiercely for all the years we did not see. When we
disentangled, Ifeoma knelt on one knee to hug my girls before leading
us out to the car park, stowing our luggages in the boot, and driving
off to her house. During the drive she barraged me with questions,
which was not her style really; maybe the excitement of seeing me
again brought that on. I nodded and then nodded to her questions
and the next thing I knew she was shaking me awake.

*   *   *

So by about 9am, we were safely ensconced in her house at
Edgeware. Being a Saturday, she took her time and laid out an English
breakfast, as she informed us, and was quite relaxed at playing the
perfect host. This was surprising and I said so, for I had never cast
Ifeoma in a domestic role. I took my cue, however, and relaxed and
we had a leisurely breakfast. Afterwards, Ifeoma cleared up while I
put the children to bed for the much needed rest. When I came back
Ifeoma took the first shot at getting the ball of discussing our past
rolling.

'Remember Prince?'

She was comfortable in a blue leather sofa, clutching a glass of
pure orange juice. I stretched out on a rather dainty chaise lounge
while struggling to maintain my grip on a glass of water spiked with
a sliver of lemon, guaranteed to aid digestion. I creased my forehead
at Ifeoma's question; why was it that problems cause people to lose
their equilibrium? Well . . . I suppose that's why it's named problem,
designed to confuse. I answered her anyway.

'Are there two Princes, no be our Rock Star of Jamaican descent?
Ifeoma no confuse me o as I *dey* plan meet am to see *wetin* you see for
im body.'

'Forget it, you won't. Do you know that that snake went and
impregnated his ex-girlfriend and expected that I'd not take it to
heart? We were going to get married for goodness sake. What nerve!'

I stared at Ifeoma with my mouth open, then caught myself and closed it quickly before saying, 'You were going to get married? To a Jamaican? Aah . . . this *dey* serious o. So what was his problem?'

'Nothing. That we should go ahead with our plan. He was even annoyed by my anger! Gift, this lady gave birth to his son only last week! How did that happen? I have been going out with him for donkey years and I am not even going to talk about the abortion.'

'Abortion?' I looked around askance, then, 'whose abortion?'

'He wasn't ready to settle down then.'

Ifeoma's eyes clouded and so she looked away.

'So how did you find out?' I asked steering us to a safer ground. Ifeoma took a deep breath before answering, her voice however was unsteady.

'He told me that we could not see this weekend because he will be at his son's rave.'

'What is rave?'

'Jamo speak for party.'

'Mmmh. So . . . Just like that?'

'Just like that. Mostly because he did not think it was that important. "The bird's not gonna trap me with no child, mon. You're ma woman" he said.'

'Was it through insemination then?'

'No, "But it meant nathing . . . just ma old woman . . . I helped her, mon . . . she wanted to carry ma child, you dig?" were his pathetic attempts at explanation. Didn't that sound like the greatest dribble ever spouted?'

'Nobody can top that, I tell you, but Ifeoma when could this have happened?'

'I have buried it Gi, please don't resurrect it.'

'Buried it? You better dig it up. Come on Ifeoma, what am I?'

Ifeoma looked at me pleadingly, but I ignored the eyes.

'Remember the day I called you mistakenly while you were out working?'

'Yes and made me promise to keep a secret which you never came round to telling me about, by the way.'

'That was what I wanted to tell you but . . . but . . . , anyway you got raped and then, look Gi it is over.' She stopped and lowered her head. 'Now it's like it never happened, like something I dreamt up.'

'Now you are scaring me, Ifeoma.'

'Maybe I need to talk about it really, but maybe sort of another day? It hurts Gift.'

'Eeem . . . Well . . . In so far as you don't wake up in the middle of the night and murder us all, then lets.'

Ifeoma smiled and shook her head at me before speaking, 'Gift you are really a good mood-lifter and I love you dearly. I wish you were available then. Anyway back to Prince. I suppose ' . . . to your tents oh Israel . . .' made sense now. Maybe, it would not have been a big deal to his type of women and probably why he couldn't place my anger. But . . . I'm done with him, anyway. Love my foot!'

Oh yeah. You don't get so hot under the collar when you're done with somebody, but this was not the time to go into that, so I suggested.

'Well, maybe his love for you wasn't that deep. But if I remember correctly you didn't really care that much about him either.'

'But I did, I just didn't realize it and when I did I rejected it as it did not fit my image of myself and what I wanted to represent, it still doesn't, which was a baffle for me. I love him Gi.'

'I never met him, but in my estimation the two of you did not fit, not background, not aspirations. Now, both of us are living testimonies to love's inability to conquer anything, so re-check that love. But what is wrong with men? What do they want from us women exactly? Or maybe it should be what is wrong with us women, we seem to always pick the wrong men?' Ifeoma stretched the lower part of her face which represented "search me" but said nothing. Eventually she said,

'You are probably right. But tell me Gift, on a more serious note, what kind of permutation led you to trot off to Italy to prostitute for that leech of yours?'

'Have we finished with you already?'

'Didn't we agree to put it in the cooler?'

'Oh.'

'Well. My journey with Osahon, my sister, is a long story.'

'Are you trying to fob me off? You have been telling me that for some time now.'

'Alright, take it easy, unless you want the abridged version.'

'No way. I want the gory details. It will help to fan my hatred.'

'Your hatred? Of who?'

'Of whomever.'

I started my story with care detailing how I was even breathing during that period.

I drained the last of my water and then kept quiet, staring at nothing. Ifeoma, looking visibly subdued was also staring at nothing, but nonetheless lost in thought. I took a long look at her before pitching my thinking.

'Ifeoma, Osahon's treachery has scarred me. I allowed my body to
be treated despicably in the interest of laying the foundation stone to
our life together, but for Osahon, it was just like any other business
arrangement. Out there you had to be constantly on your toes or
you'd be devoured.' Ifeoma nodded with her mouth pursed like she
was saying "really? You don't say." I ignored her and continued.

'Tell me, Ifeoma, who will this not destroy?'

Ifeoma, who suspected that the question did not require any
answer, gave none. She had not even looked at her friend since the tale
came to an end. It was not so much the tale that made her reflective,
but how much her friend had loved, how she had worshipped Osahon
and would not brook any argument against him. To be told that she
lived in a fool's paradise, that she had used her teeth to peel the bark
of bamboo in vain, as the Igbos would say, could not be equaled. It'd
gnaw at you all your life. But what do you tell that person, what kind
of consolation was appropriate, and even if you find one, how do you
word it?

I directed my gaze at Ifeoma, to see if she was sleeping, but she
was not so I concluded that she must be building the fire of hatred as
she had mentioned. When I still did not hear anything from her after
a while I decided to give my tale a neat ending.

'Much as my escapades were not something I will overcome in a
hurry, I will advise you to move on, forget that Prince of yours and all that
he made you do, he was not worth it, take it from me as the truth.'

'You mean with all your problems which have not ended yet, you
still have it in you to advocate forgiveness?'

'Please don't misquote me,' I rounded on Ifeoma immediately,
'I did not say anything about forgiveness, but if I should continue to
remain bitter, then I assure you I will most certainly be destroyed. Then
what will happen to my children? When I said move on, I didn't mean
forgive; I only meant that you should get on with your life. Nobody's
worth making us live in the past, tomorrow will always be better than
yesterday.' I heaved a great sigh, kept quiet while searching for more
things to say. 'Mind you the anger will not leave of its own accord,
you'll keep working at it and over time maybe it'll go, but you had to
make that first move.' I sat back finally, exhausted. *Osahon was an evil
that should have been avoided by all means.*

'Alright I will try and work out how not to worry about Prince
anymore,' Ifeoma conceded. So we sat there with our respective
thoughts, then Ifeoma suddenly asked, 'Between the two of us, who
has committed the most atrocity: debasing your body or killing a
defenseless child?'

I gasped. Had she gone mad? How had she managed to reduce such big issues to a comparative game!

'Ifeoma I don't know. I had decided to abort this pregnancy when I first found out, but really I am not sure anymore. These days the boundary between good and evil is being constantly eroded by placing personal pursuits foremost but . . . look Ifeoma I don't know,' I stated flatly.

Ifeoma was not the crying type so I shouldn't have fallen for the bait of that question. I got up and went over to her, to hold her. She cried for a long time and when she finished she went and replenished our drinks then said, 'I think you are being too cool about this whole issue with Osahon. Much as you've valiantly masked your pain, I can still glimpse it in your eyes. I advise that you let all the emotions; anger; loss; hurt; grief, or whathaveyou, out. That way, you will not have a breakdown in the future.'

'I have stewed in them long enough to roast so I am open to suggestions,' I announced while straining to adjust my bulk. I couldn't recapture the comfortable position I had before and that irritated me.

'Well . . . why don't you write a book and share your experiences; it will serve the dual purposes of an 'emotional elixir' for your soul as well as alert other well-meaning girls, intoxicated by love, to be wary of smooth operators like Osahon.'

I burst into laughter.

'You know being born and brought up abroad has turned you into a white man. So you want me to publish my story for the whole world to read? Because it is supposed to free my soul? Have you forgotten that I am going to be part and parcel of a community while raising my kids? You are asking me to further alienate myself and family with a book. Ifeoma let me tell you, no matter the level of sympathy I hope to garner with the book; I would have used that same book to bury myself. I am quite sure that my neighbours would not appreciate that either. Do not be naïve, my sister, sympathy is all well and good but I will definitely keep my story to myself.'

I went into another paroxysm of laughter and spluttering. I told Ifeoma that the imagined proceeds from the sale of the book would probably bring Osahon to my heels for his own share of the goodies, after all it was 'our' story. We made it happen, remember?

'Don't worry, we Nigerians have built-in survival mechanisms that help us defeat our problems and forge on, otherwise you'd be trampled by others trudging on. There was never a safety net for anybody, you make yours and that I intend doing, but not with a spiky net in form of a book.'

Ifeoma nodded understandingly while deep in thought. After a while she sighed and got up, reminding me of our impending visit to her parents: they recently announced their decision to retire to Nigeria, claiming that the scorching rays of our sun on their backs would aid them to live out the rest of their lives.

*　　*　　*

During the weekdays, when Ifeoma was at work, the kids and I would roam the neighbourhood; from the parks to the corner shops, then the shopping malls, generally taking life easy. I became immediately aware that the people in London were quieter than the Italians who were constantly happy or projected the impression of living life to the brim: noisy; energetic; plucky and always on the prowl for fun.

British on the other hand were more reserved, or seemed so, and looked like they do not notice you existed, like a speck of dust in the order of things. But the most important thing for me was that they did not make me feel like a prostitute; ogling me in that knowing kind of way, daring me to step into the role, to ply my trade. This London would give one the opportunity to be what you presented yourself to be, and that was more or less your business. Just keep to the rules and you would live happily, anonymously.

As for means of livelihood . . . well, I would ponder about that much later. If only I was done with having this baby, then I'd be sure of what I was faced with, but three more months and it'd be over. About Ifeoma's offer to share her house without paying rent, I would not accept. The best thing would be to rent our own place within the neighbourhood, that way my children would be in school with their new friends from the park and I would maintain my friendship with Ifeoma. She was my rock and had given me money in the past and yes she had it to give; working hard as a property developer had made her rich in her own right, and this excluding her parent's money and her inheritance from her grandfather's trust. She never rammed it down anybody's throat, but no we wouldn't move in, it'd be better, she just did not understand the implication of having two active children in the house and a third on the way. So I'd spare her that. Let everybody make their own mess. Aside that, I had now learnt that you did not place yourself in a subordinate position however unwittingly, you would live to pay the price one day. Which reminded me that I must pay off my outstandings to her.

I had enough money to take care of my family until I was able to work. I would have to hasten and register my children in pre-school though, that would free me to look around for where to train as a Care Assistant or whatever Ifeoma called it. I noticed suddenly that it was getting colder. I got up and called the children and we left for home, to await Ifeoma's return, and she always ensured to come back with news of the happenings in the city.

*   *   *

'Guess who called today.' I knew she had some gist tucked under her armpit as soon as I clamped eyes on her in her personal sitting room where she was carefully measuring one thing or the other into two glasses. If she was not so gainfully employed, she'd win awards as a bar hand. I nodded at the quarter-filled glass she waved at me, as mine, without questioning it. She knew I was pregnant so it couldn't be lethal. But it seemed she was drinking a tad too much and I thought that I should dish a dose of her own medicine back to her. But I'd allow her to talk first.

'Who?' I asked, my brow raised.

'Erica. Erica Taribo, remember her?'

'Of course I remember her. She claimed that I edged her out of the favourite position in your heart, according to you. So what's new?'

'What's new is that you are about to relocate to the Republic of Ireland.'

'Says who?'

'Well listen first. You could settle in Britain with visiting visa, but you'll remain on the fringe of the society for the next fourteen years or so before you are able to process your Residency permit. That also meant that you will not go out of Britain for that length of time.'

I was stunned. 'Ifeoma, I suspected that there'd be a catch somewhere, but fourteen years? What does that mean really and why are you telling me now?'

'There are scarier ones; like being hounded by immigration authorities and if caught deported to Nigeria after a stint in prison. But I won't bore you with all that. I had worked under the impression that haste was of the essence then, so do not blame me for not going into the finer details lady. Anyway, I mentioned to her that you have just arrived from Nigeria, wanting to settle down here with your two kids, and the third on the way, it was at that that she came up with this unbelievable information about some kind of policy whereby automatic residency is granted to non-national parents whose children are Irish Citizens, by virtue of their being born in Ireland.'

She plunked herself down beside me, handed me my drink, took a hefty slug from hers and then continued, 'Now I do not claim to understand what it's all about, but we have to explore that option, because I cannot imagine anybody living in a country for fourteen years without the benefit of stepping out. The thought alone gives me 'madness shivers." She shook her head, as if to ward off the 'madness shivers.' I said nothing. When I still did not say anything, Ifeoma ploughed on.

'What do you think? I told Erica that we will call her back to discuss this information piece by piece later tonight, if the idea appeals to you, that is.'

'Let me understand what you are saying to me, you have agreed with your friend Erica, to palm us off to Ireland, wherever that is.'

Ifeoma opened her eyes wide in dismay while I chewed my lower lip worriedly before venturing, 'Are we getting on your nerves already then? What is really going on? What else did you tell her?'

'Come on girl, take it easy, and don't get paranoid on me. I couldn't possibly let her into your past life; you know that, so cool it.'

I kept quiet then to mull over the suggestion. When I spoke, my voice was very low.

'I was hoping that we would be neighbours, to reignite our friendship. Why are you pushing me away?'

'It is not from not wanting you around; rather I am trying to be practical here. Erica even mentioned that after five years of living and working there, you become eligible to apply for your citizenship.' When I did not react, she continued, 'You can be angry if you really want, but that, you know, will not lead us anywhere so I really believe we should explore this opportunity. And I am not palming you off to anywhere, Gift, our friendship had survived so many tribulations, living in Ireland would not scratch it one way or the other and you know that.'

'Continue then,' I murmured colourlessly.

'Ireland is about an hour away, by air from London, and even at that, it is not your regular 'hot city' and as such a very good place for your "neighbourly hobnobbing" and anonymity as you desired.'

I shook my head while rubbing my forehead with the tips of my fingers, then I sighed and looked at my friend. 'I suppose we are not destined to live in Britain then, with this fourteen-year-jail-term you mentioned. It's becoming unappealing by the minute. Ireland may not be so bad after all.'

'So you will consider it then?' When I nodded, Ifeoma stood up and went over to her laptop. 'Right, we will need all the information we can lay our hands on about this new country of yours.'

'Now?' I asked surprised.

'If they are giving out residency status and passports like it's going out of fashion, it becomes very important to get on the queue early enough, it may not last.' I saw the wisdom and opened my hands helplessly but in support.

*   *   *

As Ifeoma sat, facing her computer, waiting for it to bring up the information she sought, she turned her thoughts back to her friend; for one moment there she regretted the impulse that made her mention Gift to Erica; especially now she saw how desolate the news made her look. She seemed lost and perplexed, as if the world's problems were placed on her shoulders without her consent and for no reason. She had been so happy when Gift accepted to come over to Britain, and now she would be leaving, but she had to let go, friendship should not constrain. Besides, fourteen years was too long for anybody to stay in one place and Gift did not need that kind of frustration in her present circumstances, but . . .

'Look Gift,' she turned to her friend, 'I am due what is called my annual leave soon, maybe I will come with you. We would see the place together, if you don't like it, then we will come back. After all, lots of people reside happily in Britain without minding the long 'sentence' it does not seem like a big deal.'

'I'm sure it is not. You are not one of us afterall and therefore not exactly in a position to appreciate our helplessness.'

'That is why we will make sure that this opportunity did not slip through our fingers. Did you really appreciate the implication of what Erica said? If you don't, let me spell it out to you: Except for American visa lottery, if you win it that is, this is the best thing that could happen to anybody wanting to relocate abroad, because to acquire residency status is not an easy feat.'

'Against what we are supposed to face with here, I dare say that it's an option worth exploring.'

'Now you are talking sense, as you Nigerians will say.'

'*Oyibo* woman,' was all Gift could offer.

And so the plan was put into high gear and we never looked back. The cloak and dagger antics that were to be involved in traveling to the said Ireland beggared belief, but I conformed because I was not about to truncate our chances. Finally the D-day arrived and as instructed by Erica, we bought return Coach Tickets to Belfast from National Express instead of Bus Éireann. This was geared towards foiling any suspicion that we were going to any other place than Belfast. Our departure was at 5 o'clock with the evening coach. We arrived at Victoria Station early; to give me enough room to worry. We did not have any atom of document on us and as such had to cross the *international* boundary at the witching hour of twelve midnight, hoping that the immigration officers would be asleep or something close to that, or absent even, if our luck persisted. But it was an adrenaline pumping affair.

Ifeoma explained something to me in the region of that because I and my children did not have visas permitting our entry into the Republic of Ireland we had to go through Belfast which was in Britain but at the same time Ireland, not the Republic though. Now tell me how I'm supposed to grasp this madness! But I had shelved logic at this point.

The plan for Ifeoma to travel with us had been changed to after we had crossed over, so that if we were caught enroute, we would have somebody outside to *negotiate* for us. Now, that was neat, but it brought fresh worries for me and at the rate I was going, I might give birth and truncate the whole show altogether.

Dublin

REPUBLIC OF IRELAND

2001

When we entered the final leg of our journey; having crossed the Irish Sea in a ferry and re-boarded the National Express Coach, my heartbeat started racing, changing its rhythmic pattern of tud, tud, tud every second to tudtudtud, tudtudtud within the second. Then my breathing followed, in a quickened sequence, while something resembling fear washed over my whole body, every other minute. Very soon.

Then Belfast.

Heavily pregnant I stood with my two daughters uncertain and askance, like the proverbial chicken that surveys her new neighborhood standing on one leg, in the middle of the Belfast Central Bus Station. We had arrived, not more than a minute ago, with the coach that had been ferried across the ocean in Stena Line, before it had continued, on land, till we drove into the station.

I burrowed into my jacket as I noticed the cold, it's like this place was much colder than England and Italy rolled into one. Firmly, I clamped on thoughts about Italy that were about to sneak in. Not now please. *I am stepping into a new life so the past must remain buried.* I bent down to ensure that my daughters' jackets were properly buttoned. This kind of weather portends danger for children. Then I straightened up and looked around for signs of who could remotely be classed as an immigration officer and that tugged at my consciousness; *I must hasten and be about our business.* Not seeing anybody in that mould I was deflated but in a happy kind of way. Though I would have liked to get it over and done with, still it could be deferred or nothing at all *sef.* Maybe they were inside, I cautioned, and that cut short my euphoria. Holding my last daughter on my left hand and the first daughter instructed to walk in front of me, I dragged our suitcase that contained our meager belongings with my right hand, as we went into the building part of the Bus Station. I shepherded us deep, into the far end of the building and squeezed my girls and our luggage between a giant Coca Cola vending machine and the one vending Deep RiverRock. Feeling much safer, I looked furtively around again, but there still was no sign of anybody official. From the look of things, the station was just coming to life and that made me pause; no wonder Erica was so adamant. Now I could see the wisdom behind her instructions to not only board the night coach but to do it on a Friday so as to arrive early Saturday morning. As it were, the station workers were only just stirring and if the immigration officers ever operated in the station, they hadn't put up appearances yet. *So Gift, my dear girl, you better start looking for the black goat while there is still daylight* I told myself gleefully as my heart quietened, my breathing back to normal and the tremor waves of fear retreated.

Quickly I pushed our luggage further into the corner and left it there with my girls, instructing them, with a threat of slap as incentive, to not leave the spot, while I walked heavily out to scout for a taxi as Erica had said not to board Bus Éireann to Dublin as we might be unlucky and encounter immigration officers at the border. But what border was she talking about now? If we had crossed the high seas and were now in Belfast which was Britain and also Ireland, at what point then inside the Irish/British city of Belfast would we encounter the border with immigration officers waiting to pounce? But I willed the negative thoughts out of my head and hoped that nobody had noticed my loitering, thus causing the proverbial *using my own hand to bring disaster upon my head* to come to fruition. I snapped off my mask of dread as I veered towards a particular taxi driver who had what looked like a kind face.

The cabbie, without so much as a blink, promised to take us to our doorstep at a princely sum of 120 pounds sterling. I calculated swiftly to convert the said amount to Naira and nearly collapsed. N30, 000.00?! This was daylight robbery. I reared back to challenge the cost by asking how much the cabbie thought we paid to come from Nigeria or even from London to Belfast but stopped myself just in time. *Gift you don't have time for that, or would you rather wait and be netted by the immigration officers?* That obliterated my objection. Besides, artisans have a way of being your friend, petting you as long as there was hope of a sale, but thwart that and you became an instant enemy. Some would even go as far as directing some of the abuses to your parents, depending on how bad their day had been and this cabbie might not be any different, white man or not.

*   *   *

As we sped along, I was surprised that the driver had understood our need. And to think I was agonizing over how to present my case without sounding like a fugitive. He had stopped me with a wave of his hand while telling me that he knew exactly what I wanted. Not bad. Somewhere along the way he veered off the highway onto a narrow winding road. Cars on this road were smaller or looked smaller, or maybe it was trick of the eye seeing that the road was very narrow. I didn't know why the driver had to leave the major road that was smooth and wide. I ventured a look at the back of his head, for clues, but only noted his hushed voice talking into a walkie-talkie stuck on the dashboard. Was he trying to alert *them* or what? Absorbed in my already entrenched state of fear, I jumped, when the cabbie spoke aloud.

'We had to use the back roads you see.'

I nodded as we looked at each other through the rearview mirror. He must have noticed my apprehension.

I nodded again to show my understanding and approval. I glanced at my children, they were fast asleep. *Relax Gift, if the immigration officers are going to get you they will and there's nothing you can do about it.* Very true but I couldn't relax; truth and reality did not dissipate fear: once lodged under your diaphragm, you are done for. I shifted to find a more comfortable position; I had been sitting so far down, so as to be invisible, that my legs were screaming and the baby in my womb kicking furiously. Whatever would be, would be. I pulled up my bulk and rested my back and head properly on the backrest. It was very relaxing.

I must have slept despite of my vigilant efforts when I found us driving into Erica's compound in Blanchardstown at about noon, who, relieved to see us at last it seemed, urged that I pay the driver quickly, steered us briskly into the house and drew the curtains.

'Erica, are we still at this cloak and dagger business?' I asked wearily while looking for a space on the couch to sit down. I hadn't realized Erica was not circumspect about tidiness, but then I had never been this close to her. As students, some see it as a form of cool to be untidy. Erica in answer to my query snorted an indeterminate reply while she went about passing mugs of hot chocolate drinks to all the kids, hers and mine.

My children were especially grateful for the hot drinks as life sprang into their faces immediately and they followed Erica with thankful eyes. I heaved myself up and took over from Erica and cleaned out the journey stresses from them before feeding them as provided.

By the time I finished with my daughters and attended to my own needs any curiousity I had about this whole show had dissipated so I fell into a couch bone-tired and ready to sleep. But that was not to be. Erica came down after putting away our luggage and settling the children in front of a Disney cartoon show and announced that we were ready to start plotting.

She started right away to give me more information and I prayed that nodding would be the only requirement from me, afterall she had explained a lot before we left London.

'As you know very well, no country allows people to just flow in without proper travel document which must be processed in one's home country before setting out.' She looked at me and I nodded understanding. 'But how many countries in the world give out residency permit just like that?' She snapped her fingers to emphasize easiness. 'None to my knowledge,' She answered her own question as I looked on without any comment, 'So one must learn how to overcome obstacles if you want to live in any of these countries. But here the Irish give automatic Residency Status to parents as a result of the citizenship of their children born here. What that means Gift, is that if you succeed in having your child here, they will give your child their Red Passport as their citizen, and you will get permission to live here and bring the child up, can you imagine that?'

I shook my head no. I couldn't imagine it, but I had to say something at this point not to appear rude.

'But I did not enter this country with any visa or any form of documentation, how then will they do all these for me and my newborn? It is not as if they came to recruit me from Nigeria to come and have children for them.'

'I do not really know why they have such policy in place, but I don't see why that should worry you now. Just allow me to finish my explanation okay?'

'Sorry to interrupt you, my sister, go on,' I said in a soft voice, to convey to Erica that I was not being obtuse, just confused, tired and could do with a drop of sleep. Erica, of course, was oblivious to these biological needs of mine, she was bent on getting to the end of her educating me on the intricacies of Irish Immigration Policies, as they stood in her eyes.

'Well your questions are in order so let me explain,' Erica conceded, 'because you do not have any 'papers,' as you pointed out, you are going to declare Asylum by telling them that you are fleeing Nigeria to avoid persecution and were brought to this country by an 'agent' on his papers. You are supposed to have paid him a certain amount of money to do that. You will also claim that you did not have any knowledge of this country until the agent told you at arriving to the City Centre that you are in Dublin, Republic of Ireland. He also paid for and put you and your kids into the bus that took you to Mount Street Lower and instructed you to alight at no 79/80. And that if you get mixed up to inquire from any passerby 'where people seek asylum,' it is that easy,' Erica concluded nonchalantly.

I smiled, ironically. Of course, *it is that easy.* How could it not be? When last I was told that was in Torino by Madam Mary, and that was the hardest job I had ever faced in my life, past, present and future, drunk or sober. Now I was being told yet again that "it is that easy". It had better be, for I was not about to give birth in prison nor ready to go back to Nigeria.

'So what am I being persecuted for in Nigeria?' I eventually asked, while my thoughts were on the fact that I had two things going for me; I was truly fleeing from my death! And I know for sure that I will not share that information and secondly, the fact that truly, I had never heard of Ireland before now.

'I suppose you'll have to use my story,' Erica offered. And at my raised brow, she elaborated, 'The one I used for my interview. You can change it as you want to suit your circumstances.' As my raised brow remained raised Erica elaborated further, 'As many people as possible recycle the same story, especially successful ones like mine, the idea is to get into the process of declaring you a Refugee through seeking Asylum first but that is just to get the ball rolling. Because after that first interview, the rest is more or less a written script!' Erica got up and went to stand at the foot of the staircase to yell at the children 'Bring that noise down or I will come up there and kill all of you.'

Everywhere went quiet immediately. Erica came back and continued. 'These children,' she pontificated as she sat down, 'if you don't smack them, they don't learn.' I nodded in agreement. I supposed there's some sense there, though I never enjoyed the pain from my ear being twisted then, afterwards I never repeated the folly, so it must have its merit. The threat of the deed also worked with my children.

Erica got back on our original track. 'It is only when you attend the real interview that they will grill you with questions. I have heard that the interviewing officers are merciless with barrages of questions shooting at you like arrows, battering you into confusion.' She nodded as if she was re-living her experience. 'Even in this cold weather, you will sweat like a pig. You see, they have to be sure that you are not playing tricks.'

'You had better tell me this your 'persecution' story then so that I can start practicing, I do not intend to disgrace myself by giving birth before the grilling officers have popped the first question.'

'I have not finished, Gift.'

'Eeeh?'

'That is what I am trying to explain to you, you will not get to be interviewed. You're almost due to deliver *abī?*' At my nod, 'Then they will wait for you to do that first before giving you interview date. So you need not worry, for as soon as you return from having your baby, you will write to them to withdraw from the Asylum process, your reason being that you are now a parent of an Irish citizen child.'

Erica grinned. I frowned; it must be pure joy to be a parent of Irish citizen child, as I continued to watch Erica's grinning face.

'As soon as they confirm that to be true, they will write to tell you that your file will be transferred to the Irish Born Child Unit. You then quickly fill out all the necessary forms and within two months, believe me you will be a proud owner of a brand new Residency Status permitting you to reside in the State with all the benefits that come with it and the rest as they say is history,' she finished in a flourish. Determined to get in a word before Erica continued, I took advantage of the lull and asked.

'Are these *benefits* in addition to the Residency Status?'

'What are you talking about? Of course! The Social Welfare will take over your responsibilities, everything; they will pay your rent; give you weekly maintenance allowance, according to the number of persons in your household; clothing allowances; back-to-school allowances, in fact everything and anything that you can dream of or as may arise, and you will live happily ever after.'

'This is a joke right?'

'Joke *ke?* You no know anything oh, wait till you start then you will see,' inserted Erica to my amused stare.

'And what will I be doing as it seems they will take over the care of all our needs?'

'Nothing, oh my sister. Absolutely nothing.'

'But why?'

'Don't ask me Gift, ask the government, but before then take the opportunity on offer.'

'Then this country must be populated by the kindest of people,' I commented as I mulled over all that Erica had said for a while then asked, 'But which passport are they going to put the Residency Status in? I thought I did not have any 'papers'?'

I pounced gleefully, believing that I had found a flaw in this surprising tale.

'You will send money to Nigeria with your passport photographs and make a new International Passport that is the one you will submit. That reminds me; better bring that passport you came with so that we can destroy it. If they ever find it on you anytime, they will cancel your Residency, you might even go to prison.'

'God forbid bad thing,' I asserted quickly then continued on the same breath, 'I will keep my documents until I see all that you told me come to pass, thank you very much. Imagine destroying my 'freedom' on this cock and bull story. Are they mad in this country or what? Did they not reckon with *us* Nigerians when they put that policy in place? That *we* are like locusts, when *we* descend, *we* eat to death.'

Erica made a face at me. 'That one na your business Gift,' she inserted in a singsong voice before continuing in her normal tone, 'So what are you going to do?'

'I suppose we start from the beginning; go down to wherever place you called it and tell them 'your story' as quickly as possible before others started to flood in. I mean it cannot last, can it?'

'Oh you know it won't, there is only so much a country can take,' concurred Erica.

'So when are we going to go?'

'Aaaah Gift, take *am* easy now. Is Monday soon enough? You were being skeptical before, I could read it in your face, now you can't wait to sink your teeth into the project.'

'Project? Ooh Erica, what a word, and believe me it deserves every single letter in that word. Project indeed!' Then I started laughing, more from the euphoria of the envisaged freedom than anything else.

Erica, seeing the mirth the word evoked, joined Gift and together they rocked with mad laughter for some time, before Erica continued.

'You know that you have to be registered in the hospital for antenatal, so the earlier the better. That will give the doctor enough time for assessment before you deliver. Do you know that some people leave it too late to the extent that while still in the Refugee Office telling their stories, they are rushed to the hospital to give birth, as in right away "off the ferry to the maternity ward" it is called.'

'Oh my goodness! What type of foolishness is that? What if there are complications?'

'What complications? You know our people and their belief in whiteman's wisdom? Trusting that they'd be resourceful enough to deal with any emergencies that would arise. Besides, what complications are there in childbirth anyway? Don't forget we are a nation of strong people; giving birth is the least of our problems. Mad people roaming the streets of Lagos give births without darkening the doorway of any hospital, so give me a break.'

Erica stopped and looked at me with a frown, then said, 'Look Gift, you know you have always been a bit uppity.' It was my turn to frown, so I did, but said nothing as Erica continued, 'Yes you have, always.' I frowned again but Erica interrupted my second frown with, 'I hope you'll be able to carry this plan through. I don't want anybody to put *san san for my Garri* in this Ireland. I warned Ifeoma before I accepted to induct you. I hope she told you?'

I smiled, thinking that Erica would never change.

'I will try my best.'

'I hope so. Anyway back to your question, don't mind me *na* Naija mentality *dey* talk. In reality, though, I suppose some dangers exist, strong or not strong, giving birth is not a child's play.' I just continued to look at Erica with a smile of amusement at her indecision as to which side to be on, the posh *Oyibonized* woman or the tough Nigerian cookie.

*   *   *

Severely dressed down to look poor, as instructed by Erica, my children and I made our way to the Office of the Refugee Application Commissioner on Mount Street Lower that Monday morning, as I later came to know it, with one luggage since we 'left in a hurry,' being on the run and all. People were milling about and the queue was up to the outside main gate. I could not believe my eyes; how could all these people have heard about Ireland? News must travel fast. Then I reminded myself that cooped up in my village in the back of nowhere, absorbed in misery, did not exactly position me to hear of events around the world. And to be pampered and catered for by a country, according to Erica, was not something that should be left unexplored.

Despite getting to *this* place as early as 9am, it did not get to our turn until about 3.30pm. We were received politely, our luggage stowed in one corner and guided gently to rows of seats, where we were instructed to sit and listen for our number to be called out. As it happened, when we were eventually called, we were rushed through the process, because it was getting to their closing time. I thanked God for that. So I never did get to tell any story other than the preliminary information needed to register me which happened to include the 'agent' part of the story. I briefly mumbled about my reason for 'fleeing' Nigeria while pretending to be in pain, which nudged the interview to an end. At about 5pm, we were loaded into a medium-sized-bus and driven to a hostel somewhere in the wilderness. There, we were assigned various living quarters in forms of 2-bed flats in caravan-like homes. This was not bad at all, and I was prepared to gladly live there if that was permanent too. To think that this was just a tip of the iceberg!

The next morning, us, the new residents, were shown around; the dining hall; laundry room; the clinic; crèche for the pre-schoolers. Later, about mid-day, I sneaked out and called Erica from a telephone booth to update her about the new developments. Erica congratulated me and then advised me to 'keep to myself and not make unnecessary friends that will lead to story-telling as there are spies everywhere; gathering information for Justice.' At my prompting, she informed me that as far as Asylum seekers are concerned, 'all the agencies under the Department of Justice are referred to as Justice including the Asylum office; and, even when it seems they have accepted your stories on face value, it is believed that they carry out independent investigations of their own.'

I nodded. I, who had more skeletons in the cupboard than any three people put together was not in the habit of 'telling stories', as Erica put it, and certainly did not need to make new friends; so the secrecy of the whole set-up appealed to me very well.

I proceeded to make the best of the situation and when I went into labour, having been told repeatedly by Erica to not reveal that I knew anybody, I wisely kept quiet and my children were placed into care while I was in the hospital. Nneka, the lady that shared the caravan with us with her six-year old daughter, had offered to look after my daughters, which I politely but firmly refused. It wasn't that I wouldn't have allowed it, but I did not tell her that the officers of the hostel wouldn't hear of it and I did not push it. I liked Nneka; our friendship was born after she shared her story with me. It was one of the weirdest but most hilarious stories I had ever heard, putting my own to shame. The hilarious part came after Nneka assured me that the story was false, of course. I felt sorry for these Justice people: their minds must have been twisted to their maximum by now with the kind of stories they heard daily.

Then the baby decided that it's time and it turned out to be the most painful thing I had ever encountered, bringing back the horror of the baby's conception. I was prepared to hate this child with unprecedented relish, and if possible, give him up for adoption.

'Oh my . . . oh my . . . !'

I stopped short.

'Why didn't I think of this before?' It was so easy and yet I had failed to see it. It had to be what I'd do for there was no way on this God's earth that I was going to be stared in the eyes everyday by Osahon's atrocities. I was not sure of what went through the minds of other women during labor, but mine was spent plotting about how to dispose of this fruit of Osahon's rape.

The baby took its time and arrived two days later; lustily protesting at being wrenched from his cocoon of safety. Who would blame him? If most people were aware of the danger that was life, some would probably prefer to remain in their mother's womb. But out mine came, demanding attention.

Right away I noticed that the baby was a carbon copy of Osahon, before they whisked him away for cleaning. So I firmly shut my mind and eyes to the child, vowing to stick to my resolve and wait for the right time to inquire about the process of placing him for adoption. That was a far better solution than having an abortion I reasoned. I really feel sorry for Ifeoma with that kind of weight on her conscience.

Pot calling kettle black?

I refused to rise to the taunt. Instead, with my eyes closed, I riled against God: how could He? Why did He have to make him the spitting image of Osahon? Did He not think that I had suffered enough? Did He want me completely insane? Then in my rambling mad thoughts, I glimpsed some hope; maybe He was in support of my intention? That last thought cheered me up considerably; maybe He did, if not why did He put the word adoption into my head in the first place . . . Suddenly, I became aware that a nurse was cooing beside me and at the same time urging me to put the baby to the breast. I opened my eyes, recoiled immediately and shut them again, but too late—I had seen it.

The baby's eyes were two pointed red-hot daggers straight out of a blacksmiths' furnace, aimed squarely at my forehead, scorching as they drilled in. The pain was horrendous leaving me writhing. I heard this disembodied voice from a distance, 'My God! What kind of a child is this?' I heard the in-take of breadth of the cooing nurse before she whispered, 'Pardon me, did you say something?' I could only point, while mumbling, 'his eyes, his eyes, his eyes.'

The nurse was baffled, she took a quick look at the baby's face and then back at mine and shook her head.

I pushed the child away, refusing to carry him, or put him to the breast as the nurse had suggested. The nurse took the baby and fled.

* * *

For days I lay listless and uncaring, refusing to look after myself or to go near the baby. I was *not responding* to my environment at all, according to the doctor. And for lack of what to call it, he put it down to severe post-natal depression. I remained in that unfeeling and *not responding* to my environment state for almost two weeks. I thought it was an act, that I had staged it to get them to accept to place the child for adoption, when I eventually broached the idea, but then I found out that I was not in control at all. I could not stop myself from sliding into misery, this mushy helplessness, it'd envelope me and every attempt to pull myself out was rebuffed by invisible persons determined to keep me in this state of stupor forever. Initially I welcomed it, but then I decided that it wasn't part of the plan. I didn't travel all the way from Nigeria to the white man's land to become mad.

No!

So I struggled and then gradually I began to rally round. And when I became sufficiently aware of my surroundings, *responding to the environment,* as the case may be, I revisited the thought of placing the child for adoption. But I found out that thinking about it and actually doing it were two different ball games.

* * *

I named him Lucky. I began to realize that the depth of God was beyond human understanding, which was actually very good, for a lot of people would have started manipulating Him for their own purposes. But of immediate importance was that gradually I did not resent the child so much and my health began to improve, not that these two facts were mutually inclusive, but I got better anyway.

The social worker responsible for the placement of my children in care brought them to visit. They arrived at the hospital gleaming in new clothes and toys, obviously bought by whoever that had them. It was a joyful moment for them to behold their baby brother, with Eudora—I couldn't bear to continue to call her "Blessing"—establishing authority by letting him know that she was older and therefore his boss. They had a good visit and thereafter left. I was not interested in where they were, they must be happy, for they were full of stories, tripping on their tongues in an attempt to convey their joy.

My recovery continued to progress well, but it was almost another week before I was discharged and I went back to our caravan. Another Osahon-induced ordeal successfully overcome. My daughters came back to rejoin me after a week. With the four of us enclosed in the caravan, I began to wonder if I hadn't been a bit too hasty in my decisions to leave my village in the first place. What would I not do to have my mother with me now, taking care of situations? In the meantime I prayed that God would give me the restraint not to strangle any of my children. Being the last child in my family I had been pampered as children born late in their parent's life inadvertently were sometimes. Living with my big sister Chinelo didn't add anything to my ability to oversee a household as she took most of her household decisions. I just followed instructions and barked her children into submission with the most senior doing the job. Within the duration of my marriage Osahon did most of these things. So now I had to take care of three strangers I call my children, alone, in a foreign land. What a fearful prospect!

Nevertheless, with Nnekas help, we coped. Then one early morning at about 5.30 am immigration officers swooped down and took Nneka and her child away and later deported them. The quota of her story had capped, I suppose. That was a blow but life usually did not stop because of obstacles, you soldiered on. Not too long after, following a succession of visits from the public healthcare nurses and a social worker, our approval to live in our own place came through. It was music to my ears and as soon as the said 'paper' entered my hand, I marched off to Blanchardstown to see Erica, the claim of not knowing anybody completely buried in the pit of my mind. With Erica's help, we scoured the estate agents and finally succeeded in finding a three-bedroom house in Donegal. I wanted us to live so far away from the city that nobody would know my past and I would not be in Osahon's route to anywhere. Erica, who was not privy to any of my life-secrets, was surprised at my decision. More like a village she had complained and then gave up persuading me, adding disparagingly that nothing about me surprised her anymore and good luck to me.

Donegal

2001

Lulled by the rocking of the Bus Éireann coach conveying us to Donegal, we fell soundly asleep. When I jerked awake, hours later, I felt disoriented. I was always disoriented these days, it must be the combination of my current life combined with the various medications to combat my post-natal depression, but who wouldn't be overwhelmed and tired anyway? But never mind, this quiet place would sort me out in no time. Inside the station, the driver parked the coach haphazardly, with the rear jutting onto the next parking space. The remaining passengers alighted tiredly: it had been a long journey. I came down with my children and headed for the boot located in the belly of the coach, to retrieve our luggage.

Lucky was still fast asleep so I strapped him to my chest with a baby-harness leaving my hands free to hold the girls as we went in search of a cab that would take us to our village. Compared to my first arrival to Ireland, my steps were firmer. I was no longer a fugitive, and very soon my Residency Status would enter my hands and then "the rest would be history" as Erica had said.

Sighting the outskirts of our new abode, I smiled happily. I was glad that I chose Glenncolm; with her rolling hills; lush vegetations and the deep blue sea undulating regally, I knew that it was suitable to the kind of lifestyle I wanted to live: quiet and next to nowhere. A soothing balm to my bruised soul. Nobody would know me here and Osahon in the best and most of his efforts, could not locate us. These thoughts and the calmness of Glenncolm started seeping into my being and I could feel the effect considerably.

John, the cab driver, as he introduced himself, helped us with our luggages into our gleaming three-bed house. I had not had time yet to think about it properly, but the people of Ireland seemed to be a kind people; because since arriving in the country, though uninvited, from the Belfast Coach Station to the officers in the Asylum office and then hostel, through to the doctors and nurses in the hospital and finally to the strangers on the streets, they were always happy to see us foreigners amongst them. Always interested in our well-being with a kind word on offer when necessary, otherwise waving, nodding and smiling suffices. We couldn't have chosen a better country!

*   *   *

The first week was idyllic and sailed by effortlessly, but, by the second week, loneliness hit with a sledgehammer, knocking me off my gleeful pedestal. Here I was, alone, in a remote village in a foreign country with three toddlers, ages ranging from two months to three years and six months who depended on me morning, afternoon and night. It was no mean feat to be able to attend to all of their needs, including mine, and still remain sane. I did not know a soul, did not have any intention or inclination to knowing any soul. So I must find the means to cope on my own, in this self-imposed exile.

By the third week, we established a pattern of sorts; wake up in the morning and have a crying session: I, for no discernible reason other than the combined effects of all my troubles, coupled with the newly acquired periods of thrashing away half the night looking for the elusive sleep, while the children, I suppose, from a combination of seeing their mother crying and from hunger. When we had our fill, I'd make breakfast consisting of Weetabix for Frances and Coco Pops for Eudora, while Lucky's was a combination of breast and baby milk, which mercifully always knocked him back to sleep.

Then we'd loll around doing nothing. The girls would play with the few toys they had acquired since arriving in the State and I would half-sit, half-lie, on the couch staring into nothing until hunger pangs drove the girls to cluster around me with Lucky screaming his head off.

Lunch consisted of spaghetti loops in tomato sauce or something in that neighbourhood and Lucky's another round of breast and powdered milk and once again off to sleep, thank God. He wasn't old enough to babble and whine like his sisters and he was a good sleeper. He probably sensed what was good for him otherwise he'd suffer: for the blazing hatred I felt for him at birth may seem to have disappeared, but I could feel some traces of it cavorting in my veins waiting to erupt.

Dinner was a combination of crisps, chocolates, biscuits and baked beans and or cereal yet again, but none of us were complaining.

I hadn't ventured out of the house since moving in save for sneaking out under the cloak of darkness on three occasions to replenish our supply of fresh milk. Every other thing came with us, courtesy of the Asylum hostel of County Kildare. As if they knew. Besides, there wasn't much happening outside to draw me out, so to say, and it was always raining. Maybe this was their own rainy season. But everyday? It would soon abate, was my constant refrain, because no matter how much rain relishes falling, it must come to an end one day, I consoled while standing by the window peeping out on a particularly nasty day. That was a new habit I had acquired; peeping out through the window, scanning the neighbourhood, for any sign . . . *For any sign of what or who?* I had asked myself repeatedly but had not found an answer.

By the fourth week, I knew I had to do something or spaghetti loops with his brother baked beans and all what not would start sprouting out of our ears. We had to have properly cooked meals to supplement. Very early the next morning I woke, defying all the forces of whatever that had caused my apathy, had a good wash, did same for my children, fed them and after peeping severally to confirm that nobody was paying the remotest of interest in us and therefore was not lurking about, we came out quickly, closed and locked the door, and trouped down to the city centre, with Lucky snuggled comfortably in his harness, Eudora in her buggy and Frances trotting alongside, clutching the buggy like her life was dependent on holding on.

The nodding, waving and smiling accompanied us till we veered into the butchers for inquiries.

Glenncolm city centre consisted of one building, long and rectangular, housing most of the offices and shops.

I chose the butchers, there were no customers in there, and pushed us in with a smile creasing my face as I sought information on how to locate an electronics shop. I had realized that we needed a diversion from the walls of our parlour and a television set had come to mind. So, on this trip we had two birds to kill with one stone.

The butcher, Fergal, did not seem to realize that we were in a hurry; he was determined to make the most of the rare sighting of the black family and didn't get to my question right away.

'Ah Ms. Everything alright with yerself and the little ones?'

Widening my smile, I answered in the affirmative. But he wasn't done yet.

'Where about are yous originally from?' This asked, while coming round to inspect us properly under the guise of handing lollipops to the kids.

'Nigeria.'

'Nigeria! Me mam's uncle Thomas,' he crossed himself quickly before continuing, 'was a priest. He lived somewhere in Africa called Eye-hi-al-a.' At my questioning look, he added, 'It's in Biafra.'

'Oh.' I smiled, wider still. That must be Ihiala. I knew that a big Holy Ghost Juniorate was stationed there. 'Your mam's uncle is a Holy Ghost Missionary then?'

'You got it right in one count Miss. A missionary he was.'

'Still living there?'

'Lord no!' Accompanied again, by another sign of the cross. 'He died thirty years ago of malaria. Well before my time. God rest his soul.' Another sign of the cross followed.

Before his time? Was he trying to be funny or what? But I held my peace. Then took a closer look at him again and realized that his hair must be from hair-dye and apart from the heavily lined forehead from permanent frowning, he was actually young, mid-twenties maybe. But before I could state our mission once again, Fergal beat me to it, he was only getting started.

'Me mam's uncle was the oldest of them lot and his mam, God rest her soul,' he crossed himself again, 'had twelve of them. Me mam's mammy, my Nan, you know, was the seventh in line.' I was quite sure that I did not need this history but did not know how to steer him away from his determined course. He must have read my mind for he said, 'I must not prattle on so, but if you don't mind me saying so, like, you must come out often.' He nodded 'yes' to his suggestion, then, 'No need to lock yerself in. Yous all are welcome in our village. So what can I get you?'

'Sausages, chicken laps, shin beef,' he reeled, as he went back behind the counter to re-arrange the different meats as he mentioned their names, though he was re-arranging pig feet as he mentioned chicken laps. That had me confused, but I rallied round quickly not wanting to give him the opportunity to launch into another family history, this time probably mine.

'We are looking for where to buy television.'

'You'd be after going to the city. You can't get them 'tricals here.'

'To Dublin!' I had slept through the journey to this back of beyond and so had missed the opportunity of seeing any city.

'Lord no. You'd want Donegal city.'

I thanked Fergal profusely with more smiles splitting my face before asking, 'How do we get to Donegal city?'

'Are you sure you don't want anything here?' he asked crestfallen.

'I will buy some chicken laps when we return,' I offered, hoping to remember to be on the look-out that I did not get the pig feet. Fergal came round the counter and firmly took command of the buggy and I had no choice but to troupe behind him.

When we got to the bus stop, there was no shelter, unlike most of the ones in Dublin. It was just a navy-blue iron pole with a round-bulge half-way up stuck on the ground with the bus number written on the bulge. Fergal stopped when we reached this pole and instructed me to buy the television from O'Grady 'tricals. 'It'd not be hard to find, they are right beside O'Tooles', the best fish and chips in Ireland. I'll tell the driver where to set yous down.' And so he abandoned his business to stand with us at the bus stop, issuing running commentaries on everything and about everybody living in Glenncolm, including Una who was after coming back with pregnancy from running wild in Dublin.

Una was his sister!

I was dumbfounded. I left my village and country, and even Dublin and her environs for this tranquil village and here I was being regaled about everything inclusive of the ones I wanted to hear and the ones I did not care about. I had to be careful. If a whiff of my past escaped into this atmosphere I'd be ostracized. I shivered and inched away from Fergal. I didn't ever envisage that *Oyibo* indulged in gossip too.

'Ms. You'd want to cover yerself so. That coat'd cover no 'grel.' I looked at him, sure that Fergal was not all up there. But nothing escaped him. It was a mistake coming out today. Now everybody would know about us and could easily trace us! But I nodded, hoping desperately that the bus would show up. I was beginning to despair. Why wouldn't Fergal go back to his shop and leave us alone? He was being helpful, yes, but so what?

'Fergal,' I called, 'won't you go back to the shop? You may have customers waiting.'

'Not to worry Miss. Nobody comes at this time. I know me customers.' I nodded again, and smiled inwardly when I sighted our bus from afar. Fergal, after a long natter with the bus driver, helped to put us in the bus safely before he waved and trotted back to his shop. And then the driver started his own questions. There was nobody else at the bus stop, but he was determined to wait even for those that were yet to make up their mind whether to go on the bus that day. So there we sat, I with a smile and a nod, occasionally needing to verbally confirm answers from the driver's questions, which started with the weather as the ice breaker then, "where about are you originally from?" and "how long have you lived in Ireland so?" That had been the two constant and consistent questions at first encounter with the Irish. Then if they wanted to extend the conversation, would follow those two with the "do you like it here so?" one. But my demeanor never gave them the opportunity to linger or maybe they themselves were not really interested in the answers to their questions. Since I did not need the complications of friendship, I was never really interested. Ifeoma was enough. Erica I could stomach. And Nneka was gone. And that reminded me of the need to contact my people back home to let them know that we had settled down finally after a change of country and about Lucky.

I was always reluctant to call home, my parents specifically. The wound I inflicted on them was still raw, and calling them would keep reopening it. But I'd call them, at least to let them know the basics.

In Donegal City, I paid for a 32" television set; Sky satellite cable; then for the delivery and connection fee. The cable would be installed the next day. I did not have any telephone number, land or mobile to enable them to contact me. I used their phone to call Éircom for the installation of a telephone line and purchased a telephone hand-set. Finally, we left the 'tricals shop with their advice ringing in my ears to not forget to pay the T.V license at my local post office. It's a punishable offence to be caught without one; either a substantial fine or a jail term is applied. For buying a T.V! What was that? In Nigeria you buy your T.V and all that comes with it, put it up and that's that. Anybody wanting you to pay for a T.V license would have to tell you his contribution towards the purchase of said T.V.

License indeed! But here they were talking about jail term and that was enough to put the fear of God in me.

We perambulated about in the city, calling on various shops looking for nothing in particular. In one shop known as Tesco, which sold everything including 'tricals, we bought a toaster; that'd add flavour to our breakfast. Then in Dunne's Stores, I stocked up on more warm clothing, nighties, socks, trainers, etc., for my daughters and babygros, bibs and all whatnot for Lucky. When Lucky started fussing we went into Macdonald's and warmed and fed him his bottles while the girls were happy to tuck into 'happy meal' for kids. It came complete with toys. I ate a MacChicken Sandwich meal, not to be left out. After eating and resting, we once again trudged on as I was determined to stock up on all that I felt we needed to aid our hibernation.

Alighting at Glenncolm bus stop, I espied Fergal gesticulating
wildly at us. I was tired and courtesy or not, was not ready to waste one
second with Fergal. But I reckoned without his determination. He ran
over and helped me strap Eudora into her buggy, with Frances clinging
on the side rail as usual. And with him in the lead, we marched back
into his butchery where he proceeded to pack: 1lb of chicken laps, 1lb
of mince—'You'd like it,' I was told—and 1lb of stewing beef. He rang
up the total and I paid. I didn't think Fergal would take kindly to the
reminder that I hadn't ordered any of those.

As punishment for his brazenness, I left my daughters in his shop,
and went into "your local post-office" as instructed by the 'tricals
people, to pay for the T.V license. Who would have thought that
nipping out to buy a T.V for pleasurable consumption could lead to
a jail term if one were not careful? An account was created for me by
Noreen, the yellow-haired post lady. I tucked the receipt carefully into
my purse with the intention of pasting it to my front door—for ease
of inspection. I went into the supermarket and bought spaghetti and
the sauces that go with it: now that we had been inflicted with mince.
Then, onions followed and before I knew it, I had stocked up some
more. If truth be known, I wouldn't say before I knew it with a straight
face, I suspected that nobody would see our faces in a long while after
this outing, if we got home without any incident. This was hoping that
Fergal would not misinterpret my constant smiling for what it was not
and came calling to bring us more mince.

I paid for my purchases and went back into Fergal's. Though the
smell in Fergal's shop was not inviting, it was still better than scrabbling
outside, in the view of the whole world, to pack our purchases. So I
knelt down with one knee and proceeded to unpack the contents of
the trolley into the various Tesco 'for life' and Dunnes Stores' 'always
better value' bags we had purchased earlier in Donegal city.

'You can bring them trolley home.'

'Pardon me.' I twisted round, to be able to see Fergal.

'I said you can bring them trolley home with yer.'

'You mean take it home with me just like that?'

'Yes.'

'And nobody will arrest me?'

'Lord no! What are you like? Arrest you for what?'

I smiled. 'Don't mind me Fergal.'

I straightened up and loaded the rest of our things into the trolley,
thanked Fergal, and then wondered at how to push the two—the
food trolley and Eudora's buggy. Finally I unfastened Eudora, folded
and threw the buggy on top of our purchases and marched off with

the two girls on each side of the trolley trotting along to match my baby-stride. Fergal walked us half-way home before going back to his shop. Business must be slow in that shop of his.

Not wanting to lose the momentum, I prepared a quick spaghetti Bolognese, fed the children and then worked on the house. By the time I finished, our house was squeaky clean and I bone tired. Very welcoming because then I'd be sure to fall off to sleep as soon as my head touched the pillow. But that never happened. I didn't get to sleep till about 3 am as usual, but was jerked back awake at about 5am, by an unexplained nightmare. I remained awake, afraid to go back to sleep, listening to the night noises, while examining the content and sequences of the nightmare. Finally, I abandoned that fruitless exercise for a more worthy one, sipping from a bottle of my preferred tipple: Californian Merlot, while switching my mind to thinking about Ireland and her people.

*   *   *

Gradually the household established a rhythm. With Fergal's advice I went to the only crèche/Montessori in the village to place my two daughters and they could stay as late as 5pm at a good rate. But there was a drawback; Eudora had not been toilet-trained yet and so they would not take her in, I was informed in a firm but polite tone. And there went my hope of coping with Lucky alone. Eudora was not the easiest person in the world. I left with her, vowing to come back in one week to put her in school with or without her cooperation: She must become toilet-trained by force. The hope of charting a new course for our life with minimum disturbances would not be truncated even before it had had a chance to be explored.

*   *   *

It was slightly over a month after establishing our rhythm that Lorraine, the local welfare officer, came to visit. I was ambivalent about this visit. What does she want? Would she notice my glazed look and realize that it was from lack of sleep and drinking? I didn't like this idea of officials *spying* on me and my family, but if it had to be, then it had to be.

I was highly strung and couldn't relax as I would not want to be seen in a bad light.

My worries were unfounded, I felt initially, when the officer came. A very friendly woman, but who wanted to know everything inclusive of when my husband would join us. At being told that he did not exist, she suggested that I upgrade my status to lone parent—our benefit package would increase slightly. I wasn't too sure that I needed to upgrade. What we were being given was enough. Then the friendliness vanished, when Lorraine suddenly realized that the television in the background was a brand new 32" one. Then the grilling started.

'How much money do you get from other sources?'

'Other sources? Like from what?' I retorted as a nasty thought insinuated itself *or have they discovered that I used to be a prostitute and have started plying my trade here or what?* What was this woman trying to get at? I became visibly worried which did not help.

'How much does your husband pay monthly as child support?'

I frowned, this woman *sef.*

'None.'

'Then how much extra do you get in addition to your welfare allowances and from where?'

This woman would not let this other sources blend with the air?

'None,' I intoned weakly.

'None? So where did you get money to live in such a grand style: to install an expensive television and cable?'

The question raised my hackles instantly. The shock that had gripped me initially fell off and I went on the offensive.

'What right do you have to barge in here to harass me about our living expenses?'

'I am only doing my job. If you're on benefit but have other means of income then you must declare it. Because, you may not even be entitled to welfare payments if you have a healthy means of livelihood. Welfare payment is means tested, and you must be earning below a certain average to be on welfare,' Lorraine finished, her eyes shinning.

My anger evaporated. So the woman was not being nosy afterall. She was simply doing her job!

I back-pedaled and explained how our money came about: clothing allowances for all of us; buggy allowances for the three children since they were all under four, I only bought one for Eudora, Frances can walk, if we ever go anywhere, which was rare, and Lucky had his harness; nappy allowances for the three of them; weekly allowances for food and the transport money for our trip down to Donegal—they probably expected us to use the airplane the money was that much, instead we had used the coach. Then I added, lest she thought that I was hording the loot, that because I had been ill, I had been unable to do any of these things in full hence the accumulation. All these had tumbled out in one gulp and I hoped that they were enough to satisfy the lady. Thank God I left my life savings totaling 15,000 GBP and our passports with Ifeoma in London. Their discovery would have facilitated my being thrown into jail for real. They seemed inclined to do that at the slightest chance.

At the end of the figure reeling exercise, Lorraine wanted to inspect the house and I told her to suit herself. I sat with my children, quaking, hoping that nothing untoward would be discovered, since I was not exactly sure of what they were looking for. But Lorraine refused to go on the inspection alone. So I gritted my teeth and led her round. Finally, she left with the promise to get back to me after she discussed with the welfare officer in charge of our hostel in Co. Kildare for confirmation.

These people are not serious, I thought, but I was not worried. The only money I came into the country with was less than 200GBP and that had since finished. Whatever money on me came from the state, so nothing to fear about. But that also got me thinking. Okay, so if you're on welfare you'd have to live a certain kind of life; the kind of life that the limited amount of money given could support. And to think that I had offered Lorraine a choice of Merlot or Chardonnay or even the harder stuff! Brandishing a matured Bushmill in ignorance. 'Oh Lord,' I sighed before laughing. Now I could see the catch. Getting out of welfare as soon as possible would be my next project. My lifestyle and the kind of things I'd want to own would not go down well with them officers and I was not ready to accommodate anybody's sniffing. Looking for what they did not keep!

Donegal

JAN. 2002

Tiredly, I plodded about as I cleaned and buffed in preparation for Ifeoma's imminent arrival from London. As I chased the dusts here and there, my thoughts were also flitting alongside, here and there, in rhythm with the dusts. It had been more than six months since I had *successfully* settled my family in Glenncolm and had since procured both my son's Irish passport and my Residency Permit. The fear of not knowing had gradually evaporated. I had a lot to be grateful for and something to celebrate. Life could not have treated me better. But for some reason, there seemed to be a blemish in the horizon of this idyllic new life in the form of a depthless hole in my soul. A sort of meaningless vacuum.

I had realized early on that the choice I made about the kind of life we'd lead would alienate us, but that was alright, you can't eat your cake and have it. But now, for some reason I wasn't so sure afterall, because the euphoria of my newly acquired lifestyle had turned to ashes in my mouth. I stopped chasing the dusts and sat down on the sofa. Suddenly, cold fingers of sadness gripped me, snaking through my body, as if carried in the bloodstream, spreading everywhere, overwhelmingly. The nightmare that started after our arrival to Glenncolm, had not abated and usually left me tired and listless the next day. With my children clamouring for attention, needing one thing or the other, I couldn't hide, I had nowhere to go. I was trapped!

As my mind dwelt on my pathetic life, I slid slowly from the sofa down to the floor and gently rested my head on one of the sofa throws that tumbled down with me. Tears clouded my vision and slid down my face, but I was not crying, it was just self-pity.

I had been up since 5am and dared not get back to sleep, so I decided to clean the house, from top to bottom instead, and had continued after I returned from taking the children to school. Lucky, mercifully had slept after his breakfast and it was such a relief. But I was no longer sure that I could handle this situation. Bearing Erica's advice about friends and my aversion to exposure, I had no friend except Fergal and the offshoot of that decision was brutal loneliness. Now the invasion of my sleep by all the demons in the form of thousands of giant, dark and fat furious rats with pincer teeth, who chased after me, morphing into fierce, horrible lions with several heads, all of which were Osahon, baying at me were not helping the matter. At some point all the lions would morph into one single red-eyed, wild-looking Osahon who in one fluid stride would capture me and curl his talon-like fingers round my neck, squeezing. Usually here, I would wake up panting from my near-death marathon run, drenched in sweat and shaking uncontrollably. The curious thing about the whole affair was that in whichever form, Osahon, the mastermind, kept barking for money. How nasty could any one person be? He dealt with me in real life, sucked me dry and threw me out, but that wasn't enough now he's invading my dreams, still demanding for more! And there was nobody to share my hell with. So I suffered both in the night and in the day.

After my nocturnal encounter, during the day, I would be the shadow of myself, scared stiff by the littlest of noises, dreading that the rats, the lions and the crazed Osahon were all still after me. So to stabilize my day, first I'd take tiny shots of whiskey; two really, otherwise my nerves would not steady as to do anything for the rest of the day and that luxury I did not have. Next I'd chase down my depression prescription with chilled glasses of red wine. Thereafter, I'd steadily drown my sorrow in cups upon cups of spiked coffee, taken in small gulps. I had the whole day and the rest of the night to consider so I was never in a hurry with my cache, but how I seemed to consume so much baffled me. Finally I'd slump to sleep only to wake from the pursuit of my neighbours, brandishing broomsticks, calling me a prostitute and a witch. There was no respite and I couldn't pinpoint what had gone wrong with the idyllic life I had envisaged in Donegal.

This had been going on for months and I dared not confide in anybody for fear of being confirmed mad. Post-natal depression was bad enough.

So this Ifeoma's visit would be a welcome relief. At least with her, I'd have somebody to confide my latest predicament to while hoping that the fearsome animals and my demented neighbours, of the day-time-mares, would know to keep away.

I heaved my body up from the floor and stretched to restore the flow of blood before continuing with my cleaning. I still had to go to the shops for purchases, to enable me to whip up a simple meal for my visiting friend.

When I finished cleaning I got ready to go to the shop. I unlocked and opened the door, having spent over ten minutes scanning the road, and darted out, looking furtively up and down the street as I hurried on. I went into Fergal's and from there scanned the road where I had just come from, to ascertain that nobody was following me. Then I scanned the forward road, to confirm it clear too before darting out and into the supermarket. At the back of my mind, I knew I should not be doing all these but I couldn't help it. I had to be sure that nobody from my past was anywhere near before I ventured out. I was not about to jeopardize this new life however dismal.

*   *   *

Back home, I unpacked my purchases and having decided earlier, on a simple *tagliatelle carbonara* meal on a bed of vegetables, I went about assembling all that I would need. I rustled in my secret store and brought out four bottles of red wine. I remembered that Ifeoma preferred Sauvignon, but what I wasn't sure of was whether it went with *tagliatelle*. Ifeoma always matched her food with this wine or that wine, recalling our student days in Unilag, when we went to all those high-brow restaurants in Ikoyi and Victoria Island. Then my thoughts flashed back to when I was a wine connoisseur of some sorts in the good old days, when I was Gift, a child of light, destined for greater things. I shook my head to shake off the nostalgia. There was no need to look back with regret, it had happened, it had happened. I couldn't wind the hand of the clock-of-life either backward or forward. So I had to lie on the thorny bed as I had made it without complaint. If only I could jump over this time and get to the future.

Ifeoma

Ifeoma arriving, took in what she was seeing, and realized Gift was either seeking to recreate her village or she was hiding from something. But she decided not to pursue it at the moment. She was welcomed noisily by the children, with Gift hovering like a mother hen, looking suspiciously out of sync. Was she drunk?

Finally they settled the children in for the night and Ifeoma got up from the squeaky couch, where she had ensconced herself after dinner, went and sat on the one facing Gift. She was ready to be told what was going on.

'Gi, are you alright?'

'Yes. Why do you ask?'

'Well, I don't know. You don't look okay somehow. Your eyes shine suspiciously like that of a drunk, but one that is trying to hide that fact.'

'Well. You know how it is. You are okay but at the same time you are not, if you follow my meaning. Just that I have these constant nightmares like all the demons were after me. And during the day, I keep looking behind my shoulders for him. I keep seeing faces from the past that would expose me. And my neighbours did not want a prostitute in their midst. My life seems delicately unreal; a fragile glass ready to shatter at anytime. However, I am trying to take things slow, one step at a time and I am drunk.'

Ifeoma nodded.

'Is that why you chose this village, to hide from him and your past and drink?'

'Partly for that and partly for a bit of peace and quiet, that's all.'

'But are you sure that you have recovered from the trauma of the birth. That your post-natal depression is not being aggravated by this place?'

'Fifi, you know me, I can only say no to your advice if it did not suit my purposes but I have never deliberately shut you out and you know it. If there is anything, I will let you know. Just that somehow I do not feel comfortable living in the city. This place suits us very well, for now. I drink and take more than my prescribed medication.'

Ifeoma ignored that last part and asked, 'Why do you think he should be looking for you and what will happen if he finds you?'

'I don't know.'

'Look Gi, this is unlike you. You don't look strong anymore, I mean in spirit. Are you sure you can continue to cope alone with these children considering your numerous demons?'

'I will keep trying. If it gets too much for me I chuck it all in.'

Ifeoma nodded, as if what her friend said was the kind of conversation you hear on a daily basis, while she chewed on the information.

'So what exactly did you say your neighbors want from you and where the drinking and the taking of more than your stipulated prescription come in? And what kind of chucking-in are we talking about here? You could handle drink effortlessly, that I know. What I don't understand is why you can't seem to do that anymore and why you are abusing your medication.'

Gift didn't say anything, her head resting on the back-rest of the sofa, eyes closed.

'Talk to me, girl,' Ifeoma bellowed.

My eyes flew open.

'What was that all about?'

'What was that all about is that you have three children, all below five, who depend on you and you think you can drink and abuse your medication? Gift what is it? Talk to me, tell me what I don't know already.'

I sighed, swiveled my neck back and forth.

'Ifeoma, it's really bad and I don't know what else to do. I drink to steady my nerves and I take more than my prescription to push for more effect. I really do not know how my life nosedived and with three children. It preys on my mind day in, day out and I do not see any solution soon. And then on top of that I hardly get any sleep in the night with Osahon chasing me around till dawn demanding for money. While during the day my neighbours take over if I happen to close my eyes for a second. I am surprised that I am still sane.'

'That you're still sane? My God Gift, listen to yourself. You are no longer sane! I concede that it is tasking to find yourself in unfamiliar and difficult circumstances, but Gift you have to sit up and take notice. Do you not realize that you have three little children?'

'You have said that before and if you must know, they are part of my problem. I cannot cope, I mean I did not bargain to raise three children alone Ifeoma, three! But at the same time I am scared that if I seek for help they would take them away.'

'There's no point going over how you came to be in this mess, my friend. If you cannot look after yourself, not to talk of them, would they not be better off in care?'

'That's a cruel thing to suggest; sign away my children? I have always told you that you are not African?'

'Please give that a rest. How are you going to sort out these problems then?'

'I don't know. Do you?'

'Yes. And don't start that your business of my being a Whiteman.'

'OK. How?'

'Tell your GP or your Public Healthcare Nurse or your Social Worker. They'd arrange for assessment and counseling if need be.'

'Counseling? Ifeoma counseling? Have you gone mad?! In any case what happens to my children while I luxuriate in this counseling thing?'

'They'd have to assess you first to determine whether you needed counseling, your children may not need to be taken anywhere.'

'Thanks. You see, that's why it looks as if I don't listen to you sometimes. Look at me Fifi,' I stood up and flung out my hands, then twirled around for a comprehensive view, staggering in the process, 'Do I look mad to you?'

Ifeoma peered at me and shook her head no, before adding, 'You may not *look* mad but your behaviour isn't exactly that of a rational person and you just acted mad now with all that twirling. Anyway what is going on in your mind, do you know?'

I shook my head no.

'So why won't you allow professionals to take a look and sort you out once and for all? Afterall, you know, as well as I do, that all these problems are in your head.'

'I'm sure I love my children Ifeoma, it's just that they cramp my life at the moment, but even at that I can't just hand them to anybody on grounds of madness. I will never get them back.'

'But nobody said you're mad, Gift. You have not grieved properly for all that happened to you and I warned you about blocking them out; they are your realities, Gift, and you must learn to live with them whether you like it or not.'

'Fifi, I know you are right, but what do you seriously advise me to do?'

'Contact the people I mentioned earlier and confide in them. I am sure that some sort of solution would be found for your state of mind, and if need be, foster your children temporarily while they take care of you. That is if it has reached that stage which I doubt. But you must reach out for help. This absolute secrecy position you took is not helping matters at all.'

'Do you really believe that I'd do that?'

'No.'

'Good.'

'I can only tell you what I think from where I stand. But it's really up to you at the end of the day to do something. However, if you're not careful they'll still take your children from you. You can't continue like this without being found out.'

I nodded, crossed my arms across my chest, as I thought. Finally I got up and poured myself another glass of wine before turning to my friend.

'Let me sleep over it and see how I feel in the morning. I know that if I get to sleep, just for one full night, I'll be alright.'

'Well I am here. I will take the children off your hands and you can get all the sleep you need. Do they come during the afternoon sleep, your demons?'

'Not them, my neighbours instead.'

Ifeoma laughed. 'You are even beginning to talk crazy.'

'Try and be me for one hour and see how far you'll go before going crazy.'

'I can never be you for a minute. You were born mad Gift and you know it.' Ifeoma stretched her hand and took my drink, drank it down, and got up to pour some more for herself before announcing that she definitely needed a drink herself to be able to sleep with all these problems swirling around.

Gift smiled wanly.

'You see what I mean.'

'On a more serious note Gi, I'll always be there if you need me, let us just hope the demons and the vermin and your *neighbours* would know to take a hike.'

That didn't need any reply, I simply got up and went to lie down on the same sofa and held my friend in a fierce hug. She responded likewise, and we held each other for a long time. Two women in a solidarity hug, merging strengths, drawing and giving hope that it'd be enough to confront the unknown. It was very comforting and I was glad that Ifeoma came.

The impact another adult company had on me was profound. Ifeoma's presence gave me strength. We explored the Glenn and all it had to offer. A small farming village with few houses scattered here and there with spectacular hills. But what took our breath away was the deep blue sea. One could never imagine that seas were actually blue. We hiked during the day and joined the locals in the pub in the evenings to drink, having employed a local nanny to look after the children. I did not get any respite from my assailants but I did not have to worry alone.

However, Ifeoma remonstrated on the second week that she had had it. Being neighbourly and friendly with the sheep and ewes was no longer satisfying, she needed to be in a city. She's a cosmopolitan babe and this Glenn of nowhere was enough.

So we drove down to Dublin seeking the "drop of city" and stayed in Conrad Hotel, not too far from St. Stephens Green. Ifeoma paid. We took advantage of the hotel's proximity to the National Concert Hall and took in two performances. On Saturday night, we went to Tripod, a nightclub, located in a Gothic looking building at the end of Hatch Street and danced till dawn. Erica linked us to Hatch Hall reception centre for asylum seekers where we got a cheap nanny for the children.

Then we hit the shopping scene with a vengeance, daily tramping round the City Centre, window shopping at Brown Thomas, Pia Bang, Laura Ashley, Clerys, Arnotts, etc., etc., trying out clothes of various styles and shapes, cooing over shoes, drooling on handbags, and finally rewarded our efforts by purchasing pampering lotions and potions, fabulous fragrances and marvelous make-ups.

When we were not shopping, we toured the city with the hop-on-hop-off tour buses, listening to the droning tour guides as they detailed historic edifices of Ireland.

By the weekend Ifeoma came up with the brilliant idea of all of us booking a one week touring holiday to see other parts of Ireland. Erica and her children joined us and it was one week of non-stop movement, amusement and noise. The children hooting about with abandon. Frances kept coming back though, to inquire 'are you alright, mum?' which made Ifeoma frown at me fiercely, before adding, 'you must do something about yourself woman, before you infect your children with madness too.'

'Oh please. Don't start again. I've heard. I am only human you know?'

'Yes, but you have a responsibility to other humans too, who happens to be your young and helpless children and you're instilling not only fear but insecurity in them however inadvertent, with your adopted behaviour.'

'Are you now saying that I do all those on purpose?'

'No, but your refusal to try and heal is stupid.'

'I will do something, I promise.'

'You had better. You claim that counseling is for white people and refuse to avail of it. But you'll be surprised at how much you'll gain if only you'll listen to me and go if for nothing else, at least, to test the ground.'

'It is okay. I will do something.'

And then Ifeoma left and took her profound presence, but I was determined to live, so I took her talk to heart and tried to clean up. I paced my drinks and took the exact amount of my medication. It didn't work. I fell back to my old routine, if not even worse. Then one morning I was shaken awake by Frances to tell me that Lucky was eating his feaces. I sat up and realized that I was lying on the floor of our living room. What was I doing on the floor? Didn't I go to bed last night? Then I remembered that I no longer go to bed to avoid the demons who had taken up residence in my room. But why were Frances and Eudora not in school and what was all that nonsense about Lucky snacking on his feaces?

'Frances!'

'Yes mummy?'

'Come closer.' She did and I held her hand to pull myself to a sitting position, pried my eyes open and quickly closed them. It was too much. Then I started to massage my forehead, in a circular motion, and then extended it to my nose, then my eyes. I tried again and succeeded in keeping my eyes open.

'Why are you not in school with your sister?'

'We have no breakfasted. We no have lunched pack and our teacher tell us not come without food because we beg food and we have not bathe since and our class mates said we smell and . . .' I nodded while covering her mouth with my hand to stop the flow of indictments.

'Alright.' I got up and went and retrieved Lucky's nappy where he was still busy serving himself and tried to remember when I fed him last. That proved too much so I abandoned that. Instead I took all of them into the bathroom and gave them a thorough wash, cleaned their teeth and dressed them up in clean clothes. I took them downstairs, rustled in the food cupboard but couldn't find anything but some out of date sausages. No wonder they were hungry. Frances had mastered the art of *cooking* their cornflakes if they were in stock, which they weren't.

We went shopping after eating our out of date sausage meal, and stocked up. I could barely make it to the shop: my head was banging without mercy and my eyes out of focus, in a bid to pop out, but with gritted teeth I made it and back. I switched on the telly, and each child, armed with crisps was firmly sat before it with the instructions to not move. I then went and had my own bath, dressed up in track-suit and came back down with Calpol for Lucky, to diffuse the effect of the feaces, hopefully.

I went into the kitchen and prepared Jollof rice and chicken which we all ate heartily. Who knew when last they ate like this? I wondered, but shrugged it off carelessly before sitting down to watch TV with them. Then,

Let me ask you Gift, what is going on?

What do you mean? If you have been part of me, then you should know.

Really? Then let me tell you what I know. What I know since being part of you is that you are a child of light, forthright, confident and focused. That got you far enough. Then fiam, *every thing went up in smoke in a twinkle of an eye.*

And so what? I ask you Gift. And so what?

Is that why you have lived half-alive, half-dead for over a year now? A very selfish and destructive life. Look at your children. What chances are you giving them in life? What exactly are you preparing them to become? Drunkards? Layabouts? Answer me, Gift.

If you were in Nigeria would you have chosen to wallow in self-pity because you failed yourself? Who would have been paying for this kind of lifestyle: Your drinks, roof over your head, feeding, utilities, clothing, food on your table and so on and so forth? Tell me who?

If you want to live stop this nonsense right now. Give your children the chance of making life-sustaining choices by being brought up in a conducive environment. I hope you realize that you are a daughter of a merciful Father and each time you come to him with your failure He is ever ready to set you right. Do not be so arrogant about life. You're nothing without Him.

I was shaken with fright and shivered with cold by the time the voice withdrew its presence. In all honesty, I had never for once thought of my children or their feelings. What the effect of my behaviour would have on their lives. But could my behaviour be equated to arrogance? Selfish maybe, but arrogance? That I couldn't understand. However, one thing was clear, if I was back home, it would be considered extreme luxury to take a full day off to mourn your past. So what was

I doing floating around for a year, a year that I couldn't recall? So much so that my children are feeding on poo. 'God . . . . I am so sorry. Please forgive me . . . Forgive me Father, Please!' As I had continued to whisper, asking for forgiveness, I started whimpering for the loss of my life; for inadvertently maltreating my children; for the pain I had caused my parents; for everything that had happened to me since meeting Osahon. It all converged in my head and gave vent to tears.

My children, one by one, looked at me and then back at the TV, then at me again. Torn between continuing with their own favourite past time or listening to their mumbling and crying mother. At last Frances got up and came to peer at me, then sat down and started crying. Lucky came next and joined in. Eudora did not bother: it was almost part of our daily life to cry. So what else was new? When I did not stop crying, after the usual duration, they gave up. Frances went back to the TV. Lucky climbed onto my lap and started cleaning my tears. I was touched by this gesture, but this made me cry harder. My tears were flowing down in rivulets and Lucky was cleaning as fast. When he couldn't contain the flow with his hands, he stood up and started licking the tears. I had to smile at that and pulled him off my face, sat him down on my lap before telling him that I will stop crying. Then he said, 'Mummy, I love you.'

When did my son start to talk? Oh . . . . Oh . . . . ! What have I done? Yes, I knew that I lost control of my life, but how could I have failed my children so badly! But I didn't want to pursue that train of thought anymore. And I didn't want to cry again either, so instead I responded, 'I love you too, son.' Lucky looked closely at my face, confirmed that I had stopped crying, then snuggled up against me, placing his head on the crook of my left hand while stretching his leg across my body, his bum still on my lap.

There and then I promised God, myself and the children, in that order, that I would turn a new leaf going forward.

Easier said than done I came to realize as the day wore on. The urge to drink was unbelievable. My whole body was trembling. At about two pm I couldn't hold on anymore. I must have a drink or I'd explode. So I filled a tall glass with wine and downed it in one gulp, smacked my lips in satisfaction, but that was not enough, it seemed to intensify the craving. How was I ever going to stop? In desperation I shouted at God,

'Where are you? Are you not going to help me? You can't just sit there and watch me ruin my life and that of my children. Didn't I say that I will stop with a promise to mend my ways this morning? What else do I need to do? Please help me God, help me, please.'

I waited to feel God's help, at least in stopping the urge. Nothing happened. The prayer must have been intercepted by the devil, for God obviously did not get it.

I must have nodded off to sleep for when I woke up my whole body was on fire from cramps. A bottle of Jack Daniel was three-quarters gone. And I was lying on a wet bed. Who could have poured water on my bed? I tried to sit up, but gave up on that ambition immediately. It was easier to reconnoiter from a low level. And I was not in my bed. I was on a hard, wet and cold surface. My mouth was gummed together, so also were my eyes. But despite the roar in my ears, I could hear the sound of the TV going. So I was somewhere in the house, in the livingroom or the kitchen or the utility room or the guest toilet. These were the various locations in the downstairs part of our house.

I extended my hand to feel the floor. That'd help me pin down the exact location, but my hand instead encountered a body. Lucky! I scrambled into a sitting position defying all the roaring and splitting going on in my head. His body was covered with his blanket from his room and he was not wet. So what was he doing here? I touched myself and the smell told its story. The wetness was my urine! What day was it anyway? I crawled to the television and after several attempts was able to get the Sky channel and the date and time winked at me from the bottom right of the screen; 20th and then, 22:15pm.

Quarter past ten in the night, twenty-two hours after I vowed to clean up. I had stayed clean after the vow and only took my first drink by two pm and that was as far as I could remember.

'God you are certainly keeping close watch,' I sneered. I crawled to the couch but couldn't lift myself onto it so I sat there with my legs stretched out straight before me and hid my face in my hands.

Gift, you can't do this alone.

Immediately, I rounded up on the voice and screamed, 'Fuck off you.'

And my utterance startled me. I didn't train myself to curse and never did.

'What am I going to do?' I soft-pedaled, asking in a defeated voice.

Go and look for help.

'OK. But who? I don't know anybody here.'

How do you know people? Seek.

I nodded and seek I must. This thing had got out of hand.

I used to love life. How could I degenerate so much? To the extent that I now urinate on myself. I, Gift Nkiruka Ofoedu, the bringer of light?

No!

'Osahon you can't win all rounds!' I shouted.

Suddenly I was energized enough to get up and gingerly zigzagged to the kitchen. I knocked the pot of Jollof rice off the cooker accidentally, but was surprised to find it empty.

'At least they ate,' I murmured.

Lucky stirred but went on sleeping. Poor boy, he must have joined me on the floor in solidarity. I stared at my son and thought of the fact that I might not be able to carry him upstairs in my condition. I'd just have to put him on the couch instead.

But the main task at hand right now would be to try and keep myself going till morning. How not to drink, at least not enough to conk out again. Or maybe I should try and sleep by drinking like that again. Because keeping awake would put me directly in the path of temptation. As I contemplated the idea, another thought gently insinuated itself into my mind. How come I didn't get my usual dose of nightmares? Or was I too out of it that their antics could not penetrate? Should I start doing that every night?

Don't be silly. What kind of solution is that?

Then another thought struck: But I was always dead with drink all the time before and it never deterred the demons. So how come?

I picked up the pot and the cover, steadied it on the cooker, covered it and moved slowly to where Lucky was. I half-carried and half-dragged him to the couch heaved him onto it and covered him up. Not a murmur from him, Lucky had always loved his sleep. I sat down again to catch my breath then dragged myself to the base of the stairs and looked up, a very daunting task, but it must be done. I crawled and finally got myself into the bathroom and stepped into the shower. I just let the water run over me for several minutes before I reached for my sponge and body wash. I squirted the body wash on my head and started to massage my body only to realize that I was still clothed. I struggled and peeled off the clothes, dropped them on the bathroom floor and continued with my bathing. When I finished, calmness settled on me but I was still drunk, that I knew. My head still pounded furiously and I was not steady on my legs but I had work ahead of me. I had nursed myself long enough and whatever was ailing me should get ready for a battle.

I toweled briskly, rummaged in my laundry bag and pulled out a black track-bottom and a sleeve-less t-shirt, dressed up and went down again this time to plot a strategy, but first I cleaned my wee off the floor. Thank God it wasn't the carpeted part of the house. I moved Lucky further into the couch and sat down to plot, telling myself that if the temptation to drink became too much I'd take some Valium, as much as was needed to knock me off immediately.

I felt a presence and woke up, still groggy from sleep, but I knew immediately that I wasn't drunk, nor did I take the said Valium and therefore must have slept off without any help from the stuff, and most importantly, no nightmare. And I must have slept off almost immediately because I was sure that I didn't plot much as no solution came to mind. I opened my eyes and it was Frances. She was staring at me in a peculiar way.

'Mummy, are we going to school today? We haven't not since?'

'You will today.'

My head was still pounding, much more than the previous night, but I had crossed a threshold towards recovery. What was a little headache? And no nightmare yet again!

But it was not easy; I fell off more than I retained my seat. At one point, in desperation, I enlisted the help of my daughter, Frances, to watch and stop me from drinking. But Frances could only do what she could do, when she remembered, afterall she was barely over four. Finally I decided that it was not going to work, not the way things were at the moment. There was no way I'd claw myself out of the hole I was in, it was too deep. A much more serious step should be taken, must be taken. I needed real help; it had passed the stage of self-help. And so very reluctantly I went to see my GP and the hell that was our life for over a year acquired worthy opponents! But most baffling was my resistance to their urging to get out of the house and socialize. 'What was out there to seek, I always countered? What?'

But eventually I gritted my teeth and ventured out. I returned about thirty minutes later, triumphantly, with three different packages of chicken legs, minced meat and pig legs! Housed in one blue cellophane bag. It was a step in the positive direction.

The next day I ventured out again, but this time into the supermarket, cum the general purpose store, to buy some sort of accompaniment to my yesterday's purchases. I came home triumphantly again with rice, pasta and spaghetti. On my third foray I met Una, the village wild-child who came back from her adventure in Dublin pregnant!

*   *   *

Una made herself scarce but yearned inwardly for company so was happy to have met Gift and she was different from the rest of the gang. Gradually they nurtured a friendship and when Una felt comfortable she opened up to Gift about her so—called adventure in Dublin. It transpired that after her Leaving Certificate, she had headed to Dublin, the city of lights. And there flitted from job to job; sales girl in Penneys; waitress in a pub; sales assistant in a spa and numerous others. She made enough money to live life to the brim, but living life to the brim came with its own brand of troubles. She fell pregnant, but luckily it was for her boyfriend. But the bad news was that he didn't want to marry yet and as for a child? Forget it! So there she was, stuck with a pregnancy alone in the city of lights. It didn't take her long to realize that she should go home and so she returned to the Glenn to *clear her head* and sort her life.

                    *   *   *

Two kindred spirits wanting their heads cleared and their lives sorted. So we joined forces. I dug in truly and continued to claw my way out of the darkness that was my life. The Hikers Club of Donegal, such a grandiose name for a motley collection of certain kind of people, sucked any excess strength that was left by the treadmill. We hiked any mountains, more of hills than anything, but mountains they were, that was close enough.

In the gym, I continued to sweat out my darkness on the treadmill. These activities kept me busy and pushed my depression at bay. My past life was still mine, but I was learning to circumvent it. With Una's added friendship that brought her family into the equation I was able to work hard on getting better.

But life was not all about walking and hiking, we needed to do something to define us as members of the world. So we decided to look for jobs. But that became a problem. We were not really trained to work as anything other than doing odd jobs here and there, and hopefully, climb into more respectful positions later, if we were dedicated enough. But the new life we mapped out for ourselves did not include hiding in the hills of Donegal serving behind the pub counter or the butcher's.

And so we sought for and were admitted to train as Funds Administrators with the local FAS office. Towards the end of our training, which lasted six months, Brendan, Una's man and the father of her daughter, Kathy, came looking for her. They made up and she planned to move to Dublin after the training.

Una's wedding, which took place in the Glenn to stop the wagging tongues, left me empty afterwards. I had lost a friend, well, not really, more my prop, for the friendship would be maintained. It was Una's partnership with me that aided my not falling back to my old ways.

When she finally left the Glenn for Dublin, I became even more determined to cast my past, in its entirety, behind me and move on.

When I saw the need for four Funds Administrators advertised in a Dublin newspaper by a recruitment agency, I knew that the hand of God had finally returned into my life, nudging me gently, keeping me in line with my new assured self. He put me on the road to recovery in the first place. And when I got the job after a series of grueling interviews, I packed my family, once again, and headed back to Dublin. When we had fully settled in and I was about three months on the job I withdrew from the social welfare benefits. I felt that I was ready to stand on my own two feet and with my investments through Ifeoma I knew that we would survive.

One year into this tranquil life in Castleknock, Dublin, Osahon came calling.

He *found* me?

OBINNA

Una and I left the office discussing other things, crossed the Luas track and walked towards Harcourt Street to Café @ Sol. We chose a corner seating for two and ordered our meal while returning to our unfinished conversation, with Una trying gallantly to convince me.

'You have to get a solicitor immediately, Gift. There is no way around this. At least, even if he is to be given access to the children as their father, it would be on mutually agreed terms and not for him to waltz his way in at will. Now that he has found his way to Ireland and to your house, he could do that you know?'

I nodded, munching my tuna roll while thinking that Una did not know anything. Who was going to mutually agree with Osahon for access to the children? But I didn't blame her, she was only going by what she was told, which wasn't much.

However, Una's badgering eventually saw me head to the Free Legal Advice Centre where I was informed, after much calculation, that I'd have to be earning below certain level for me to qualify for free legal aid. I thanked them and left and that ended my quest for legal representation.

Finally I responded to the summons with my own affidavit written by myself, littered with half-truths and at times blatant lies. This was in line with Osahon's which was also riddled with lies. I sent it off like that. But it was okay by me, because that way, I didn't have to tell anybody my story.

Our life continued as normally as it could but two months after sending off my representation, the appointed date for the court hearing arrived.

I was up with the birds that morning but a little subdued. I did not have the appetite to hum my favourite Enrique Iglesias *Hero* as I stepped into the bathroom and had a brisk shower. I took my time though to dress up, careful to appear lawyerly, since I was going to represent myself.

Ifeoma, my friend, had flown in from London the night before, to lend her support, but chose to stay in a hotel in the city because she had scheduled a meeting with her cousin who was on a working visit to Dublin and would meet me in court later. Her cousin being in Ireland had increased the number of birds she had intended to kill with one stone to three, Erica and myself being the first two birds. I shook my head, Ifeoma and her time, always economical with it, rationing it. I suppose, if you're working for yourself you had to be disciplined about time or you'd achieve nothing.

I finished dressing and studied the outcome in the long mirror stuck to the inside door of my wardrobe. I saw this very confident lady in a navy wool midi-skirt with a side slit, which hugged my figure flatteringly, topped with fitted white cotton blouse. I finished it off with navy-blue court shoes. I applied minimal make-up and sprayed on Laura Biagiotti's Roma parfum, brushed the brushable parts of my burnished-copper and black Ghana-weave hair style and was ready to face the day.

I dropped my children at their various schools and informed their head teachers that Erica would collect them after school. I then drove back to my house to pack the car, preferring to travel on the bus. I opened the door and stepped out again but automatically, as I had learnt to do over the years, looked up to scrutinize the face of the sky which happened to have turned gloomy, looking rather unhappy to say the least, threatening to pour its tears on poor earth any minute, but I was not deterred, this was my day of victory. I felt it in the marrow of my bones. When it started to drizzle, a prelude to the torrents to come, I knew that the gods had decided in my favour.

I recalled how I used to rush out to embrace the rain, welcoming it with arms spread out wide, gulping it, romping and splashing, splattering in the muddied flood, as a young child. And how I reveled in the exhilaration such rumpus brought afterwards; the calmness in all its goodness. Rain had always been a good sign for me; it had brought many a good tidings to my life. It cleansed the old and ushered in the new. It washed away the horrid and in its stead the pleasant. But the light drizzle would most certainly turn into a deluge by the look of things so I turned and quickened my steps back to the house, this time was not for romping. Unlocking the front door I stepped in but stopped a moment to think about where best to start the search for my umbrella.

Finally, I located it between the presses and the sink, retrieved it gleefully, went out and relocked the house before hurrying to the bus stop, spreading open the roomy umbrella from AXA. My steps were jaunty, springy, and euphoric even, for today, I was going to be given the certificate to life, to freedom; a testimony that I should go ahead and live again, fully, without fear. On arriving at the bus stop, I nodded greetings to my fellow commuters clustered together away from the rain in the confines of the bus stop shelter.

When our bus arrived in Dublin City centre, I alighted and decided to go for a cup of coffee in Clerys; to melt my frozen blood as well as to fortify the body for the journey to Smithfield. As I ascended the stairs to Café Iguana, I tried to see where it could go wrong, but however much I stretched, I couldn't see it. So I took the liberty to conclude that everything would be fine from now onwards. I queued, bought and paid for a tall Mocha and then with a cheerful disposition I sat at the back of the restaurant to savour my drink and watch people do their thing.

As I sipped and scanned, my eyes caught sight of a fellow that had just strode in and my vision immediately clouded over, believing this person to be Osahon. I hadn't seen that many black men in Dublin who were as tall. Not that I felt scared. No I didn't. I was no longer afraid of him. He had done his worst—the court case.

Then the guy turned, with his tray of goodies, to search for a seat in my direction and I saw his face clearly, a very handsome face. It was not Osahon's. Osahon's face could not be qualified with that term—handsome. Though it never did any harm to his chances of attracting women in their droves. He had his own personal magnet, but it wasn't in his face. This man was handsome and attractive and he was not Osahon. Good!

I studied him from under my lashes. Since he was heading towards my table, I couldn't look at him directly. The guy, apart from handsome, had a lot of things in his favor; the kind of things that gladden my heart, the chief of which was sophistication. And the quality of his finesse was highlighted in his casual but powerful dressing.

As I surveyed him, still under my lashes, I realized that the guy must be very much aware of the reactions and the offshoot emotions that he evoked in his audiences: the women—desire and men—jealousy. I then wondered about what atrocities he must have inflicted on his women and shuddered. Or maybe he was just your regular man. But my psyche had been saturated with weird imaginations inherited from my past, just so that I would not be accountable to my subsequent snobbish action if approached . . .

'May I share the seat with you, mam?'

'But of course,' I responded gently, and inwardly congratulated myself: I had truly been cured of my *menphobia*, before now I would be getting ready to vacate the seat. If I was no longer seated there, I would not be expected to respond to any advances, was my reasoning at such rare times when I ventured out alone.

Now it seemed I could respond to encounters with men candidly without thinking that they were interested in me for paid sex. Or that they were going to rip my heart out like Osahon did, if I so much as nodded to them.

I may have overcome the first hurdle, but I had to be very careful to not show too much enthusiasm. Or without being aware of it, activate the predatory hawkish stance of a former prostitute on the prowl for custom: poised to pounce; be-in-there-first-otherwise-lose-out attitude.

And I was no longer a teenager either, fired by hormones and youthful exuberance. I was now a full-grown woman and a mother of three children and so must have my feet planted firmly on the ground and not be carried away again by love. Though, I had come to accept that my Osahon-experience was particular and therefore should not be used to stain all men, I just did not want to be misinterpreted based on any actions on my part. I sighed inwardly.

Falling deeply in love then may have made me open to certain vulnerability in relationship to my lover, but there should always be a choice in everything people do, even under the influence of love. Empowering your lover to relate to you in a destructive manner was a choice I made myself, foolishly or not. If you put your life into somebody's hands, in its entirety without restraint, be that man or woman, the outcome may not always be pleasant.

Your life is your life, letting people share it did not mean handing them the reins to propel you according to their wishes; that portends suicide. That was what I did.

You need to be in a loving relationship. This made me remember Ifeoma, who believed that it'd be easier to wring water out of stone than to get a man that would love me and my baggage. I swallowed a smile. She never minced her words, that Ifeoma. But she's a true friend indeed. I just hoped that the rain would not make her late to court.

The man in question, settled himself comfortably on the seat opposite me, looked at me pointedly and murmured, 'What a day.'

'Oh lovely, isn't it?' I beamed at him and was surprised at the frown on his face. I watched him look outside through the window as if to confirm to himself that we were speaking of the same environment, for he apparently could not see anything lovely in the current weather judging by the furious rain pounding the streets outside. When he finished his survey he turned and looked at me closely, probably to ascertain that I was not crazy or something. My smile still in place I said, 'I know, you must think me addled or something, with it raining cats and dogs out there but, believe it when I say that it is a lovely day, it is really a blessed day.'

He looked closely at me again and then shrugged.

'Okay. I take it you mean metaphorically, right? In that sense, then it is a lovely day for me too: I met you.'

The smile slipped off my face immediately, but I did not cringe at the memory the last three words evoked. I just nodded, and then looked away, but instead of allowing sadness to swamp me I indulged in what I had not done for over five years now: envisioning myself lost in the man's arms, drinking in the euphoria of being loved again, by a kind soul, hopefully.

Then I chided myself: *he is too handsome and bound to be too vain, be careful here.*

I sneaked a peek at him again, still from under my lashes, and concluded that he's probably an actor or a model, but not based in Dublin: I would have seen him on billboards or something. Dreamily I stirred my beverage, a little smile lurking at the edges of my mouth, hiding my warring heart over what could or could not be. Then his voice brought me back.

'Lady, if you could share the secrets of your joy, it may help me this day. This nasty weather transmits loneliness on its wake.'

'Oh, you won't understand. It took me years to get to where I am today and take it from me it wasn't an easy journey.'

'Then that is a journey worth undertaking, my dear, if what I see represents the end result. By the way my name is Obinna Ikejiana. May I treat you to another drink?'

His deep velvety voice enveloped me in a warm embrace even as he stretched his long, strong finger, with manicured nails, for a shake.

I proffered mine which disappeared in his. He then enclosed it with both of his. With my hand trapped in between his two he studied my face before leaning forward.

'And may I ask what sowed such bliss in your life?' he asked.

I ignored the deep look, the burning sensation in my hands and the blast from his eyes while the inquisitive question floated between us. I was not about to fall for another sweet talker, not again, and so I withdrew my hand before answering him.

'You may not ask, actually. My name, however, is Gift and I must beg to take my leave for now. I need to be somewhere within the hour, maybe some other time.'

'I will not detain you longer than you wish then, but I will be very happy to have your telephone number, I may convince you to go for the coffee then.'

I smiled and gave him my mobile phone number. Things may not always be as they seemed I thought as I sailed out of the restaurant leaving a cloud of Roma parfum behind to titillate Obinna's nostrils.

*   *   *

And he was thoroughly titillated while he watched her glide away.

'Gift! My goodness; how do parents come up with names like that,' Obinna exclaimed to himself as he ate his food. Who could have known at birth that the name would befit her to the last ounce? For she really looked like she'd be a gift to any human. Such an exquisite lady, spreading sunshine even in a deluge. He made a mental note to see her when next he was in Dublin. To see if she could take away the loneliness that was quietly creeping in, taking root in his life.

He'd begun to feel the full weight of his thirty-five years on earth this past year. He had always thought himself to be a born bachelor and nobody would accuse him of not living his life to the brim. But lately certain kind of disenchantments had besieged him, to the extent that he felt a bit jaded scouring his cherished bachelor scene these days; it was getting rather tiring. Unbelievable!

He never believed it then or rather he chose not to, when his father and later his older siblings, had told him to take it easy on what they called his non-stop jollification or he'd crash; burnt out at the peak of his life.

Why should he? With life abundantly swamping him at every angle? Forget it. He was not going to slow down. And for what anyway? He had queried. His father told him that if he played too hard too early and too long, he'd be bound to have an unsettled marriage. Because then he would go into it with very high expectations of what should be which he had unconsciously absorbed over the years from the various women and which he may not find in one single woman—the wife.

He had quipped then, that was, in case they had not noticed, that he wasn't about to be tied into a rut by any one woman, not then, not ever. He was born to love them and leave them.

But as the time went by, he had felt very silly to have said such a thing: it made him sound irresponsible; especially when it turned out that he was a cool responsible man, with integrity. In the love zone he had even become a one-man-one-woman man.

During the lifespan of any of his relationships, he tried to be everything a woman would wish for in a man until the itch struck and he was ready to move on to the next chick. It never seemed to last, that was the problem. He got bored, easily. Maybe his family's prediction was beginning to come true.

Now he was tired of the fast life at thirty-five years of age! Well before his prime, or was prime not from forty-five? He wasn't sure anymore. Maybe this Gift would point him to the right direction. Show him how she was able to achieve such a state of contented cheerfulness despite all odds, for he did not espy any wedding band on her fourth finger, yet she was happy! And she did not attempt to gulp him either even with his subtle invitation.

She was worth looking up; she had a lot of explaining to do: like what informed her cheerfulness even as she was no spring chicken. Well, she didn't look old but women's biological clock seemed to have shifted post; now starting to tick from cradle!

Usually the indeterminate pungent aura of spinsterhood followed women around when they got to certain age. And the fear of being left on the shelf in addition to other kinds of life issues combined to embed tinges of desperation to their behaviour, which began to manifest at what they considered the eve of their sell-by-date. He was not trying to lay blame here, life and the accompanying obstacles were not meant to be tackled alone, if one could help it, just that the aura put him off.

Obinna shook his head in amusement, women! They came in all shapes and sizes and with all sorts of baggage tucked safely out of sight until you came close. But this Gift seemed different; there was a sort of restrained air about her which was intriguing; a mysteriousness that stirred his challenging mode. She was not only regal and beautiful, she also seemed peaceful. It remained to be seen, though, how all the other characteristics, which could not be seen at a glance played out; characteristics that were better observed over a period of time. Or maybe that was a new ploy in the scene which he hadn't been aware of? Cheerfulness at all odds. He would definitely look her up, she was one captivating lady.

*   *   *

Unaware of the commotion and subsequent chain reactions I had set agog in my table-sharing-companion, I swam to Smithfield negotiating precariously in view of the slippery roads and at the same time maintaining a deepening sense of loss. What wouldn't I give to have certain aspects of my life cut off and burnt, leaving a clean slate? Look at this most handsome man for instance, would he ever in this world want to be acquainted to a former prostitute? Not to talk of making me his girlfriend. Prostitutes were employed to do certain kind of job and once done, discarded like they had a plague of a specific nature. You don't make them your girlfriends or wives.

If I didn't go off in the wrong direction, now housing a scorched and blackened skeleton in my cupboard, would I have met and married Obinna or somebody like him? Would fate have intervened, brought us together?

If I had graduated and followed my career path, the career path I had mapped out for myself, what would have become of me? What would I have become? A career civil servant? Would I have veered into politics as I once dreamt of, enroute to being a Senator? If only I had stuck to what I knew . . .

Family Court

SMITHFIELD, DUBLIN

2005

Going through the security scanner at the entrance to the Family Court in Smithfield, I shrugged off my reminiscing coat, to search for the room in the Court where our case would be heard. I didn't know whether I was required inside the court right away or not. Not being sure I took a seat outside Room 2 to await further developments.

After sitting out there for a while, I became aware of the reduction in the volume of noise inside the courtroom. The shuffling and the conversation levels had considerably toned down. Maybe it's time to go in. Something different must be happening or about to happen. So I got up quickly and moved towards the closed door, pushed it open and went in while thinking of Ifeoma and why she hadn't appeared yet.

'The business meeting with her cousin couldn't possibly have extended from last night till now?' I mumbled grumpily as I went in, searched for and sat beside a smartly dressed lady at the back of the room who turned out to be Ifeoma. We raised our brows in acknowledgment, grinned and quickly faced forward to the sound of c-o-u-r-t. Everybody stood up and I in amazement stood up too. I never thought it really happened like this in real life.

When the judge sat down we all took our seats again while I immediately trained my eyes on the judge's face searching for any sign of what his decision would be after the hearing. But I discerned nothing. There was no indication whatsoever of the direction of his thoughts.

The court registrar, sitting directly beneath the judge, shuffled some papers before him, adjusted his glasses further down his nose, then looking above the rim to the wall opposite him, read from an open file on his table, the cases to be heard that day. Ours was number one. When he finished calling out the cases, the judge called on the solicitors concerned to present them succinctly and dismissed every other person not connected to the case.

One of the men sitting with Osahon stood up and introduced himself as Mr. O'Donoghue, but I could only see his back, since he was facing the judge, and he coughed before he started to present his client's case. I realized that he was Osahon's solicitor. But because he was backing me, I couldn't hear most of what he said, but the few I heard told of Osahon's misfortune at marrying a woman who did not pay any heed to what a true family unit should be or how it functioned. In any case, he was here to ask, on behalf of his client, that the court redress the anomaly by giving his client the opportunity to perform his role as a father to his children, failing which, the court should grant him access to his children as well as mandate the defendant to cooperate towards his securing his Residency Status on the basis of being a parent of an Irish Citizen Child. He referred to certain documents, already tendered as exhibits, inclusive of our marriage certificate and the birth certificates of our two daughters, to corroborate Osahon's claims. He did not present any birth certificate for Lucky; that would have given the game away, I thought unemotionally.

I processed these informations, as simply as I could, because the solicitor's presentation was fraught with so many high-sounding legal words that I'd need to either go back to school to study law or engage a solicitor of my own to be able to absorb the full import of what was being said, neither of which I could do now.

I did not like Mr. O'Donoghue's voice: it was thin and squeaky. And each time he started a fresh point, he hacked out this nasty cough that grated on my nerves. But I kept at trying to decipher his words, then I heard my name.

The full import of not having a solicitor suddenly settled on my shoulder like a boulder. At the time, I did not think beyond sending off my responses to Osahon's submissions. In any case, it never occurred to me that I'd be required to speak in court. Right now, I had to respond or explain to the good judge why I denied Osahon everything.

I shot up, seemingly propelled by anger, and moved towards the judge. Osahon should not think that lying would get him far. When I got to the long bench, occupied by Osahon and his lawyer, I edged in but giving them quite a good distance.

I closed my eyes and took a deep breath, exhaled quietly and then opened my mouth but then had to close it. I opened it again, yet nothing came out so I closed it. I looked around and realized that all eyes were on me but I couldn't speak. So I sat down. I didn't know how to start and even if I did, I wasn't composed enough. I had never in my life had course to exchange so much as a hello with an officer of the law at whatever level. And now I was expected to stand before a judge and speak! How easy can that be?

Determinedly, I got up again and heard somebody exclaim, 'Your honour it is not true. It is not true. It . . .' Then the voice tapered off and a hush fell in the courtroom with all eyes boring into me. I looked straight at the judge who was frowning at me. Realizing that I was the one that spoke, in the strange voice, I cleared my throat to ensure that I did better.

'It is not true, your honour.'

'Yes, you have said that Ms. Ofoedu. Can we hear your own version of events?'

I nodded, but that was all. The judge nodded at me. Maybe in response to my nod or to encourage me.

After a while I muttered. 'Osahon misrepresented everything, everything. All he had his solicitor say were lies, all lies. I am going to . . . I will . . . I will . . . I can't . . . I can't . . .'

I stopped again and then looked around. They were all still looking at me but this time with distaste. I wasn't sure that it was so, but that was what I saw. They had seen through me, through to my dirty sordid past! Exposed before them like a vat-full of vomit. This massive dose of humiliation coursed through my veins like an IV injection. My body shrank from the revulsion on their faces and I couldn't utter any more words. I felt my body slide, as if in slow motion, until I sat in a slump. I put my face down on the back-rest of the bench in front of me and started crying without decorum. The tears cascading down my face were dredged up from the depth of my soul. Osahon had wounded me and here he was rubbing salt and pepper on the raw wound. How terrible and unfair could life be?

What was I expected to say? The way Osahon's solicitor had marshaled out his case has already condemned me. What could I possibly say to alleviate the damages even though I knew they were all lies? I couldn't hope to counter them with further lies and I would die before I divulged the truth. I was so incapacitated I could only cry. I botched it with Osahon then and now I had botched it yet again in court. I continued to cry slumped on the long bench, but something made me raise my face to look at the judge, though his face was still closed, it had softened somehow. As I continued to stare at him, tears cascading freely, I heard 'he beat me up and raped me.' That strange voice again? I nodded at the judge as if endorsing the assertion.

I didn't know how long I sat there hunched in misery, crying. But then I became aware of being led out of the courtroom and of being made to sit down and of being patted on the shoulder by somebody. Somebody gave me a paper napkin while the earlier hand continued to pat my shaking shoulders. I was sandwiched between two bodies.

I cleaned my eyes with the paper napkin and looked up sideways to my left and encountered Ifeoma's face. Her own eyes were glistening with unshed tears. I was saddened even more. It must be very bad if Ifeoma was on the verge of tears too. Ifeoma was not known for such feminine inclinations. She was a veteran of knowledge and facts and always had answers for everything: so employing one of these *womanly-ways*, like shedding tears in time of helplessness, would not be considered a solution to knotty problems by her. I then swiveled my face slowly to my right and encountered a solemn face of a white lady who I did not know.

'Are you alright Ms. Ofoedu?' the solemn lady asked in a kind but hushed voice. I took awhile, to test whether I was alright, before nodding.

'Do you want a drink, maybe a glass of water or something?' I shook my head.

'Right. Then we will have to go back in for the judge's summation.'

'Summation?' I repeated, askance. I may not be a lawyer but summation is summation—summary which would be followed by conclusion.

'But I haven't said anything yet. How could he summarize without hearing from me?' Well he is a man, I told myself, he must have decided to side his fellow man.

'He is not ruling on the case, if that is what you are thinking. He only wanted to give instructions on what he wanted all of us to do and when to converge for the next hearing.'

I nodded without understanding. I covered my nose with the now soggy napkin and blew it furiously. The solemn lady extended another napkin which I accepted, this time with a murmur of thanks. I cleaned my eyes, this was not the time to pat them delicately so as to not smudge the shadows and the mascaras. I then got up and smoothened my skirt, which had ridden up to my thighs before they thought that I was trying to ply my trade in court! Meekly, I went with the lady back into the courtroom with Ifeoma guarding the bench outside for when I'd be brought out again for another session of crying.

Dazedly I stared at the judge who cleared his throat and went into a long and winded explanation of what he now expected from the plaintiff and the defendant, how he wanted it and why. Apparently he had stopped the hearing when the voice had helped me to mutter that I was beaten and raped. Anyway, he wrapped up his speech by ordering what he called a section 20 report. He stood up and we all rose again at the bailiff's c-o-u-r-t.

I, though thoroughly confused, rose too and went out with my minder, whose name was Eileen, when it was our turn to leave. Outside, Eileen advised me to go home and think about what the Judge said and to listen very carefully to the social worker when she called on me. She'd be able to guide me as to what to do next. I thanked her and she left while I sat down with Ifeoma on the bench, each of us lost in our own thoughts.

I swallowed the metallic saliva that had collected in my mouth and then changed position now resting my head on the wall behind the bench and closed my eyes. I needed to appraise the situation in view of what transpired in court; I had to give it to Osahon, a real smooth operator, that one. Only God knew what he told those lawyers of his. But does this mean that Osahon is going to score yet another goal against me? I didn't begrudge the Judge his suspicions, he was free to pursue the truth, if he felt it wasn't forthcoming, but . . . As I chewed the turn of events Ifeoma intruded.

'Gi, what do you want to do? You have to make up your mind about doing something, and that something had better be the right thing this time around. It is not a matter of you and Osahon trying to win an argument anymore, you know?'

'Fifi, I will give this a serious thought. Before the first visit of the social worker I will have worked out the direction I want to go.'

'Fine. Are you coming with me to Erica's?'

'I do not feel like visiting with Erica today.'

Ifeoma smiled, extended her hands and we embraced, then she stood up.

'Fine. I'll advise you to think about what was said today and make your decisions. You have suffered enough.'

I nodded in response, my mind far away. Ifeoma continued unperturbed, she knew that I could hear her.

'I will go directly to the airport for my flight back to London after Erica's so we won't see again, you know.'

I nodded.

'Take care then and I will call you when I reach home. OK? And while you're still at the vacillating stage, find a solicitor,' Ifeoma flung at me as she marched out like a soldier, and she would have made a fine one but for her height. Then she came back and said, 'Look Gi, go away from this place. Your staying on will depress you more and more and delay my leaving. Please.'

'Ifeoma I am actually alright. You worry too much.'

'I don't.'

'You don't usually but you are now. Go, I will be fine and call me in the night.'

'I will. Bye then,' Ifeoma murmured hugging me once more before she took off swiftly. I waved enthusiastically, to show that I was not being depressed by the place. But after a while I took her advice and quietly left the court premises.

Erica

On reaching the gate that led out of the court premises, Ifeoma called her car-hire driver, Padriag, to alert him that she was on her way to the car park. By the time she was completely out of the gate and on to the road, he drove up to where she was and she slid in and sat beside him telling him to take her to Blanchardstown first before the airport.

Padriag was exceptional and knew when one was not in the mood for chit-chats, she thought, as she sighed, stretching her legs while her mind veered to Gift. The problem with Gift was that her ears were just for decoration. But she didn't want to think about Gift now so, decisively, she banished her thoughts and replaced them with Erica. Another troubled friend. But in Erica's case she was determined, this time, to ask questions as to why exactly her Refugee Status was cancelled and she was now on the verge of being deported!

*   *   *

Erica was relieved to see Ifeoma. She thought she had left for London when she didn't come, as she promised, at about two pm. Ifeoma, when she had sat down, explained that the hearing took longer than she had anticipated. Erica nodded. There was no need of asking Ifeoma about it, she wouldn't tell her anything. She hoped that Gift fared well and filed it away to remember to ask her later.

It seemed they were all being besieged by problems all of a sudden with the exception of Ifeoma, of course, but who, however, found herself in the centre, tugged first to the right for Gift and then to the left for her. Though she seemed to lean more to the right. However, Erica had learnt not to be angry about that anymore. What made Ifeoma like Gift more than herself, she'd never know. But she had accepted it as one of those things. Ifeoma refused her offer of drink or food, but she provided tea anyway before they went straight to the heart of the matter.

'We have hired a solicitor who promised to try his best to sort out the problem. It may be tough, he had told us, but we'd just have to keep our fingers crossed,' Erica informed Ifeoma as she placed a tray of tea, in her best crockery, on the table in front of her.

'But what happened exactly Erica?'

'Well, our Refugee Status was based on a lie: they found out and cancelled it. But in the process of investigating that, they (social welfare, and to be honest I don't know how those people got involved but they did) found out that we work, but not in our names which they termed impersonation or identity fraud, another set of offense on its own.'

'But how do you work without it being in your name and you were not detected up until now?' Ifeoma raised her brows in a question mark, to accompany the voiced questions, while her thoughts skidded ahead; how low could anybody sink? And to think that Nigerian leaders are being accused of corruption. Now given a level playing ground some people do not even have the decency to play by the rules.

'Some people got their Residency Status but do not live here so we used their documents,' Erica enlightened. Ifeoma frowned, trying to process the information before speaking.

'Let me get this right: You have your own Residency Status which permits you to work here but you chose to use another person's paper to work with right?'

'Mmmh.'

'But what do you hope to gain . . . ?' Ifeoma stopped as it fell in place.

'Oh . . . Oh . . . That way you'd remain on social welfare without anybody being the wiser and save your salary? Is that what you are telling me?'

'About right.'

'My God, Erica!' Then she stopped again and lapsed into silence, her eyes never leaving Erica's who stared back unfazed. Eventually Ifeoma looked away. Choosing to examine the surroundings instead.

She swiveled her head to the right and then to the left, taking in the livingroom and all that was in it. At a point during the surveillance she realized that she was becoming angry, very, very angry. But she reined in her anger, though she couldn't stop her lips from stiffening. Finally she brought back her gaze on her friend before asking.

'So what did you do with the extra money you made? This place contradicts this enlightenment.'

'That's the whole idea,' Erica crowed conspiratorially, 'You see, we have to be very careful so we send the money back home to acquire properties and stuff, you know. If we start showing signs of affluence here the social welfare officers would just come in *gbam!*'

Ifeoma nodded as if in agreement, but then she asked, 'So you live and work here while you remit your money to Nigeria? A country which you only visit, say once a year and stay for about a month at a time?' Ifeoma shook her head perplexed before continuing.

'This is unbelievable. But how do they even allow you into Nigeria?'

'Ifeoma sef, we go through Ghana *jare*?'

'Oh. Ok. So now that you've been found out what next?'

Erica took a long time before answering and when she did it was in a sort of I-don't-care-kind of tone.

'Well they have done their worst. We were summoned for hearing, some sort of local court, and the ruling was that we should refund all that they had spent on us since we started working. In addition we have been withdrawn from any kind of social benefits except for the children's Child Benefits. I suppose they have no way of knowing how much we have amassed and didn't want to deny the children unnecessarily.'

Ifeoma didn't like Erica's tone of voice or what it spewed out but still she did not want to lose her cool.

'So your request for loan from me was to not only pay your solicitor but to refund the benefits?'

'I told you I'll pay back, so . . .'

'It is not about that Erica,' Ifeoma said in a very quiet but dreadful voice, 'and I am sorry but I have to be critical here. How could you even deem it right to defraud a country that has been so good to you? Is there no limit to your greed? I find it difficult to appreciate what you and your husband did. But there is no need crying over spilt milk now I guess, the harm has been done.'

Ifeoma got up and started pacing up and down. And Erica was following the pacing, gauging the extent of her friend's anger, but at the same time thinking, why was Ifeoma agitated? Everybody was doing it here, or was it because they found her out? It's chicken-change for the State's pocket *jare* so what's the stress? She clicked her tongue in anger and that seemed to break Ifeoma's trance.

'I can't say that I know what drove you, but I hope that you'll take this as a lesson and mend your ways. You have consistently placed an unusual amount of value on material things. Such attitude fuels greed which in turn would get you into all sorts of fraudulent acts as you no doubt know now. You are lucky you were not sent to prison. I suppose it has never occurred to you that a good name is better than money?' Ifeoma stopped her pacing and started gathering her things, thinking, Erica had been a social climber even as a student back then in their university days and would not mind stepping on one or two toes to get what she wanted. But how had it come to this, resorting to thieving to satisfy her wants? She may have to rethink her relationship with her in future. This type of person would not think twice about hurting anybody in her misguided deals. It's a pity that it took this to open her eyes.

She straightened up to be scorched by the fury in Erica's eyes, but she was good at cracking tough nuts, just that she hadn't cracked it on Erica's head yet. She stood up completely and looked down on Erica squarely waiting to take her cue from her next action or utterings. It was time to put her to a befitting position and friendship be dammed. And the bloody woman was not even remorseful!

'I don't blame you Ifeoma, all your life you've been rolling in untold luxuries. What do you know about want? Tell me?' Erica blazed, but Ifeoma ignored her and continued to stare at her like she was a cockroach to be squashed.

'You see, you don't have an answer to that. So don't judge me.'

Ifeoma still didn't answer. Then she flicked imaginary lint off the sleeve of her leaf-green cashmere top, dusted her bum that was encased in a darker shade of leaf-green Balmain denim trousers, before walking to the door that'd take her out of the house. Erica jumped up from her seat in hot pursuit.

Ifeoma opened the door and then turned to her former friend.

'Is that all Erica? Is that all you could say in your defence: that you were poor? Your justification for being a fraudster and a thief was because you were poor? Give me a break, Erica. That excuse is so pathetic that it's laughable. I am surprised at you not drumming up a better one, because you wouldn't recognize poverty even if it stuck on you like a second skin.' She looked at Erica again, up and down, and then added, 'I do not have what it takes to judge you so I won't, but I believe we human beings are imbued with the mechanism to choose between right and wrong. So you can smear your name and that of your children as much as you like. As for me I am out of here and for good.' She opened the door, stepped out and gently closed it on

Erica's misery of a face and stood awhile taking the cold air into her lungs to clear her head.

Erica flung the door open and screamed at Ifeoma who carried on walking, 'Come back here you rich cow. Where are you going? To that snooty Gift? No be am? Don't go and marry, be playing aunty to all our children. Old cargo like you. And let me tell you what you don't know, you're not the one that watched your father kill your mother in cold blood because of money. So you can say whatever you wished and see if I care.'

As she shouted, her voice got smaller and smaller and her body slid down until finally she saw herself slumped on her doorstep. She didn't think Ifeoma had the right to attack her no matter what she may have done. She was her friend; they'd been friends for a long time.

The image of her bloodied dying mother appeared and refused to disappear as was usual. She sat there and cried for a long time, so long that her ribs ached. Finally she cleaned her eyes and reverted to form—put back the shield that had helped her bury her pains.

She had gained so much from being Ifeoma's friend; all-expense paid holidays, both for her and her family, cash gifts which had helped them to finish a block of four flats that they rented out back home, expensive clothing for herself, her children and even her husband. Was she going to lose all that? She had lived in this country for three years and Ifeoma never showed her face, but only two months of Gift's arrival, two months! and she was in hot pursuit. Only God knows how much Gift got from her; that she was not number 1 in Ifeoma's friends list ground her intestine to no end.

But what medicine did that Gift use on Ifeoma? What? Ifeoma should just not annoy her, because she was born with a diamond spoon in her mouth, did she not realize that people born with tarnished spoon or no spoon at all, had to claw their way to the top, otherwise remain downtrodden for life? What did she know about want? What could she possibly know about poverty? Nothing! That's what and that's why she should not stand in judgment of her. Her dead mother was a testimony to the powerlessness of poverty.

You are going about this the wrong way you know?

'I don't know any such thing,' she rounded mutinously.

And you were relatively not from a poor home, not afterwards. You should let your mother rest in peace.

'I say shut up, you fool. What do you know?' she snapped again at whatever that was still trying to inveigle in some sort of sanity.

However, Erica got up from her doorstep to stare at the disappearing car bearing her friend of many years away. The feeling at the pit of her stomach was ice-cold dread. She stood there, for a long time, staring into space long after Ifeoma had disappeared, her arms folded across her bosom as if to ward off the unsettling spell that suddenly enveloped her.

As she felt the bite of the cold she shivered, feelings having started to flow back into her body. Still in a daze, she went and sat down on the very chair she was on before and during the *event* and held her face in her palms as she replayed the scene again. Finally she sighed. She supposed that the best thing would be to go down to Gift's and sort things out with Ifeoma.

She'd have to find a way to mend this rift because for one her husband would not find it funny, and she'd rather not know how unfunny (her dead mother was a testimony to that kind of funny).

Ifeoma had been a good source of income on her own; this was a safer line of thought. She had never said no to her demands all these years, however outrageous. If that side dried up too what were they going to do? No! She'd have to change her singing tone.

Then stealthily it slithered into her consciousness that really she had come to like Ifeoma as a person and did not only see her as her bank. It was no longer because of what she could get out of her. When did that happen? She tried to see if she could ascertain when, but couldn't. And when divorced from Ifeoma, even with her retinue of other friends, there already existed a gaping hole and it didn't have anything to do with money. Ifeoma had always been a caring friend, though from a distance, who took on her friend's problems and joys like they was hers. In a world filled up with piranhas, she was an angelfish. She changed her sitting position. God would show her the path to follow. He would deliver her family from all these tribulations. Wasn't it said that the evil-one would always try to destabilize the children of God, but that "no weapons fashioned against us shall prosper"? After affirming the quotation with other such assertions, she then sealed it with, 'Satan you are liar. You won't get me,' as she went to her room.

Slowly, she climbed the stairs, lost in thought. She must go and see if Ifeoma went to Gift's place at once. She had to tackle this new problem as it's still hot. She went into her room and sank on her knees for a heavy prayer session, but she didn't fare long as she was swamped again by grief from the past and she collapsed into a crying heap.

*   *   *

The wind that carried Erica's last comment brushed past Ifeoma's left ear, as it rushed by, but she veered her head off its direction. She had known Erica for donkey years now. She knew her parents, who both came for her matriculation and convocation, so which mother was she talking about?

'Scheming little scoundrel,' she hissed and closed her eyes, relaxing her posture and her tautened lips. But Erica's words kept reverberating in her brain. She couldn't relax. So she opened her eyes and sat up to ask Padriag about the possibility of Erica's comment being true, but changed her mind and told him to take her to Gift's place.

Osahon

Having put the finishing touches to his case, Osahon left his solicitor's office, which was not too far from the court. Skirting the Luas line, lost in thoughts, in took an aimless walk. Something was worrying about that judge's section 20 shit, though he did not let on to his solicitor about the worry.

What if . . . ? He dismissed that. No. He knew that there was no way Gift would tell the world what she did. How could she? She dared not. How would she raise her head in public again?

No chance!

And this Ireland of a place looked like it was small, likely everybody would know everybody, so who would want her as a neighbour? Nobody, because she would be expected to snatch their husbands or boyfriends and even the future ones for the unmarried and the boyfriendless. He had trusted in his instincts on those grounds and lied through his teeth and it paid off, now . . . He shrugged and continued walking through Abbey Street towards O'Connell Street, chewing his lips, still agitated.

Women do not have ears; otherwise Gift should have given him what he wanted and some cash to save herself this embarrassment. By now he would have brought his family to Ireland, settled down and faced his life. Instead here he was traipsing the four corners of the court. Stupid bitch! He had warned her. Now with this court order the shit was about to hit the fan, definitely. And in his favour, he knew.

But as he continued to walk his mind cleared and clung to other thoughts brightening his demeanor. He crossed O'Connell and entered Talbot Street before emerging on Gardiner Street, heading towards his hostel. He was now suffused with happiness, secure in the knowledge that after a long-time of badness, goodness would follow. He had suffered, for almost two years now, but it has come to the time of favours now. Good news only, all the way.

'Mark it somewhere, I tell you,' he mouthed to nobody as he searched for the key to the entrance to his hostel. He would get Ezra to take him out this night for a celebratory drink.

This is a security post as far as he was concerned, reception my foot, he thought in annoyance as he gruffly accepted a letter he was handed which looked suspiciously like the ones you get from *Justice*. He scanned it disdainfully.

'Stupid people,' he muttered, as he went up the stairs to his room and settled in to sleep.

He needed to maximize the off he took from his various money-making activities. He had hoped to have quit the evening job by now, but having to pay his lawyer did not afford him that luxury yet, thus he had continued to deprive himself of so much of sleep from having to wake up early to be at his post to distribute the free daily papers; then double back to do cleaning in a hospital with *dagbo*—forged paper that Ezra got for him. So he'd use sleep to kill himself the rest of the day and by the 5th of next month he would be installed in his own house paid for by the government and all his accrued allowances paid to him. Then he'd ask for them to pay for his return flight to Nigeria to bring his family. He'd make the most of what was on offer; it's not his fault that they were foolish in this country!

*   *   *

He woke up late in the evening very refreshed. There's nothing like a good sleep to restore a man's sense of being, he thought, as he groped for and called Ezra on his cell phone to invite him for a drink. Ezra would cough out for the outing; he just didn't know it yet. He took a long and leisurely shower and dressed up smartly, and was about to switch off the light on his way out when his eyes fell on the brown envelope. He picked it up and opened it.

'Justice.' *I knew it.* 'So what do they want this time?' he asked angrily as he tore open the envelope and ran his eyes quickly through the letter then sat down and read it again.

'Motherfuckers! What do they mean by this?'

He read the letter again and placed it on the table. As he thought about it, he began to calm down. If truth be told, he acknowledged to himself, who'd grant him Refugee Status on that contrived bullshit he

spewed? It'd be foolhardy of them if they did. In any case he did not
need the bloody Refugee Status.

'Who tell them say I be refugee?' he spat, '*Na* their papa be refugee.'
He cursed. Anyway he didn't come to Ireland to be a Refugee. It was
just something he had to do to hold himself till he won his case which
was more or less a month away. So to hell with the *Justice* people or
whoever refused to declare him a refugee.

'Do they know me? Look at this people oh. Do they know who
they are dealing with? Anyway I don't blame them. Na me find their
trouble. If I didn't come here would they have the temerity to declare
or not declare me a refugee? Bullshitters!' he screamed as he banged
and locked his door, enroute to his rendezvous with Ezra, his anger
monumental. He'd deal with the fucking letter tomorrow.

*   *   *

They spoke in elated voices as they maneuvered their way to Bolton
Street. Osahon had told Ezra his version of what took place in court
that day and they were analyzing it hither and thither on their way to
a local watering hole owned by a Nigerian, no less. They reached their
destination still on high and the place was already throbbing with guys
eating and guzzling, their voices notched up an octave. Discussing
Nigerian issues variously, ranging from happenings in the political
arena, to the economy, and to what those wild-boys were doing in the
Delta area—the oil hot-spot.

They sat down and waited for the waitress to take their orders
while listening to the arguments. Osahon had never seen why he had
to kill or be killed because of oil that nobody knew how it came to
be where it is. So he did not join that group. Politics rankled him:
politicians brought out the worst in him because they were cheats;
reaping where they did not sow!

So he twitched his ears to capture yet another point of view—those
discussing business.

'What business can anybody do in Nigeria now?' he scorned, 'These
people *sef*, when did they visit that country last? Abi they no hear say
that that man Obasanjo has made sure that anything importable was
banned.'

He shrugged, topping it up with a loud hiss. But if these fools
allow people back home to lure them out of their hard-earned Euros,
hard-earned, he could attest to that, with promises of selling whatever
they wanted to send to Nigeria, that'd be their problem.

He interrupted Ezra who had waded in on the political side and demanded that they order for their *chop* before he was fed up with this place and all these fools. Ezra beckoned to the waitress who came over wiggling her non-existent waist which irritated Osahon. When people did not have anything to flaunt why make it so blatant that they don't have it? Stupid girl.

When she reached their table he realized that she was not even a girl by a mile and this annoyed him further, an old cargo like her should know better. But his anger turned to surprise when he was given the menu with an array of mouth-watering choices that included Starch and Banga soup. His very own people's food, in a restaurant owned by an Igbo man in the Republic of Ireland? Wonderful!

His good humour returned instantly and he placed his order expansively accompanied by three bottles of Star beer direct from Nigeria.

'Na wah for this Ireland,' he mouthed and at the same time patting Ezra to attract his attention and to once more ask him to place his order. Ezra was getting on his nerves right now. What was this sudden interest in Nigerian politics? Is he planning to become a politician? Little man like him? He should finish with his mission here in Ireland first before embarking on another. Politician *ke*, see him with head like that of grass-cutter. He *wan* be politician!

'Ezra abeg order your food, we didn't come here for political rally joo.'

Ezra was surprised at Osahon's tone. What had set him off like that? On the other hand he wasn't surprised as such: that man was always incensed by one thing or the other. He ordered his food, however, and they fell to as soon as their orders hit the table. Osahon who had regained his good humour when he set eyes on his favourite food, started from where he stopped on their way, to regale Ezra about his day in court inclusive of the latest *distaste* from Justice. His voice turned slightly menacing at that revelation. Ezra looked up.

'But you don't care, so why are you angry?'

'I am not angry, my friend! I am only trying to update you.'

'OK,' was what managed to escape Ezra's mouth through the bushmeat he was crunching. He nodded for emphasis and licked his fingers noisily. Osahon frowned.

'My friend are you that mannerless or what? How can you be licking your fingers *fiam fiam* like that in public? Please I am trying to eat.'

Ezra nodded again but this time in pacification. He had learnt to take this, his new friend Osahon, one minute at a time. That's the best way. He's so full of anger; every little thing bounces him off. But Ezra liked him; he was a man full of himself. He didn't take nonsense and that is what made a man. That's what he needed to be able to catch one of those women who abandoned their husbands for the sake of house and welfare payments. If he managed to get himself hooked to one, then he'd stop paying rent and they'd take care of his food and other needs as well.

He'd been trying valiantly to emulate Osahon without success. He blamed his height, but Osahon had told him, that he could achieve anything he wanted if he put his mind to it, height or no height. Had he not heard of Napoleon or Mussolini? Osahon had asked him. After that Ezra had decided to focus on working at his confidence. Then he'd do his first run on that big-bottomed Remilara that lived in Tallaght with her two noisy children. It'd be a straightforward journey into the City from Tallaght with the Luas. There would be no need to go after Rita, whom he really loved. But Navan was too far out to serve his purpose now, besides she still *dey do inyanga*. Maybe hitting on Remilara would make her come running to him.

Osahon had taught him to be mean when it came to women matters: it usually maneuvered them towards the desired direction, he had claimed. Ezra chuckled. Everybody had turned mercenary in Europe in an attempt to survive, even in the affairs of the heart. Whoever said that love was blind must be a joker.

He turned to his friend even as he wondered whether questions while eating counted as mannerless.

'So what are you going to do about that letter from Justice?'

'I will ignore them.'

'But you must respond within a given time or . . .'

'They asked me to respond within fifteen working days or they'll take it that I accept their decision. But I am not going to bother with them anymore. I know that before they get to my turn again, I'll have finished with the court case and be on my way to my own house and all that goes with it.'

'You're right. There is no need to even respond at all.'

Ezra envied Osahon no end: him with his Irish Born Child. How he wished that he came in early enough. He would have made sure to *give* somebody belle; by now he would have been living in his own place, taken care of by the State. Some people were born lucky. Look at him that came only yesterday, he's already going to be sorted out. Ah . . . Irish born child! He shrugged the envy away and concentrated on his bushmeat.

Gift

I exited the courthouse and strolled along the Luas track, Smithfield receding behind me as I headed towards Abbey Street, my thoughts in chaos about the new development. The rain had long since given up its assault but I did not notice. My tread was slow because my legs were heavy with thoughts. My shoulders stooped. The euphoria of this morning was like in another era. What was I going to do? The Judge must have seen through the lies in my submissions: my vehement denial about not knowing Osahon from Adam! Osahon did not present like a mad man. And men do not go about claiming any woman as their wife and the children they did not father as theirs.

I had made a fool of myself in there. Smart judge. That was why he was there I suppose: to see through such nonsenses and stop it. But why only mine, what of Osahon's nonsense? I had to think about this apparent injustice playing out before me, before continuing with another train of thought.

This social worker had a tough job ahead of her for there was no way I would relinquish an inch to Osahon, not anymore. He had had his time and he squandered it. Or maybe this social worker woman would serve as the route to my salvation? I stopped short and beamed. OK, if I tell them what happened, at least they'd see that he was a beast, not to be allowed near us. Then, maybe I'd begin to heal and search for myself. But . . . I'd get my own solicitor to help me marshal out the facts.

My steps lightened and became springy even. A bubble of joy exploded at the base of my spine and flowed into my stomach and from there started criss-crossing all over my body. All the weights lifted and a state of well-being settled in on me so much so that I was floating on air.

I came up to O'Connell Street, but turned to the bridge towards Trinity College instead of towards Burgh Quay and the bus 39 for home.

I couldn't go home in this state I was in, and I knew just the medicine!

Shopping, and on Grafton Street. Heaven!

Oh Gift you are truly free.

'I know,' I responded as I hurried towards Grafton Street on feather-light legs.

I love to window shop, though not averse to treating myself to something nice once in a while. Right now happened to be one of those once in a whiles. I had to have something and I knew what that was. I headed straight to Brown Thomas to get it over with first before inflicting myself on the rest of the shops.

When I stepped inside the dimly lit but inviting Brown Thomas interior, I came face to face with my coffee companion of the morning when the Irish weather was showing her nasty side, according to him. His smile was wide and full of warmth: the type used to welcome a long lost friend. He must have forgiven the weather, it having become sunny now.

I gave him a calm smile back, the type I feel goes straight to the recipient's core and settles warmly. I followed it with a mellow 'hello,' but this time there was no handshake, I'd rather not. I then excused myself and made straight to the Sisley Paris counter, for the whole range of Eau Du Soir; parfum, perfumed bath & shower gel, scented soap, scented deodorant and moisturizing scented body cream! I threw in the Fleur Champagne Perfume for good measure. I had coveted them for so long, the hunger had to be assuaged and this was the perfect time so I did not equivocate. I gathered my purchases and headed firmly to the payment counter. Court ruling or not, I deserved the treat.

*   *   *

Obinna, who was still at the entrance, gazed at Gift as she wove her way to the check-out. Suspecting her next move, having seen her collect what looked like the whole items on display, he employed his long-legs and cut her off at the check-out, offering to pay for the goodies.

'I'll rather you do not, Obinna. Thanks anyway,' was my clipped reply.

'Why?'

I looked up at his face and smiled but did not respond. I extended the cash I had already counted out to the cashier, collected my receipt and my purchases and then turned back to him, smiled once again before asking, 'What better time to take up that offer of a cuppa than now?'

Obinna opened his eyes imperceptibly wider, and then nodded. I knew that'd throw him and it did. A ghost of a smile grazed my upper lips and dissipated. However, I hoped he'd not attach any meaning to my suggestion. And he had better hurry up before I lost my nerve. I hadn't been to a proper date in a long time and did not want to vacillate now; so many impediments could rear their head and mar the opportunity.

But even as I was gingering myself up, I wondered about what could be going through his mind. Would he think I was being too forward, which did not befit a well-nurtured woman? Anyway that remained to be seen. I had come such a long way; I should not destroy the moment with misgivings and imagined assumptions! Then he spoke.

'I am not very conversant with Dublin; I barely found my way to Brown Thomas. Could you suggest a pleasant and quiet place for the cuppa then?'

'Bewley's is down the road, quiet I could not guarantee, not at this time.'

'Well, we will take it from there.'

So we left Brown Thomas and strolled up to Bewley's Continental Café and were sat on a corner seat for two.

'Would you rather eat?' Obinna asked while thinking: this lady was being very uncharacteristic. And he would very much be interested in knowing what the story was. Which Nigerian lady would rather pay for something that could be hers if she so wanted without being short for it? And then turned around to take up an offer that had barely left his lips this morning without demur of any sort? It did not add up. There's something not right.

He'd better be careful; women these days were full of all sorts of trickery. *Oh yes. But what would propel her into tricking you? Did she know you before?*

Maybe not, he thought in response, but he would still be on his guard, there's nothing wrong with that.

'No. Thank you, but I'd rather go for something much more flamboyant than coffee,' I responded.

Obinna groaned inwardly. Now what? He did not know how to react to the request. Good thing he had finished his business in Dublin, if this lady wanted them to get drunk, he was all for it, though it would put a big question mark on his earlier deductions and intentions. He wasn't about to settle for a drunk! How sad really, they could have been perfect for each other. He concealed his disappointment, however, and signaled to the waiter who was hovering and they placed their orders.

'So Gift, what do you do?'

'Funds administrator. I took the week off.'

Beauty and brain. A good mix. Rare, but well appreciated. And she only asked for half a glass of Bloody Mary. Good. Masking his thoughts, he asked instead, 'In anticipation of victory for whatever you were celebrating this morning?'

'You could say that.'

Obinna nodded while continuing to look at me. I looked back, unabashed. If he wanted to stare, I was equal to the task. There was no point pretending to look at every other place but his face. I also wanted to look at his fine features, as I knew he was taking mine in.

It may not be expected of a woman, but I knew that I was no longer a woman in that sense. The vagaries of life had peeled that veneer of feminine cunning off me. I could follow any rules I wanted, if and when I wanted to.

I sipped my drink gently though, some manners did not peel off that easily, and I would have been on my third glass if all my femininity had peeled off. But in deference to his presence, I decided to respect myself, there was no need to show off that I was a skilled drinker, acquired from birth as a palmwine connoisseur, and honed to perfection during the lost years of my life.

Conversation flowed smoothly between us with no discerning awkwardness. An onlooker would think we'd known each other forever. We both watched as something developed between us. But I knew that it would not last. Not if he had the full details. He had told me about himself in a nutshell—a negotiator in the upper echelons of United Nations, stationed in Austria. Last in a family of ten! Born and brought up in the US.

I had raised my brows at that and in turn told him that I was divorced with three children. I had to let him in on that early on, I was not going to hide the fact that I had children, but I demurred from inflicting him with the heavy stuff.

Being an Igbo man going by his name, what I had so far revealed should be enough to make him flee for dear life. Our Igbo men were not known to stray far to marry and they preferred nubile young things from their village or not too far from it.

I made sure my eyes were trained on his when I made my revelations, but his only concession to my big news was a frown and a nod. Well, seeing that he was such a sophisticat, he would make himself scarce after today; he does not live in this country afterall.

'You must have started early then.'

'Early enough. I had my first at twenty-one.'

'Good for you, one more and you're done.'

'Really, how did you come to such conclusion?' I asked, arching my face up for a better look at him again.

'I didn't, it was in your eyes.'

I had to laugh out loud at that and then said, 'You'd probably die in penury if you were working as a psychic.'

'Maybe, maybe not, we wait and see.'

We ended up having a meal afterall and we're now walking it off in St. Stephens Green Park. It was a very relaxing walk. For me, I corrected, I couldn't vouch for him, though I could not detect any itchiness on his part. But then not everybody reflected their thoughts on their faces, or became fidgety with negative thoughts, and him being a skilled diplomat and such. But he did not show any signs of wanting to leave, so he must be attuned to the atmosphere or to me as the case may be.

We took in the ducks; waved at the pigeons; admired ourselves in the slow-flowing lake; sat down to gaze at the grasses and the beds of flowers with wonder. Two goofy lovers on hand-holding stage. It suited me well: I didn't want to go beyond the hand-holding stage yet. One step at a time.

'I hate to break this, but I must leave,' I eventually said regretfully.

'Would you mind if I see you home?'

'Don't be daft, didn't I just tell you that I have three kids?'

'But . . . I am not complaining, why should you?'

'Well, just so you'll know and stop wasting your time, I am not looking for a boyfriend or for a man, or for any sort of relationship at that.'

Seeing Obinna's arched brows, I relented and apologized.

'I'm sorry to round up on you like that; just that I have a lot of things going on in my life at this time; I don't want to complicate it.'

'Which you have resolutely refused to share with me, I notice.'

'You shouldn't be in hurry to hear it; it may not be to your taste.'

'We will wait and see.'

'Thanks for everything, but I'd rather go home alone. See you when next you're in Ireland. You have my number?'

'Just like that? Anyway, my offer to take you home was just that, no insinuations there.' He had stopped, making me do the same as I nodded. Then he continued, 'Since you took the week off, could you spare some hours of it and wave me off tomorrow? Please don't say no.'

'Alright. Where do you stay?'

'My flight isn't till six pm. Where do you live?'

'Castleknock.'

'If my knowledge of Dublin is anything to go by it's somehow on the route to the airport so why don't you give me your address. I will come up to your place then we leave for the airport from there, if that's alright. That would save you from coming into the city and having to head back out again.'

I arched my brows, in an amused retaliation, but gave him my address and then hurried off, still amused, very much amused. This man's a very determined one. It seemed there was no stopping him once determined.

'We'll wait and see,' I murmured to myself, as he was wont to say.

I quickened my steps to Burgh Quay and boarded bus 39 from Hawkins Street to Blanchardstown which passes Castleknock.

In the bus, going home, I daydreamed unashamedly about Obinna and me, my over-active and fertile imagination unleashed to its maximum. I dropped off at the Sunflower Crèche in Castle Grove, not too far from my house and was hard put refraining from hugging Lucky's teacher, who had always been kind to me. Though I had not given her any cause to suggest unhappiness in my life, she seemed intuitive, she must have smelt it off my aura—suspected that I was suffering somehow. Some people were born that way. But she had never said a word to me, probably expecting me to set the ball rolling, before she could offer her shoulder.

But I never set any ball rolling because as I had continued to live more and more in Whiteman's land I had become more and more self-reliant, like them. Their method of problem solving was far removed from what I knew. For all intents and purposes, I was a classical case for therapy or counseling or whatever—their way—but I would not heed them—as a proper Nigerian. You did not open yourself up just like that; attending counseling sessions to churn out your life secrets. God forbid! That would not happen. You'd automatically be branded mad and that would amount to *social* suicide; your life and social relations up in smoke. Do we even have counselors back home? Oh well, I am sure they must be out there somewhere; one of those services you never seem to notice their existence until you needed them.

If I were at home, my father would have sorted me out a long time ago with talk talk and talk. My mother on the other hand was not the type for long talks, she'd either ignore you completely or just hit you on the head with that word that would galvanize you. Maybe it's the same thing with therapy, really. But the danger here was that you'd be letting people officially count you as not all there upstairs.

'Not me and them,' I whispered at the same time shrugging as if to ward off the unseen advances of the white man's therapist creeping in to counsel me. I had come so far, I did not have much further to go, then freedom.

I smiled widely at Siobhan, Lucky's teacher.

'My, some people are happy today,' she chirruped in her thin voice. Intuitive she may be, but she wasn't blessed with the type of voice that should befit a therapist.

'How did you guess?' I asked my voice laden with joy and laughter. Siobhan laughed out shrilly and I winced inwardly. She definitely wouldn't cut it as a therapist with that voice.

'I am not guessing Gift. It's written all over your face.'

'Oh.'

Intuitive indeed.

We stood out there for awhile talking before I finally breezed off with Lucky squirming under my armpit. The tyke never seemed to want to go home, even if he was studying for his leaving cert!

I hummed while I made dinner for my children who in turn were full of exuberance. Children, eeh, so easy to please, so easily made happy. They were happy just because I was happy. If only they knew the extent of my happiness; that I met a man who was interested in me as me and not as an object of paid sex and did not mind that I had three children. *Ewoh!* That was too much.

Sadly, nobody to share this bit of joy with. Ifeoma must have flown back to London after visiting Erica. We'd speak later in the night, but the distance would make the story sound silly.

What if it doesn't amount to anything?

'Spoil sport,' I remonstrated in response. But I believed I should heed it anyway. No need to set myself up for any heartbreak. Or maybe I'd tell Una. I couldn't keep it to myself, the pressure would suffocate me. I'd wait and see, though. I had to smile at that. I had resorted to re-echoing Obinna non-stop since hearing that quirk.

Then Frances, piped up.

'Mummy, Aunty Ifeoma.'

I didn't hear the house phone ring. Oh, it must be my mobile which happened to be in my bag in the living room where the children were watching television.

'Bring the phone up to me, dear.'

'Which phone?'

I looked up with fright. Did I conjure her up or is she real? I moved closer and touched her.

'Ifeoma. You're real?'

'I know I should be in London, but what do you mean by am I real? It seems all you babes in Dublin have some nuts loose all of a sudden.'

'Why are you still around. What happened?'

'I think there's something seriously wrong with Erica.'

'I thought we agreed to live with her excessive greed. That was serious enough or you didn't think so?'

'Gi, it's more than that. I don't really know what to make of her claim. She said . . . I think we'll have to go to her and hear it together . . .' Ifeoma stopped, looking pained.

'If you are lost for words then that is out of the ordinary. Let me get ready.'

*   *   *

Erica opened the door for us, her eyes red from crying, and her general demeanor listless. But I could swear that her face tightened when she saw me.

We made ourselves comfortable and looked at Erica expectantly. She hadn't said anything to us since we came in. Ifeoma, not one for dilly-dally, cleared her throat.

'Erica, you said something that I needed you to clarify.'

Erica looked towards her and looked away again. Then her shoulders started shaking . . . she was sobbing. I looked at Ifeoma, who was already turned to look at me, and we both shrugged. When Erica's crying did not abate I went over, drew a dining-chair, and sat opposite her to console her. The aura of sadness that was around Erica was tangible. I could feel it and it made my eyes water.

Ifeoma looked at Gift in amazement and hissed. Then, 'Gift are you crying? Why? Please don't add to the confusion.'

Then she turned back to Erica.

'Erica, it is enough. What is the problem, tell me?'

I cleaned my eyes and calmly patted Erica's hand in sympathy. I had to because the circumstances under which we found ourselves in required a soft touch to negotiate, and I was not even privy to what it was yet. And Ifeoma was too hard and might not be able to wheedle the story out of Erica. I nodded at Erica encouragingly while still holding her hand.

'Erica,' I implored, 'I know that in your ladder of friendship I did not rate high, but if I tell you that I understood your pain without knowing what it is, believe it, because I do. Don't cry anymore. Problem shared is said to be problem solved. Now I can't say that we will solve whatever problem that would arise or has risen, but you won't know that if we don't hear it. Do stop crying.'

Ifeoma looked at me and rolled her eyes heaven-wards. I ignored her.

It probably didn't have anything to do with my impassioned speech, but Erica after one final bout of heaving shoulders and loud blowing of her nose into the hem of her shirt started.

'My father killed our mother when I was young.'

Then she stopped. What kind of a thing is this? I looked at Ifeoma who was looking at me already to ascertain that she heard what I heard. Then I turned to Erica again, then at seeing my hand tangled with hers I snatched it off hers immediately like I was stung. What kind of a joke was that? Where did she get that from? I didn't get the chance to digress further, Erica continuing, said, 'and for your information I am an Igbo girl.'

Erica had told us she was from Kalabari and that is in Rivers State, but compared to what preceded it and had been floating before us it was no big deal.

'We are four of us siblings, three girls and a boy, who is the last, after me. We lived in our village with our mother, our father lived in Nnewi,' she turned to Ifeoma, 'your home town,' and Ifeoma nodded. 'My mother was a petty sub-sub-contractor; supplying sand, gravel, cement, stone, and anything that could be required in building sites. After the major contracting job had been awarded, the major contractors will sub-contract just a small bit out to relatives to help them make ends meet and said relatives in turn would sub-sub-contract it out yet to another needing relative. My mother sometimes would be required to supply one or two barrows of sand. So it wasn't anything substantial. But it was something.

'My father, who seemed to time it well, appeared without fail to collect the proceeds. Initially they used to fight about it because my mother felt cheated out of her income which she would have used to look after us properly. Especially when she claimed our father used her money to chase other women. Our father never listened to her arguments; he'd simply beat her to submission. But being a woman, she found a way. When she collected her pay, she'd skim off some before my father arrived for the weekend. And to be sure that he'd never find it, she hid it in our school bags.

'On that day my father, probably suspecting my mother's ploy, arrived early. He must have parked his car further away from our house because we did not hear him drive in.

When my mother at her return sighted him and so could not hide some of the money she flew into a rage. My father ignored her rage, plucked her handbag, took the whole money and turned to leave. As you may have guessed, this terrible fight followed. Before we knew what was happening my father had boxed her face so forcefully, to get her out of his way, that she fell hitting her head on our centre table. He hissed and went off while we crowded around her. Their fights were not new but my mother always got up to hold us all and cry, but this time she didn't and never did. She had died. The base of her skull had shattered on impact with the center table. We clustered around her and cried the whole night. The next morning my eldest sister, then fourteen, went and called my mother's brother, some distance away from our own village.' Erica stopped, her head bent down studying her hands like they belonged to somebody else. I looked at Ifeoma; tears were all over her face. Good.

Then Erica resumed but in a very low tone. But our ears were so stretched at this point that they could absorb any sound, no matter how muted.

'One of my mother's brothers took us with him to Onitsha, where he lived with his family, but a year later I ran away to PortHarcourt and was found by Sr. Christopher wandering the street. Did you know that when you are ordained a reverend sister, you are required to take a new name, but that of a man?' She looked at us for confirmation or not of her finding, but it was difficult to switch from the painful narration to the antics of the reverend sisters. But Ifeoma and I managed to look at each other with a frown before returning our gaze on Erica. Who I was forced to acknowledge must be on the edge of madness, if that was the sort of question she could come up with at this time. When we did not show any inclination to her reverend sister men-name game, she continued.

'Sr. Christopher took me with her to her cluster—The Sisters of Grace—who had a Convent on the outskirts of Port Harcourt city. After I had got over my shock and subsequent nightmares which took close to a year, I was fostered out to my current parents who later adopted me when I turned twelve. I had told Sr. Christopher, who became sort of a mother to me that I did not remember much about my past, but that all I knew was that fire had engulfed our house with my family in it. I did not know how I escaped or how I got to Port Harcourt or where I came from but that I had walked for weeks to get there. I was only ten then, you have to bear that in mind, so it was possible that I may have forgotten. Anyway she accepted my story, and made all the rest tiptoe around me. But they were good to me.' Erica stopped again, probably to recollect and savour the goodness of the reverend sisters. Then suddenly, 'Remember Peter? Whom you guys assumed was my now and then boyfriend?'

We didn't answer. We just stared; because she had floored us and we were still scrabbling about on the floor and therefore not too keen on raising our heads up: we didn't want more inflicted on them. But she answered regardless.

'Well, he is my younger brother.'

We nodded. I don't know of anybody that could say anything under our current situation to be able to pull us out of the moat of sadness that enveloped us, that had hedged us in together, squeezing life out of our emotion-laden hearts. So we didn't add to or subtract from the weighty revelation nor try to climb out of the dark moat rather we wallowed in it shamelessly until Ifeoma summoned enough courage to dispel the saturated dangerous atmospheric condition thus freeing us with her actions.

*   *   *

Erica's palaver had nipped my Obinna euphoria and reduced me to a hand-holding nurse. It was a horrendous thing to have happened to anybody, anybody at all. Such horror would live with you forever. Imagine having to wrap up such an incident to continue with life as if nothing had happened. Deep in the mush that was her revelation certain disquiet started settling on me. But Ifeoma stepped in because left to me I'd probably stay there holding Erica's hand, and told her, in not-to-be-argued-against voice that she should get ready to come to London one week from that day, when she'd come back for her and her two kids. She needed the one week to get an appointment with a psychiatrist or a therapist. Either of them would do.

I nodded, now its Erica's turn for Ifeoma's cure-all-remedy—counseling.

And she stayed with Erica! That is till her husband returned before she would check into a hotel, to leave for London, first thing in the morning.

Erica needed a support system, but Ifeoma should do for now. So I left. I needed to go; in any case, the minder I had hastily engaged for my kids would need to go.

I got home and thanked her for accepting to come at such short notice, and she left. Maybe I should listen and employ an au-pair as suggested by Ifeoma. Because bringing somebody from home was out of the question, the Irish termed it slavery, but in all honesty maybe we are a little over the top with our treatment of our househelps. They forgot that they were living in the land of rights and rules of law. Anyway . . . I sent my children to bed and while getting ready to go to bed myself reflected on the events of the day, life in general and the particular brand of life where a man would kill his wife in front of his children for money, no matter how inadvertent.

The next morning I got the children ready for school and dressed up myself, with the intention of nipping into Erica's on my way back. I felt remorseful for all the time I had kept her at arms length. But remorse wouldn't do her any good now, I had to fashion out a way to incorporate niceness and companionship into our future relationship, she needed all the camaraderie she could get.

Then I remembered Obinna's impending visit and was of two minds about what to do. Should I drop the children in school and risk being with this heart-throb alone or should I allow them to stay? We could all have a good day, thus affording me the opportunity to observe his take on my kids. Remembering my earlier vow that any relationship I embarked on would have to be inclusive of my children, I decided to let them stay. They did not have any other person but I in this foreign land and I was not about to abandon them like their father did for any man. So Obinna had to be for all or not at all. I resolutely made calls to my children's schools and excused them for the day.

I set to and spring-cleaned my already squeaky clean house. I was never tardy about house cleaning but I gave it a once over, in case, then set about doing wonders to my body with my yesterday purchases. When I finished, I stood before the mirror in my room to survey my effort; turning here and there, eventually I made a satisfied face at my image. I got into what I would consider a stay-at-home casual, but which I knew did wonders to my shape. I was a killer in the gear and was ready to face the world, again. Since there was no fixed time for Obinna's arrival, we had to cool our heels for God knows how long.

I called Erica instead: she might sniff out that something was cooking, even in this dark hour of hers, to know how she was doing and she told me, in a very heavy nasal tone, that because she had opened up a past she had slammed a door on long time ago, she did not know how she was feeling really. I told her to hold herself and I'd see her later. My request to speak with Ifeoma or her husband led to her informing me that Ifeoma had left already and that she, Erica, was not in the mood to be with her husband in the same room. That had me baffled and I said so. She laughed a hollow laugh and told me that her husband's presence irritated her at the moment and that's that.

'Erica, what do you want me to do for you now?'

'Nothing really, but you can pass by later in the evening. I want to be on my own for now.'

'Please Erica, don't be alone. It is not good.'

'Gift, don't make me laugh. If I am alone what would happen, kill myself?'

'Well you never know.'

'Don't be silly. If we all killed ourselves at every little problem that presented itself, there wouldn't be anybody remaining in that country of ours.'

'Please get your husband to be with you. You don't have to talk with him. Have you not heard of companionable silence?'

'This Gift *sef*,' Erica snorted before she added, 'Ok. See you in the evening.'

I rang off and breathed a sigh of relief; that was a close call.

When Obinna arrived at about 11 am, I thought that the time for his flight had been brought forward. But it was not, it was still at 6 pm. He wanted to spend more time with me, he had answered to my query. He would have arrived sooner, he told me, but he didn't want to wake us up!

'Mmmh.' I couldn't say more than that. I would just have to take it in, one chameleon-stride at a time. Then he handed me a bunch of flowers which he had hid behind him. White man to the core, this Obinna. But what did I expect? With him born and brought up abroad? I was bemused and at the same time awash with quivering feelings. This was something I was not used to.

Giving flowers was not part of my growing up culture, nor while I was living the life in Unilag and certainly not while in Italy. I conceded that on Valentines Days toasters deluged me with flowers in Unilag but somehow, there was nothing intimate about that, it was just fun to give and receive flowers. It made us *feel* superior at imitating a foreign custom, like you were now up in the world. But if there was any kind of feeling behind the flower-giving-gesture, it was lost on all of us.

This was a different time, and a different person and so the gesture was packed with emotions.

I took the flowers and smiled; that breathtaking smile that supposedly made my admirers weak in the knees, according to Ifeoma who had took on the job as guard to scare off my unwanted *toasters* back then in our university days.

'For me?' I murmured, putting my nose on the bloom, 'How nice of you.'

I had watched enough movies to react accordingly, but I did not have a vase to place the flowers in, it's not my regular thing, so I floundered before marching off to the kitchen to rummage.

*   *   *

It turned out to be a day that'd be etched in my mind forever. Obinna was easy to talk with, yet again, and to crown it all, he was not inquisitive. Gradually my natural self emerged and took hold of the situation. I regaled him with stories about my growing up years—being poor; about my village and about my first time in the city; living and studying in Onitsha Urban with my big sister Chinelo. About my parents; my best friends and my brother ThankGod. All the things that made me happy. My aim to be a Senator which was thwarted by my marriage. I skirted round that *tiny* subject of marriage and continued nonetheless. But Obinna noticed: a surreptitiously raised brow gave him away, but he said nothing, so I continued.

When there was a lull, Obinna kissed the back of Gift's hand to assure her that he was with her and not to worry unduly. He had noted her reluctance to talk about her marriage. He believed that if you were divorced from your spouse, there must be issues, but then he was not interested in those issues, at least not now. He kissed the back of her hand again for solidarity and encouragement.

Then it was Obinna's turn to regale me about his existence. And he didn't disappoint: starting from birth to date. For lunch I made jollof-rice which was heartily enjoyed by all. We strolled around the estate and the children were treated to sumptuous ice-creams. When we waved him off at the airport later that evening, an aching gap was instantly created in all our hearts, including Lucky's who started wailing; he didn't want Obinna to go.

'Mum, is uncle Obinna our daddy?' Frances piped out.

'No baby, he is not.'

'How come we don't have a daddy?'

Trust Frances to bring up awkward topics. Then it occurred to me that my children had never asked about their father before, not once, which was rather strange. And the way the ears of the other two had stretched out, like that of a fennec fox, betrayed the fact that it must have been a coup: planned amongst them but to be executed by Frances, the inquisitive one. Being the oldest, it was only right that she led the squad.

I thought through the question and decided that maybe it was time they were told that they had a daddy, like every other child. Nobody could be born without a daddy, even if the conception was concocted in a Petri dish!

Oh Osahon . . . What really went wrong for us? I wailed in my soul, remembering how being wrapped up with love felt, but it turned out not to be love on his part in any case. Or it was love, but Osahon was not equipped to handle the full scenario. Otherwise how could an expectation that something would go wrong, but had not happened, elicit such jealousy with devastating consequences?

*   *   *

'This woman, you're positively glowing! Tell me what the secret is?' Una whispered on Monday morning when I came to work after my one week off. I smiled from ear-ear before whispering back.

'Gist *dey*, just wait till lunch break.'

Una's patience was sorely tried, but she restrained it. On the dot, she came over to watch me put the final touches to my struggles to beat the deadline to submit a Credit Appraisal Memo I had been battling with since morning: with my mind weaving in and out of the office every other second to Obinna, it was quite a struggle. The customer was desperate for the loan and Alfie, my supervisor, who was all for the loan was puce with worry that I may not make it.

'Gift when am I getting your report for GRECO?' he had asked about a hundred times in a hushed voice. Finally I gave him a different response: 'Very soon,' and qualified the soon with, 'It's about ready, sir. I am after putting finishing touches on the spreadsheet.' And said in an affected Irish English and with a sweet voice.

The problem with the memo was that the company's audited account looked dodgy and I wanted to be sure of my facts before bringing it to Alfie's notice. He would not thank me for losing him this deal if I was wrong. So I had donned my looking-glasses and with a fine-tooth comb probed the account. And that had delayed my pacifying Una's gist-thirst. But she wouldn't settle down.

'Woman, you have to give me something,' Una hissed.

'Stop whispering girl, Alfie is not in the office,' I responded, but that was a mistake, Una would probe without mercy now.

'Fine. So what's the story?' Una's voice now restored to the usual volume, queried. But it wasn't much different to her whispering voice, anyway, she was that soft-spoken.

'A beau Una, a beau.'

'Get out of here!'

'But it's the truth girl.'

'What are you like this woman? You took one week off to deal with your ex-husband and came back with a beau? How did that happen?' she fired but with a huge grin splattered all over her face. She was happy for me. 'A healthy gossip is the spice of life you know? Give it to me neat,' she added in case I'd not deduced that yet.

'Which one do you want, the compressed or the convoluted version?'

'You know my choice, but . . .'

'No but, you gossip monger. We keep it for our lunch break.'

'Not even a pinch?'

'Alright just to put you in the right mood. He is a hunk, as they say.'

'Oh my word! Gift . . .' Una's face was a picture.

'Keep your shirt on Una, we haven't done it yet.'

Una visibly relaxed and then whispered, 'Thank God,' with such a relief in her voice that I couldn't help laughing.

'Una you can be such a prude sometimes.'

'I know this will sound old-fashioned but you would have died a romantic death if you had indulged so soon.'

'I know, Una. Rather unfortunate really, but he'll have to eat sand first before I'll let him smell my knickers.'

'Wouldn't that be rather too harsh?'

'We wait and see,' I pronounced before continuing with my work once more. Una took the cue and went back to her section. It was an open plan office, though, so she could still see me and each time our eyes locked she'd mouth, 'hurry up girl,' at me, and I in turn would mouth back, 'easy, girl. The gist is not going to run away.' Not hearing me well, she'd frown and I'd frown back.

'Yes! I've found it,' I announced gleefully, with relief. I was really getting bothered that I may have delayed my boss and our customer for nothing. Una got up and came over to me dragging her chair along.

'What did you see?'

'The bulk of their revenues were mostly on Debtor Account (Receivable) that is almost one year old. In certain kind of business, there'd be nothing wrong with that. But for GRECO it shouldn't be so, also their physical cashflow was not what it should be.'

'Which was why they needed a loan Gift,' Una pointed out.

'Yes, it seemed so at a glance. But they retail fast moving goods. Why are they not collecting as fast then?'

'Good question.'

'Bearing that in mind I worked backwards, because if you look at these figures, you'll notice that not only were they not collecting as fast as they sell, but they seem to remunerate their shareholders unnecessarily high.'

'In that case we should work out a programme for recovery and ask them to stick to it to free their cash instead of asking for a loan,' Una completed.

'Good woman yourself, as your people would say. So we elect you to tell our dear Alfie.'

'Thanks a million, but I'd rather not. You work directly under him, so do the honours,' Una retorted.

I hoped Alfie would thank me for being so diligent, while hoping that the GRECO guys would see what we saw. They looked rather a sharp bunch. Like the types that would hide their money in Cayman Island to avoid paying taxes.

I double-checked my findings, printed just one copy of the memo report and along with the company's Audited Account, and went to see my super. I knocked and at his bidding I went in.

Alfie wasn't a supervisor for nothing. He picked up on the default immediately and explained further implications to me. But I wasn't really paying attention, I was itching to get out, my gist was getting cold and I knew Una would have scratched herself raw by now with impatience.

Finally I was able to extricate myself and rejoin Una. We gathered our things and left for our spot in Café @ Sol on Hatch Street, to dissect Obinna piece by piece.

PART SIX

The farther I run away from the place where God dwells,
the less I am able to hear the voice that calls me the Beloved,
and the less I hear that voice, the more entangled I become
in the manipulations and the power games of the world

Henri Nouwen
The Return of the Prodigal Son

...Court Ruling

SMITHFIELD, DUBLIN
OCT. 2005

I studied Ms. Flynn, the social worker, with the tail of my eyes while wringing my hands, unable still to marshal my story to flow sequentially. The woman, to her credit, did not look ruffled or angry at my reticence despite having called on me three other times. Eventually after much squirming, I deduced that there was no need of beating about the bush; it's either now or never. So I took a measured breath in, let it out slowly, carefully, as if to not ruffle Ms. Flynn's blouse, and then in a gentle voice, I launched into the tale.

One hour later Ms. Flynn, seemingly holding her breath for the duration of the tale, let it out in one fast rush, breathed in and out, her nostrils quivering at the rushed job, before turning to stare deeply into my eyes like she was seeking for the truth. I stared back steadily, calling up my long-ago staring skill acquired when staring contest became our favourite pastime as children.

Even as I had trivialized the narrative to make it palatable, I knew why Ms. Flynn's unwavering gaze was on me: probably to see if she could make head or tail of this bizarre tale and to determine who was telling the truth, I or Osahon.

I must concede that listening to my voice dispassionately reeling out the story sounded unreal, weird even. How much more fantastic could it sound to a third party? Even Osahon did not know the whole story. His part in the saga was as a king seated on his throne eating from the sweat of his subject, me.

Finally, Ms. Flynn smiled, briefly, before relinquishing Gift's eyes. Who was telling the truth here? In her line of duty she had heard and seen many things bordering from the mundane to the bizarre but this, she must admit, took the biscuit. She sighed inwardly before voicing her thoughts as questions.

'Ms Ofoedu, are you sure? Are you sure these things happened? All that you have told me did they happen, truly?'

Going by Ms. Flynn's demeanor, I surmised that she must have gleaned some elements of truth from my narration, even though her tone was laced with uncertainty.

'But of course, Ms. Flynn. Could anybody make such things up?'

'I have to ask because this is a total departure from your earlier responses. And, as you are very much aware, they are extremely contradictory to your husband's version of events too. Having lied under oath once in court, the veracity of your claim must be thoroughly pursued. What would you have me believe?'

'It was unfortunate I started on the wrong foot in the court, but I have realized that two wrongs do not make a right. So I am sorry for my lies and I apologize for them whole-heartedly. It will not happen again. This time I am telling the truth.'

'If all you have told me is true, then we have to go through the story one more time. Please take your time and think about what you are telling me. Any element of untruth must be weeded out. Be specific with dates, phone numbers, pictures, if available, names of any person or persons whom we could speak with, to corroborate your claims. We have to be sure of our facts, before we take any further steps with the case.'

I nodded while hunched over miserably, not willing to look at Ms. Flynn's eyes again. Narrating the whole saga seemed to not only have sapped my strength but also to have brought back the old memories. And now to have to remember every detail that could help was not appealing. But I had to do what I had to do with the hope that some profit would come out of it as I was really tired of Osahon-related problems resurfacing to torment my life. Ms. Flynn seeing my miserable face, when I raised it up finally frowned. 'Gift, are you alright? Are you sure you're ready for this?'

'I don't know anymore, I really do not know. I am starting to feel overwhelmed again.'

'I know, it may seem a bit hard on you at the moment but it will become easier with time. Besides, you must consider what will be the best for you and your children.'

I nodded. She was right.

'I will get you all the information you need; it may take a little while to organize.'

It was Ms. Flynn's turn to nod before she spoke.

'I'll start my investigations right away and call me as soon as you have some concrete information for me. However, I may call on you from time to time if I need to, to re-clarify your husband's claims in light of this new but contrary information.'

'That is alright with me,' I responded and so with Ms. Flynn's prompting I re-narrated the tale from the beginning to the end but in a subdued tone.

Another hour passed before Ms. Flynn was satisfied, her demeanor triumphant as she prepared to leave, gathering her things. She extended her hand for a shake as she got up. I got up myself, grasped the extended hand in a fierce handshake, as if my life-line was etched somewhere there. Ms. Flynn winced and looked pointedly at me before nodding at our clasped hands. Embarrassed at my over-enthusiastic handshake, I smiled in apology and released her hand. The combination of tension and relief must have stiffened my fingers!

'I will leave now to get on with my investigation. Do remember to keep your contact with your husband as minimal as possible. I do not need to remind you that there are highly volatile and contentious issues at stake now which, if not properly handled may constitute potential violence. So be careful of where you go and who you go with.'

I nodded. Then she scribbled something on a piece of paper and handed it to me.

'That is my direct line in the office, my house number and mobile. If you notice any slightest thing out of sync, anything at all, call me, OK?'

I nodded again.

'Be careful and make sure you look after yourself and your children.'

I nodded yet again.

Ms. Flynn nodded too, then, as if it was an afterthought added, 'and good luck.' Still drained from retelling the story and from the mention of violence I could only continue to nod at Ms. Flynn's words. I escorted her out and stood there to wave her off.

When I came back to my living room, I sat down and mulled over Ms. Flynn's words. I tried to shake off the cloak of fear which her words had inadvertently evoked by way of rationalizing it objectively: Osahon had taken me to court to plead his case and as far as he was concerned, he had me cornered and was expecting to win hands-down. After all was said and done, the long and short of it was that Lucky was his son. But if he failed, as I was hoping that he would, could he turn violent? I had seen firsthand what he could do when thwarted, like when I went against his will and left my job as a prostitute. But what could he do if he failed in his bid this time? Could he unleash violence on me again? No answer came immediately to mind.

*   *   *

My initial instinct, after Ms. Flynn's departure, was to call Obinna with the hope that the soothing effect of his voice would infuse some verve in me, but I changed my mind and decided to wait till our nightly call. I was too disconcerted now and he might sense it in my voice, and since I was not about to reveal that kind of stuff to him, I may well let him be. But my mind was still in turmoil, I couldn't settle. Finally I decided to ring Ifeoma to arrange for a short stay with my children at her place after the hearing—to allow things to simmer down. There's nothing to be gained from tempting fate.

Having made that decision, I became reasonably calmed, feeling the oppressive cloak of fear slightly lift from my shoulders as my contingent plan took root in my mind. I could practically see the proverbial light at the end of the tunnel getting close.

'And not too soon too,' I murmured.

I was surprised, however, to take a call some minutes later and it was Obinna. Though his deep massaging voice floating down the line was calming, somewhat restoring my sense of well-being and security, I was still a bit nervous.

'I had to speak to you, babes. I couldn't wait till tonight,' Obinna murmured but, at my response I could feel my nervousness in my voice and he picked up on it immediately.

'Gift?'

'I am alright Bino, or rather, it's nothing I can't handle.' I had used my pet name for him to make him relax, but obviously it didn't work, judging by his next words.

'I think you should tell me what is wrong or I will be in Dublin by morning and please don't make me do that, you know how busy I am right now.' I smiled, a knight in shining armour? How quaint.

'I am fine and everything is alright, really,' I pacified, but as I prepared to launch into some story that would make him believe me an involuntary sigh escaped my lips and I stopped. 'Obinna it's my past life threatening to overwhelm me again, but honestly everything is under control, we are fine. In fact maybe by the time we see again it will be over.'

'How can you be sure?'

He paused, but I didn't say anything. Afterall I wasn't sure and I didn't want to reassure him too much. It'd raise his protective hackles which would bring him to Dublin quicker.

'Has something gone wrong with the case? I thought you said that everything was under control. I know I have not really paid attention to that part of your life but it was for a reason so if there is something wrong let me know now. I . . .'

'Oh Obinna you can never know how much I miss you. How much I miss being with you, being held in your arms but . . .' I stopped, for I was yet to get over the fact that I could speak out my feelings freely. My relationship with Osahon didn't involve much talk in that direction, not from me anyway. But with Obinna it was different, his was more physical. He didn't mind holding my hand in public or dropping a kiss on my hair, forehead, ears, lips, anytime anywhere or stopping even to envelope me in his strong arms in a warm embrace. He had made me tactile and more expressive of my feelings too.

'It is Ok really,' I continued, 'it is not something that'll make you come all the way to Dublin, not now anyway,' I amended. Obinna kept quiet, then asked, 'So what exactly is the problem?'

Hearing the depth of his feelings, transmitted through the line, I had to tell him.

'I finally opened up and told the court appointed social worker what I endured while married to Osahon and she was of the opinion that it may alter the direction of the case, probably in my favour.' I stopped. He was so quiet that I thought the connection had cut us off, 'Obii are you still there?' I asked, rattling the handset. Nothing from the other end but I held on.

When he spoke, I became alert immediately. He had not previously shown any interest in what transpired in my marriage—exhibiting what I had referred to as his white man's *I don't want to pry* attitude.

Initially, his I-don't-care-attitude had worried me: shouldn't he want to know? But later I assured myself that it was for the best. If he had started to pry, a lot of un-revealable things may come to light and I didn't want that. So I had got used to that. Now he was playing a different tune and I was unable to sing along because it was not scripted. His question refocused me and I pulled my thoughts back to the present.

'So what did you endure in your marriage?'

Silence.

'Gift.'

'Yes.'

'What happened?'

'Nothing much really.'

'Nothing much really could not alter the direction of a case Gift.'

'Well, a lot but . . .'

'What did he do to you? Was he cheating on you or something?'

This Obinna *sef* with his *oyibo* mentality. Since when did the cheating of a husband become a divorce issue?

'Worse than that.'

Silence.

Then.

'What did he do, Gift? Tell me.'

'He was abusive and violent.'

I heard a sharp intake of breath, but he said nothing. This was getting out of hand. Why was Obinna asking these questions now? Did he hear anything? Did he encounter somebody who made him want to know? What now? When he finally spoke I could feel the pain in his voice bleeding through my ear to my heart. How could anybody feel another's pain this deep?

'Please tell me everything now; what did he do to you?'

'I am sorry Bino, but I really do not feel like talking about it any more.'

'But you told the bloody social worker.'

I shrank back at the vehemence in his voice and the swearing. Obinna was so well-mannered, that things like swearing seemed beneath him. He must be highly incensed to have degenerated to that and rightly so. We had known each other for some time now yet I still acted skittish when it came to Osahon issue.

And that made me take stock. My goodness! Was it only two months since meeting Obinna? I could have sworn it was longer. I had been so enveloped in the aura of love radiating from him that I had not realized how short the duration of our relationship was; with him always on the phone, had even flown out thrice to see us since, so looking back really in love terms we've known each other long enough, but in real-life terms not long enough for him to know everything. But the closeness that had developed between us was incredible, so incredible that I felt he had actually earned the right to know. I could not imagine life without him. It was like we were meant to be with each other forever and we hadn't even made love! It had worried me that he wasn't pushing for sex, but I had also come to accept that it'd happen at its due time, because the electricity charging between the two of us had to be assuaged one day. His living far away in Austria helped. I stopped; I had to respond because he seemed to be waiting for an answer.

'The bloody social worker is not my boyfriend, Obinna, and can we please give it a rest? I promised to give you the chapters and verses of everything about my life before now but it must be when I feel the time is right.'

'And when will that be?'

'Is this some kind of inquisition?'

'No.'

'Good. Please ease up, you're not helping matters.' I could hear his sigh. But really, I could tell him nothing at this stage. Sensing his dejection I soft-pedaled. 'Bino, please don't take it to heart. When the whole palaver is over and done with, you'll know everything.'

'Mmmh,' was his only reply. I felt his unhappiness and swiftly I moved to reassure him further. 'What do you say to our visit to your place after it is over, maybe for the Easter holidays? The social worker felt that it'd be best if we keep a low profile, if we win the case, that is. She is of the opinion that he may turn violent.'

'Turn violent! What are telling me Gift? Maybe I should take that trip down to Dublin afterall. You are beginning to really freak me out.'

'Babes, it's still more than two months away.'

'I know, but what if he decides to come round to the house anyway? You don't know what will happen. I think I will come down so that we can arrange where you and the kids will move to, a safe place, you do not have to wait till after the case.'

'I don't know whether he will or not, but I want to bet that he won't come because right now he thinks he is going to win. I don't see him doing anything to jeopardize that position.'

Obinna nodded, acknowledging that she's right. Then he remembered that he'd be away to the US around March which would coincide with the time, but decided not to pursue the argument further as he had noticed that Gift tended to get more stubborn if she felt hedged. He'd find a way.

'I am sorry baby, but I will be away to the US by then. We are having a party to mark our parents' 50th wedding anniversary. I have been meaning to invite you and the kids to go with me, now is as good as any time. What do you say?'

'Can you imagine your family's reaction to me and the kids? I will not dream of spoiling what is obviously a family affair. No thanks, Obinna, I won't risk it.'

'Gift.'

'You know I have a point.'

'OK. I think I will come down to Dublin next week. We can discuss this security situation properly then.'

'Don't worry about that, I should be able to sort something out, or well . . . OK no problem, we can discuss that when you come down then as well as our trip to your end.'

'Are you sure?'

'Yes. We may stay for over a week.'

'Right. I will be glad to have you guys forever.'

'Don't be hasty with words, Obinna.'

'Gift, have you ever thought of what you have come to mean to me? The depth of my feelings for you?'

'Oh Obinna . . . but please . . . don't go there yet,' I pleaded; 'let's just take it one step at a time ok?'

Obinna did not say anything anymore and I kept quiet too.

'Babes, I will speak with you before you go to bed. Be careful alright?' He finally murmured managing to bestow a sense of mixed guilt and sadness on me.

'I will. Talk to you later. Then I hastened to add, 'I care about you, you know? More than you'd ever believe.' But he didn't respond.

I could understand where Obinna was coming from: he had been doing everything within his power to move the relationship to the next level, whatever that is, but I was content for it to remain on the current level and couldn't envisage what the next level would be, or rather I chose not to. But first things first, I had to untangle myself from Osahon.

However, I decided that from now, I'd start showing Obinna how much I really cared about him too, that'd help to reassure him that he was treasured. I sat near the phone staring into space wondering what the future held, after he rang off.

*   *   *

Resignedly, I called Ifeoma who congratulated me on my decision to unburden myself, this with the belief that my finding the courage to face reality and live life again would help to locate me on the route to true healing. She then advised that I must try and go for counseling as well: to nail the process perfectly. She crowed triumphantly like she had single-handedly shepherded me towards the ultimate goal of healing. This, in a way, could not be far from the truth. She had continuously pushed for me to speak up and unburden my soul. I thanked her from the bottom of my heart for being faithful to our friendship, standing firmly with me during my highs and lows, without judging. Ifeoma accepted all the thanks without any shame and warned me to stick to the footpath, as it seemed to be a better route and had served me well until I veered into the express road. We both laughed.

Then I intimated her of Ms. Flynn's fears.

'I don't think he will try anything stupid, but if it'd make you feel any better come over to my place for a while though you guys will have to be on your own. I'll be away in the States visiting my sister and to attend a family function.'

Everybody seemed to be hopping off to the US all of a sudden, I thought before responding, 'I'll let you know of my decision then, but not to worry, Fifi, everything will turn out alright, I hope.'

'Anyway, you have my keys, whatever you decide.'

'Safe journey. I will keep you appraised.'

And we rang off.

I felt uneasy which was increasingly bordering on agitation: Obinna's reaction had unsettled me. Look at me hoping to lift my drooping spirit by talking with him earlier, instead he lowered it even further.

I called ThankGod who was the only person in the world that knew, in great details, the extent of my relationship with Obinna and told him of my intentions. Ifeoma knew about a beau, but didn't take it serious and therefore did not ask me anything except what I chose to tell her, which was practically nothing.

ThankGod's advice was not something I did not know already: our men were not known to be adventurous when it came to marriage, he said, but since Obinna was still talking to me, after being aware of my status then I should give it a chance. He also assured me that the idea of telling him about my past life when the court case was over was OK but that I should bear in mind that it might kill the relationship, and as such to be prepared and try not to hurt too much if it disintegrated.

I pondered my brother's words, wondering about how one arranges not to hurt too much, but didn't wonder for long, what was there to wonder about really? One did not control such things.

I rang my parents afterwards. Things were speeding up alarmingly, it was about time they were informed that Osahon had located us. Though in the eyes of tradition Osahon was no longer married to me, our family having returned the 24 Naira he paid on my head as bride-price, he was still the father of my children and could appear whenever he was ready. It's important that my parents were made aware and now seemed like the appropriate time.

When the phone clicked initially, I did not hear anything, then these rattling noises came on and I smiled, my father must be catching his breath from climbing. But I thought they had told me that they did not need to do that anymore because mobile phone and it's connectivity was now like pure water—all over the place, now.

'Papa good afternoon, it is me Gift.'

'*Ewoh*, Gift my pikin! *Eeh*. How are you and my children?'

'Papa we are fine. What of Mama?'

'Your mother is here with me. She's fine. Are you people living well in that country?' This was always the next question, as if something must be amiss.

'Yes papa. But . . . the only thing papa is that . . . Osahon is here.'

'*Chineke napu ekwensu ike!* God should take away power from Satan! *Gift, isi gini?* What did you say? My pikin, what are you doing inviting that man to your house again? What he did to you before was it not enough, is that it?'

My father should know better than that, I thought, before responding,

'Papa I did not invite him and I don't know who did or how he found us. Anyway we are going to court here which is why I am calling.'

'Court? What court is that? Didn't you tell them that we have returned the bride-price?' I could hear my mother's voice from the background agitating to speak, as well as feeding my father with the right questions. After a considerable length of time, during which I had answered all their questions to their satisfaction, my father advised me to keep my head down and remain focused while my mother, on the other hand, advised me to book a Novena to St. Anthony immediately—the saint for hopeless cases—and that she'd do same too. I consented. There was no need of telling her that it was not likely that any saint in the church would be willing to take up my case.

My big sister Chinelo, when I told her about the court case kept invoking the Holy Spirit to take absolute control and fight Osahon for us.

I rang ThankGod back and on further discussions, he mentioned that Osahon's misfortune was only the beginning and that the next step would culminate in his total downfall and final annihilation. This evoked a foreboding feeling instantly putting me on high alert.

'ThankGod did you have a hand in Osahon's troubles? Please tell me that you did not.'

ThankGod calmly assured me that he did not do anything while advising me to do what I needed to do to win the case and not worry myself unnecessarily. ThankGod's calmness reminded me that I should not have even asked him such a silly question. ThankGod might have been stubborn and all that in our growing up years but not anymore. Now he was so matured, good-natured and God-fearing. I doubt that he'd soil his person by exacting vengeance, Osahon or not.

I asked after his family and after other chitchats we rang off.

Obinna

Ringing off, Obinna sat down to think. What was it about this woman that had lodged itself in his heart and refused to be dislodged? For all intents and purposes she'd be the last woman to qualify as an eligible contender for his hand in love. On her own, she stood a hundred percent chance: with such an endearing personality, good disposition and a kind heart, not counting her beautiful face and delectable figure and good sense of humour. But then factor in her baggage, there you begin to have doubts. But he was willing to risk it. He had a feeling that she'd be worth it. To speed things up and to mellow the chick, he had reactivated and brushed his love-letter writing skill, used during his secondary school days to soften chicks before he ate them, and wrote to her twice a week, not counting the phone calls where he whispered sweet-nothings to her nightly. He sent well-thought out gifts; perfumes, flowers, chocolates, concert tickets, lingerie, clothings for her kids, shoes, and all whatnot, all the time yet . . . She had remained elusive. And it wasn't the classic desire-because-he-has-not-*done*-it thing; he was really in love for the first time in his life. True love, if there's anything like that.

Then his thought, unbidden, veered to her so-called ex-husband and he stood up and kicked the couch, resisting punching the wall as he jammed his knuckles into his pockets. He then moved to and opened the French windows facing his back garden. The open windows yielded to the vista of the twin-peak hills overshadowing his property, this usually settled his nerves. But, after standing there for close to ten minutes, the magic didn't happen. He stepped out completely; maybe the air would do it, and walked the grounds. When he got to the edge of the stream that traversed his property he sat down on a tree stump to chew the problem.

What could that man possibly have done to her to turn her off men? He had watched her closely and had come to feel this aura of reticence about her, especially whenever he had tried to get more intimate with her—not the full thing mind you. Was it just him or was she like that with other men? He was not only jealous of her ex-husband but hated him as well for whatever he did to her. The woman he loved and was going to marry. He stopped.

Wow! When did he decide to marry her? He got up and stretched, as he looked round the surrounding forest. He stood before the shimmering lake and reviewed this sudden revelation; this innate desire that had just surfaced. He had never desired to marry anybody before now, but . . .

He chuckled at what his family's reaction would be. The baby of the family, the skirt-chaser has been hooked and by a divorcee with three children no less! His immediate elder brother would tell him that he never did anything in small measures and therefore did not expect any less from him. But three children?

Man, should you not rethink that very well? he'd ask. But the general consensus would be to go ahead if he was sure of his heart and hers. Her heart? Did he have her heart? What was happening to him? He scratched his head lost for answers before he was overcome by unexplainable emotions. He moved away from the water to sit on a stone bench and continued in thought. From the little snippets she had offered, like now, he got the feeling that she must have endured a kind of torture during her marriage. But what exactly? What do men do to their wives after love has flown or even with love flowing all over the place? Would she ever thaw enough to love him back, even if not as much as he loved her? Could anybody imagine loving somebody, wanting to marry that person without being sure of her love for you? Crazy!

Should he force her to tell him what really transpired during that marriage of hers? But how would that help his case of winning her completely for himself? It wouldn't. He'd be better off offering his support as best he could instead of antagonizing her. When everything was over they'd have time to build their relationship and life. He didn't acquire the reputation as lover boy in his he-days for nothing. He'd love and nurture her back. He'd ensure that she would never hurt again, ever. This resolve comforted him and reinforced his purpose.

He'd tell his parents during his visit home. Or should he wait till after they had visited him in Austria? No. Better to tell them and then propose to her during the visit. That lightened his spirit. He got up and strolled back to the house whistling as he edged his way to the drink cabinet. He got himself a cognac, sat down and mulled his options as he sipped the drink. He'd seek his cousin's opinion when he saw her in America on how to wear-down a resistant woman. He was not used to not getting his way but he'd be willing to learn new ideas . . . Better still he'd ask his mum.

Brilliant. His drooping spirit lifted further and he realized that he was hungry. With the house intercom, he summoned his housekeeper who lived in the guest chalet behind with her husband, to have her prepare something for him and a guest. He then called Andrew, his close friend, who agreed to join him later for the dinner. He felt relieved somewhat and a male company would aid to lift his spirits further, now that a solution, a way forward, however remote, had presented itself.

Finally, the D-day arrived and I came early to court, alone, and settled in a comfortable corner to observe events, well assured that my lawyer would get me victory. Osahon came in and sat well away from me, but I was still able to see him well so I stared steadily at him from across the room and wondered how he was going to start all over again, seeing that his bid would fail. He never liked being poor. How was he going to cope? *Why don't you take him home with you? That would solve his problems surely!* I smiled. If I should backtrack now, call the whole thing off and make up with him, what would people say? That I'd need to have my head examined for loose nuts definitely. But I knew that I did not need people like Osahon in my life, in the life of my children, and that nothing would ever make me do any such thing as backtrack.

The court orderly's c-o-u-r-t re-focused my attention as the judge took his seat. The court registrar read out the cases to be dealt with and Iguedia vs. Ofoedu was third on the list. Those not directly connected to the first two cases shuffled outside to await their turn.

I sat outside as conversations swirled, from others also waiting outside like me, past my ears, from which I gleaned the various reasons of dispute that had brought them to court as well as for others who had been or were yet to come to court for dissolution of their marriages. I thought about what they were saying and it saddened me. Very soon the court would dissolve the marriages and they'd become statistics as I'd soon be and life goes on. Nobody really knew how bitter and sad you'd be after divorcing your husband/wife, but

I guess it must be dependent on what went wrong with the marriage and who most wanted it dissolved. But nobody got married to have it dissolved surely? No sane person prepares to fail. But it was baffling to me that not being in love anymore or even infidelity, all grouped under 'irreconcilable differences' were enough grounds for divorce.

Where I came from it was not so—not for the women anyway except where you were thrown out. A mere affair by one's husband would not be grounds enough to leave your matrimonial home, especially when you were aware that traditionally your husband could marry more than one woman, if he desired. What would be your purpose for leaving him then? So that another woman would reap the fruit of your labour? Bring up your children? Or to be branded 'a loose' woman thereafter and then your fellow women, friends and foe, would no longer be comfortable with your presence in their home for fear that you'd snatch their husbands? I eyed Osahon nastily.

But was that what or how marriage should be? A one-sided power, wielded mostly by men? *Gift live with what you know, don't go sniffing at what you don't know. Your parents had a happy marriage and are still at it. In fact how many divorcees do you know? Don't let what happened to you becloud your sense of judgment.* My lawyer's tap on my shoulder nipped the train and wiped my thoughts clean as I got up and I followed him back into the courtroom, it was our turn now.

*   *   *

'In view of new information in our possession, we'll have to start afresh. We will not, however, need the counsels to re-present their clients' cases, rather I will have them re-cross-examine the applicant and the defendant. It seems there are great departures and inconsistencies which we will seek to resolve.'

The judge looked at Osahon and his lawyer before he continued.

'Counselor O'Donoghue, may we start with your client please. I want you to re-establish his case through questioning before we move to the defendant.'

I watched as Osahon strolled firmly to the witness stand. He had not stopped using his imposing figure to the limit, I observed. Well he had better hold on to his pride now, because he was about to lose it and not soon enough.

He raised his hand and was sworn in accordingly before he sat down dwarfing the witness box. I had followed his hand up and then down, then his eyes, his lips, his shoulders and finally his chest, with my eyes. That hand used to wreak wonders on my body; I mused then shook my head to rid it of such distracting nonsense. Succeeding, I continued to look at him, but this time dispassionately. I never dreamt that I'd ever be free of him physically, emotionally and psychologically, but then I had never tried until I had to.

Mr. O'Donoghue of the throat-clearing fame stood up and bowed to the Judge before turning to face Osahon on the stand to instruct him accordingly.

Barrister O'Donoghue: 'Please state your name and address in full and be concise with your answers.'

Osahon nodded and in a rich baritone gave his answers succinctly. Mr. O'Donoghue then gradually led him through his application starting from the day he met his wife, through to their marriage and ended with their decision for her to travel to Ireland and to send for him afterwards which never materialized. When they finished, the judge sought to know why they still presented their old case in view of the current gross differences.

Mr. O'Donoghue responded that his client did not put much stock on his wife's new evidence, did not read or even listen to it, insisting that his was the correct representation of facts. The truth, he said, will prevail, and he adamantly refused for us to apply for extension.

'So how do you plan to proceed?'

'As I said, it is my client's position that it is all false.'

'Even without knowing what the new defence contained?'

'Yes, Your Honour.'

The judge nodded and peered at me.

'Ms. Ofoedu would you be able to take the witness stand today?'

I nodded because my voice had closed up, but no matter, when the time comes, I'd shame the devil. My life and the life of my children depended on my ability to stand firm and face Osahon on equal playing ground. I'd keep a straight face; avoid any eye-contact with anybody. This is not the kind of story you tell looking into people's eyes. If I need to look at anything, I will look up to the ceiling. I am all alone, no friends, no family, only foes surrounded me but I'd do my best. But my solicitor, Mr. O'Brien, would cross-examine Osahon first in any case; the outcome of that encounter should buoy me.

Mr. O'Brien, my solicitor, stood up, bowed towards the Judge, shuffled some papers before him, and then reminded Osahon that he was still under oath and to stick to the facts in his answers. Osahon nodded his consent. My solicitor then cleared his throat and fired the first salvo.

Mr. O'Brien: 'Where did you procure the certificates that purported to your civil marriage and church wedding?'

Osahon: 'Don't tell me that you swallowed any single word she uttered. How could you? Are you saying that I forged the certificates? Have you ever heard such a thing before? Because me, I've never.'

Mr. O'Brien: 'Please answer the question.'

Osahon: 'Look lawyer, you were not here during the last court session, so let me tell you that she had been found to be full of lies.'

I looked at Mr. O'Brien who looked up mildly at Osahon, like he was not exasperated with his roundabout way of answering his questions, then he shuffled the documents before him one more time as if to look for the one with the right questions that'd get the ball rolling, as it seemed he was not getting through to Osahon. He found what he was looking for and moved out of his former position to get closer to Osahon.

Mr. O'Brien: 'Did you marry your wife in the court registry followed by a church wedding according to your certificates?'

Osahon: 'Didn't it say so in those documents?'

Mr. O'Brien nodded then said: 'But your parents, Eric and Ivene Iguedia, your wife's parents, Abraham and Celina Ofoedu, and your wife's friends, Ifeoma Iwuije and Faith Ofoedu nee Okereke, all confirmed to me during our telephone conversations and later forwarded sworn affidavits, that you only did the knocking on the door, which is the marriage introduction, and paid the bride price of N24. That even the traditional wine-carrying ceremony, which is the traditional wedding, was not performed. I am not saying here that your marriage was not legal. Far from it. You were married according to the local law and custom by your payment of the said N24. However, I was told that one is not issued with a marriage certificate when you do that. And the aforementioned people, who included your own parents, confirmed to me that no such document existed or should exist. Even the N24 bride-price that sealed the marriage had been returned to your family by the Ofoedu family signifying the end of the marriage. The question is . . .'

Osahon: 'So what?'

This time the judge strongly reprimanded Osahon to answer the questions. I preened.

Mr. O'Brien: 'So what is where did you get your certificates from? Are they real?'

Osahon (mumbling): 'No.'

Mr. O'Brien: 'Good. As you have now admitted, the documents are forged?'

Osahon: 'Yes.'

Mr. O'Brien: 'Your claim was that you agreed with your wife to come to Ireland to have your third child and then send for you when she had secured her residency status?'

Osahon (mumbling again): 'It is not a claim. It is the truth.'

Mr. O'Brien: 'I want you to tell us how that agreement was reached.'

Osahon (hissing): 'Suit yourself.'

The judge shook his head while my solicitor, as if Osahon had not spoken continued.

Mr. O'Brien: 'Mr. Iguedia did you agree with your wife for her to come to Ireland?'

Osahon: 'No.'

Mr. O'Brien: 'I thought not. Let us discuss your business arrangement with your wife leading to her working in Italy for fifteen months.'

Osahon: 'Don't tell me that you believed that shit?'

Then he turned to stare at me stunned. I did not blame him. It was not a tale anybody would willingly tell about oneself in public. And I guessed that he did not expect me to ever soil myself so. The rest of the audience—the judge, his solicitor and the social worker—was frozen, staring first at me then at him. They were not even privy to the full gist yet and they were stunned. They should wait for the can of worms to be opened. Bleakly I looked on ahead steadily. The shit was going to hit the fan very soon and I had better be prepared. The judge then raised his hand for my lawyer to stop speaking, he removed his glasses and stared at Osahon very hard before he spoke; 'Young man do not give me any reason to throw you out of this court, you must learn to behave yourself.'

Mr. O'Brien: 'Mr. Iguedia, I do not think you are in a position to tell us what to believe or not.'

Osahon's face tightened while looking around wildly.

I continued to watch him.

He must have realized by now that his game was up, if the massive scowl on his face was to be relied on. His optimism that the shame of exposure would keep me from talking had made him less prepared. Knowing him he'd be itching to get his fingers round my throat! *Too bad Osahon: that was then, this is now,* I jeered in my mind while staring at his tightly pursed lips.

Mr. O'Brien's voice brought everybody back to the courtroom.

Mr. O'Brien: 'On mutual consent between you and your wife, your wife went to work in Italy as a prostitute, but you failed to honour your part of the agreement. Instead you threw your two children from her out, married another woman and when she came back against your wish, you beat her up, raped her and threw her out too, with the express instruction to never show her face where you'd see it or she'd be dead. Tell me on what basis were you asking for a Residency Status . . .' He stopped, looked round to make sure we all heard the question before he finally intoned.

Mr. O'Brien: 'I have no further question your honour.'

The gasp in the courtroom resonated in my ears and head but I refused to look at anybody and the court clerk's c-o-u-r-t saw me emerging from the courtroom with the rest of them for recess. I slunk away and went and hid in the ladies toilet till the break was over and furtively sneaked in and took my seat again when the court reconvened at 2 pm. It was time for the solicitors to present their summary.

All through the recess, Osahon's solicitor scuttled about; previously secure in the knowledge that they had the case bagged, he did not seek to clarify his client's claims of holding all the aces, until the social worker's report landed on his desk on Friday the 2nd of March, with the hearing coming up on Monday the 5th. His client could not be reached. When he collared him this morning he refused to even glance at the documents or listen to him about his intention to request for adjournment to enable them to study the new evidence. He knew that this case had been shot to hell, so when he stood up for his summation, he made sure to exonerate himself first.

The judge didn't look too impressed with him, noting that they had had the chance to work with the social worker all this time. This was a feuding husband and wife; they should expect exaggerations and though they were from a different culture, human emotions invariably are the same all over the world.

Osahon stared at his lawyer in shock, *what is this man doing?* Then he shouted at him, 'God punish your mouth there. Stupid man.'

He was reprimanded by the judge again.

After the outburst and the attendant commotion had settled down it was our turn and my solicitor stood up. Eloquently, he delivered a short but crisp summation.

'What Mr. Iguedia did to his wife was incomprehensible, but as if that was not enough, when he ran short of money again, he came running back looking to extract some more, and as was his nature, in the most odious way. He craftily planned to not only worm his way into Ms. Ofoedu's life and affection, but also to secure his Residency Status and as much money as he could get, then run off again to live with his second family.

'Your honour, he abandoned his two daughters at his in-laws the very first day he returned from Italy and has never asked for nor seen them since. He not only sold his wife into sex-slavery, he wanted her to remain there permanently making money for him. When she dared to come back, against his wishes, he beat her up, raped her and threw her out warning her to keep away or die. He did away with his family at the drop of a hat. Where is the guarantee that he would not sell those children to the next sex-fiend if the money was right?! Your Honour Mr. Iguedia should not be allowed to hinge the request for his Residency Status on such a despicable act.'

Osahon got up forcefully, but the force of anger emanating from the judge's eyes on him forced him to sit back down.

My whole system locked up immediately with fear. Is he going to beat up the lawyer too? Did he not know that he'd go to jail for assault in this country? God please let him just carry his *wahala* and go. Don't let him do anything that would delay his leaving this country. I was relieved when he sat down again. However, it seemed that he was not cowed enough because he got back up and started speaking.

'I don't know what this man is talking about, your Majesty!' Osahon shouted. This drew a smattering of laughter, causing Osahon to glare around, askance, before continuing, 'That child belongs to me. I want what is rightfully mine. Given to me by God himself. That's all I know.' Four uniformed court orderlies materialized from nowhere and surrounded Osahon, pinning him down. He slumped back on his seat looking dazed. The judge peered at him from the top of his glasses, probably to make sure that he was sane. Then he shook his head, ever so imperceptibly, and nodded to Mr. O'Brien to continue. Mr. O'Brien stood up again and told the court that he had finished and sat back down.

The sum of the judge's ruling was as follows: 'This marriage has been previously dissolved by the return of the paid N24 confirmed by both sets of parents and so remains dissolved. Mr. Iguedia you may be the father of Ms. Ofoedu's children and therefore automatically entitled to the Residency Status as a non-national parent of Irish Citizen Children to provide a conducive and positive environment for children to thrive in, but in this instance I will deny you that right and this is why: You, Mr. Iguedia, are a violent man with a dubious character attested to by the facts of this case which also afforded us a glimpse into the nature of the relationship you had with your ex-wife; the atrocities you committed against her; the fact that you abandoned your first two children and the violent nature of the conception of the third, the said Irish Citizen Child, makes it clear that a conducive and positive environment would never be present. You were a vile and violent man and your mere presence in the State may constitute a danger to the peaceful existence of your erstwhile family. In light of these facts, the court will not grant you the relief which you sought.'

My gaze, trained on Osahon, was unwavering. I felt a faint tug somewhere in the recesses of my heart and I wanted to stretch my hand to smoothen out the knots on his rigid neck. But I realized that I was longing for what did not exist and nothing was to be gained from such a foolish gesture. Rather I should concentrate on taking the steps that would propel me forward and not backwards. I tried to pay attention to what the judge was saying and froze when I heard my name. What now . . .

' . . . . Ms. Ofoedu is to undergo counseling sessions to aid her walk towards restoring her dignity and self-worth.' Ms. Flynn the social worker was charged with ensuring that the counseling was effected.

I gulped some air to assuage my tortured lungs before nodding assent to the judge gratefully.

Everything over, I left the courtroom in the company of the social worker and my solicitor while keeping the tail of my eyes on Osahon who was being directed, with two orderlies on his sides, through another exit.

Outside, I discussed briefly with my minders before bidding them goodbye. I left the court premises and strolled along the road, in line with the Luas track, and as I progressed it became easier to breathe, relief coursing through my veins, mellowing me, like early morning palmwine. The cloak of fear and the shackles that had me tied to a stake in the bottom of a dark abyss fell off and I floated up to see the beauty of the world for the first time in years. Uncharacteristically, I started singing a victorious praise song out loud,

He has given me victory!
I will lift Him higher,
Jehovah!
I will lift Him higher,
He has given me victory
I will lift Him higher,
Forever!
I will lift Him higher.

I continued to sing as I marched along, even as I was aware that people were staring at me, having first crossed to the other side of the road, to ensure that they did not encounter this African *goddess* gone amok in Emerald Ireland, but I didn't care, I would have done a jig or two but refrained as I didn't want to take it too far.

Halfway up Middle Abbey Street, I switched on my mobile phone and was immediately swamped by the cacophony of ring-tones alerting me that I had several messages. I smiled; they must all be dying to share in the long-expected victory. The first text was from *mother-hen* Chinelo. So I called her and gave her the good news. ThankGod was next, then my parents, but the call went into voicemail immediately. After speaking with Ifeoma, I called Erica and Una. I left Obinna last; I wanted and needed a longer discussion.

I rang off and spent the rest of the journey thinking about him; his eagerness to love me and all that came with me, really scary and sweet at the same time. But that may be because all that came with me had not been revealed to him in all its glory. And the envisaged reaction from him when I opened his eyes eventually had constituted itself into this unwieldy uncertainty that had dodged my every waking thought and action and was now threatening to sabotage the health of the relationship.

Then I thought of all the other Obinnas that would come and then leave: all because of a wrong step that I took in the past, that had turned to hold my present captive and would continue to hold my future captive unless . . . I didn't want to envisage what lay beyond that unless . . .

You have freed yourself from Osahon, you must move on.

OK.

So what's the next step? What route should I follow to actualize this freedom from the bondage of my former life? Shouldn't this revelation of my past relieve me of the cloak of shame? Would Obinna's profuse profession of love be able to carry the weight of my shame? I cautioned myself to stop this torturing. I should stop creating misery based on imaginary reality.

Then my mother's novena order niggled its way into my thoughts; made me remember God. But I had stayed away from Him for too long, would He care to help? *You never know.* Well . . . I suppose . . . maybe it's time to factor Him into the schema of things. Time to seek His face. But I knew that I could not just barge in anyhow. That would be very bold. I thought about that for a while and decided that I had to start from the fringes; with Saint Anthony for instance, since he seemed to be the expert in lost causes, and see how far we'd go together, him and me. I grinned and murmured, 'OK St. Anthony over to you, just help me!'

Having handed the problem to one of the Heavenly Hosts, my whirling thoughts began to calm. It's always good to have somebody to share your burden, even an unseen somebody. Feeling much better, I tried my parents again and their line was still dead so I went on to catch my bus home.

Osahon

Osahon's mind was in a chaos—between reality and unreality. What happened inside that court was yet to clear in his head. How could that stupid woman open her dirty mouth to tell the whole world that she was a prostitute? Did she not have any atom of shame? Stupid bitch! How could she? He tried to shake off the strong arms of the guards but they tightened even more. He shrugged mentally, they could hold him all they wanted; he knew he did not commit any offence. Glaring and cursing or even losing your case in court did not amount to offence. But for how long would they guard him before letting him go? He shook his body again but could not dislodge the grips. He suspected however, that this delay was to make sure that the object of his anger—Gift—had left the court premises . . .

He relaxed his tensed body and when they got to their office they made him sit down where he continued to exercise patience stoically, but there had to be a limit to how much delay he could handle because he was a man on a mission and now that the court did not serve his purposes, it was time to cut his losses. Gift and the whole world could not provoke him any further. He needed to be on the move. Time was of the essence.

The walkie-talkie on the court-marshal or orderly or guard or whatever, nearest to him, crackled to life and he responded with an extended mumbling as he left the room to an inner office. Not too long after the guard came back out but with his superior in-tow. Osahon hissed, 'about time.' Then the superior officer went into this elaborate rambling about anger management.

'These people *sef*,' Osahon muttered further, but just nodded, he didn't want to give them room to delay him any further. But it looked like they were waiting for Gift to travel to Nigeria and back before they let him go at the rate they were going. Stupid people. Finally he was asked to go!

He straightened his shirt from the rough-handling. 'Nasty court-marshals,' he mumbled striding off. Now he was really in it. He rued the day he had let that letter from Justice people go unanswered. Now they had written him to give him the Section 3 option letter, referred to as Humanitarian Appeal, as Ezra noted to him. This was the prelude to deportation. Nobody listened to Nigerians when it came to appeal on humanitarian grounds he had heard. And to compound the matter, he also heard that the Minister for Justice, who must approve all such appeals, hated Nigerians with such an unhealthy intensity that it had assumed a life of its own and spread within the rank and file of the department. Well, if the Minister for Justice valued his health, he thought, then he had better shelve his anger and hatred for Nigerians because Nigerians do not hear with their ears, they were simply for decoration. The more you hate and shove them, the more they surged forward. He shrugged and came back to himself.

What exactly was he going to do next? He was not ready or willing to continue to reside in this country. Why should he? So that he would be rushing after all sorts of menial jobs just to make ends meet? No way! He was lucky that he did the Asylum when he did; at least they took care of his needs which had enabled him to save the money he made from his petty-petty jobs.

If those stupid solicitors thought that he was going to pay them their balance, then they must be joking. Fools. What did they do? Nothing. They made him look useless in the eyes of the world instead. Let them just come near him and he'd put pepper in their eyes. Nonsense!

He marched up to O'Connell Street angrily, his thoughts getting hotter and hotter. People are wicked oh. How could Gift look him in the eyes and refuse to help him? How? What did she expect him to do? How did she expect him to fend for his life? Didn't she agree to love him forever? To die for him? To do anything that'd make him happy? Where was that promise now? How could she renege so fast on her promises when it suited her? 'Women! Never trust them: fickle and faithless worms,' he ground out.

He crossed the road and sat down on the base of Larkin's sculpture, not too far from the Spire, to further examine his options even as his continued riling against that bitch, Gift. After a while he got up and went in search of a pub, he needed something to loosen his thoughts. When he reached 'Toads on the Run, Bar and Lounge,' he decided that it'd do, he mustn't drink only in Nigerian-ran watering holes.

Finally after thinking long and hard he decided to accept the option of going home. It was mentioned in that letter from Justice that some money, to resettle him back home, would be given. Together with what he had saved he'd go back and start all over again. Nigeria is a land of opportunities—one could become a millionaire overnight. He was not ready to languish in Ireland pinching cents. He'd probably die before he had made enough money to buy decent clothes not to talk of doing anything else. Yes, he'd go. And the sooner the better: his body was beginning to itch for home where he was noticed. Where his big-boyism counted.

He sneered into his beer as if it was the cause of every problem he had ever had, then he drank it down, as if downing his sorrows, then banged the glass forcefully on the table, causing men, already red in the face from drink, to look up and stare at him with that knowing glint in their eyes. He nodded at them as he gingerly found his way out in search of another lounge.

*   *   *

When I got home I called ThankGod again, he'd know if there was any problem with our parents' phone line. There was nothing wrong with their phone line, he informed me, it was just switched off.

'Switched off? Why?'

'Because our mother did not know what to tell you.'

'And what does that mean exactly?' I probed.

He kept quiet.

'ThankGod what is it?'

Then he told me. My pa fell from one of his palm trees the previous day.

'Is he alright?'

'He is asking for you.' I did not know at what point ThankGod had developed this round about way of answering my questions.

'So he is alive?'

'Yes.'

'I will come home right away.'

'I think you should bring your children.'

'That will . . .' I stopped, to think about the implication of what he was telling me, I then said, 'I will come with them.'

It meant things were not good. Maybe he was even dead already and they did not want to tell me. But ThankGod would have told me. He would not lie to me.

I ran around like a headless chicken for three days, making arrangements, and we left for Nigeria on the fourth day. Ifeoma's efficiency was monumental but she couldn't go with me. Erica was useless, she went to pieces. I supposed every death would do that to her. Obinna . . . Obinna made me feel the difference of having a good man in one's life.

*   *   *

My pa died while I was having a one-sided conversation with him on the third day of our return to Nigeria. The glimpse of the world's beauty which I saw after my victory over Osahon was extinguished and the darkness I had known before enveloped me once again, but this time it had a different hue.

My father's death stripped all the anger and shame from my system and filled it with loathing and guilt instead. My father's last words to me, in a nutshell were:

'You must go back to the beginning. By now you must have realized that money is not everything, sometimes certain type of money impedes your happiness and freedom.' He then made me promise to right my life. That was when I knew that the weight of my iniquity must have truly contributed to his death, it must have been eating at him day and night, making him lose concentration and then fall to his death. After his burial I knew that I must truly re-direct my life to what I knew, to what had given my family good value; what sustains all God-fearing children.

Therapy

DECEMBER, 2005

My victory over Osahon had long since evaporated, and with nothing acting as a buffer my many worries returned, centred on the promise I made to my father. But how did one go about rearranging life?

How do I even hope to move on with my father's death hanging on my neck; that he must have fallen to his death thinking about my iniquity. Now Obinna was pressing for information, should I tell him really? With all this playing in my mind how could I even begin to live now, just how? *Gift are we going to start all that again?* I honestly don't know. But I had promised my father and so must find a way to forge ahead. I thought maybe I'd start with the recommended therapy now, tell Obinna about my past when we visited Austria, then go to confession. My stomach churned.

I loved and I lost, but this was supposed to be a new opportunity to start all over again. But was I taking another step without thinking it through. Wouldn't it be considered too early into this relationship to traipse off to Austria to visit a man that I knew neither kin nor kith of with my whole household in tow? Afterall going to Austria was not like nipping down to Athlone. Granted, the relationship had galloped into something serious and precious, but should that warrant my letting Obinna be aware of what I did? Maybe I'd be better off telling him everything outright, face to face, than this continuous torture. What his reaction would be was not something I'd like to speculate about, just get it out of my chest and see how it went down. If only Ifeoma had been interested in the depth of this relationship, I could have asked her to hover around in Austria and step in as quickly to rescue me, but she didn't want to know, being sure that my life was over as far as snagging a decent man was concerned. She was there when Osahon happened and she had advised me initially when I mentioned a beau to keep things light so as to avoid another heartbreak. And that was what I did—"keep it light", but then it went and got heavy. Apparently, you did not control affairs of the heart, they determined their own pace and you just tagged along. Still Ifeoma refused to know, not even the name of the guy.

When you are happy and troubled at the same time, it's not a normal space to occupy alone, you need to share it. With Ifeoma's straight forward advice absent, I turned to Una at work and she promptly advised me to give the relationship a chance and if it meant going to Austria, why not? Afterall if he wanted me with three children clinging to his shirt-tail, as I kept telling her, then he must really love me. I should follow my heart unless . . . she stopped and stared at me funnily before asking, 'Or don't you love him enough?'

'I love him deeply Una. I thought what I had with Osahon then was love, but compared to what is between Obinna and me, Osahon's must be what is referred to as "being in lust" more like. Though we've not made love yet and I have not known him that long, my feelings for him run deep, so entrenched it hurts to be apart from him.'

'Then follow your heart girl, opportunities like this don't come twice,' Una advised, more like chiding really. 'Afterall,' Una added, as an afterthought, 'you cannot know how it'll turn out without really giving it a chance, you know?'

Of course Una would approve, wouldn't she? But she didn't have the privilege of knowing what I knew. So my real fears were lost on her.

Well, she knew something, afterall we cleaned up together back in Glenncolm, but that was nothing compared to what was. Glenncolm, Obinna knew about already, it's what led to Glenncolm that was pending; the nitty-gritty of my past, the portion that was locked up.

*   *   *

When Obinna called, a day before he was to return from the US to Austria and a week to our subsequent trip to see him, I blurted out that we'd not be coming to Austria, afterall. Obinna laughed and informed me that he kind of read it from my tone well before now that I'd pull out.

'You women never cease to amaze.' He then told me why he called, his voice still laden with laughter. Unexpected business problems had cropped up and would not allow him to leave the US for another month or so. However, he'd visit us on his way back, we could reschedule the trip then.

I heaved a sigh of relief before launching into other topics of discussion as well as wanting to know how his parents' celebration went. Finally Obinna rang off with, 'Baby, start your therapy first and we'll see when I come to Dublin. Don't fret too much OK?'

I nodded, then remembering that he couldn't see me, voiced out my response. At his request I handed over the phone to my children, who took turns to burden him with the extra things to buy for them from America since he was not coming back soon afterall.

I was relieved for the respite, but I also knew that this could no longer go on. I'd have to let him know about my past before we could embark on a future together. Burden of deceit was not a pleasant thing at all. In any case I had the therapy to start with first before anything else.

*   *   *

I made my appointment for three weeks hence. On that day the household woke up earlier than usual and with the speed of lightning we were out of the house by 7.30am enroute to Erica's who'd drop them off to school for a fee, twice weekly. This was to enable me attend my therapy before going to work.

Since they were found out and a clog put in their behind-the-scene wheel of fortune, Erica and her husband had become the original hustlers. They had thrown themselves into all sorts of money-making activities. Erica, besides going to school, was also a child-minder; picking and dropping her wards, where applicable, and looking after them till about six pm before hopping off to a home where she did her night duty! If you were ten minutes late picking up your children, then she'd make you pay the hourly rate again, positing that it's your choice to be early and take your children. Meanwhile, they did not need to work so much as Ifeoma had helped them to pay off what they owed the State Social Welfare and their solicitor. All that they needed, as far as I could determine, was money for their feeding and utilities. Yet they worked . . . well . . . there's no point saying 'they'—Erica worked like work was going out of fashion and there was no getting through to her and her "money is power" mantra.

I dropped off my children and raced back, packed my car and joined the bus, hoping that the bus dedicated lane and leaving early would help me make my 9 am appointment with the therapist before starting work at ten-thirty am. That was cutting it too close, but it was better than telling my boss that I was on therapy.

*   *   *

Take a deep breath in.
Then out.
In again.
Out.
Again.
Out.
Now raise your head up, eyes straight ahead. Chest out, shoulders straightened and tummy tucked in, spine stiff. Right. Now gently put your right foot in front of you, then follow it with the left. Again. Again.
There!
I know you can do it. Just keep doing that; breathing in and out gently. Head up, eyes straight, spine ram-rod. Right leg forward followed by the left leg. I did and that was how I walked smartly into, and announced my name to the receptionist at The Lords Vineyard Counseling Services. I had chosen them, among so many presented by Ms. Flynn, having pictured myself wandering serenely in this cool, leafy, orchard-tree lined vineyard.

The lady at the reception ran a pen down a list of names. My goodness! How many are we? People must be going mad around me and I wasn't even aware until I joined the queue. Niamh, as pinned on the breast pocket of her smart, cream top, looked up and smiled at me before directing me to 'Rev. Sr. Bernadine O'Connor's office; a right turn at the end of the long corridor and it's the third door on your left. Knock only once.'

I blinked at that last bit of information, as sweat started gathering under my armpit, at realizing that I was going in to see a Reverend Sister. No wonder Niamh had smiled with pity. A Reverend Sister no less! Now I'd have to tell my story to a servant of God. By implication, God Himself would be listening in. I hadn't been to confession, or to mass for that matter, since I met Osahon, and as long as I kept God at an arms length I was fine, now Sr. Bernadine was going to mar that landscape.

My original unplanned thinking was to sneak back into God's book through Saint Anthony. Even though the Anthony guy hadn't done anything so far, I was still willing to stick with him.

But you didn't choose her Gift and does it matter who counsels you? The important thing is to open your mind to the experience. You may gain something.

'OK,' I murmured. Afterall I had come this far. It was even a good thing that I was not aware of this information before now; it may have made me change my mind.

Here we go then; I braced myself, smoothened my skirt to rid my palms of their clamminess. Beads of sweat had gathered on my brow so I swiped it, gone were my affected delicate mannerisms. This was fluster at its maximum. Finally when I had nothing else to do, I knocked once on the third door on my left, as was instructed, and to the sharp, 'Yes,' from within, I opened and stepped into this very cheerful and warm room—a contained vineyard.

The room was definitely designed to soothe an aching soul. I took in the furnishings, one by one. The timberline couches were arranged in a circular form and a single patterned vase filled with flowers stood on the centre table that graced the inner circle. The second rung of the table held all sorts of reading materials; *Alive* newspapers, the *Messenger* devotionals, *Maria Legionis* magazine, psychology imbued materials and *OK!* magazines. The fabric used for the mattresses on the couches was soft butter-yellow brocade. Then here and there were red, blue and green throw cushion pillows. The window curtains were gold with bright-lemon-green stalk and bell-shaped blue flowers dotting them.

This concluded what I considered the *livingroom* section of the room while the *office* section in the same room had two deep mocha leather chairs facing a solid oak table where Sr. Bernadine presided from, enthroned on her own executive leather chair which must swivel.

The room was designed to disarm and give comfort at the same time; I was beginning to feel the calmness sneaking in on me, making me feel at home. But I was still disturbed about the curt voice that asked me in, so I remained standing, remembering to be wary again.

Sr. Bernadine stood up, and came round the oak table from the right side towards me. She didn't really have a choice about the route; her left side was blocked by a massive glass-fronted cupboard with shelves, housing books of all shapes and sizes. I watched her approach with a heightened sense of fear; my heart beat a notch faster. When she reached the *livingroom* where I was still standing, she extended her hand for a shake.

The introduction over, I was asked to sit down, not lie down, on any of the seats which I considered comfortable. I obeyed, careful to make the choice of sitting, for it looked as if my choice would set the tone of events. Eventually after much consideration, I sat on one of the mocha chairs facing Sr. Bernadine in her *office*. When she came back to her seat, she was bearing two glasses of water.

Sr. Bernadine sat down and very professionally set the parameters. I felt like crying. Maybe I should have chosen the *livingroom*. But this was serious business and should be treated as such. So I would stay in the office. I squirmed on my seat, got up and smoothened my skirt and sat down again.

'Are you alright, Gift? May I call you Gift?'

'Yes, sister, I am alright. Yes, you may call me Gift.' Silence.

Then, 'No, sister. I am really not comfortable on this seat.'

Sister Bernadine nodded but said nothing. I shifted again. Finally I stood up and went to the *livingroom* section, eyed the couches and chose a single; it wouldn't do to nod off to sleep.

'Are you comfortable now?' asked Sister Bernadine having followed me.

Slowly I released my breath before answering.

'Yes.'

After some minutes had passed I glanced up to look at the sister who looked back at me expectantly. It occurred to me then that she was waiting for me to start. The ball had been thrown into my court; it was up to me now. I had earlier tried my hand at amateur counseling by buying some books in an attempt to self-counsel in line with what I had read. So I wasn't totally at sea with the method she was intending for use: Cognitive therapy method, where you would really be solving your own problem while your counselor acted only as a guide, a helper, a sort of prompter, helping to tease out the hidden issues. And sometimes you'd be asked questions to clarify issues as you progressed. Otherwise you are the one that would do the talking.

OK then.

I thought long and hard on where and how to start, finally I started off tentatively from my childhood, not without hiccups here and there, trying to talk and arrange it sequentially at the same time. Forty-five minutes later, I was loathing leaving, but my time was up.

I stood up and thanked the sister and left. When I came out of the building I made a right turn towards Great St Georges Street wondering whether I could walk to Harcourt Street where my office was located, instead of waiting for a bus. But as I looked back, I saw Bus 19 looming up. Swiftly I turned and ran the last few meters to board the bus as it swung in and stopped at the bus stop.

'Lucky,' I gasped out as I fished for my ticket money and was very happy to find a seat.

As soon as I settled down Sr. Bernadine's voice asserted itself right away, having accompanied me unconsciously.

'For our next session Gift, we will start with finding you, using the 'who am I?' concept.' I nodded knowingly.

'You think you'll be able to look for yourself?' she had asked, peering at me from above the rim of her glinting glasses, which were winking at me. She probably felt that I had agreed too quickly to have understood what she wanted from me. I had nodded while thinking; a very strange concept and question indeed, but anything to re-locate myself would not be a bad idea, especially when the dread of venturing into the unknown had commenced without too much of a hitch. I'd be happy to explore more.

Osahon

'Why are they delaying me? Tell me why! Why can't anything be done fast in this country, eh? It has been two months now; two months Ezra, two months. What do they want?' Osahon fumed to Ezra who came to visit him as they munched on the take-away from MacDonalds, which Ezra brought with him. He had a four-pack Hackenberg beer cooling beside him too. He had to, as Osahon had previously warned him to not ever visit him with empty hands. He is a prince in his town and you don't pay homage to a prince with nothing. Ezra shrugged, swallowed chewed burger, before putting words to his thoughts.

'Osahon you have to be patient. You ran to them all the way from Nigeria complaining that your life was in danger. Now you want to go back to that same country. Don't you think that they'd want to make sure that you will be alright when you get there?'

'Mmmh,' snorted Osahon before he erupted, 'Please don't give me that bullshit Ezra, you hear me? Don't. "Make sure" my foot. Who told you that they cared a jot whether I made it alive or not? They'd be happy to see my back in case you don't know.'

'That is true. But they have to pretend that they are following international rules of the game with this delay tactics.'

Osahon glared at him. 'Ezra don't talk nonsense. What do you know about international rules?'

'A lot my friend; I am a professional Asylum seeker in case you don't know.' Osahon looked up at Ezra and fell about laughing that turned into a choking cough as a piece of burger had flown into the wrong throat as he laughed. Ezra jumped up and banged his back so ferociously that the burger flew out instantly. Osahon cleared his throat, stretched his hand and Ezra placed one of the chilled cans of beer in it. He pulled the tab with alacrity and took a deep gulp, cleaned his mouth and eyes then turned to Ezra.

'My friend you nearly sent me to an early grave with that banging on my back.'

Ezra shook his head.

'Osahon you can be funny atimes. It was the piece of meat that nearly sent you to an early grave and not the little tap I gave you. That saved your life, you know?'

'There certainly was a punch behind that your stumpy little arm Ezra. You be careful how you use it. The blow would have killed me faster than the pieces of meat so don't tell me what I should complain about.'

Then he broke into another extended shout of laughter before asking,

'And what do you mean by a professional Asylum seeker?'

'Oh that; I have been roving around Europe seeking Asylum everywhere, all in an attempt to get paper. I stayed three years in Greece. Those Greek people are confused. When you go there, then you will know that the Irish are efficient. I also spent five years in Germany and three years in Belgium.'

Osahon frowned, but before he could voice his question Ezra quickly inserted, 'Before I got my paper in Spain, after they declared the last Amnesty, I have been there four years.'

'My God! How old are you my friend?' Osahon thought about that and then followed it with, 'are you saying that you have been roving around Europe for close to fifteen years now?'

'Yes, oh. But that is nothing. Some people have been out here longer and they still don't have any paper to show for it.'

'But . . . Are you sure?'

'Osahon you be JJC, allow the experts to tell you.' He preened. At last, he in turn had something to teach his friend for once.

'But if you have your paper now why were you complaining about not having Irish Born Child.'

'Mmmh Osahon. You think I like going over to Spain every year to pay tax? Which I must do or they cancel my residency. Or you think I like paying my rent myself and cater for all my needs and every other nonsense you need to oil your life? Well let me spell it out, if I had been lucky to have an Irish Citizen Child the State would take care of me forever. You see?'

'Yes I see. But what have you gained really with all those years of roving?'

'Well I have three plots of land in prime locations in Owerri and in today's price they will fetch me nothing less than forty million Naira if I decide to sell. I have built a well-constructed duplex in my village. I am putting finishing touches to my hotel in Aba, nothing big mind you, but it will do. As soon as that is completed I am going home.'

'Look at this short man O,' Osahon exclaimed, 'My friend, you have done very well for yourself. You have really tried though it nearly took your entire lifetime to achieve that. Are you sure that that your woman in Navan will go back to Nigeria with you? I have found that our women here have turned into fake *Oyibos*.'

'Are you mad? How can I go back to Nigeria with Rita? I love her that's all but she is not marriage material. She has two children already or didn't I tell you? Who wants to train another man's pikins because of love? *Chere kam nuru gi ihe biko*. Please let me hear.'

Osahon laughed and punched him on the back causing Ezra to wince.

'My friend, are you trying to retaliate or what? Take it easy. You nearly dislocated my shoulder.'

'You little man, how can my patting your back dislocate your shoulder?'

'Please take it easy. Anyway, I love Rita but I am not going to marry her!'

'Cool it man. I am not her father. So you have a hotel in Aba you foxy fellow and here I was thinking, poor Ezra. Better give me your address in Nigeria. I may call on you when you manage to come back.'

Ezra shrugged and did not answer wondering whether he needed Osahon as a friend back home: his excessive demands were beginning to get to him. Maybe he'd give him a fake address if he persisted. He got up and cleared away the packaging of their take-away, opened his own beer and sat down again.

'So what exactly are you going to do when you reach Nigeria?' he asked Osahon to divert him from his earlier request for his address.

'You are very a sly man Ezra. See how you neatly side-stepped my request. Or you think I won't notice, eh? Well let me tell you, what I didn't notice never happened Ezra. It'd pay you well to learn the act of hiding your thoughts and feelings from your opponents. But I will not press if you are not willing to maintain our friendship. I choose my friends Ezra, they don't choose me.'

Ezra nodded and then bent down pretending to re-tie his shoelace while in thought. You'd have to choose your friends Osahon, because nobody in their right mind would choose you as a friend. You, however, have a few tricks up your sleeve and that's why I like you. When he finished, he straightened up, took a gulp from his beer and sighed before requesting for pen and paper from Osahon and gave him his village address. Let them start from there he reasoned.

*   *   *

It was drizzling, but Osahon did not notice as he stepped out of the cab that brought him to the entrance to Dublin Airport Departure on the first leg of his journey to Nigeria. His final approval from IOM—International Office of Migration—to leave for Nigeria came a week ago, but he didn't go right away, he waited to collect all that he was able to collect from the Social Welfare and other traps he had set.

Enya and Glenda, his girlfriends in Dublin, performed beautifully well towards his traveling-home-funds. Aoife, being a student did not have any money to give so he did not even bother to tell her that he was leaving the country. But the cream of the cream came from Oginika, a married mother of two, whose husband was a big time Government contractor in Nigeria. She was so besotted with him that he was hard-put convincing her to let him go. Women! Her poor husband was busy slaving away in Nigeria and did not have an inkling of what she got up to here. The poor man even contributed, unknowingly, to his going-home-funds.

Now he was ready to go back to Nigeria to salvage his life and woe betide any immigration officer at Muritala Mohammed Airport who'd so much as eye his hard-earned Euro. He had heard of the nefarious behaviours of unscrupulous immigration officers who took money off returnees under one guise or the other

'I swear I will pierce that officer's eye,' he swore vehemently moreso out of irritation as the money that was supposed to come from IOM for opting to go home never materialized. It was supposed to pay for any training he chose to undergo in Nigeria that would help his resettling back in and not to be given to the returnee as cash. Which *kin* training be that? Deceitful fuckers!

He checked in his two suitcases before going to have beer in one of the departure lounges while waiting for his flight. As he drank, he chose and discarded various tactics to employ to safeguard his cash. He chuckled as he envisaged a particularly vicious tackle. *That'd be the day somebody tried wresting money from him Osahon Iguedia. Dem never bore that person.* As he continued to drink his mind turned to Ezra and the comment he dropped the other day about his not going to train another man's children. That comment had now wormed its way into the different parts of his body, worrying him. Who was going to train his two beautiful daughters? Pretty little things, like their mother. They should be about seven and six respectively now. As for the so-called Irish Citizen Child he didn't even know whether it was a boy or a girl. He closed his eyes that were now etched with pain, 'Oh God . . . what did I do? How could I have fucked up so much . . . ?'

Osahon you had better mind your own business. You may have fathered those children, but you know that you don't give a shit whether they are alive or dead.

Yeah. That's right. Let that bitch worry about them and see if he cared. He ordered another beer. He was not going to spoil his belle on account of Gift and her children and what they'd get up to. Not now, he was going home to his true love and child. He took a swig of his beer as another thought snaked into his mind. Maybe he should even leave that one to stay with her parents and start all over again, that way he'd not be encumbered in any way by anything or anybody. Why must he be saddled at all?

'Mmh,' he snorted

This idea began to taste more and more viable. Of course, freedom always had a viable taste. How could he not have considered this before now? *Wonders shall never cease to happen Osahon; you are getting soft in the head.*

You are right. As the idea continued to grow in his head, he brightened up, became happy even, and that was not a state he had seen in himself for a long time now.

Gift

Twice a week and four weeks into the therapy, we had a breakthrough; we pinpointed a deep-seated *weakness!* It came out that I was consumed by, mind you without my being conscious of it, and suffered from what Sr. Bernadine referred to as 'Avaricious Consumerism.' Translated, it meant irrational and baffling love for material things to include money, wealth and even physical appearance, so much so that everything I ever wanted was turned into these huge needs that must be met. And as such I became obsessed with the ambition of becoming wealthy in every sense of the word so as to not only be able to live ostentatious lifestyles but be among the haves.

At this point in our discovery, mostly explained by the good sister, I felt that I needed to put mouth into words by voicing out all that was gathering in my mind in my defence: Where was Osahon in this 'Avaricious Consumerism' equation? As I recalled it, he was the beginning and the end of my problems. Before I met him I was fine. But the good sister still had more words in her mouth so I left the playing field for her. Let her finish then I'd tell her how it was.

As if she hadn't caused enough havoc to my mental state, Sr. Bernadine went ahead to drop the final bomb with; when such an irrationally high level of desire was placed on material things, for some people it may lead to their suffering from or likely to breakdown including depression, being anxious, drinking excessively and may even resort to drug use. Oh yeah. So I did what I did to satisfy my innermost desires and when the dream was thwarted I became depressed and the resultant actions I took I could tell better than the sister, it emerged. Osahon may have featured substantially in the whole saga, but we would concentrate on my role, she said, so as to: identify, and then examine said roles minutely before we could look for solutions.

When Sister Bernadine finished, I did not say anything. Instead I trawled my past gathering events and actions like fishes from the depth of the ocean. So the desire to be rich, to have material things and fame was the culprit all along, that calcified into a life ambition and goal at realizing that it was within my power to better my life? But had I not mapped out a route to my goal and worked hard towards achieving them? I didn't expect luxury to fall on my lap like manna did for the children of Israel in the wilderness. I knew better than that. So, at what point did that same desire, who knew my plans, was very much aware of my walk towards attaining them, diligently through hardwork and labour, suddenly turn around to accuse me of changing the agreed mode? When did I, on my own, decide that get-rich-quick-route was better? How could I absolve Osahon like that? The idea that I was the architect of my own downfall was galling to say the least. Only a mad man would plan for his downfall! I should not sit here and take it like a fool. I must say something in my defence.

'What of my love for Osahon? It was the catalyst you know?' I finally inserted.

The good Sister, without so much as a blink, asked me to desist from fighting myself. 'Go home and think towards the direction we were headed and see what surfaces. Everything is in our mind Gift: knowledge, wisdom, worldview, values, desires, everything, and the route to the choices we make are supposed to be instilled in us through our socialization process or the way we were brought up. It is supposed to help point us in the right direction, and our job, based on what we know is to make the right choices as seen in our actions. These resultant actions are physical but what determines the route? That step, taken to actualize the decisions, the choices, where did it all begin?' She tapped the side of her head and then her chest.

'So you see, deliberations, thoughts, decisions are internal and precede the physical manifestations that are actions.'

I nodded but stubbornly persisted, 'I know I said yes to working as a prostitute, but did I choose to break down?'

'You did Gift, but you will tell me about that when you are ready.'

I had been in more trouble than I cared to acknowledge, but could I get away with cursing a servant of God? Because, believe me, this woman had gone too far. I chose to break down? How nasty of her to suggest such a thing. But I didn't let on to my thoughts.

I was sad and it showed in my steps which became hesitant as I left to board a bus to my office. After my second cup of coffee, taken successively, I was still subdued and increasingly sad. Una, sensing my mood, gave me a wide-berth after the perfunctory 'Hi Gift' greetings in the manner of white man. I ignored her. I wasn't sure I should be at work in the first place. I needed to sort out all the thoughts darting about in my head and the office was becoming very crowded and suffocating. I wanted peace and quiet. During our lunch break I informed Una that I'd rather go to St Stephen's Green Park for a walk than eat at Café @ Sol. Una offered to go with me, as well as share her sandwich. Her mother-in-law was visiting and had sent her off to work with a sandwich in tow, Una informed me. I shrugged. We left together anyway.

We got to the park, chose a secluded corner and sat down on a rusted-iron bench, not too far from a witch-doctor look-alike shack by the children's play section to munch listlessly on our lunch. Una's appetite must have gone in sympathy with mine and a pensive demeanor clothed her.

As we chewed, I felt Una's tail of eye on me, urging me to put her out of her misery even though her white man "mind-your-business-aloofness-mantle" implying disinterest, supposedly, was still visible. When I couldn't bear Una's tail of eye on me anymore I told her what was troubling me. Una didn't have much to say other than to suggest that I give it time, complementing that with, 'you know a lot of people had been to therapy without success but then a lot came off triumphant,' the important thing being that I must desire to do it willingly and in that desire comes acceptance and then application of self. Maybe I'd be among the triumphant ones, was her conclusion. I looked at her with raised brows. Una too? Imagine. She's actually doing Sr. Bernadine on me. I frowned then nodded. Good talk. But she wasn't the one being bashed by Sr. Bernadine's words!

At the close of work that day, I left for home with the cloud of subdued air still clinging onto me. Throughout that evening it hung thickly around me, floating ahead of me in the house like dust motes, my children gradually became subdued too and till they went to bed, it did not dissipate. How easily our actions and moods affected the children, I thought as I tidied up for the night. Obinna called and his call did not distract me as expected, but we talked far into the night, nonetheless.

The next morning I woke up still unsettled and sad, implying that the downcast had invaded my sleep as well. Listlessly, we prepared and left for our various destinations.

Somehow, I got through Tuesday and Wednesday and by Thursday morning sharp; I presented myself to Sr. Bernadine and launched immediately into my self-defence. Somebody had to speak up for Gift, especially seeing that I needed to open Sr. Bernadine's eyes. She had continued to get it wrong.

'I was bitter, very bitter towards Osahon. This was a man I loved with all my being. We were one. I put my life on the line, on hold, debased it, so that he will be happy and have all he ever wanted at his disposal. Then he betrayed me, raped me and cast me adrift. The anger, resentment and bitterness would not go. I won't let it go!'

I looked up to note score one, but Sister Bernadine observed me impassively. I shrugged and powered on. Sister Bernadine could think anything she liked.

'I was remorseful about what I did. You have to know that: the weight of the shame had never left me. I have walked with my head bowed down so that people would not see my face; with my eyes darting over my shoulders now and then because of fear of Osahon and his threat. I was too ashamed to communicate with my parents meaningfully since the incident. Now I could not even do anything about my dad. He died you know?' I eyed Sr. Bernadine malevolently for failing to see what Osahon did to me. She didn't say anything in view of my revelation so I continued.

'What I did became a barrier, too monumental to ascend, so as to start afresh, so much so that it had coalesced into a hole, a deep chasm, in my soul. I knew everybody in my family were disappointed and ashamed of me.'

Sister Bernadine, so far, had not shown any visible sign of applause. I could now see why a glass of water was always available when people make speeches. I needed to unclog my throat and free my voice which was sounding hoarser as I spoke. So I got up and went over to the *office* section and, from the good Sister's big-oak desk, took one of the glasses of water and sipped while studying Sister, sitting regally on her throne, from under my lashes.

I finished and returned to my seat with the now half-filled glass, which I placed gently on the side stool that either was not there before now or I hadn't noticed. I resumed the explanation that would exonerate me and bestow the full blame of my actions on Osahon.

'Then being able to live with the enormity of what I did was another issue. It lent its weight to the other facts and my mind became heavier. The rabid fear, of being discovered, constantly preyed on my mind, day in day out. Lucky's birth added its own dimension. I didn't want him. I never wanted him, but he forced me to, so I accepted him.

I like him now though. Don't get me wrong. I love him now. All my children. The three of them. But . . .

'Well . . . Finally all these pressures conspired with my already fragile mind to tip me over the edge. The weight overpowered me and for more than a year, I could not say what my life was because I didn't know. But I overcame all of that,' I finished triumphantly and looked up at the good Sister who looked back as if in waiting. Neither disgust nor pity, nor grudging respect. Nothing. Was this how it usually was?

Oh well. I acquiesced mentally. It's like the good Sister was not impressed by my sufferings and subsequent triumph. I rubbed an itch on my cheek and then at the back of my neck.

'Now tell me Sister, why are you blaming me?' I had to ask because Sr. Bernadine did not look as if she had any talk in her mouth. My question, however, elicited an amused half-smile; she then followed that with, 'That was an interesting choice of word Gift—conspired. But first tell me why you chose to become depressed,'

I looked swiftly up at Sister Bernadine aghast.

'I did not choose to go mad sister.' I spoke sharply, but then soft-pedaled. 'I have been trying to explain all these to you, what is the matter?'

'You have indeed tried. Alright Gift, let's put it this way. Instead of trying to exonerate yourself, why don't you humour me and let's see what will come out.'

I took my time, to digest what she said before I cleared my throat, took another sip of the water and then started to humour Sister Bernadine as requested.

'Well . . .' Then I stopped. How do you humour somebody by blaming yourself? I kept quiet, looking for a gap, and then ploughed on regardless.

'When we are hurting, which at the time would seem like the weight of the world was placed on our shoulders, weighing us down, we still have choices in terms of the actions we engage in to overcome these life-challenges that causes the hurt. The weight of and the solution to the problems lie within us. Whether and how we wanted it solved is still within our circle of influence. But we'd need to make that personal decision to have the problem solved in the first place. The decision so taken would propel us to the path of solution that would bring healing and freedom. But first we must reach deep into the inner recess of our mind to draw from that inner strength imbued in all of us to accept that there was a problem and that we need help. The next step would be to seek for a solution. The process if properly executed would oust that problem. Mind you it may take months, years even, we may fall back many times, but once we have determined that the thorn must be removed it would be invariably, otherwise you'd remain in the quagmire, the bog that'd never let go.

I was beginning to like my psychoanalytical ability. I smiled, warming up to my theme, but sadly my time was up and I had to leave. I waited for Sr. Bernadine to pat me on the shoulder for the amazing revelations, but nothing was forthcoming, rather a faint smile hung on her lips and then she nodded. That was still something, I told myself as I got up to leave for work. I had long since concluded that Sr. Bernadine most times seemed to be communing with the spirits instead of listening to me.

*   *   *

'How do you feel today?' Sister Bernadine asked, looking kindly at me.

'Oh grand, Sister.'

'Good. So what do you have for me then?'

Without preamble, I launched into my analysis, Sister was not one for tête-à-tête, but I was surprised that I was personalizing it.

'ThankGod, my brother, never had a dream and was seen as an obstinate mule with no agenda for the future . . . Or maybe he did have a dream, just that nobody bothered with ThankGod or his dream. He ended up being somebody, whereas I, the star of the family, ended up being nothing. I that was supposed to bring light to the family ended up coating it with tar. Now my name is mentioned in whispers in that eye-rolling kind of look reserved for *akalogolis*. The good-for nothings.'

'You know that for a fact?'

'It must be. That's how it usually is.'

Sister Bernadine nodded. 'Alright,' she intoned without any inflection.

'All because of that good-for-nothing-he-goat, Osahon.' I had to take a swipe at him, I couldn't resist, but I stopped immediately. 'That, that . . .' Then I stopped again and very slowly raised my eyes up to stare into Sr. Bernadine's eyes in awe.

'You know, I think I've got it wrong all along.'

'You did?'

I nodded.

'Then enlighten me.'

'What had Osahon got to do with it?' *Maybe that was where it all went wrong. Attributing and blaming my problems on the other.*

Look at me analyzing and pontificating about making choices and the route to its actualization without once applying it to my problem. As it turned out, I had no business blaming Osahon or any other person at that. It was left for me to retrace my steps;find my dream and re-route the process of achieving it. When I get to the beyond what would I tell God? That I stood still? That I debased my body because Osahon made me? Very silly.

I should do something, must do something or be extinguished forever. So I spoke.

'I should not have chosen prostitution as route to making money in the first place, and when my life with Osahon ended I should have found another route to life instead of wallowing in self-pity and delusion which led to all sorts of problems for me.' I focused on Sr. Bernadine and asked, 'It is my life we are talking about now, right?'

'Right,' Sr. Bernadine murmured without batting an eyelid, like my question wasn't silly.

'So first and foremost I should stop blaming somebody else. Secondly I should stop running because from what I can now see, it would never get me anywhere either. What has happened has happened.'

Sister Bernadine nodded again sagely, before commenting 'You have actually come a long way Gift. This therapy was to help you discover yourself and get your perspectives right; to begin to apply your knowledge-based thoughts to yourself. You should stop distancing yourself from your environment while allowing only your emotions free rein. It was unhealthy. They should co-exist, your thoughts and your environment, one validating the other. I'm glad to say that you are making the connections. You did admirably well.'

I was elated to be patted on the back at last, for finding myself by myself. This journey had brought new insights; the chief being to stop deluding myself that Osahon made me do anything or that I did it for Osahon because of love. I did it for myself! So now I'd chart my dream anew and follow it going forward. I noted that the portion of my psyche that harboured resentment and hatred had emptied itself and became hollow. It was a very rewarding feeling, a feeling that gave me inner strength. A feeling that made me realize that I had come to the end of the torture era and was poised for a new life. Obinna flitted in and out immediately in my mind.

This is not about men, Gift. This is about your life in its entirety. So don't be so myopic.

I agreed.

*   *   *

I celebrated my victory over Osahon and the success of my therapy with Una and a couple of our colleagues, even though they were not aware of my palaver. The good-will feeling did not abate and I carried on being happy.

Erica

Erica came with her children to visit on a Saturday. The five children, Erica's two and my three, immediately got busy clamouring upstairs while I sat mutely with Erica in the livingroom snacking on my provided tit-bits like strangers in a train station cafe. I noted that Erica, inspite of her effort to appear glamorous, by donning the most expensive of garbs, with gold accessories and all whatnot, cloaked in perfumes with *names*, still looked somehow scattered and disheveled and lacking of something. Maybe her tendency towards being dirty did not allow her to attain the sophistication she craved. And to think that her husband was always impeccably appointed, opposites most certainly attract.

Erica busied herself surfing the TV channels as she nibbled and watched Gift from her hooded eyes, thinking: What was it about this lady that she did not like and had thus restrained their friendship for so long? Was it because she always carried herself well, properly groomed, and soft-spoken, everything that she had hungered for! Was that it? Was that why she hated her even as fresh undergraduates then? Ifeoma had money, Gift dirt poor, yet she carried this air of sophistication as if she was born into it.

Does poverty deter sophistication?

No.

But hadn't they come a long way, nursed each other through one thing or the other, long enough to bury the differences and move on? Wasn't it time they considered being friends if they both worked at it? But how would she approach the suggestion after years of ignoring each other? Maybe she'd start by showing interest in her therapy and the reason for that, maybe . . . She cleared her throat.

'Ee em Gift.'

I turned to look at Erica.

'How is the therapy going?'

I was startled. To my knowledge Erica had never shown interest in anything I did. Why now? *Careful girl, she's fishing.*

'It is going well, I guess. Or rather it is going to be alright ultimately.'

'Why are you really doing it?'

'Because I had a rough time within the duration of my marriage.'

'So?'

'How do you mean "so"?'

'You had a rough marriage and both of you went your separate ways, is that why you should shout your secrets from the roof-top? What is the meaning of that?'

I arched my brows in surprise.

'If you live in a country where the citizens cut off their ears, you join them and cut off yours.'

'Oh yeah. So you're in therapy because that's the done thing in Ireland?'

'Far from it Erica. My soul was hurting. I needed to heal, but I was not. Back home it is different, with a lot of things vying for your time; you just have to keep going. But here, it's a different thing altogether. You're lonely and you feel isolated and naked, so much so that your thoughts would rub you raw and it's painful. But we cannot continue to detach ourselves from a society where we've made our home. Anything on offer that we perceive may help fit us in should be grabbed with both hands, we'd be the better for it.'

Ifeoma should hear me spouting so!

'Mmmh,' Erica murmured, but said nothing. She'd need to crack Gift into two to be able to extract what she really wanted to hear. Like what really happened between her and lover-boy, Osahon, and why was there so much gap in her life's chronology. Five years on and she's only just going for counseling?

I eyed Erica from under my lashes, who stared at me with that kind of eyes that knew that she won't be told anything further. I looked up and stared back, my own eyes indicating that this was as far as she could get out of me. We looked away at the same time. Then I suggested that maybe Erica should avail of the counseling services herself. It may help to straighten her jumbled psyche and probably help to reduce the confusion in her life and the constant forlorn look she always carried around her. What happened to her was horrendous and maybe that's why she loved to chase money so much. But she needed to sort it out and live without the burden of her father's atrocity on her shoulder.

Erica looked at me to see if I was poking fun at her. Realizing that I was not, she sighed in acknowledgement.

'Maybe I should Gift. Thanks.'

I nodded. I didn't need friends beyond Ifeoma and maybe Una, but my relationship with Erica had just notched up a step and both of us realized it.

'I want to invite you to our church service on Sunday,' Erica said.

'Why. Are you people doing something?'

'Something like what?'

'I don't know. Why are you inviting me to your church service?'

'Relax Gift, it is not a war. I know you're a Catholic but I have not seen you attend mass since you came to Ireland so I felt the need to invite you; to try something different.'

I kept quiet. If only you knew why. I could try her church, maybe it would help. I had enlisted St. Anthony, but he probably couldn't help because since asking him I had still not desired to or been compelled by any forces seen or unseen to go to mass.

'OK Erica, we will go with you next Sunday. Just call to remind me before then.'

Erica was surprised at the ease with which Gift accepted. Catholics were the hardest to convert. This was a victory. She must give her testimony as soon as she got her into their church!

'Are you sure?' she ventured hesitantly, she had to be sure.

I laughed.

'Erica you invited me to your church and I accepted then you turn around to ask whether I was sure. What kind of thing is that?'

'I was surprised that's all.'

'Don't be. We will be there come Sunday.' This probably was the best way to inveigle my way back. God may not even notice my move until I was in.

Obinna, a staunch and practicing Catholic, was baffled at my continued refusal to attend mass each time he was in Dublin and invited me. And was even further confounded by my refusal to make love to him. It didn't make sense to him. But I, in turn, was confounded even more when he told me that it was a relief that I had refused because then he would have broken the pledge he had made to God where he'd stop chasing skirts and God, in return, for his turnaround would direct a good woman his way.

Wow!

Was he being real or was it just to make me think he was something else? I mean it's not fashionable these days to mention that you go to mass every Sunday! I hadn't pressed for clarification though. I sighed and ate more biscuit. Erica was lost in a world of her own too.

So we sat, with a friendly air floating around us till Erica departed with her children and my children clustered around me for our Saturday evening treat—telling them our local folklores. I always tell them stories as were told to me by my parents. It kept the thoughts of home warm in our hearts. Mine maybe. The children could barely remember that much.

During the rest of the weekend I tried to apply the wealth of insight I had imbibed during the therapy and noted that really, there was nothing in my upbringing, past and present that led to my going astray. I pursued happiness through a route that was unconventional, tramping on the values that were sown into me. And because I kept justifying my actions by casting blame left, right and centre, to just about anybody that could be blamed, I had avoided responsibility and accountability. But it doesn't work like that. You own up to your misdeeds, accept responsibility and make concerted efforts to atone for them. It may be a life-long atonement, but it'd have to start from acceptance, then solutions would open their doors.

The bottomless hole that had dug itself somewhere in my heart, in my life, occupied by hatred, anger and remorse, that had weighed me down then but which had now emptied, had remained empty. It should have been filled up with happiness and all that went with it. It did not and I did not know what to fill it up with, thus making me even more weightless and anchorless. I thought the space having been rid of the bad stuff would be filled up by goodness. So attending Erica's church may help or at least help to begin the process of anchoring me.

*   *   *

That Sunday Erica drove into my compound, parked and called me on her cell-phone to hurry up. I had been ready with my children earlier, so I hurried us out amidst questions of why we were going to aunty Erica's church. They only ever went to church with uncle Obinna, they reminded me. But I assured them that this was also in order, that they'd enjoy it. They accepted my pronouncement with alacrity but wanted to know if I'd take them to Conrad Hotel for lunch as uncle Obinna usually did. I said no but we may go to MacDonalds if they were quiet in church. They promised solemnly. I didn't think that that particular feat would be achieved, but then they had always been good for Obinna, he had told me, so maybe.

Up at the end of O'Connell Street, after the Garden of Remembrance, we veered left into Gardiner Street and halfway through Erica turned into a side street and parked. I did the same behind her and got out to survey my surroundings before shepherding my children after Erica and hers into Mount of Glory International Church, Inc.

'Oh, they have started praise worship already,' Erica threw back at me as she quickened her steps climbing the stairs. I didn't respond, struggling, as it were, to match Erica's energetic pace.

We were led to our seats by two ushers amidst the thundering drumming and clapping accompanying the praise worship. I surveyed the set-up and moved my children out of the direct path of the throbbing drums. I wasn't about to have their eardrums blown. Erica mouthed something and gesticulated wildly at me and I responded with a wilder gesticulation, head shaking and then finger pointing to my ears and surroundings. Erica shrugged. I shrugged back while continuing to stand up with my children to gyrate to the praise worship songs.

Then my children were whisked away before my very eyes by another set of ushers. I looked up as to confirm that Erica's children were getting the same treatment and realized that they were not even with her. Probably that was what Erica was trying to convey to me earlier with the arm-flailing.

I had to look at my watch again. 'Is this really the time?' I murmured, while looking over at Erica's direction, but I might as well not have bothered, she was in the spirit-realm and nothing happening on earth at this time could bring her down, going by her behaviour. I had to take solace in the fact that my children were not with me to agitate for food. We had been in The Mount of Glory International, Inc. for three hours! And things did not look as if they'd abate soon.

Eventually we were released and I made for the exit, but found myself surrounded by various women welcoming me to the service and to their church, this was in addition to the official Church welcoming routine, which we had endured towards the tail end of the mass, service I mean. I pasted a smile on my face, murmuring and nodding accordingly. The pastor came over and everybody fell back. He welcomed me and my children to the family of God—his church. Then he prayed for me; imploring Jesus on my behalf to grant me all my heart desires in full, 'in the mighty name of Jesus,' he thundered at the end of the supplication. I murmured my Amen while surreptitiously scouting for an escape route. Erica came round with five take-away packs of jollof-rice but I refused telling her that I had promised my children McDonalds afterwards.

'You can be infuriatingly snooty atimes Gift, you know. Is this food that everybody is eating beneath you?'

'I don't know any such thing, Erica. Besides, why should I be made to languish in the church all day and then be given rice to make up for it? It is not a harvest and bazaar, nor fundraising, and I will eat where I want to.'

Erica suddenly laughed.

'It's alright Gift, I understand where you're coming from. You Catholics have the briefest of service.'

'Mass and three hours for no reason is trying.'

'Mass. No problem. I'll see you at home later.'

I nodded and directed my children out and into the car and sped off.

As we drove into our compound two hours later, Erica also veered in grinning. Were they just coming from the service? I wondered.

'Erica, don't tell me that you people are just coming back?'

'Yes oh. You missed. We had a love-feast.'

'That explained the presence of the packed lunch.'

'No, we do that every Sunday. The love-feast came afterwards. A member was celebrating her engagement.'

'Oh. It went well then if you are just coming. It's almost six pm Erica.'

'I know but that is alright, Sunday is for God.'

'Tell me, is it like that also in Nigeria. I mean the long service?'

'Oh yes oh, but you bring your own food sometimes.'

'But why can't people be let off early to eat in the privacy of their homes?'

'We celebrate life everyday culminating on Sunday. You won't understand Gift so leave it.'

I nodded and then looked Erica up and down again. I had wondered in the morning why she was the way she was, dressed to the teeth with gold occupying every available space on her neck, wrist and fingers but had kept my peace since almost everybody was equally decked, but now I couldn't help myself.

'I can see where you got your penchant for high-fashion of gold jewelries and laces. All the women in your church were decked out to kill.'

'Don't mind them *jare na so dem go dey* owe money all over the place to be able to meet up.'

'They do?'

'Yes oh. Some of them even change boyfriends like wrapper if he wasn't performing.'

'They all looked married to me,' I ventured keeping a straight face.

'It doesn't stop them. Besides, most of them have their husbands still back home in Nigeria.' I nodded and started walking up to the house.

'How do you know all these things by the way?' I threw at Erica as I resolutely marched towards the house, hoping that she was not planning a visit, I was too tired.

'I be you *wey don* turn to house-rat, *wey no de commot,*' Erica retorted and then added, 'I just wanted to be sure you people got home safely.' I laughed as I waved her off.

'Thank God,' I murmured with relief while stepping into the house with my children and immediately dove onto the sofa to recover before attending to them; they had run up to their rooms.

My mission had failed woefully; attending Erica's church did not seem to hit the mark as I really could not see myself sustaining the whole set-up, I did not dig their way of service, aside having most of the women straining to out-dress each other. After much rumination, I decided that I may have to take the bull by the horn myself and go back to what I knew. Unimaginable aspersions may be cast on the Catholic Church, yet she still has her ways and I want to believe that any devout member would always reach God from there. Yes I'd go back for it seemed all this round about way had not done me any good.

... The Hand of God:

As I laid back on the sofa trying to catch a nap having changed out of my Sunday best and mediated between Eudora and Lucky, as usual, my phone rang. I sighed and got up. It was Obinna, calling to alert me of his arrival itinerary to Dublin from America. He had spent six weeks afterall instead of the proposed four. I itched seriously to see him, to melt into his warm chest for comfort.

The relationship had fully taken off, but I was determined to have my feet firmly rooted to the ground, because the last time I was swept off my feet brought untold anguish and I was still paying the price. This time around everything should be as I would want it whenever I could get away with it. It's left for Obinna to worry about me instead of the way it was with Osahon. It's a man's duty, as I knew it, to look after his woman. Let him woo me and everything that went with it. The only ugly patch was my past. But that should be dealt with in due course.

＊　＊　＊

Obinna came and left and our life continued with me getting deeper and deeper into myself searching for something that apparently wasn't there, otherwise I would have found it. One Sunday, I woke up, got ready and went to mass just like that. To my utter surprise, it felt like I never left, well . . . not really. The second Sunday of attendance was even more comforting and yet more torturing. The third Sunday in a row I knew that something had to be done, I could not continue like this, but how do I approach that 'something' that must be done?

I asked painfully as images of my life as a child and mid-teenage years flashed across to coincide with this powerful overwhelming shame washing over me. It was an awful feeling; how did I ever get to immerse myself in something this dark and all because of what? I shifted uncomfortably twisting to look around; trying to see beyond people's faces; maybe they were staring at me, loathingly.

Don't start that your paranoia here Gift, what are people supposed to see even if they deigned to look at you. Your soul?

Then I turned back to face the altar again before sliding down quietly to kneel in thought; whatever made me remember the past and how it was must be telling me that I was being prepared to become free again. My life was about to change for the better, guided by the invisible hands of God. Growing up, going away to school, living abroad both past and present had widened my worldview, improved my knowledge, my thought processes, my perceptions, decisions and actions arising therefrom. And somewhere along the way, I must have dropped some views that I considered obsolete, but I never gave up on my belief in the hand of God: always directing when and where He wills. Even if I had stopped attending mass—but that was because I didn't know how to face Him—I wanted to believe that He must be why I was here today. So I hunched over and started praying: asking God to forgive me all that I had ever done to hurt the temple that was my body, but that belonged to him, all that I had ever done to further nail His son onto the cross. Then my mind wandered off.

When I brought it back, I apologized to God for that, and then veered off again on how God manages to deal with all his children all over the world with their different antics. I couldn't fathom that, was not supposed to anyway, so I continued with my praying.

After I had attended four successive Sundays without receiving, I went to confession. There was no point in joining to cook a meal and not partake in the eating of it. I had kept away for over six years, what if I had died during that time where would I have ended up? In hell? That did not go down well at all. I have what it takes to live a good life in Christ why was I still denying myself? Like my mother had pointed out, I have the rest of my lifetime to atone for my mistakes, but why should I not do that with the support from the spiritual food and drink that was meant to nourish my soul—the Eucharist? Maybe I should go for this confession in another parish, that way the priest would not start looking at me as a wicked sinner. I processed this thought and felt that it must be coming from my lack of conviction of God's power to regenerate lives which informs why I was still skulking about, so when Saturday came round I went but lost my nerves and ran back home. Then I turned right round and went back but sat at the back of the Church instead. I couldn't go any further. I was really paralyzed by fear. Eventually the light went off in one of the confessional cubicles and our parish priest came out and at seeing me he changed direction and walked towards me. 'Gift, were you waiting to confess?' he asked before noticing tears streaming down my face. He stopped speaking and sat down with me.

I cleared my throat and said, 'Father I don't think I can confess today.' He nodded.

'I don't really think God will forgive me anyway.'

The priest nodded again but said nothing. So we sat there in silence. After a while he said, 'You do know that God sees our innermost thoughts?' I said nothing. 'And that He knows already that you need Him in your life.' I still said nothing but after some more time had passed I cleaned my eyes, got up and went into the empty and dark confessional. Minutes later the light came on and I bared my soul to God through his servant, clutching onto the hope that the restorative power of the Grace of God would help me to recover.

As a child my first confession was with anticipation and ease, I practically flew to the confessional, eager to tell God my sins. As I grew older and knew sin, my heart palpitated so much, my feet laden, as I approached the confessional. This time around I did not have the words to explain my loss of courage but I overcame and I was better afterwards. The priest reminded me that even before we were formed in our mother's womb, even before we were good or bad that God loved us and will always, but we have to choose to come to Him for His grace to flow into our lives and heal our wounds.

And if I thought I was relieved after my therapy that was nothing. The confession was the ultimate elixir for my soul and my body. I was so relieved that I sat in the church for over an hour doing nothing. Just marveling. Finally I said the prayers for my penance and left.

Over the days, the emptiness that I had hitherto experienced started to lessen and my soul and body were being filled up by something which I can not even describe. Now don't sneer, it was not like right away, but somehow I felt better with my thoughts. I could even vouch that there was a glow about me, which emanated from every pore of my body. I no longer see it as an ordeal to go for odd early morning mass now. While growing up it was the bane of our lives, daily morning mass attendance, but our mother seemed to either not notice our groaning, from having our sleep interrupted, or she didn't care. Now it seemed like no ordeal at all.

So except for the promise to Obinna, to let him into my past, I must say that my thoughts felt less severe and condemning.

Obinna

AUSTRIA, 2006

So one bright Saturday morning, in Dublin at least, with promises of rain hanging in the air, on the first day of the two weeks Christmas holidays, I took one week off work, packed my children and we left for Austria. The time had finally come for the inevitable. It was either now or never. No more secrets, no more hiding. I had chosen to be free, in every way.

During the flight I was apprehensive. How would I start the narration? What would be Obinna's reaction to this amazing tale? Would I ever see him again? Would I ever have a man in my life again; somebody to share with, to laugh with, and to cry with, a companion, somebody to face the highs and lows of life with?

I knew that if truth be told it's not a possibility and rather ironic that I'd be using my own hands to strangle myself. But I had to do it, if for nothing else, at least to see how far his love for me could stretch.

But one thing though, I had made up my mind to make love with him, as I was not sure that I'd get another man after this relationship died. I wanted to have something to look back on during the lean years.

Complete nonsense, what was I even thinking about? Had I gone mad? I had been given a clean slate of life besides, as a serious Catholic sex should be within the confines of marriage. So no sex period.

Then I saw the sign and then the announcement telling us to fasten our seat belts and prepare for landing. A wave of something washed over me and I clenched my fingers then balled them into fists. But somehow I managed to fasten my seat belt as instructed and at the same time tell Frances and Eudora to do same. I then leaned over to fasten Lucky's who beat my hand off and in an aggrieved voice told me that he could do it himself ending it with, 'I am not a baby,' but now said in an admonishing tone. I didn't even give heed to any of that his macho behaviour this time around, I had a crisis looming and I needed to not only divert my troubling thoughts but of immediate importance was to still my hands which had started trembling. But Lucky was ready to wrestle me to the ground, if possible, to assert his independence, so I gave up while keeping an eye at his efforts.

From nowhere however, a thought flashed. *Why don't you leave it till the last day of your stay?* I grasped it immediately and grinned. But of course. We'd enjoy our stay and then wham! It was a lifeline thrown by whoever and instantly my fear receded, my slide to the pits of misery now derailed and I was instantly rejuvenated. Yes, I came to tell Obinna something but there was no rule that said it must be said on the first day. The bottom line was to ensure that it was said within the duration of the trip, full stop. I became visibly calmed as the plane started its descent.

As we clattered to unbuckle ourselves, gather our things, in readiness to disembark the plane, two ladies approached and at the confirmation that I was Ms. Ofoedu, proceeded to help us disembark while informing me that they were sent by Mr. Ikejiana. I didn't say anything other than to raise my brows ever so slightly: Obinna's thinking was always one step ahead of mine. I certainly needed help with my children and the luggage but didn't realize it'd start from inside the plane!

* * *

Obinna himself was waiting at the arrival lounge and as soon as we had crested the door out of the inner arrival gates, he stood up and marched forward to envelope me in this extended bear-hug then followed it with kissing while my children were hanging variously on his legs. He released my mouth and stared at me before murmuring.

'God! I love you so much Gift.' I smiled, looked deeply into his eyes and murmured, 'How are you Obinna?' With our eyes still locked on each other he murmured back,

'I am fine now.'

'I love you too Obinna. Much more than you'll ever know,' I purred. Obinna opened his eyes wide, then nodded with a huge smile spreading on his face before looking down to attend to my tykes before they tore his pants off him. I had never said that to him before.

The ladies that helped us off the plane were joined by two men who relieved them of the luggages and then we all proceeded towards the exit. I walked regally, head held high beside Obinna while holding the girls. Lucky holding Obinna.

By the time we got outside, a BMW Seven Series was whining there with our luggages being loaded into the boot and one of the two men behind the wheel. Obinna opened the back door and I noticed a toddler's car-seat and wondered wether he had a child of his own which he had not told me about or else he borrowed the car from his neighbour. Well, it didn't matter this is a week of revelations and Obinna's couldn't match mine. He buckled Lucky onto the car-seat, without a murmur from him, which was amazing, then Frances and Eudora next to him, properly seat-belted. Then the two ladies got into the car, one in front and the other beside the children and they drove off.

I turned and looked at him quizzically, but before I could formulate a question another car took the stead that the other had vacated. This time it was a Mercedes Benz SLK 350 driven by the second man. Obinna took my elbow and drew me towards the back seat and as soon as we had settled in my eyes lit up as I saw an opaque glass rising up and eventually cutting us off from the driver. I had watched films so I knew luxury when I saw one, but come on Obinna, what's with the impression? I turned to look at him again with my brows almost touching the roof of the car. Obinna looked at me and enveloped me again in another hug whispering, 'I miss you so much. Why won't you be mine?'

I didn't answer. I couldn't. I hugged him back instead and we held each other, our hearts pounding in unison.

Finally he drew back to study every inch of my face, like he was seeing me for the first time or the last time. I was becoming very hot all over and this scrutiny was upping the heat level.

'Bino, what's with the scan?' He didn't answer, instead he opened some cabinet, or was it a fridge? and brought out a bottle of champagne and two glasses, pulled at another something which turned out to be a sort of table, popped open the drink and poured. He gave me one and holding the other proposed a toast.

'May we always be together?'

I nodded, held his gazed and responded, 'May we always indeed.' After sipping the drink in silence he took my glass, set it down and pulled me to his chest and held me again in his arms. I wriggled down and made myself more comfortable—virtually lying down with my head resting on the croak of his arms while we whispered sweet nothings to each other.

When we drove into Obinna's place, almost an hour later, I was drowsy by the combination of the drink, tiredness and the knowledge that I was truly loved, but even in that state I was completely flabbergasted by Obinna's house. If I wasn't such a cool customer, I'd have had my mouth open in stupefaction, the kind that would have flies diving in and out without your being aware. It was practically a palace or something very close to one if it's not already. I looked at Obinna and frowned. If he was doing all these things, hiring the cars and the palace to impress me, he had over done it big time. But why would he want to do all that for? And how could he live here alone anyhow?

But for some reason, Obinna did not seem to get the bad vibes emanating from me. Did he assume that all this would appear natural? Was I supposed to accept these displays of wealth without murmur?

No be you dey find luxury before. Now you don see am wan run eh?

Yes. But not like this!

'Pardon me?' Obinna asked.

'I wasn't speaking to you.'

He nodded but threw a peculiar look at me, before he opened the door, got out and stretched his arms to help me out. I got out and looked around, maybe we had branched off for him to show us the sites but there was no sign of the BMW. He led me with his arms now around my waist up the stairs and to the first layer of the house. Not knowing what to call this part of the house I assumed it to be the patio or the entrance hall but quickly I amended that. None fitted the space and then *swish* the door opened and a man stood there, officially attired and bowed from the waist down but still ram-rod. Probably nothing like that but that was how I could best describe it. Then I looked beyond the man and encountered a smaller version of Captain von Trapp's mansion of the famed musical drama 'Sound Of Music.'

Maybe all houses in Austria were built like this seeing that 'Sound of Music' was supposed to have happened in Austria, I thought. Nonetheless, I marched in with Captain von Obinna beside me without missing a bit. Then suddenly I remembered them and turned swiftly.

'Where are my children?' My voice laden with panic. Maybe he was a trafficker. He had lured us to Austria to sell us into sex slavery? No wonder, how could one so young be so rich? Or maybe he was into

419, a con-business in form of letter-scam that was rampant amongst some unscrupulous Nigerians who schemed money off others both foreigners and natives in a bogus manner.

Obinna frowned and looked at me.

'Are you alright?'

I shook my head but said nothing.

'I am sorry. I didn't mean to get you worried.'

He led me to what seemed to be another estate within the original one and there my children were quartered. They had all had a bath to wash away the travel weary, and were changing to go down to tea, I was informed. While one of the ladies, from earlier, was struggling with Lucky, the other was getting on much better with Frances and Eudora.

'Lucky, would you want me to dress you or you'd rather do it yourself?' Obinna spoke breaking Lucky's struggle.

'I want to dress myself.'

'Good, you do that. Angelica please go and check that their tea is ready.' Angelica nodded and got up immediately leaving Lucky to dress himself. Just that one, he was always very slow and two, the shoes were not always on the right foot and the trouser lopsided, but nobody would accuse him of not dressing himself like the independent gentleman he was aiming to be. We all trouped down after the children had finishing dressing up. They took their places as directed in the dining room and I noted that it was just for the three of them. Obinna, who had not relinquished my arm, led me out through the facing door while instructing the lady with the children who was not Angelica to let Lucky eat unaided. That way there'd be peace. Lucky nodded vigorously at the turn of events. He had won hands down as a master of his own while gleefully making faces at his sisters. Obinna must have noticed my hesitance and murmured, 'Let them be, you can come back and check on their progress.'

'As if I'd find my way back there.'

'I will accompany you so don't worry.'

'But Obinna, why are you living in this ridiculously big house, alone?'

'It is an investment, but until I decide to sell it I don't mind living in it. Actually, I only opened up this section because of you and the kids, otherwise I live in a very compact section of the house, where we are heading to now so that you can freshen up before tea.'

'I am?'

'Yes you are.'

So we went to the said compact section of the house, if anything, it was as spacious.

*   *   *

Obinna's itinerary for us, packed into just one week, was mind-boggling, but like he pointed out, we mustn't attend all. We attended most though. The children were in seventh heaven and I was transported to Olympus. We watched the Berliner Orchestra with Dupont conducting as a family. Then we went alone without the children to see Cherie the Cellist. It was poignant and very romantic.

We always cuddled, smooched and kissed and that was that. Obinna never made any attempt beyond those again and I was happy. I could not imagine what would have happened if he had made a move and I had rebuffed it again. But I would have had to rebuff his attempt; I had my promises and vows too.

After dinner, on our last night, on popular demand, we trouped down to the cinema to see 'Happy Feet' yet again, it was the children's favourite and Obinna indulged them anything within reason. When we returned, he elected to put the reluctant children to bed. Halfway up, they wheedled a promise out of him to read the bedtime story to them, and they would sleep like angels immediately afterwards. He did it always with flair, in any case, and had been doing it since coming in contact with the children, even when he was not sleeping in the same accommodation with them, it'd be done in advance. So it wasn't any problem for him. Besides they had confided to him, that I had not mastered the art of reading bedtime stories with the accompanying acting, singing, mimicking, etc., that he, uncle Obinna, used to bring the story alive.

I was glad at the turn of events that way; I would pack in peace for our flight back to Dublin the next morning. It would also afford me the opportunity to arrange my thoughts and assemble all the facts, a promise was a promise and it was now time to deliver on it. Finally we both returned to the quiet living room, Obinna in anticipation and I in resignation.

I looked back on our relationship and realized that I could no longer honestly look Obinna in the eyes without feeling guilty. He was loving, caring and nothing was too much for him to do for me and my children. Our stay in Austria was even more of an eye-opener to how love worked, at least in his estimation—mine was jaundiced. And I was so afraid all through; because I expected him at any moment to ask me to marry him. He'd have to be made aware of the full situation, give him the opportunity to see things as it were.

I sat on a sofa opposite Obinna in preparation to shatter my life once again, but he protested, preferring me to sit on the same sofa and very close to him, as in being ensconced in his arms. But I didn't think so and stayed put before launching into the narrative I knew would plunge my life back to the depths of despair yet again. But one thing was for sure; I knew that the darkness that had enveloped me previously would not return; it was not the same circumstances. This darkness would entail more of a regret, a regret of what would have been, which would forever play in my mind's landscape over and over and over, like a broken record. It would be too much for any one person to live with, but I knew that no matter the pain I'd not tip over the abyss again. I had made my bed, now I had to lie on it and with the Grace of God bringing fresh dews into my life every morning, this pain would be less. Obinna was really everything any woman would want, need and require in a man, plus more. But enough. I cleared my throat and started. Obinna, you see . . .

Epilogue

CASTLEKNOCK, DUBLIN

2007

As soon as we had finished unpacking I called Ifeoma.

'Fifi, I told him last night.'

'Where are you now?'

'At home.'

'OK. So what did he say?'

I snorted a sigh.

'Nothing. Just silence. It was like somebody died.'

Then I kept quiet myself as if to demonstrate to my friend how the silence that surrounds death worked. Ifeoma prompted.

'Gift, please get on with the story. What happened next?'

'When I sat on the sofa next to him to start the story, he protested, he wanted me to sit beside him so that he could hold me. I refused of course, knowing what I knew.'

'You are perambulating.'

'Ifeoma please stop. If I want to perambulate, sniff and even cry I am entitled. Or didn't you realize that my heart is broken?'

'I am sorry to be prompting you,' Ifeoma apologized, then, 'but I must say that I didn't expect your heart to be broken again Gi. I mean how many times can one's heart break?'

When I didn't retort back immediately, Ifeoma hastened to reassure me.

'Please don't take that to heart. I was only trying to make you . . . '

'I know Ifeoma, don't apologize. I am not mad at you. I was pondering your question. And I think that one's heart can break as many times as it is knocked but the intensity may differ. My heart did not shatter last night; rather it was filled to the brim with regret. Regrets about what could have been if I had met him first. He was the best yet and I love him, so much that I don't know how I am ever going to fill the void that was him in my soul.'

'Mmmh . . . Gift, he walked away in silence. Anyway, what exactly did he say afterwards?'

'Nothing. He just sat there like a carving and stared at me, shaking his head now and then. Then after almost an hour, Ifeoma, get that, an hour of silence, staring and shaking his head, occasionally accompanied by a sigh, he drained the remainder of his drink, nodded at me curtly and went out. That was it. The last I heard was his car pulling out of the compound.

When I got tired of waiting for him to come back, I went to bed. In the morning we dressed up and just as I was wondering about what to do the doorbell rang and a cabbie had come to drop us off. The driver was told to do so, he said. So we left and that was that.'

'Oh Gi, how awful and painful. I really do not know what to do to take some of the pain off you . . . to lessen the intensity of the ache. But Gift, in a way really do you blame the man? Just take a critical look at the situation and tell me, if you were him what would be your reaction?'

'Fifi we won't go into that, I am not a child, neither am I a fool. If my son, Lucky, should bring an intended home with similar checkered past, I would fight tooth and nail for him not to marry her. So I do understand, just that that doesn't make it any less painful: Am I ever going to remain a plaything? Somebody that nobody wanted to love and cherish?'

'Well, that doesn't present a blissful future and to add to your gloom I don't know of any man that would marry you except, maybe, a white man. Okay maybe a Yoruba man and . . . em em em, a widower. In fact I don't know. If only I was a man, maybe we won't be searching for anybody . . . ' We had to laugh at that before Ifeoma continued.

'But in all honesty, Gi, it may really not be that bad and as you know things have a way of sorting itself out eventually. Your intended will come at the appointed time, just don't give up hope.'

'Amen to that,' I intoned.

'Anyway I am inviting myself for a visit, say by the end of the month. That will be three weeks from now. Would that give you enough time to mourn or would you rather come over to London? That may aid your snapping out of the dismal situation faster.'

'Nothing will aid me. I don't even want anything to aid me. I'd rather wallow. Thanks though. I would have loved to visit London, but no, maybe during the summer; we can all book a mega-holiday to somewhere exotic.' When Ifeoma's chuckling subsided, I decided to give her something to really chuckle about.

'He didn't know what he missed you know by not holding on to the relationship, like my expertise in certain quarters for instance.'

Ifeoma roared and while still spluttering commented, 'Now I can safely say that you're not only mad but your bloody heart is solidly intact, not one jot out of sync. Bye and hold on to the good humour, it would save you yet,' she added as she clicked off.

*   *   *

At the arrival gate, we sighted each other at the same time and we both broke into this jaw splitting smile while moving towards each other and then hastened to cover the last distance and then embraced.

'Are you growing taller or what?' Ifeoma asked looking up at me.

'No. I think it's you, you are reducing in height more like, you imp. How was your flight?'

'Fine thanks. And your heart? Your eyes are a bit dull, are you sick or is it the general love malaise?'

'Ifeoma it hasn't been easy. It isn't so much the malaise than the facts of the matter. I have been besieged by all sorts of scenario none of them pleasant. Other than that I am Okay. You don't expect my eyes to be sparkling at my age. I am no spring chicken you know.'

'Yeah, practically in your dotage. Anyway, we will hit the town in a very mean way, you'll be begging me to go away in less than a week I assure you.'

I helped her with her luggage and we sped off into town.

After dinner that night, we settled down to natter, relegating my second heart-break to the back burner.

'I followed Erica to her service one Sunday like that.'

'Oh. And?'

'And nothing. I found it . . . I don't know, it wasn't my thing and I didn't go back.'

'That'd put you further down Erica's book I'd say.'

'On the contrary. We are actually trying to gradually build a friendship now. Imagine that? After all these years we are only getting to know each other.'

Ifeoma swung round swiftly to look at me, making me burst out laughing answering her unasked question.

'Of course not. You think I'm stupid? Never!

'You had me worried for a moment there.'

'For some reason I don't think we would ever be as thick as thieves as to let her hear my story, but she's okay. I suppose you know that already.'

Ifeoma just nodded sipping her wine. After a while I commented, 'I think you should *really* forgive Erica.'

'Really? Why?' Ifeoma asked surprised and I shrugged before speaking.

'I don't know. She was your friend and you won't teach her anything by keeping your distance, two wrongs do not make a right.'

Ifeoma nodded but said nothing. I looked at her and looked away. Granted, friendship should not be based on material acquisition, but Erica is what she is, Ifeoma should accept that. Then I wondered, if I was Ifeoma's friend for her money, I should be rolling in real money by now, but . . . oh well, I wasn't that kind of person. *Of course you weren't, you'd rather prostitute.*

I shook my head to dispel the mean thought while countering, 'But Ifeoma you knew what Erica was as far back as the onset of your friendship, you told me so yourself, why then are you holding it against her now?'

'Erica had no business being a fraudster because of material wealth.'

Considering what I had given her. Ifeoma concluded in her thought nastily.

'Because she was associated with you plus the handout? That's very arrogant of you, my dear girl, because I do not think that it is right to dictate your friends lives because they are not as well off or because of the material things you give them.'

'Have I ever dictated to you?' Ifeoma retorted hotly while thinking that Gift was spookily on the mark.

'Maybe because I don't sponge off you and so you do not have that kind of edge over me.' Ifeoma turned and looked at me for a long time before speaking.

'You know, there has never been any need to be nasty to each other, we shouldn't start now. But I must let you know in addition to the aforementioned that my real anger towards Erica was not because of as my friend she should not steal, but because she is a human being who should discern between good and bad. I don't have to cavort with thieves either, it's a choice I have to make for myself.'

'Ifeoma you should look inwards first before you continue to crucify Erica, and remember, to err is human and . . .' the pain that shot out of Ifeoma's eyes, that furrowed her forehead stopped me in my track. I cut out my speech and turned away. It's not like I had planned to remind her of her own failure but . . . Then her face cleared but before she could say anything I spoke. 'Fifi you must believe me, I'm really really sorry, it was not my intention to hurt you, and I retract the comment immediately. I am sorry.' She sighed but nodded assent.

'If I didn't know better I'd say that Erica had bribed you.'

'She didn't. When she started visiting me, often, I had to take it up with her immediately; let her know up-front that if the reasoning behind the current move was to wangle her way back to you through me then she had better put that plan out of her mind because it'd never work.'

'And what did she say to that?'

'She admitted that it was her original intention but had to reconsider and let it be, adding that if the two of you were meant to re-unite again it'd happen, one way or the other.'

'Gift!' was all Ifeoma said after laughing.

'I know. I should employ this type of warrior-attitude when it came to men, but remember that all things being equal and disregarding a lot of things, I have only ever gone out with two men. I still have time to practice.'

'Sure but from a very disadvantaged position,' Ifeoma reminded me while draining her glass. Then she added, 'If you are up to it lets go and see Erica then.'

'Ah Ifeoma, no. I don't have the energy to separate a cat-fight. Do go on your own please.'

'In that case I won't go, afterall you started it, I never planned on calling on Erica, at least not on this trip. And you must know that I do not engage in cat-fights, it's beneath me.'

Seeing that my face had set like a roughly plastered wall she begged,

'Please Gi.'

'Is it that important to you?'

'No.'

'Then we leave it for next time.'

'Oh, that's OK then. Your bringing it up had made me want to get it over and done with now, but it can keep.'

'But nobody said I should go with you.'

'Yes, but I'll be glad if you do.'

'Are you afraid that she might beat you up? Because she won't.'

'Gift please go with me to Erica's. Stop winding me up.'

I couldn't help laughing as I got up to go and get my children ready.

*   *   *

Ifeoma was alone in the livingroom bored; her visit was winding down and they had exhausted all that there was to do in Dublin. She sighed and sighed again, undecided as to what to watch on the television. Gift was out at the back spreading her washings and her aloneness was beginning to make her restless. That was a feeling she didn't like because the next thing now her reflections would go deeper inwards and uproot certain thoughts. She hissed and got up deciding to join Gift in defeat, on a chore she detested with a passion. The doorbell rang and she shrank back in surprise and then became elated; somebody at last to the rescue.

She turned and headed towards the short passageway to the entrance door only to be stunned by the presence of an unexpected visitor at opening the door.

Obinna Ikejiana, her first cousin and best friend, stared at her with a great confusion and a slight frown creasing his handsome but sad face. Ifeoma stood there with several emotions wracking her face too.

She recovered first, however, and led him to the living room, pointed to a sofa for him to sit down and proceeded to mix drinks for the two of them to still the fear that was foremost of the emotions, but her hand was trembling, so much so that she could not hold the glasses successfully. If Obinna was sent to get her that meant only one thing; something had happened to her daddy. They knew that only Obinna could do the job . . . *Hold on Ifeoma, you don't know that . . .*

Not one to beat about the bush unnecessarily she decided to take charge. 'I take it mummy told you where to find me. But you didn't have to fly all the way to Ireland; you could have called me, you know? Anyway, now that you're here, please don't keep it from me. What has happened?' Her daddy had had what the doctor called a 'threatened stroke' a while ago and they were constantly worried for him. Though he had told them to cease worrying with, "it's nothing the sun in Nigeria will not sort out." But Ifeoma had not ceased worrying; he is her one and only daddy.

'I didn't speak with aunty Grace and your daddy is fine as far as I know. And like you pointed out I could have called you, but . . . . what are you doing here yourself?'

Ifeoma closed her eyes and tried to still her pounding heart, to assert some sort of control but she was still trembling. So she had to employ logic to her thoughts: She knew that Obinna would not play with her, he knew her well enough to not do that. So if he said everything was fine, then everything must be fine. She kept repeating that. Finally she managed to calm herself somehow and cautiously looked up to focus on his eyes, for any sign that would make her doubt his words. She saw nothing other than pain but from what if not her father's death? Then she said, 'I am fine Obinna. Thank you very much for asking.'

Obinna shook his head and smiled but said nothing and so Ifeoma continued, 'I forgive you as I can see that you're still in the throes of love-induced sadness, but if you ask me, either make up with that girlfriend of yours from whatever seemed to be the problem or move on. Life is too short to moan and carry long faces around and it's not like you at all. So why are here then if I may ask since you are not looking for me?'

'I came to see Gift.'

'Gift? You came to see Gift? How come?'

She stopped and opened her eyes wide as realization hit her.

'Oh no Obinna, come on, it's not you, right? You're not the boyfriend are you? 'No Obinna you are not. It is not you. No, you're not!'

She shook her head before continuing, 'But how could I have missed this?'

'No it's not you.' She shook her head. Oh Lord, how on earth am I not going to be forced to take a side, howonearthaminotgoingtobeforcedtotakeasidehowonearth . . . the buzzing was too much forcing her to stand up and made to go and look for Gift, but halfway there she yelled out her name instead and returned to the livingroom and sat down mauling this new challenge.

Obinna looked at Ifeoma speculatively as he searched his memory for the clue and how he could have missed the connection. Yes he had chosen not to discuss Gift with any of the family yet except his mum because he wanted to be sure of what he was doing until the new twist. Did his mum tell Ifeoma or what? No, his mum wouldn't do that. So where could they have met as to warrant her visiting from London . . . then it clicked . . . Unilag. That was the only common denominator from Gift's tale. As he made the connection he now fully turned his eyes and thoughts on his cousin who appeared very agitated. Did she know of her friend's past? Was that why her face was in such a horrendous scowl? Was this an indication, a taste of what he's going to face in future and forever: trying to gauge people and their reactions if they stumbled on Gift's past? Would he be willing to spend the rest of his life imagining the snicker of distaste and disgust that he was sure their being privy to that information would elicit? But he reined in that angle of thought, he had gone through that before and came to terms with it himself and so he was not going to do that again. He should be able to weather any storm that would arise from Gift's past. It shouldn't matter; because he loved her, had since their first encounter. The last four weeks had opened his eyes to the pain that was her absence in his life; a life that was increasingly becoming empty, a gaping void, until she came along. But life's not perfect and true love should be able to overlook imperfections, be it from nature or nurture, if the people involved were willing to try. Love should be able to overcome, to conquer. Surely?

He had made up his mind to look for his love which was what brought him back to Ireland today. At least she was honest about her past. And that should do for him. Afterall at the end of the day, it's still between the two of them, and nobody else.

Ifeoma had been his best friend within the family from the time they were children; staunch supporters of each other, even though she was not an easy customer. Would she be able to support him this time around? He shrugged inwardly. Time would tell, but he hoped, prayed even, that she would be on his side, because as it stood he was prepared to stick to his decision. Unless Gift herself decided otherwise.

He nodded in answer to Ifeoma's question, but did not elaborate. Instead he asked, 'Where is Gift?' Ifeoma flicked her head towards the back door and they both turned when the said door opened and Gift entered.

*   *   *

I had come in through the back door into the kitchen and made for a corner to keep the large plastic bowl I had used to ferry the washing while asking, 'Ifeoma, was it the doorbell I heard awhile ago?' No answer. I straightened up and walked towards the livingroom with my mouth shaped to ask the same question but then this apparition blocked my way I looked up and froze, my mouth was still poised to speak but no words came out—it was Obinna with Ifeoma beside him. I looked from one to the other and then rested my eyes on Obinna, with thoughts swirling about. I searched their faces for an answer, an answer to a question I hadn't even formulated, I couldn't even formulate, but that would have been "Obinna why are you here?" Should I have formulated it? But I wouldn't formulate it or ask the question because I didn't want to raise my hopes. I was done living in a fool's paradise. I was a tainted woman, and tainted women should not hope for reprieve, not . . .

But Obinna saved me any further soul-destroying condemnations by moving quickly to stand in front of me. I lifted my face up to be able to look into his eyes; to search it for any sign. As I searched his face my eyes clouded with pain, he lifted his hands and cupped my face with both his palms and so we stood there and stared into each others eyes, my hands flapping at my side not sure of what to do with them; keep them beside me or hug him? But then we must have seen what we were both searching for after a long time of staring into each other's eyes, because he removed his hands from my face, opened his arms wide and I stepped in. We held each other in a tight embrace that looked like there was no tomorrow. Then he murmured into my hair, 'Oh Gift. Oh Gift,' each 'Oh Gift' coinciding with a squeeze that was stronger than the last one, suffocating me, but I did not care that I wasn't taking in enough air, that my throat had clogged up; that I couldn't speak, so I nodded instead. I now inhabit a space with somebody who wanted to be there with me.

I am home.

I took a very deep satisfying breath in and at exhalation I murmured, 'Thank you Lord.'

*   *   *

Choice.

Freedom.

These two words have the power to explode in your face and drown you, if you are not careful. In retrospect I now know that the real power to quality of life is not in the freedom to choose, but in the making of choices that give freedom. I had applied my own understanding of freedom to choice in pursuit of that that was supposed to bring me untold happiness, but really what did I do . . . ?

Gift.

The End

Lightning Source UK Ltd.
Milton Keynes UK
UKOW05f1941221213

223525UK00001B/53/P